MAGIC TREE HOUSE®

MUMMIES IN THE MORNING

MARY POPE OSBORNE'S

MAGIC TREE HOUSE®

MUMMIES IN THE MORNING

THE GRAPHIC NOVEL

ADAPTED BY

JENNY LAIRD

WITH ART BY

KELLY & NICHOLE MATTHEWS

A STEPPING STONE BOOK™
RANDOM HOUSE 🏠 NEW YORK

Text copyright © 2022 by Mary Pope Osborne
Art copyright © 2022 by Kelly Matthews & Nichole Matthews
Text adapted by Jenny Laird

All rights reserved. Published in the United States by Random House Children's Books, a division
of Penguin Random House LLC, New York. Adapted from *Mummies in the Morning*, published by
Random House Children's Books, a division of Penguin Random House LLC, New York, in 1993.

Random House and the colophon are registered trademarks and A Stepping Stone Book
and the colophon are trademarks of Penguin Random House LLC. RH Graphic with
the book design is a trademark of Penguin Random House LLC. Magic Tree House
is a registered trademark of Mary Pope Osborne; used under license.

Visit us on the Web!
rhcbooks.com
MagicTreeHouse.com

Educators and librarians, for a variety of teaching tools, visit us at RHTeachersLibrarians.com

Library of Congress Cataloging-in-Publication Data is available upon request.
ISBN 978-0-593-17479-1 (pb) — ISBN 978-0-593-17476-0 (hc) —
ISBN 978-0-593-17477-7 (lib. bdg.) — ISBN 978-0-593-17478-4 (ebook)

The artists used Clip Studio Paint to create the illustrations for this book.
The text of this book is set in 13-point Cartoonist Hand Regular.

MANUFACTURED IN CHINA
10 9 8 7 6 5 4 3 2 1
First Graphic Novel Edition

This book has been officially leveled by using the F&P Text Level Gradient™ Leveling System.

To Georgia and Ada McCulloch
—M.P.O.

For Krish and Alya —a truly magical
brother-and-sister team
—J.L.

To April, our amazing art director, who
has been with us through thick and thin (and
deadlines). Thank you for everything you've
done to offer assistance and advice; this series
wouldn't be the same without you.
—K.M. & N.M.

CHAPTER ONE
Meow!

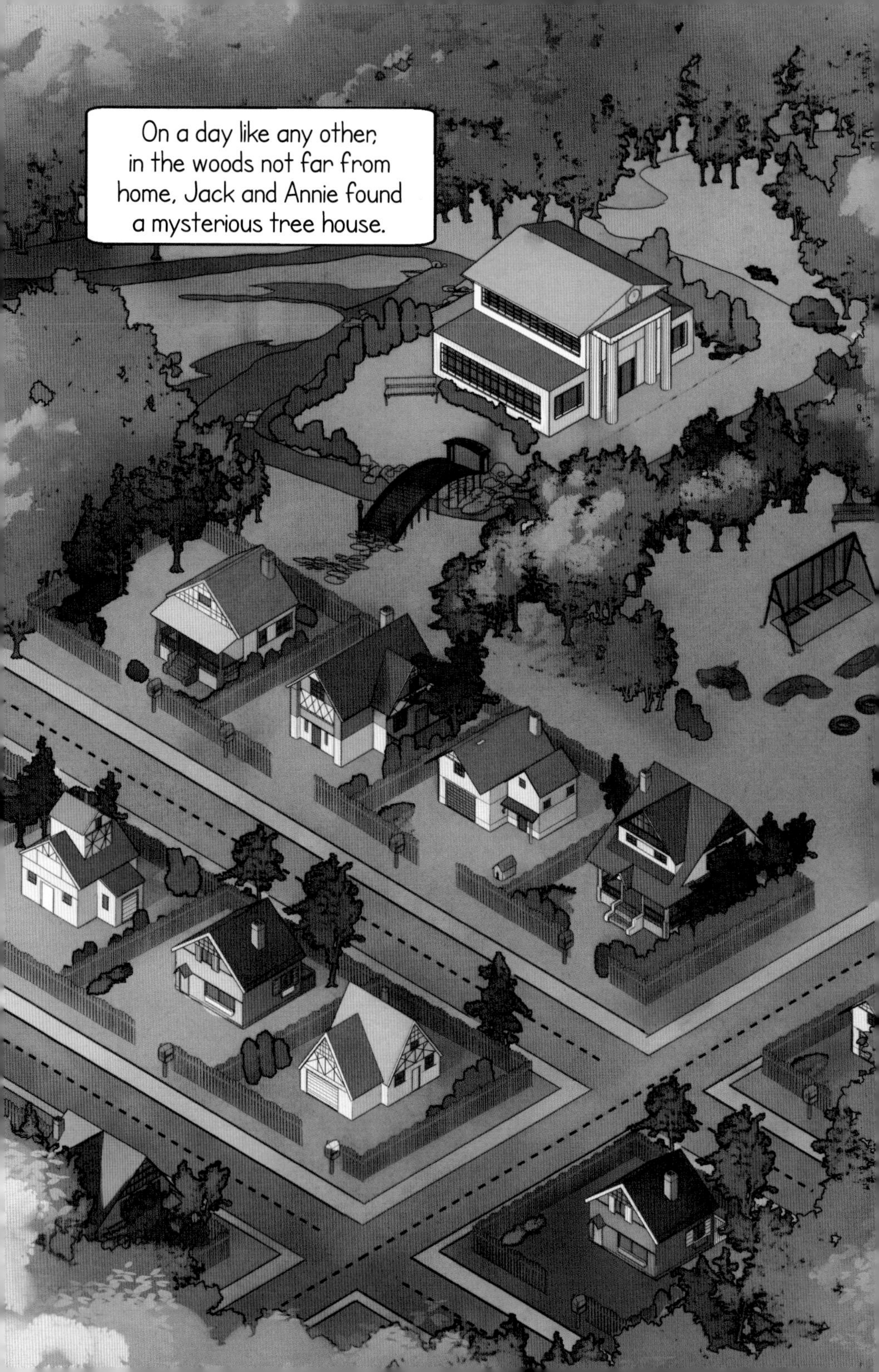
On a day like any other, in the woods not far from home, Jack and Annie found a mysterious tree house.

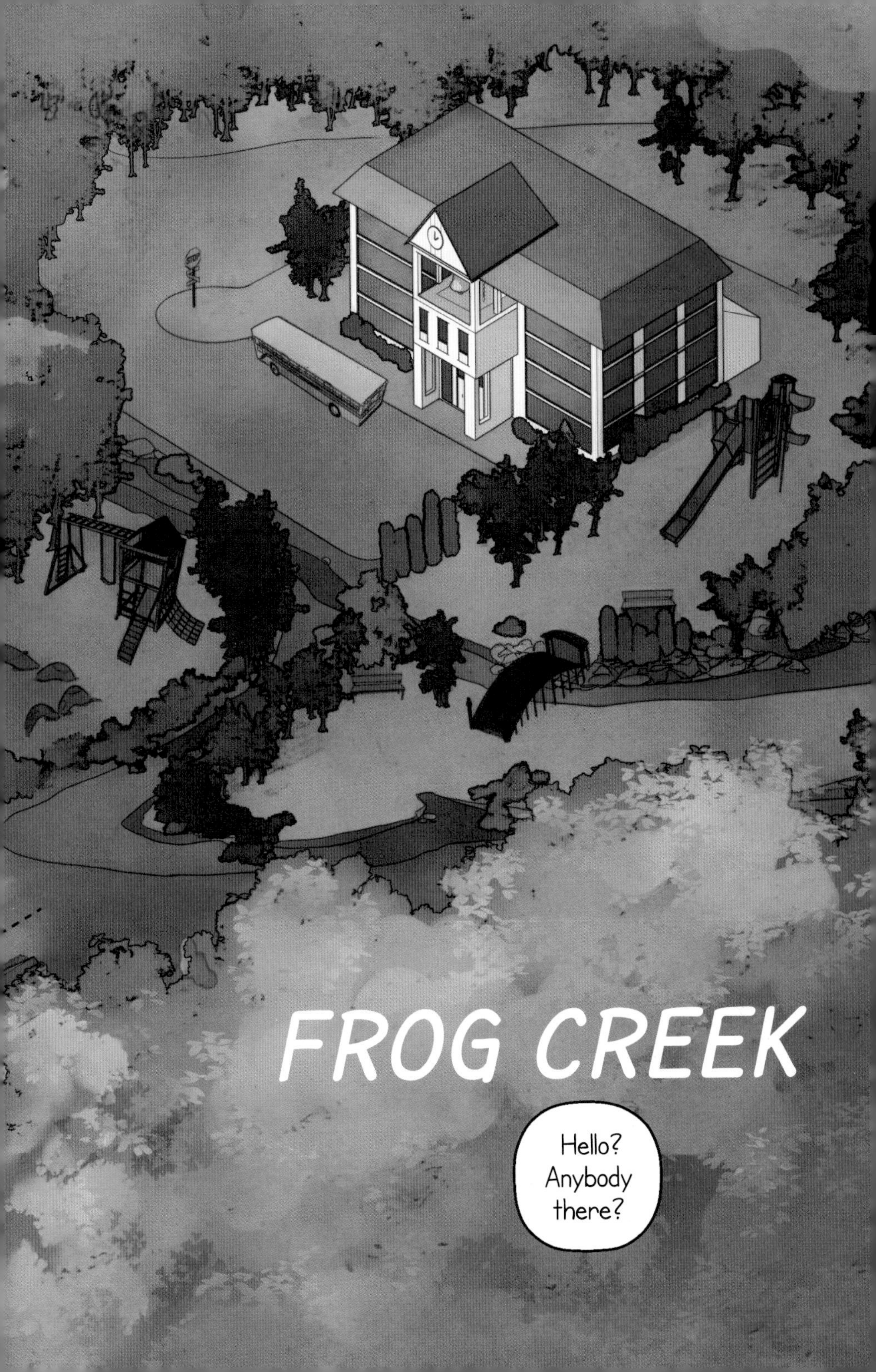
FROG CREEK
Hello? Anybody there?

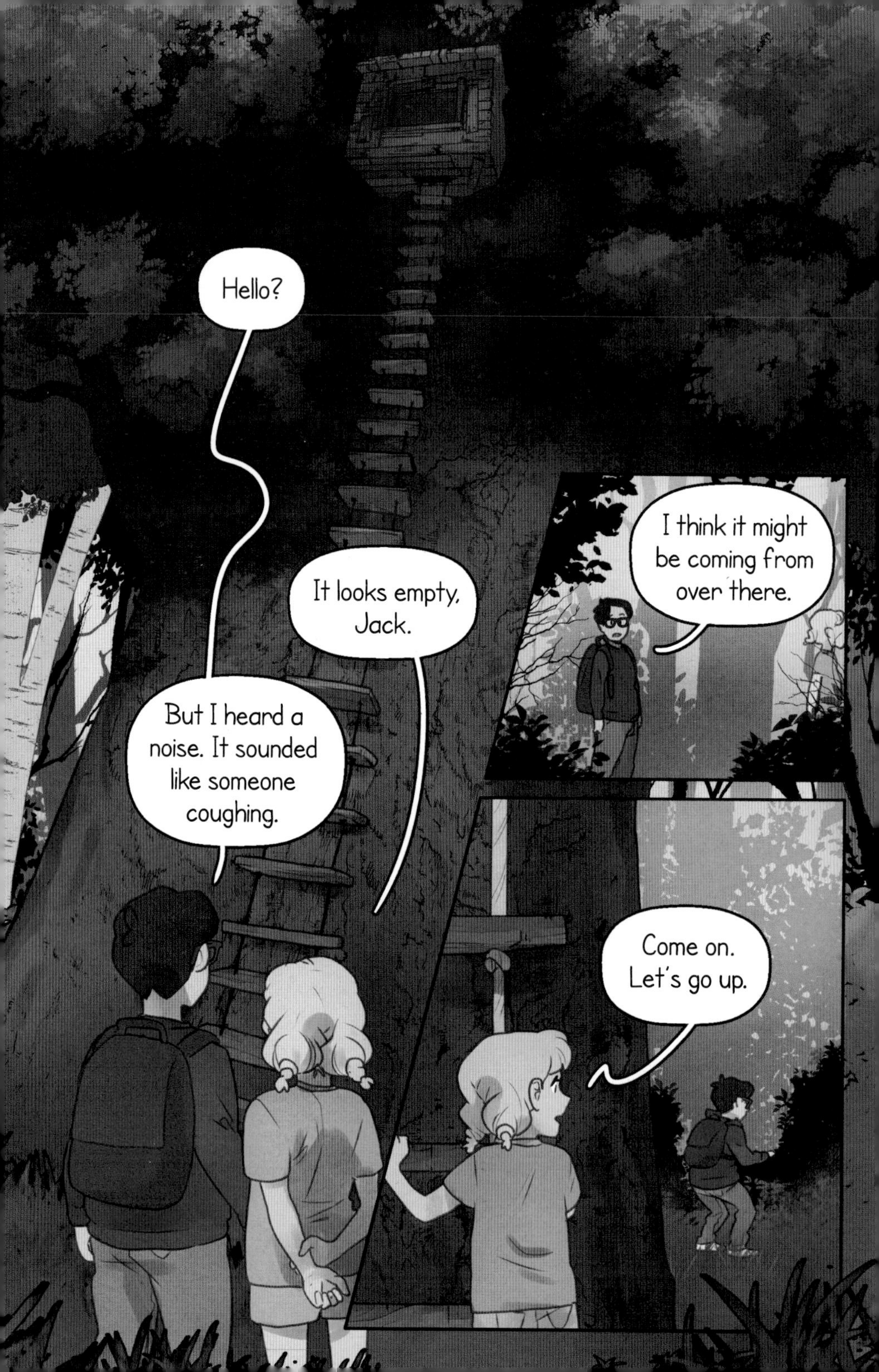
Hello?
It looks empty, Jack.
But I heard a noise. It sounded like someone coughing.
I think it might be coming from over there.
Come on. Let's go up.

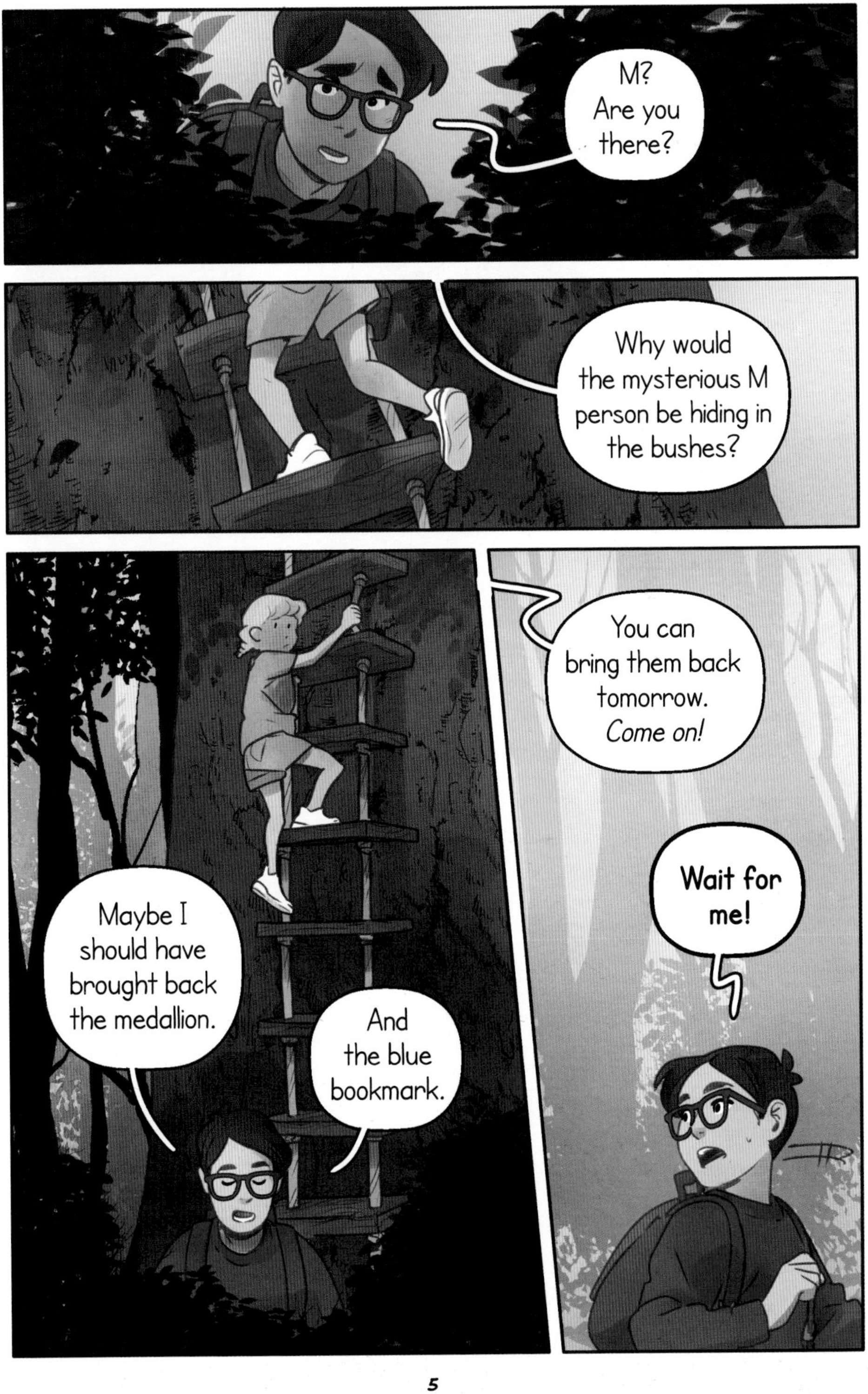
M? Are you there?
Why would the mysterious M person be hiding in the bushes?
You can bring them back tomorrow. *Come on!*
Wait for me!
Maybe I should have brought back the medallion.
And the blue bookmark.

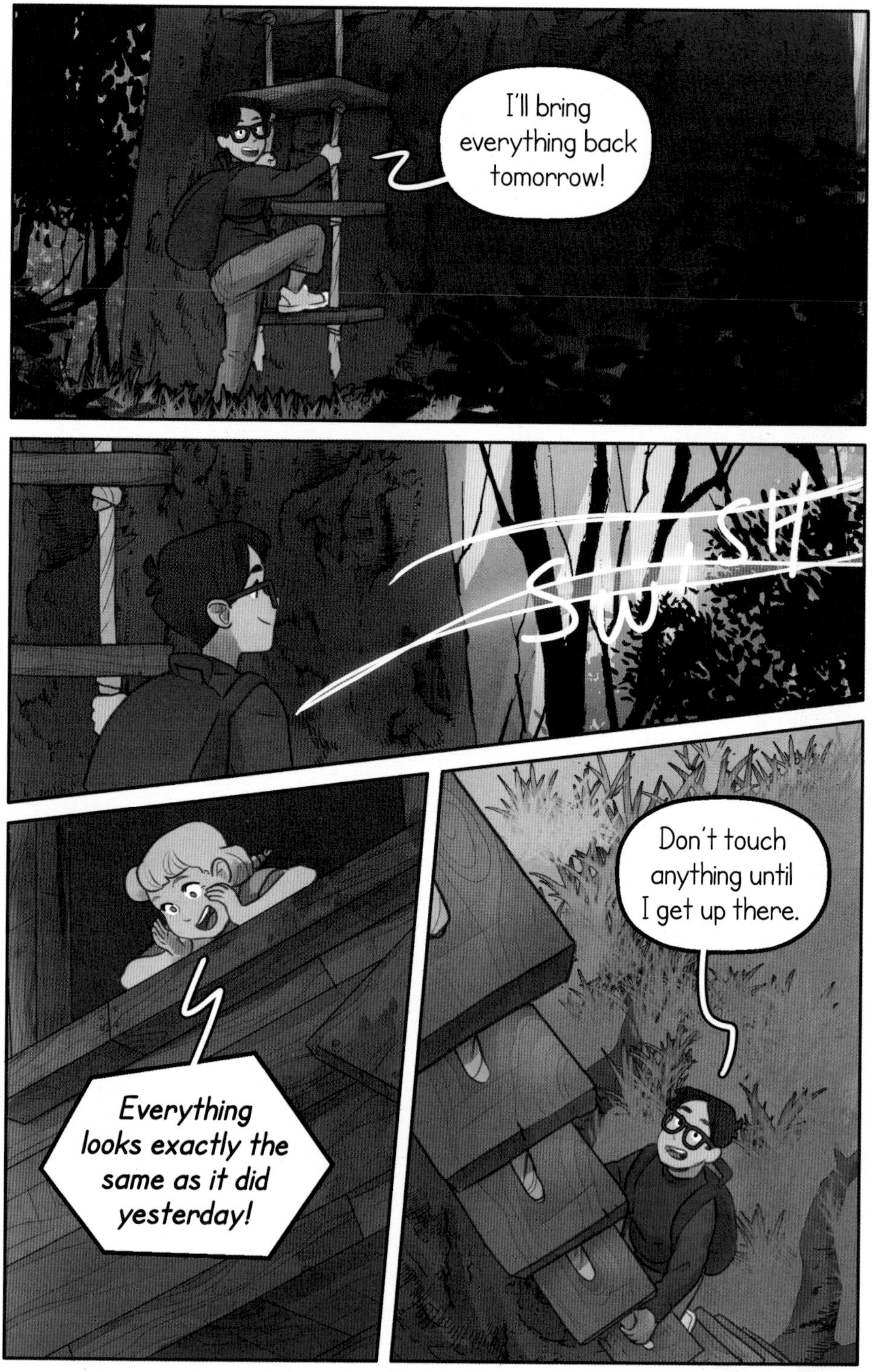
I'll bring everything back tomorrow!
SWISH
Everything looks exactly the same as it did yesterday!
Don't touch anything until I get up there.

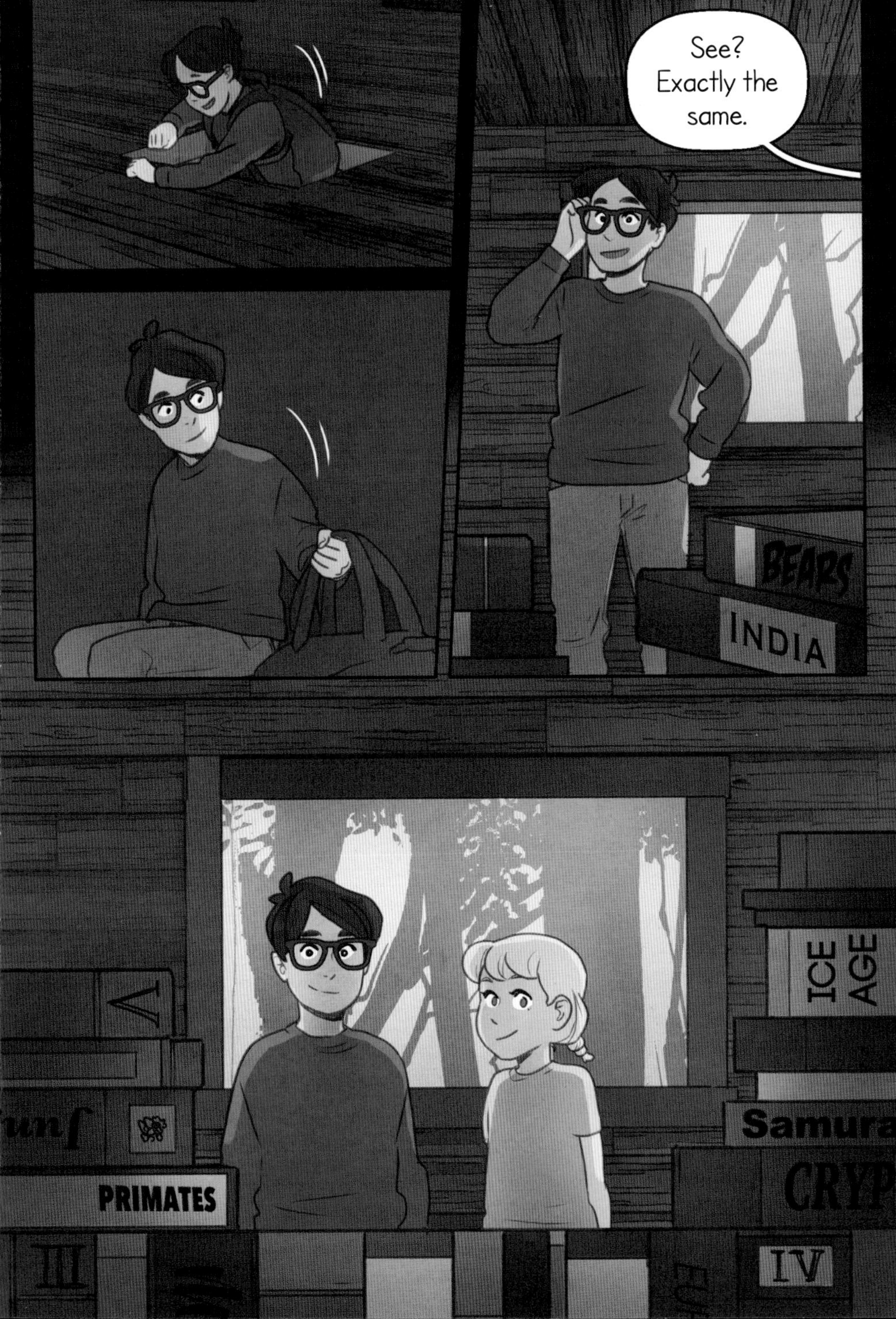

See? Exactly the same.
BEARS
INDIA
ICE AGE
Samura
CRYP
PRIMATES
III
IV

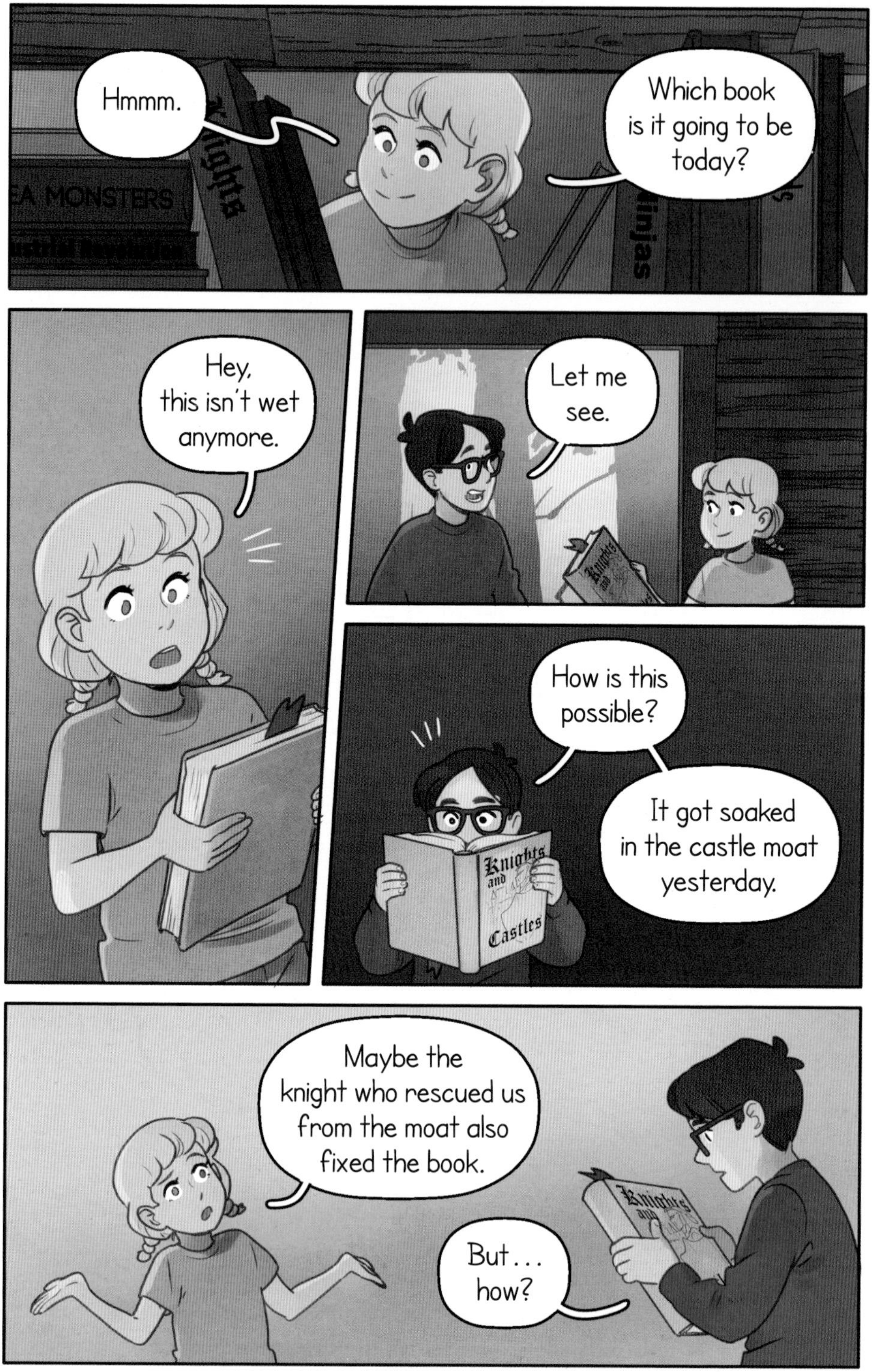
Hmmm.
Which book is it going to be today?
EA MONSTERS
Knights
Ninjas
Hey, this isn't wet anymore.
Let me see.
How is this possible?
It got soaked in the castle moat yesterday.
Knights and Castles
Maybe the knight who rescued us from the moat also fixed the book.
But... how?

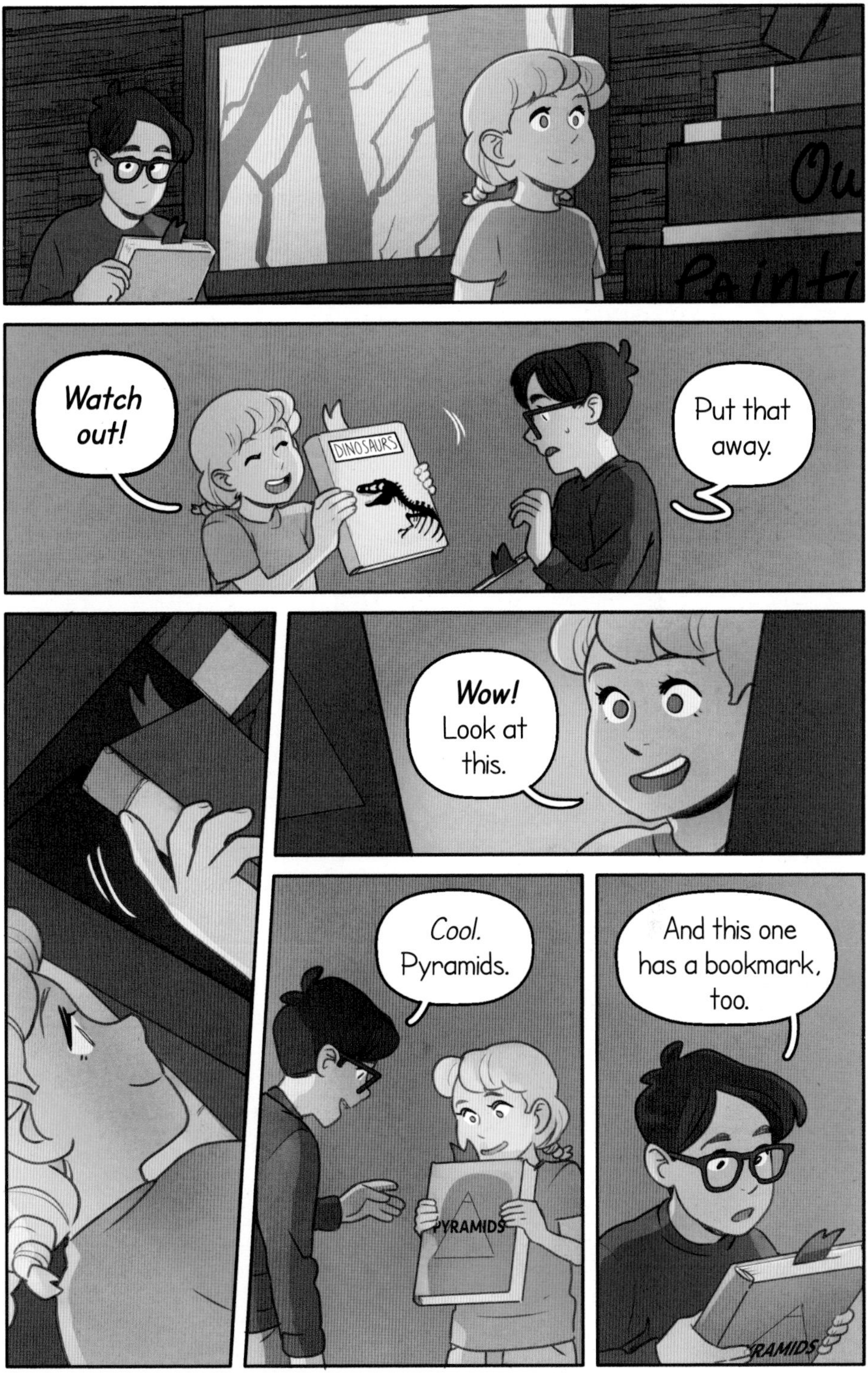

Ou
Painti
Watch out!
DINOSAURS
Put that away.
Wow! Look at this.
Cool. Pyramids.
PYRAMIDS
And this one has a bookmark, too.
RAMIDS

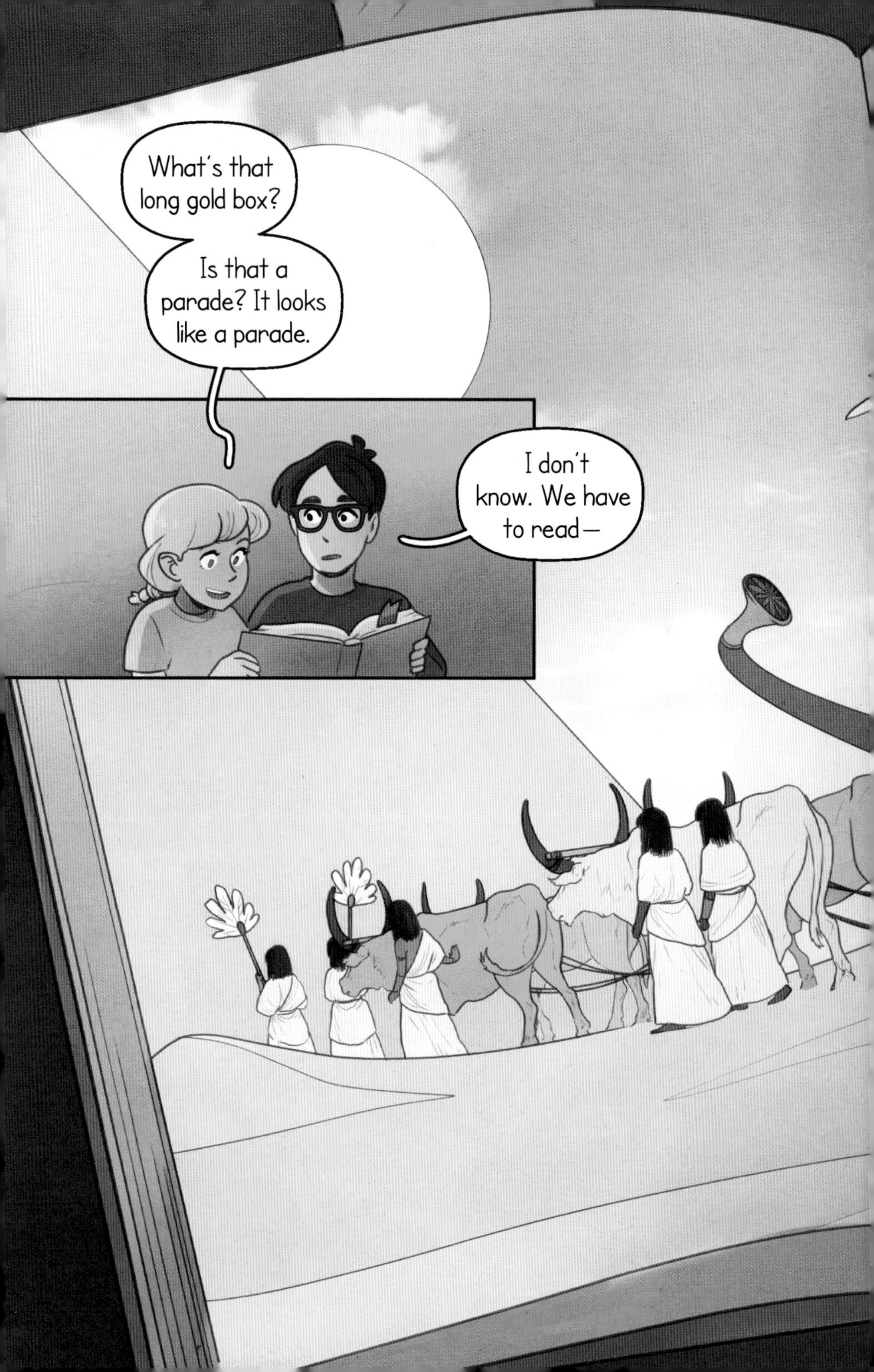
What's that long gold box?
Is that a parade? It looks like a parade.
I don't know. We have to read—

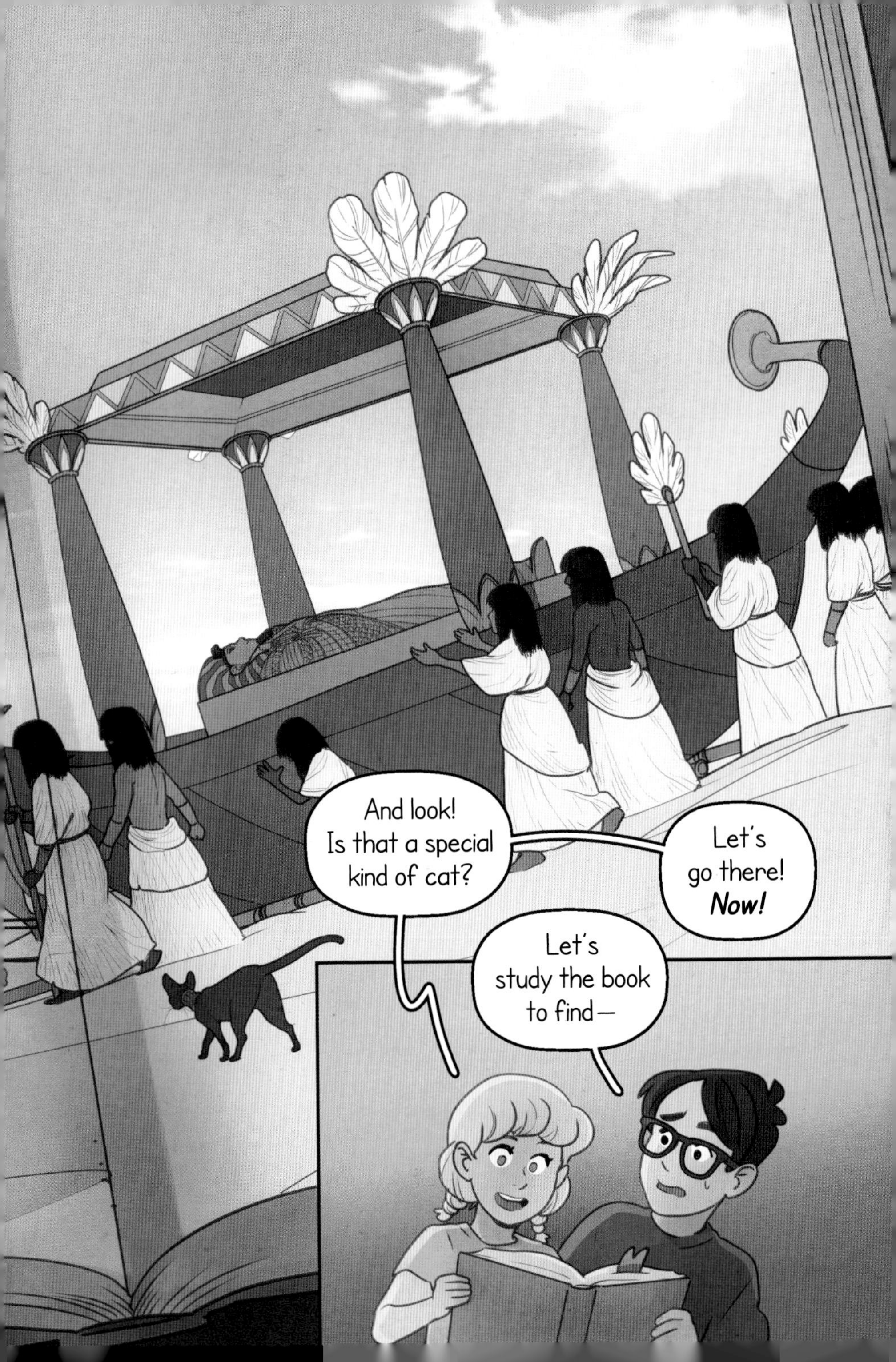
And look! Is that a special kind of cat?
Let's go there! *Now!*
Let's study the book to find—

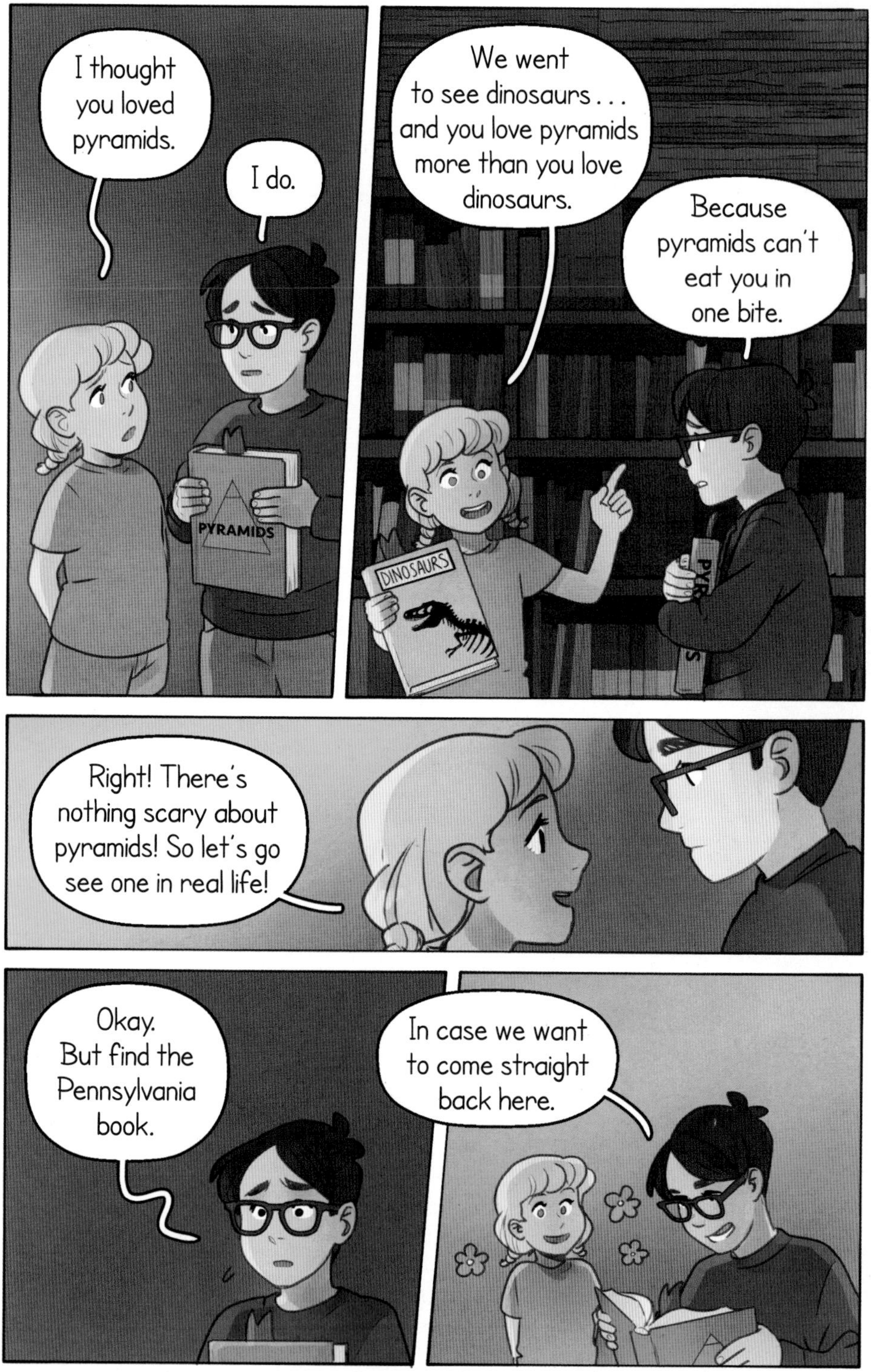
I thought you loved pyramids.
I do.
PYRAMIDS
We went to see dinosaurs . . . and you love pyramids more than you love dinosaurs.
Because pyramids can't eat you in one bite.
DINOSAURS
Right! There's nothing scary about pyramids! So let's go see one in real life!
Okay. But find the Pennsylvania book.
In case we want to come straight back here.

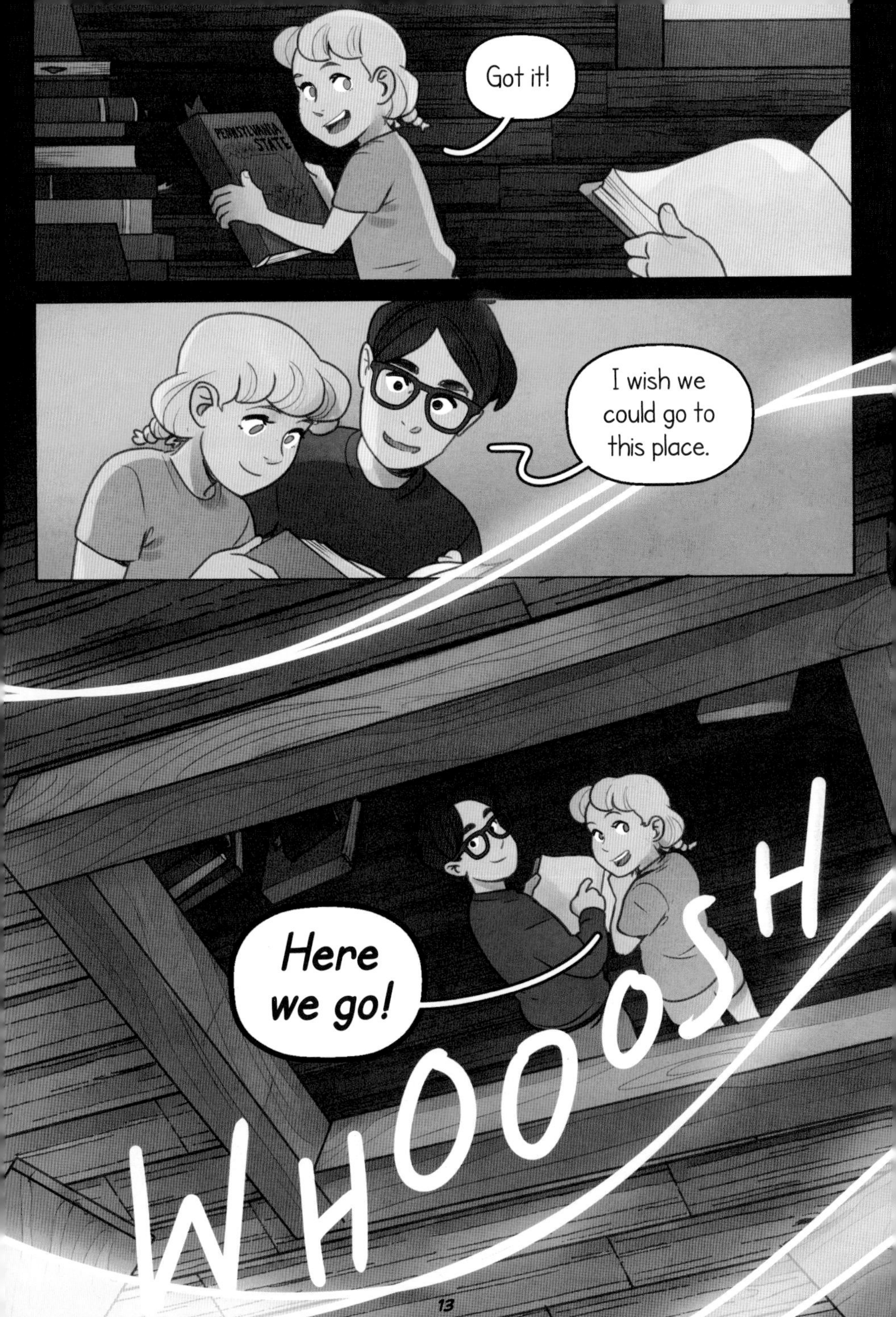
PENNSYLVANIA STATE
Got it!
I wish we could go to this place.
Here we go!
WHOOOOSH

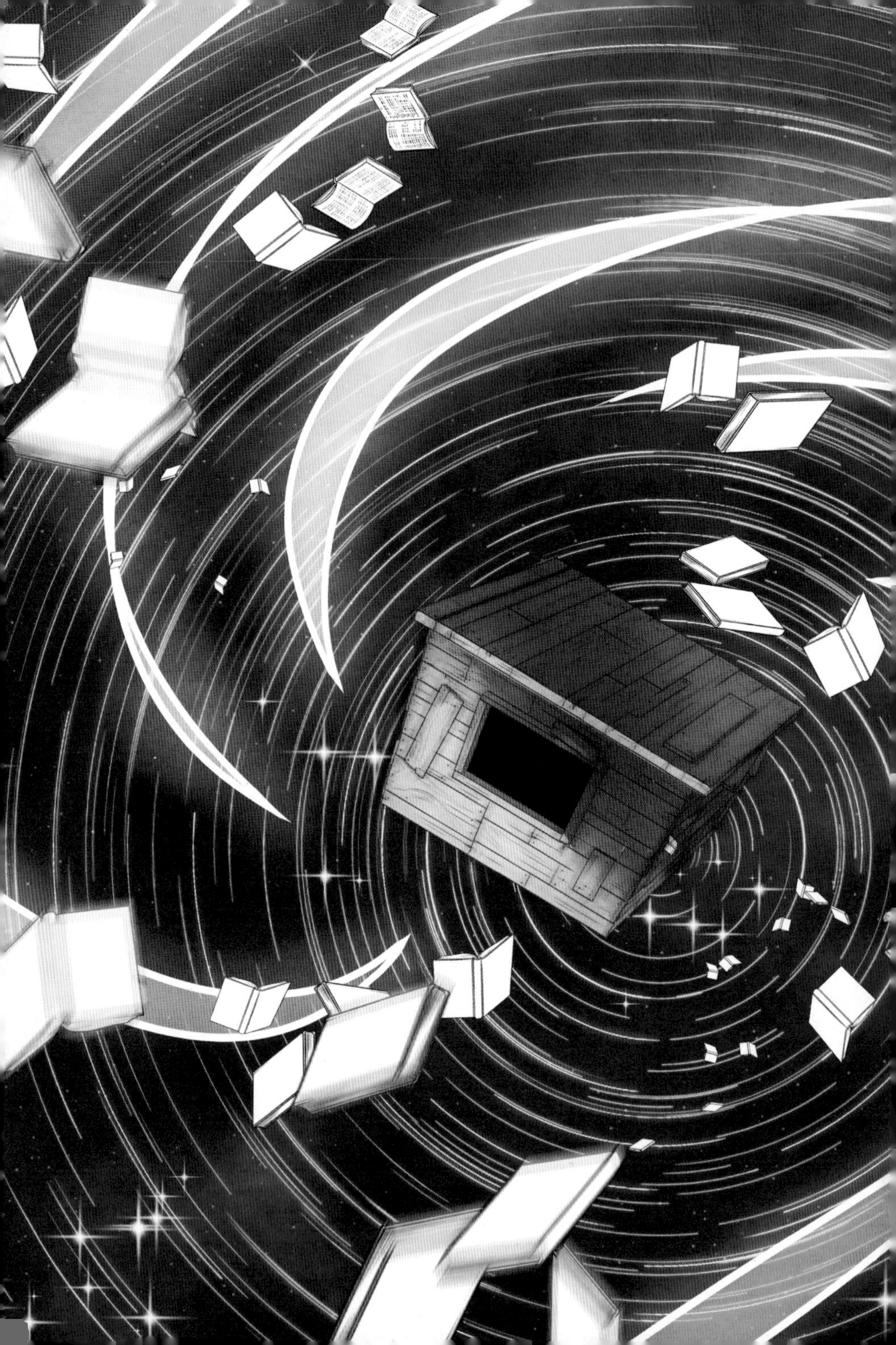

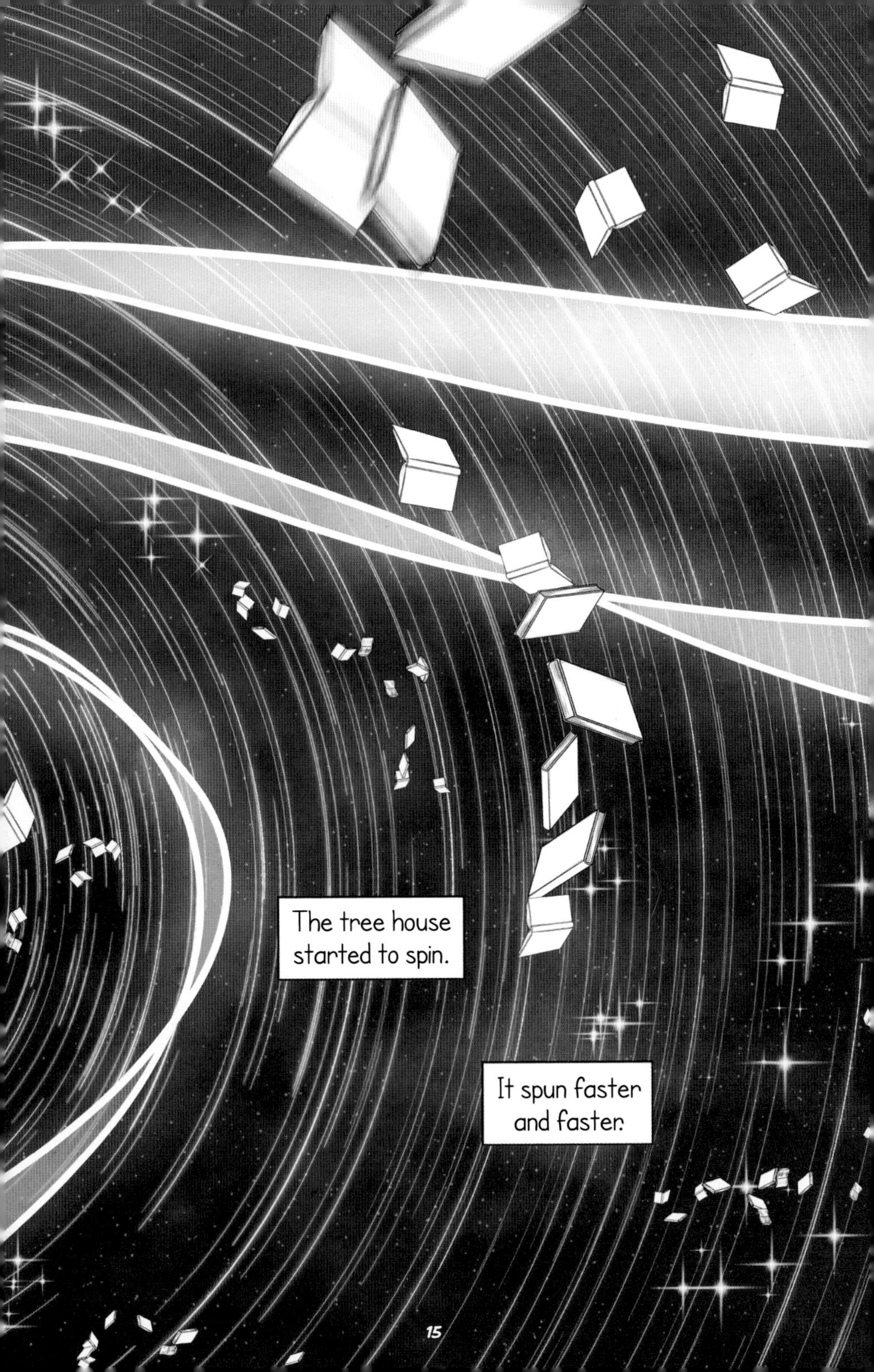
The tree house started to spin.
It spun faster and faster.

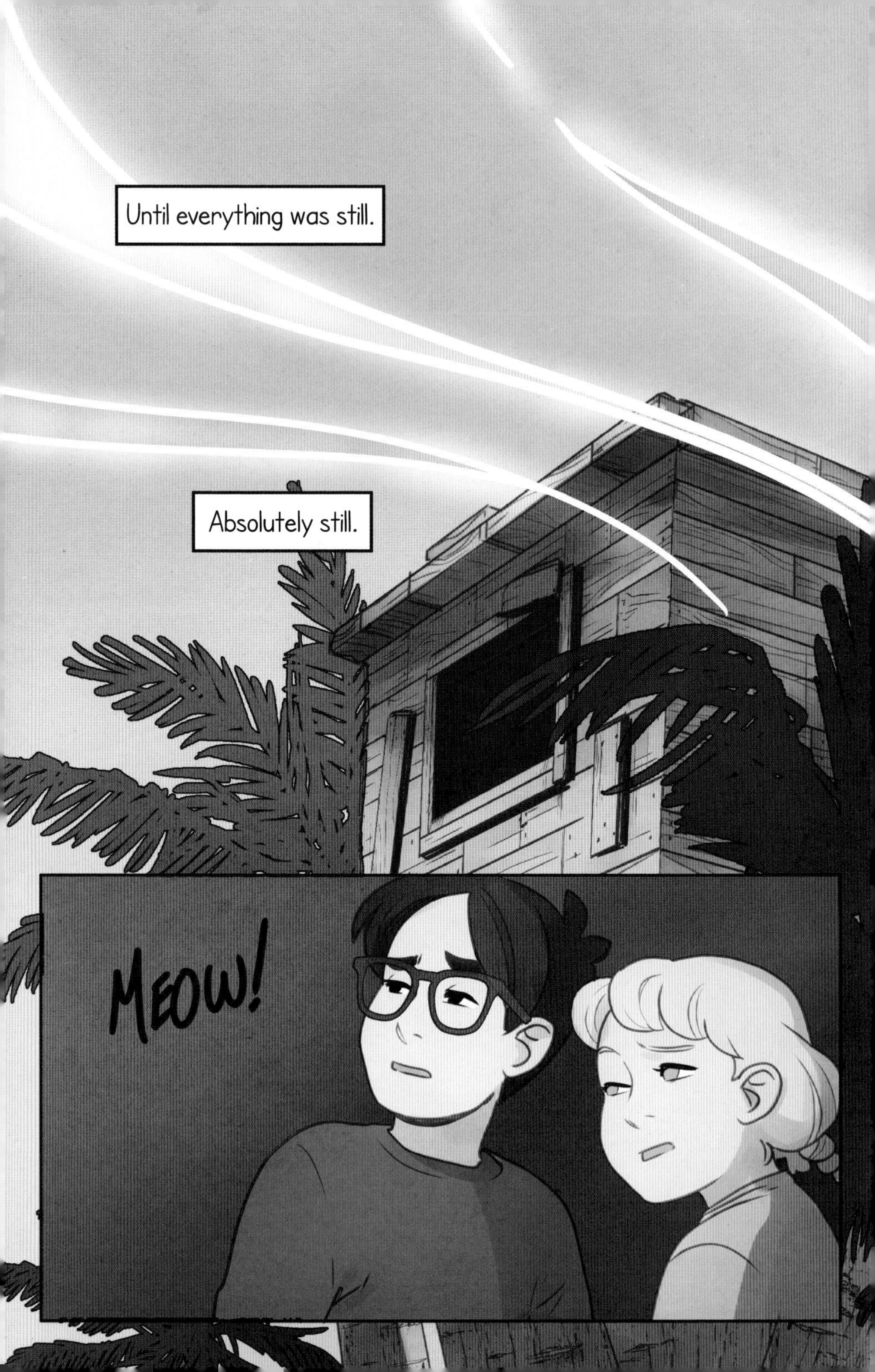
Until everything was still.
Absolutely still.
MEOW!

CHAPTER TWO
Oh, Man. Mummies!

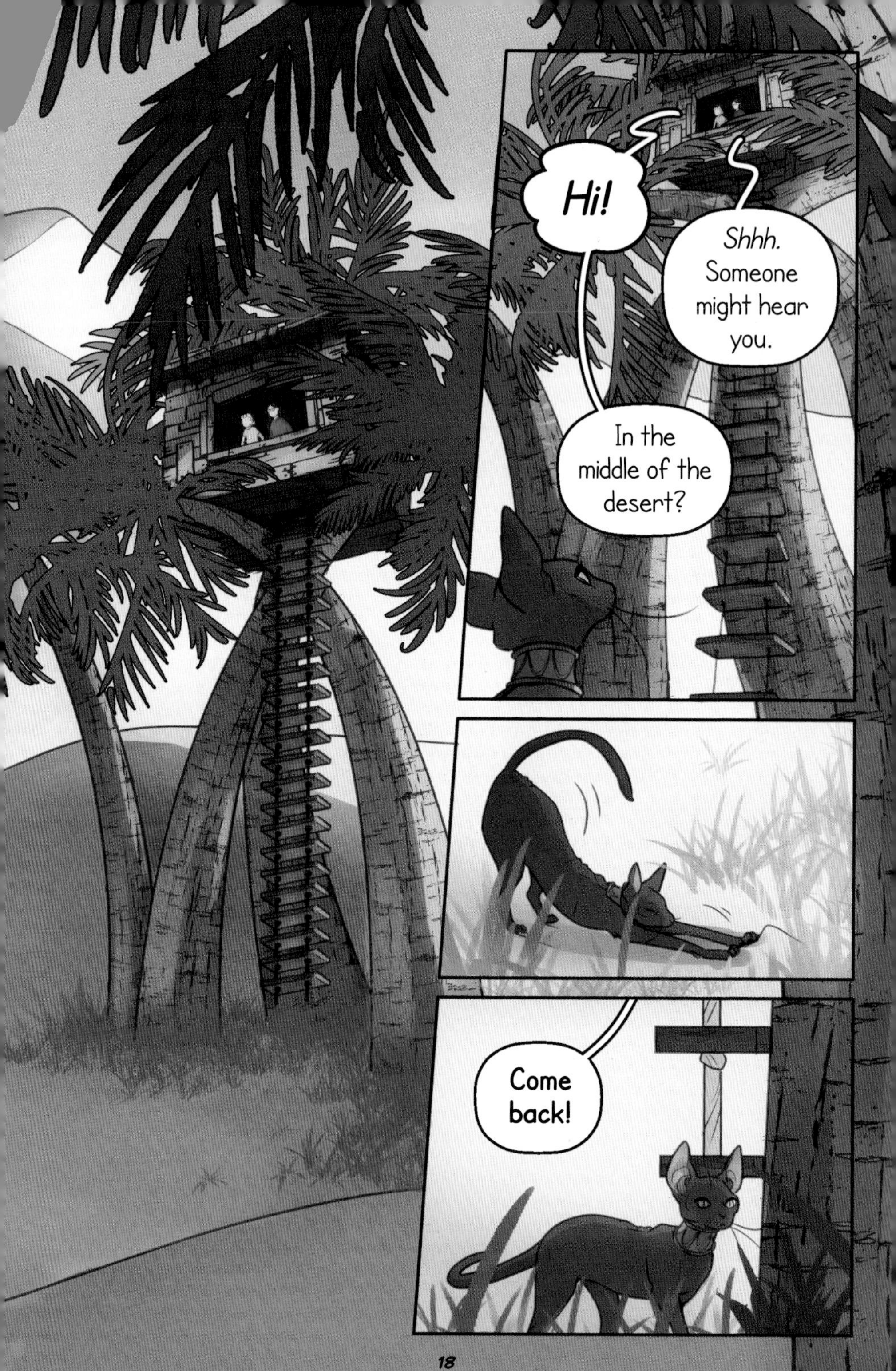
Hi!
Shhh. Someone might hear you.
In the middle of the desert?
Come back!

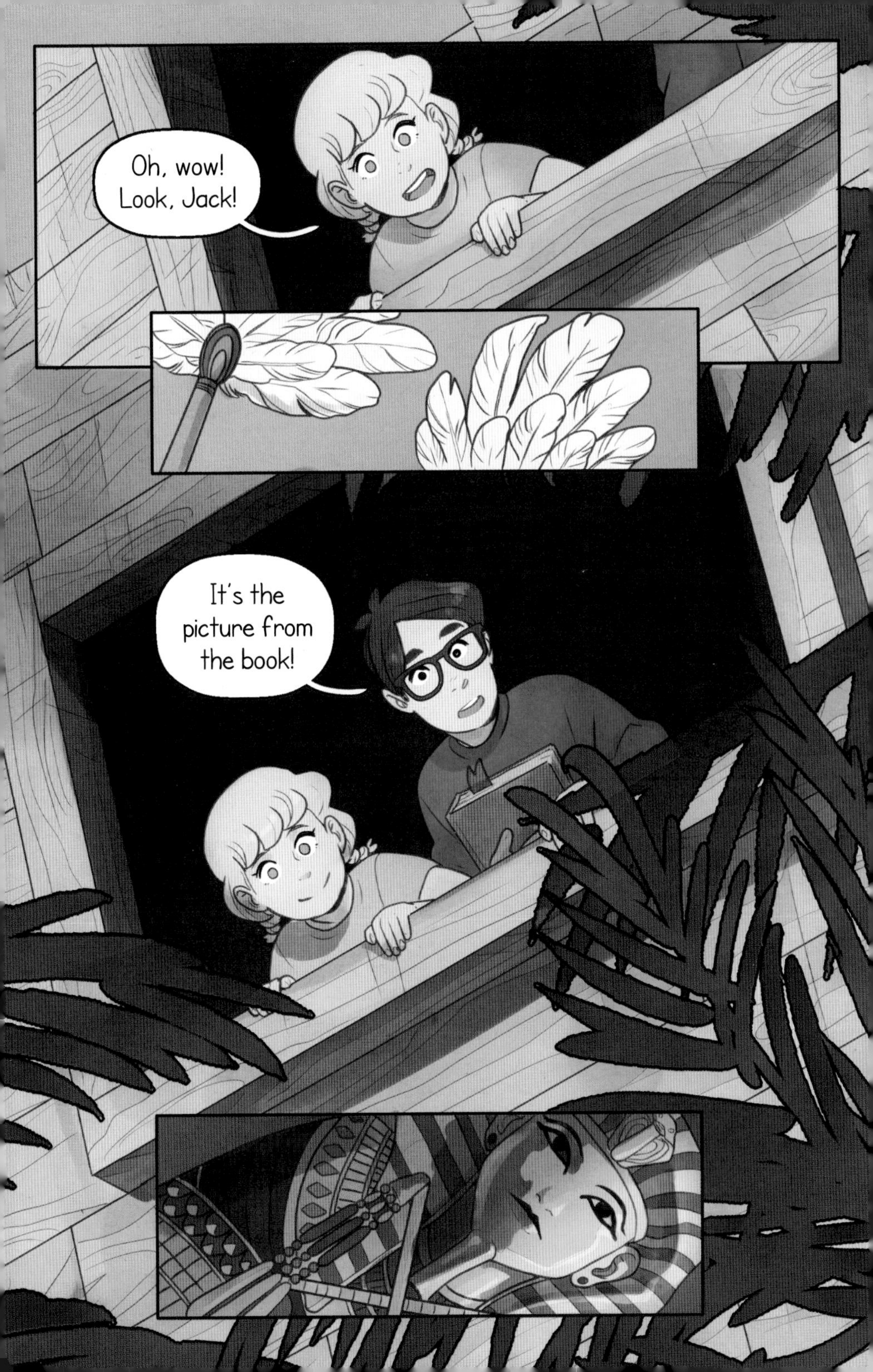
Oh, wow! Look, Jack!
It's the picture from the book!

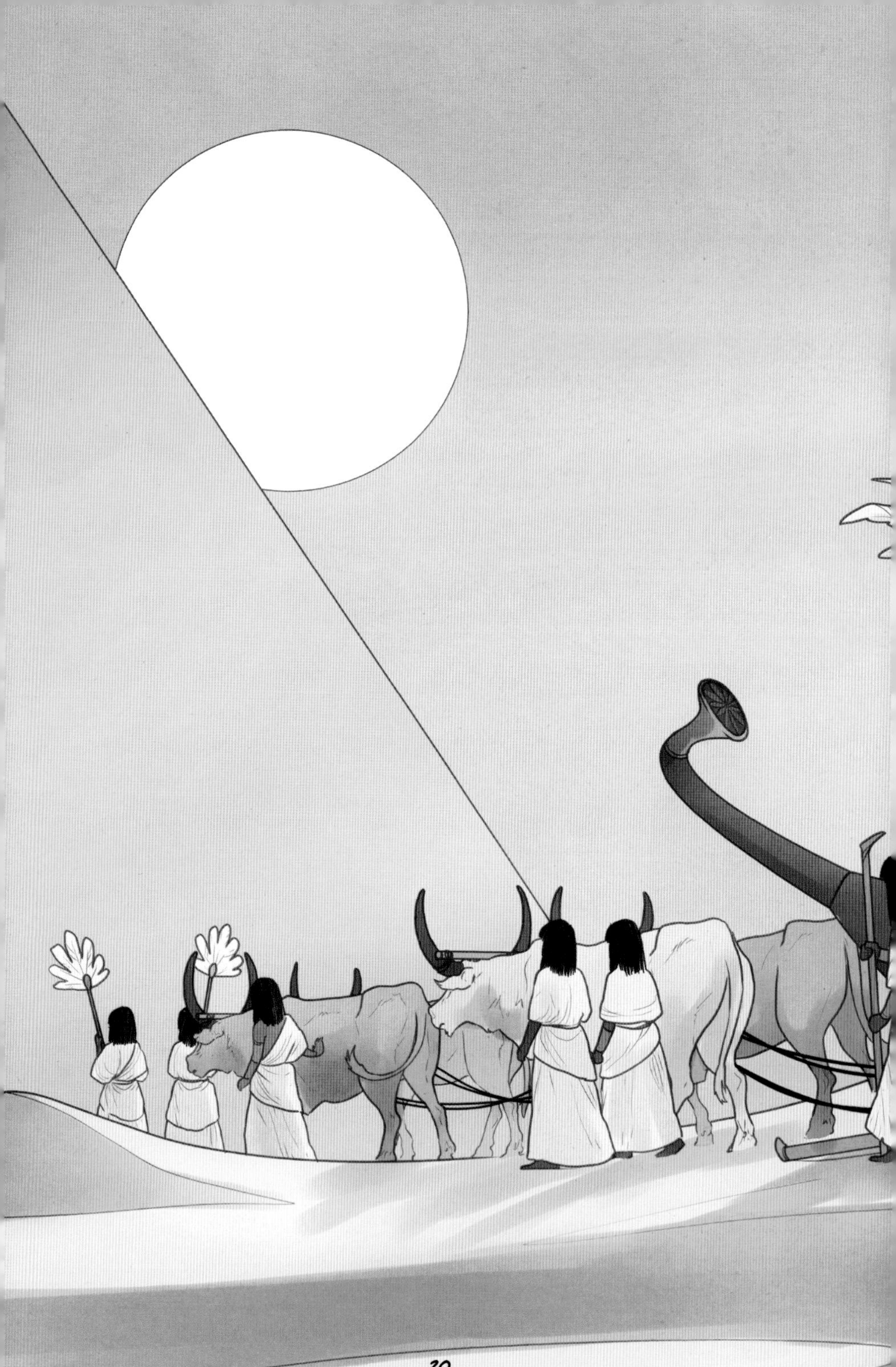

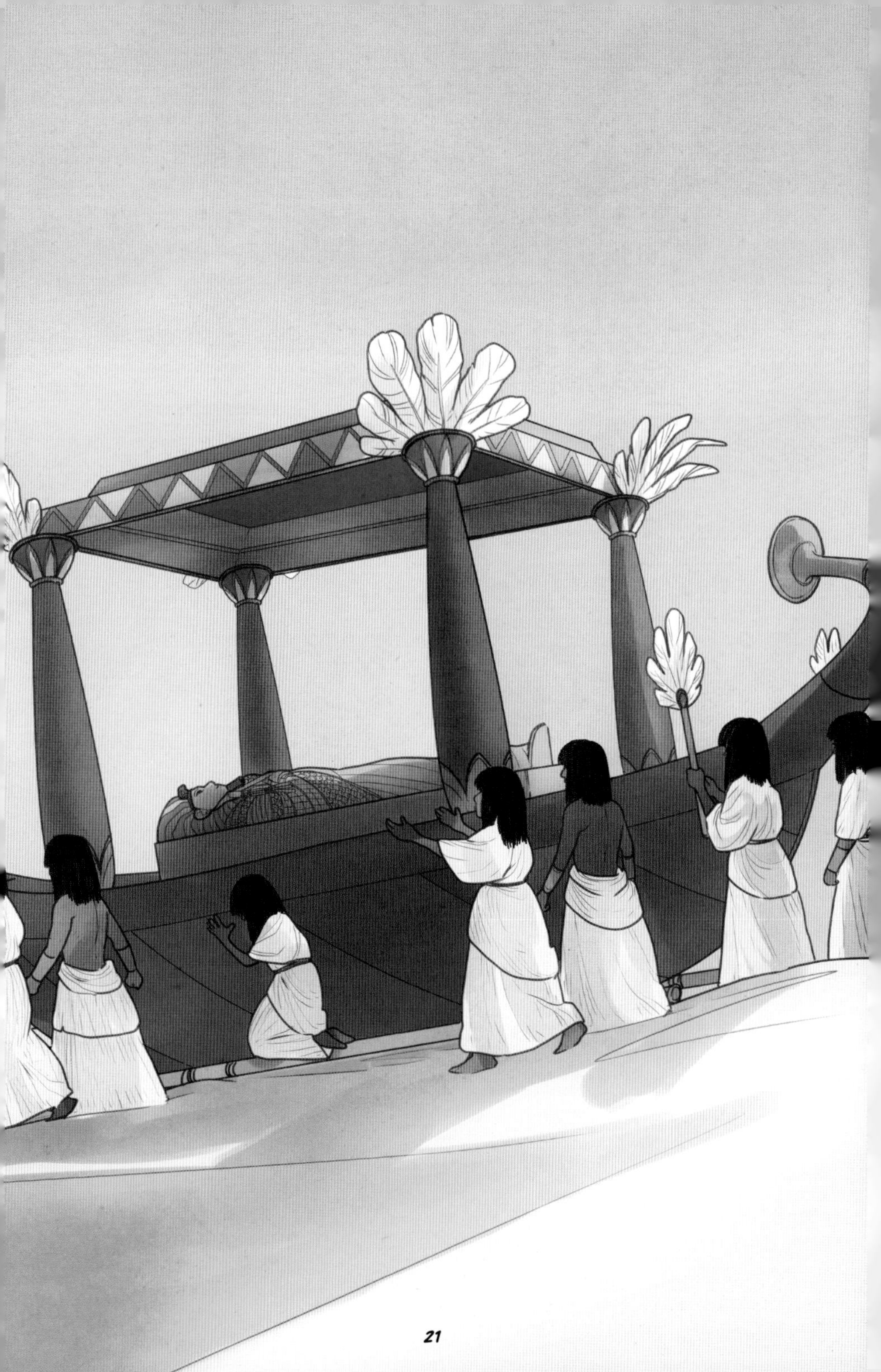

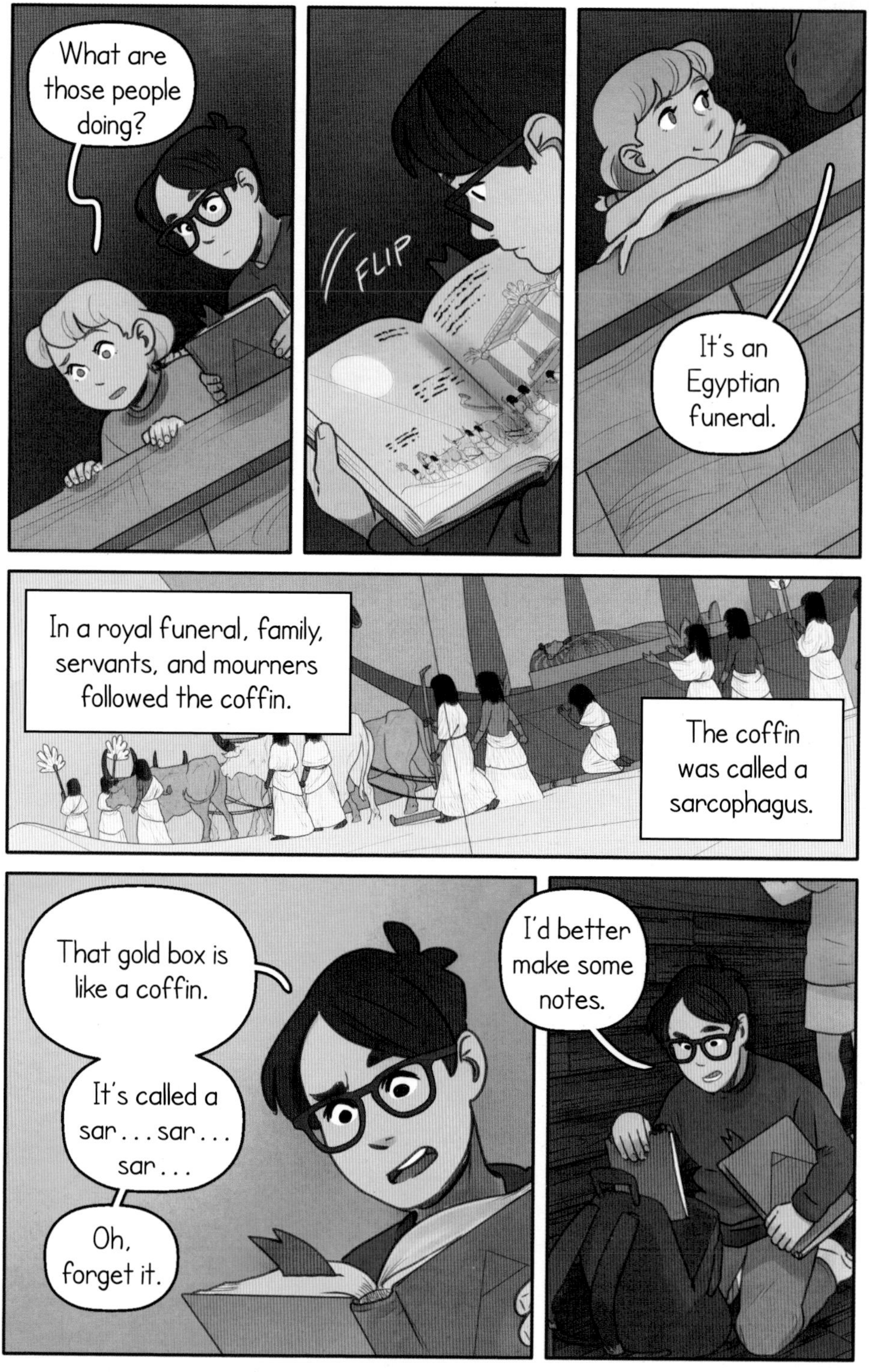

What are those people doing?
FLIP
It's an Egyptian funeral.
In a royal funeral, family, servants, and mourners followed the coffin.
The coffin was called a sarcophagus.
That gold box is like a coffin.
It's called a sar . . . sar . . . sar . . .
Oh, forget it.
I'd better make some notes.

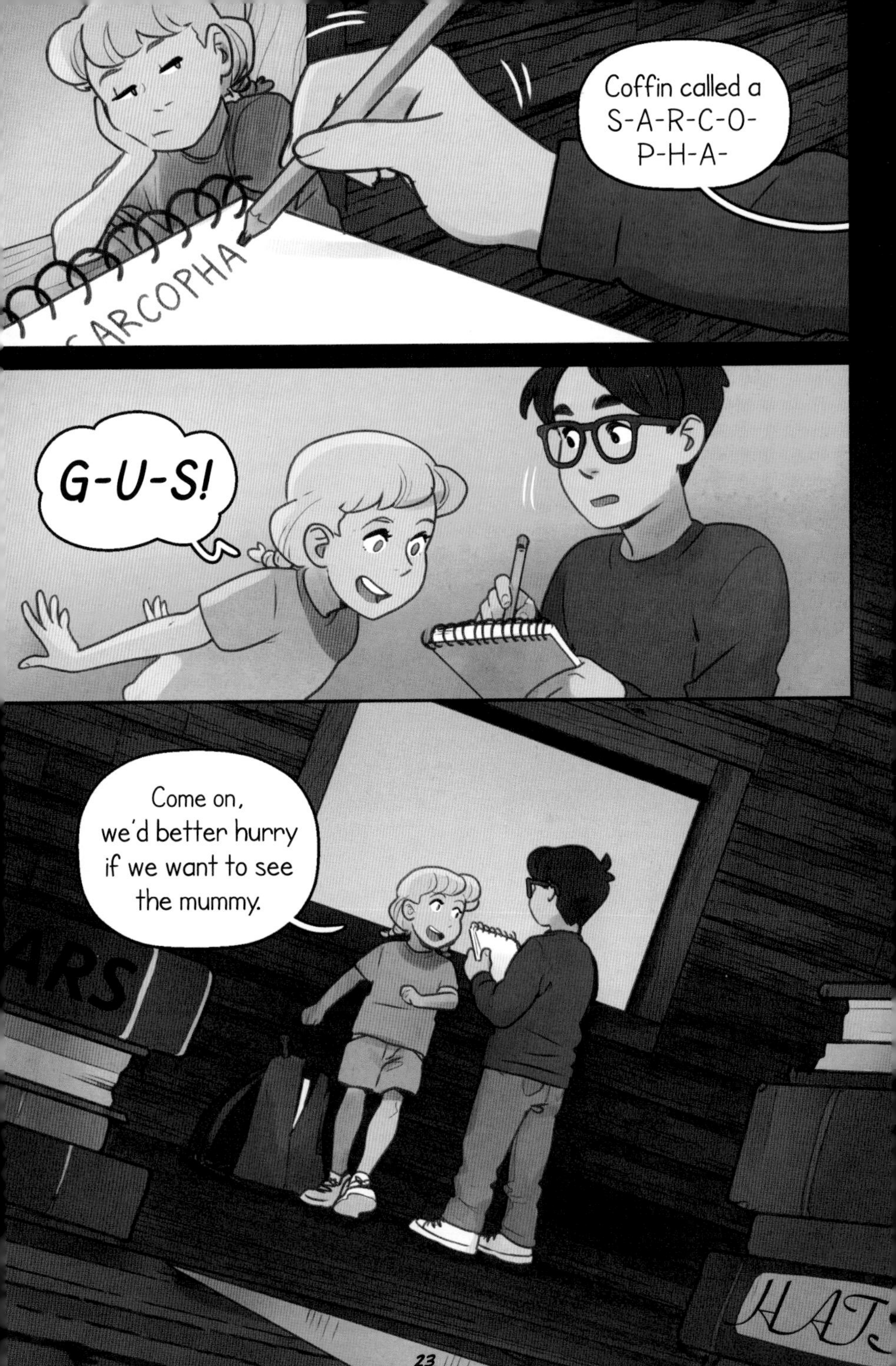
Coffin called a S-A-R-C-O-P-H-A-
SARCOPHA
G-U-S!
Come on, we'd better hurry if we want to see the mummy.
ARS
HATS

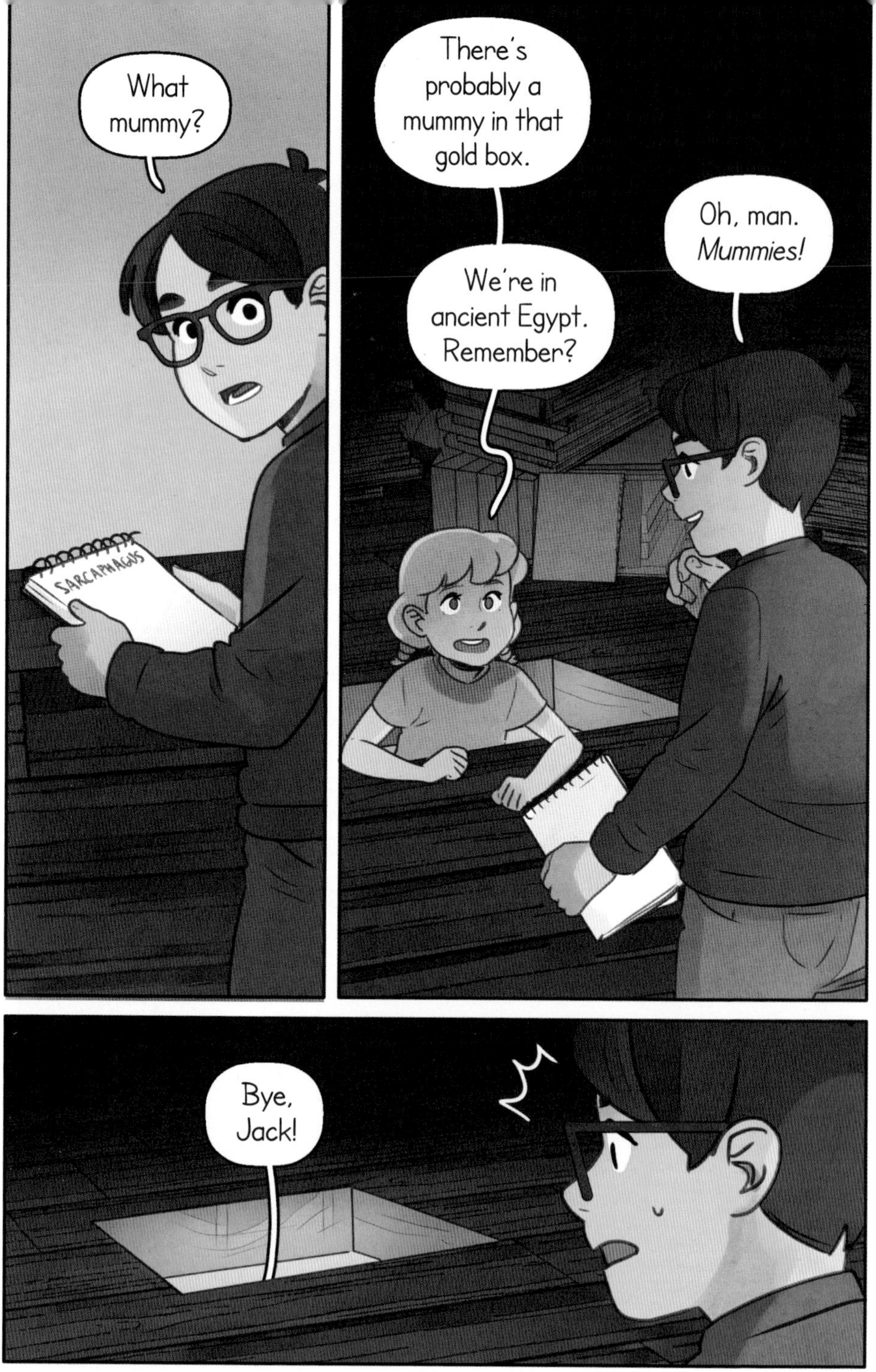
What mummy?
SARCAPHAGUS
There's probably a mummy in that gold box.
We're in ancient Egypt. Remember?
Oh, man. *Mummies!*
Bye, Jack!

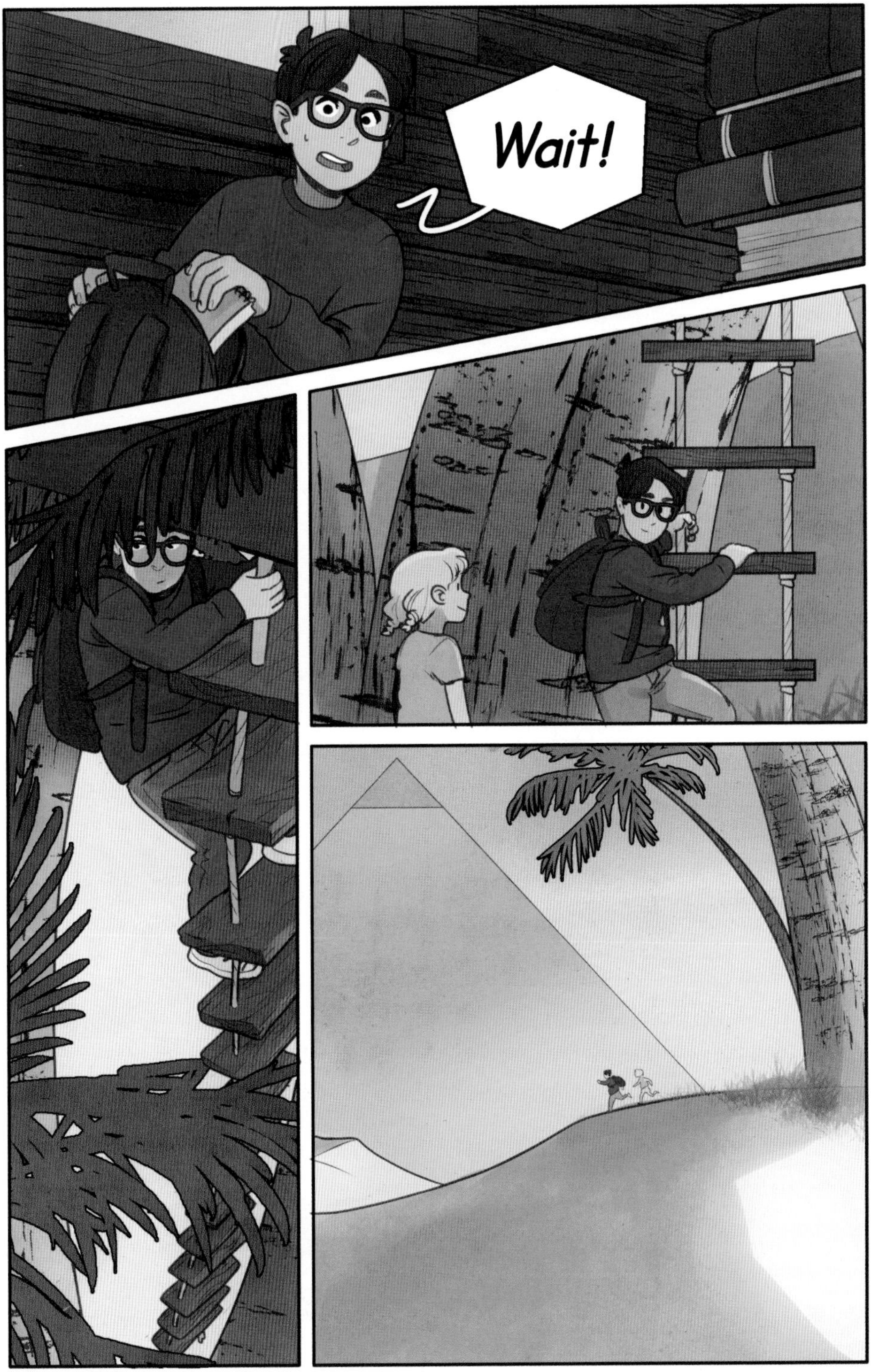
Wait!

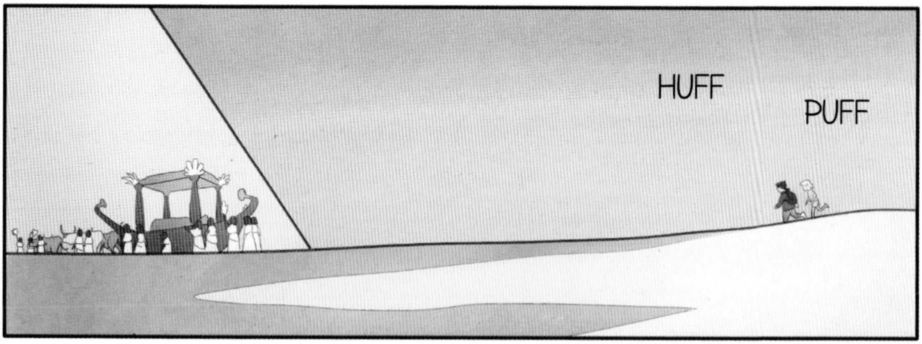
HUFF
PUFF

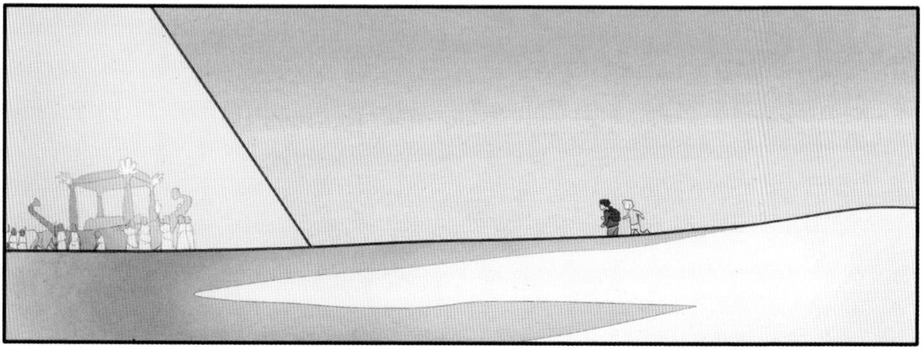

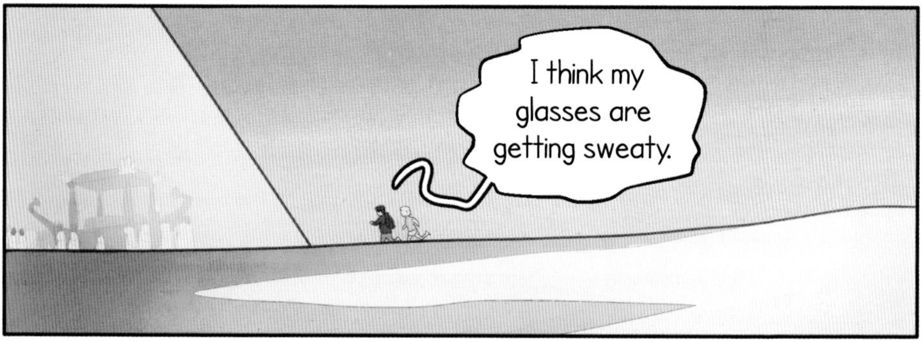
I think my glasses are getting sweaty.

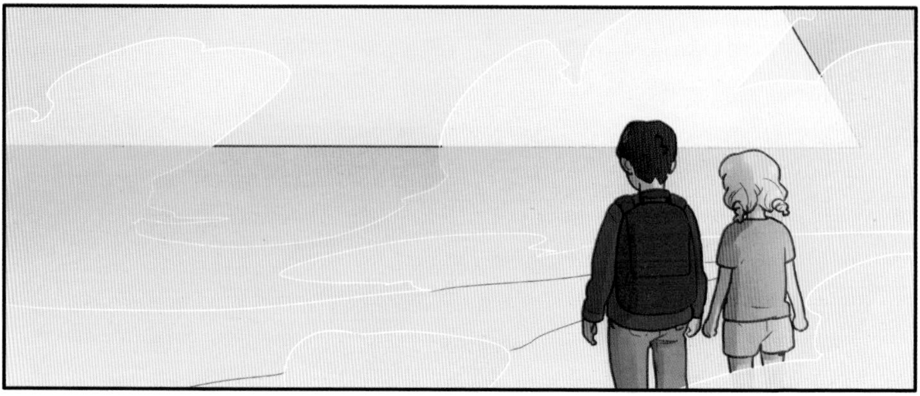

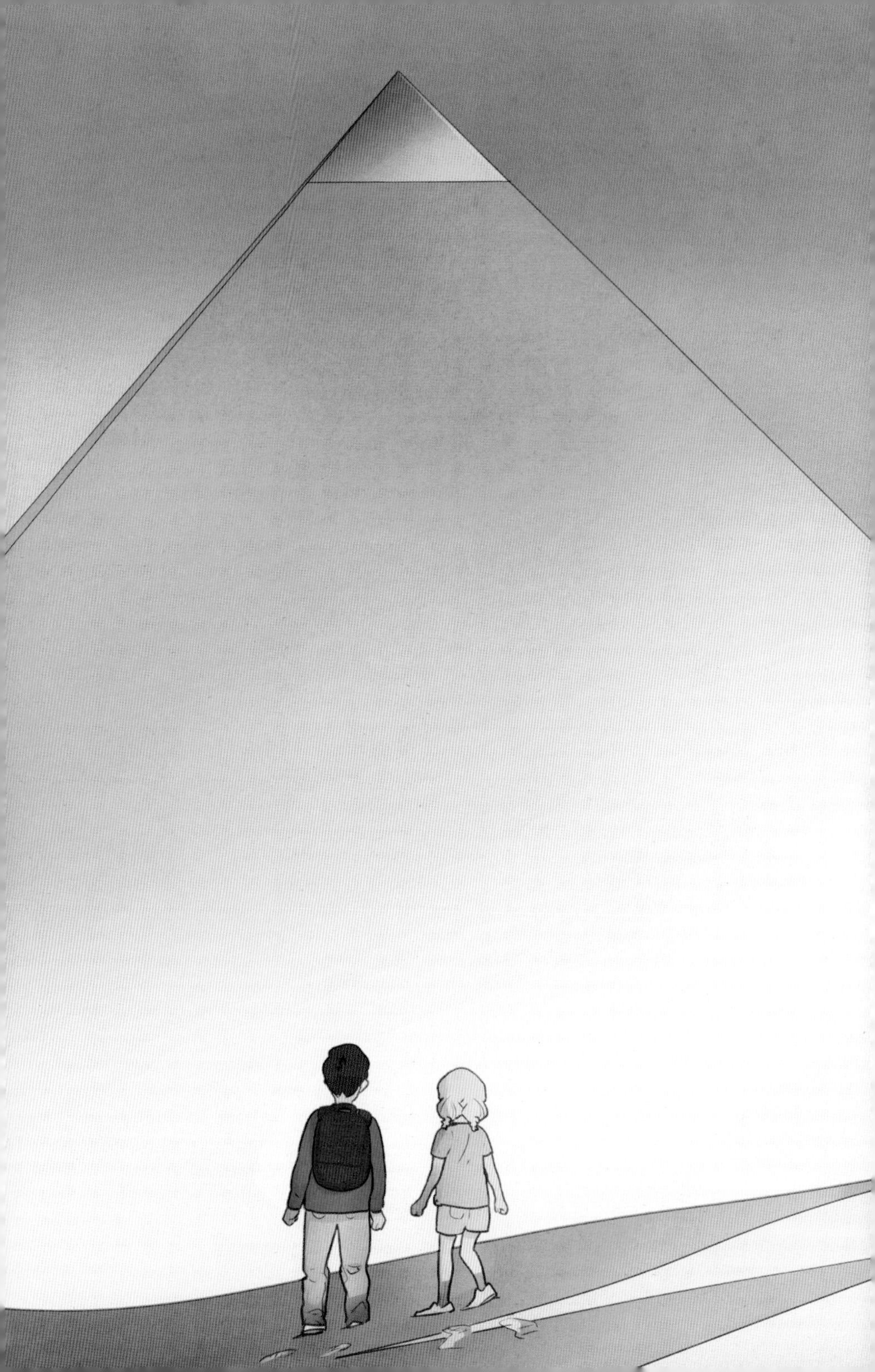

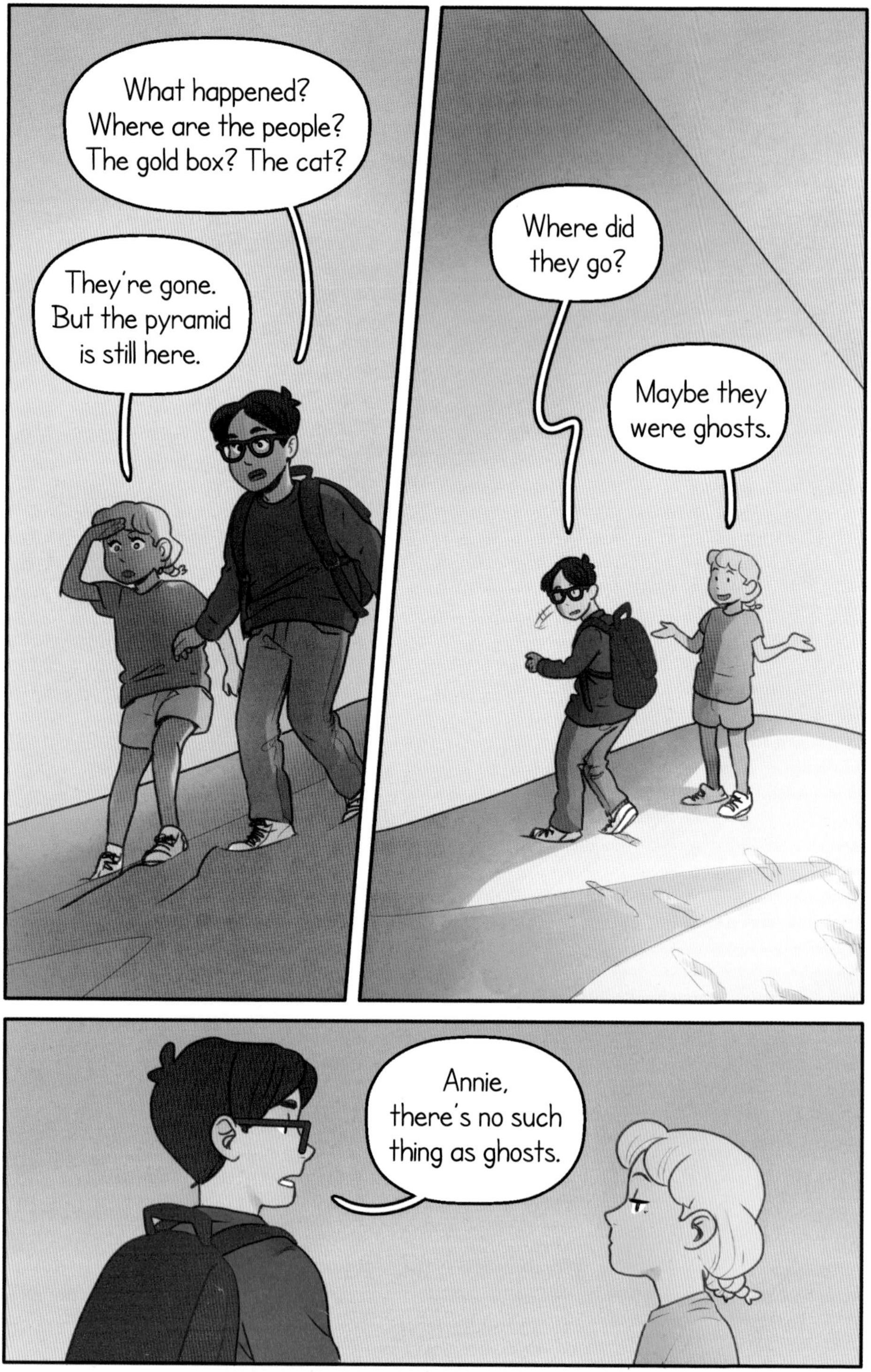
What happened? Where are the people? The gold box? The cat?
They're gone. But the pyramid is still here.
Where did they go?
Maybe they were ghosts.
Annie, there's no such thing as ghosts.

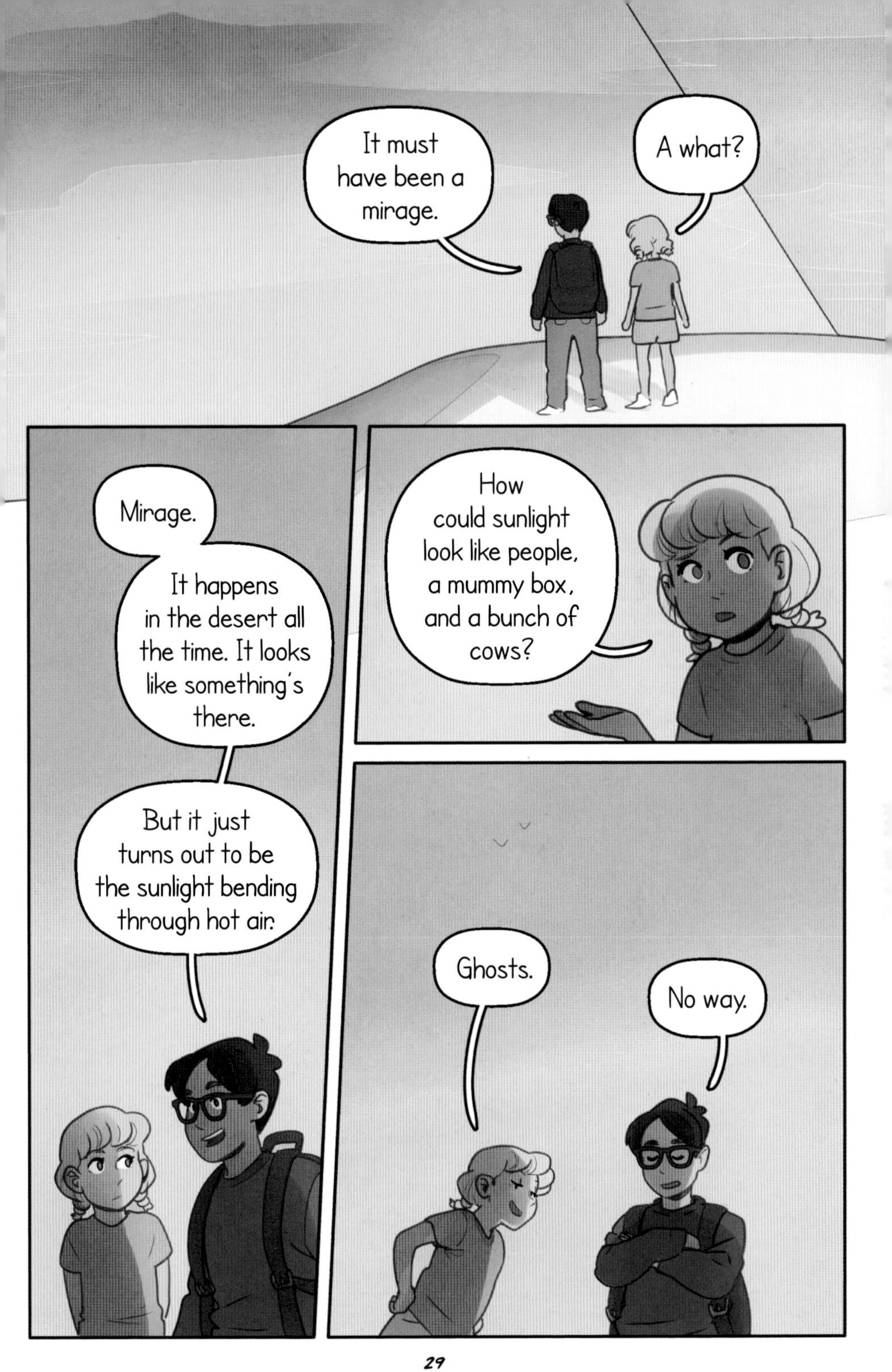
It must have been a mirage.
A what?
Mirage.
It happens in the desert all the time. It looks like something's there.
But it just turns out to be the sunlight bending through hot air.
How could sunlight look like people, a mummy box, and a bunch of cows?
Ghosts.
No way.

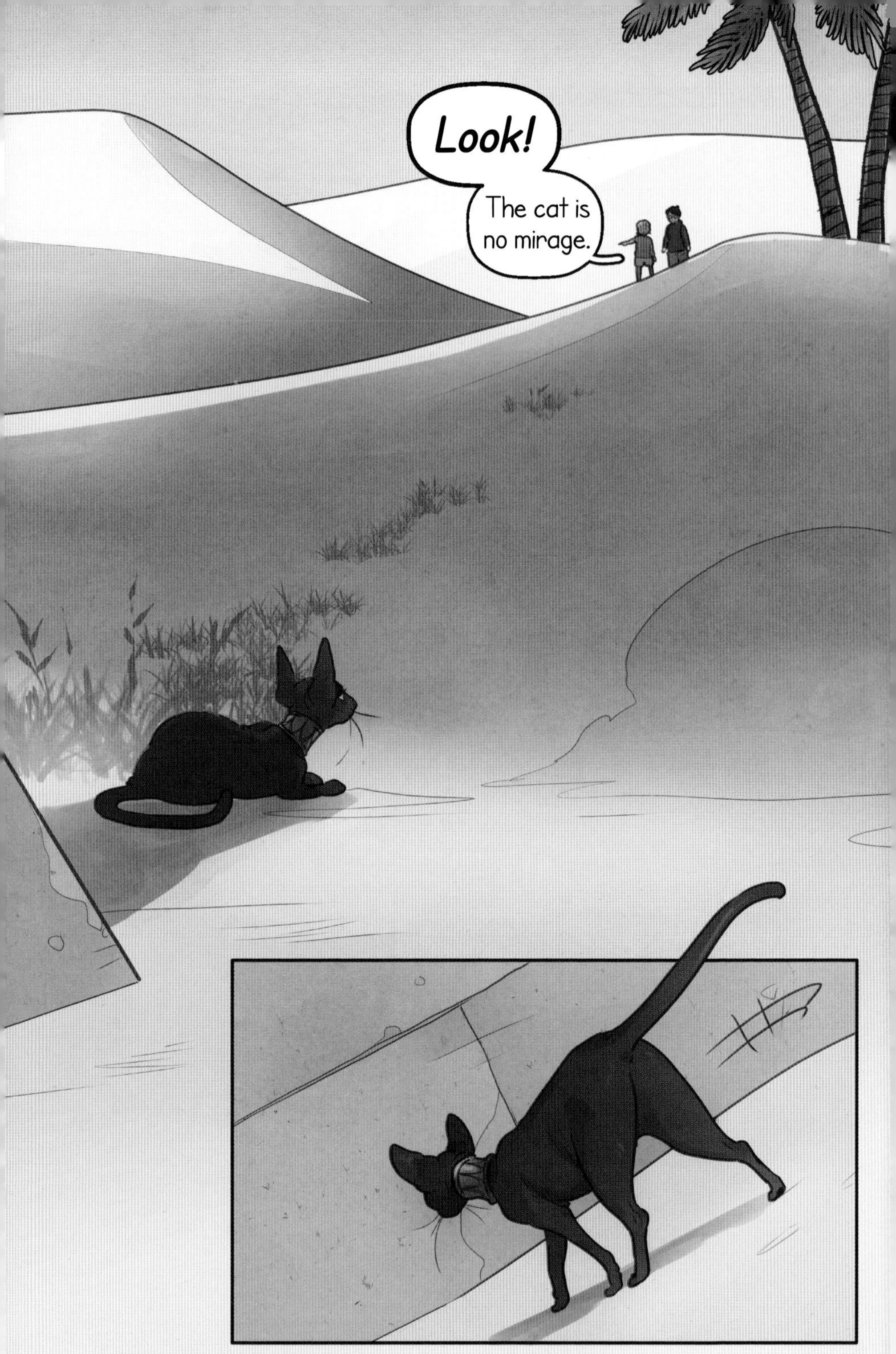
Look!
The cat is no mirage.

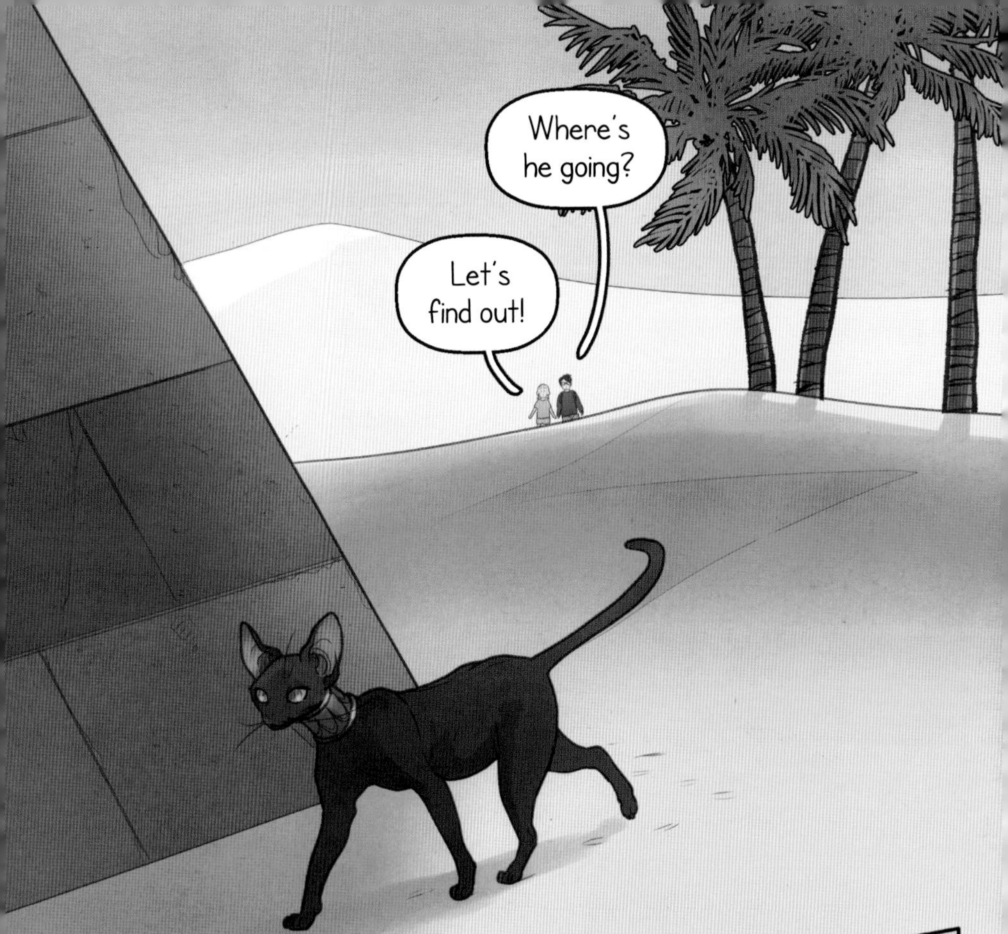
Where's he going?
Let's find out!
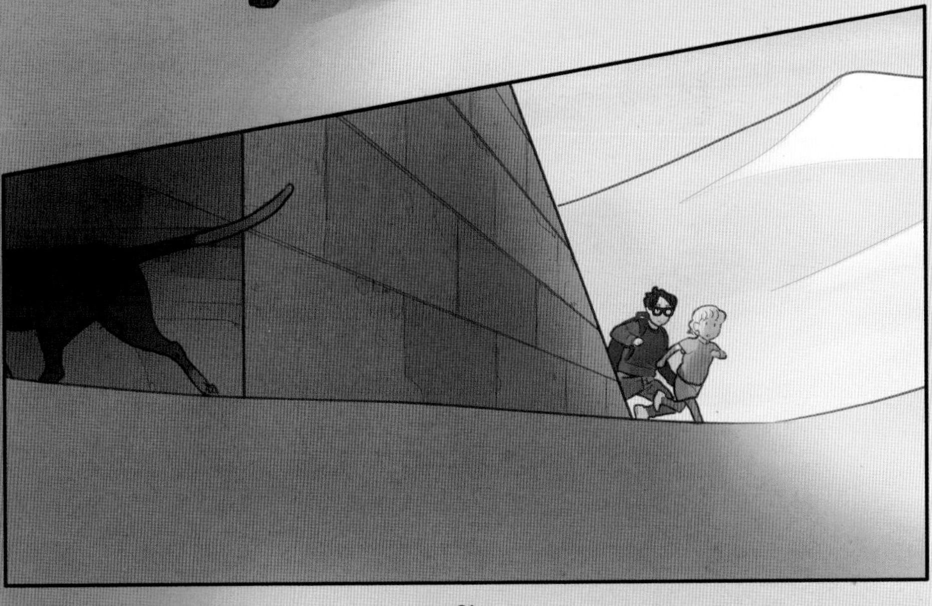

CHAPTER THREE
The Pyramid

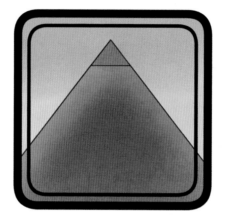

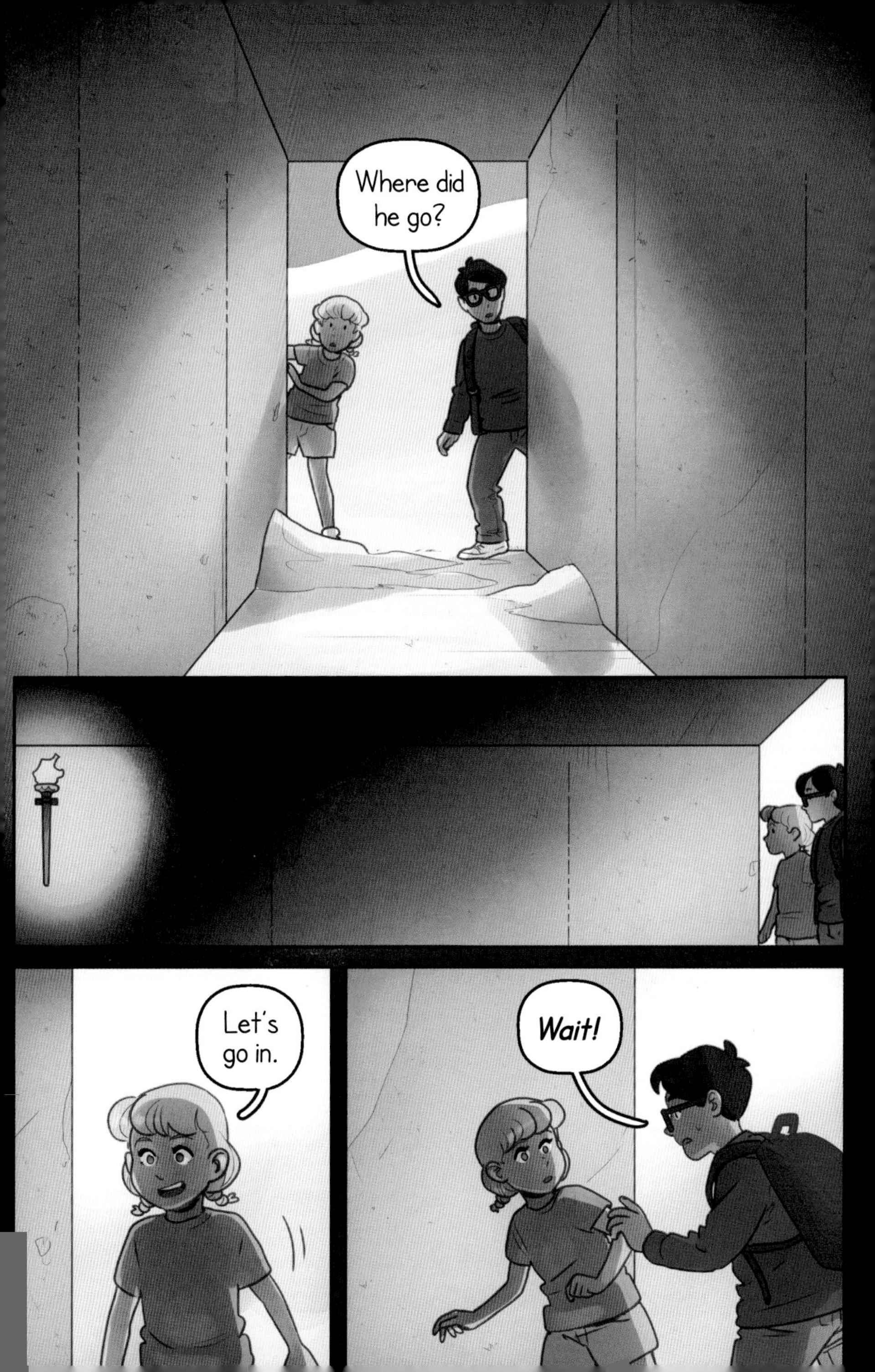
Where did he go?
Let's go in.
Wait!

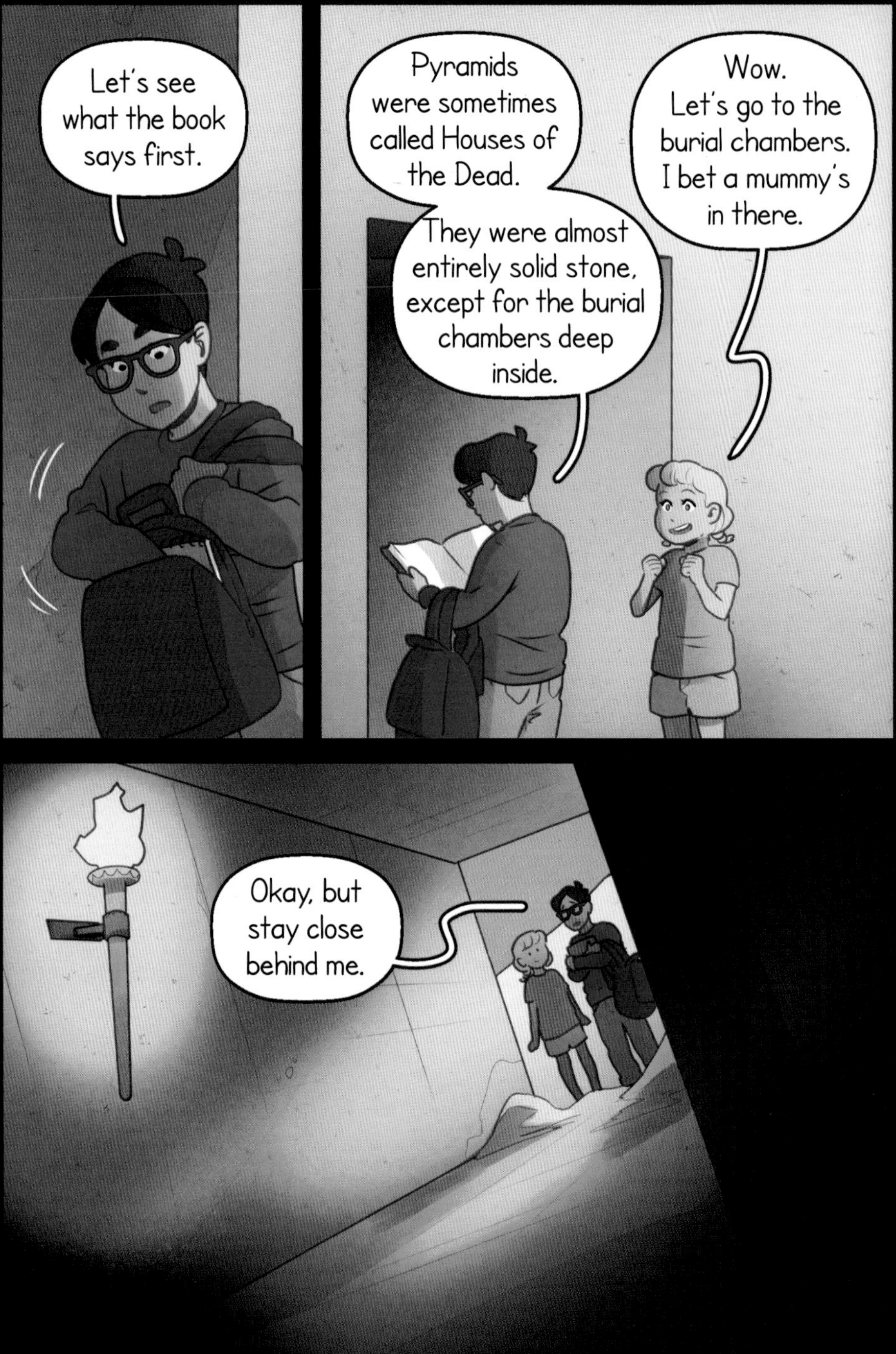
Let's see what the book says first.
Pyramids were sometimes called Houses of the Dead.
They were almost entirely solid stone, except for the burial chambers deep inside.
Wow. Let's go to the burial chambers. I bet a mummy's in there.
Okay, but stay close behind me.

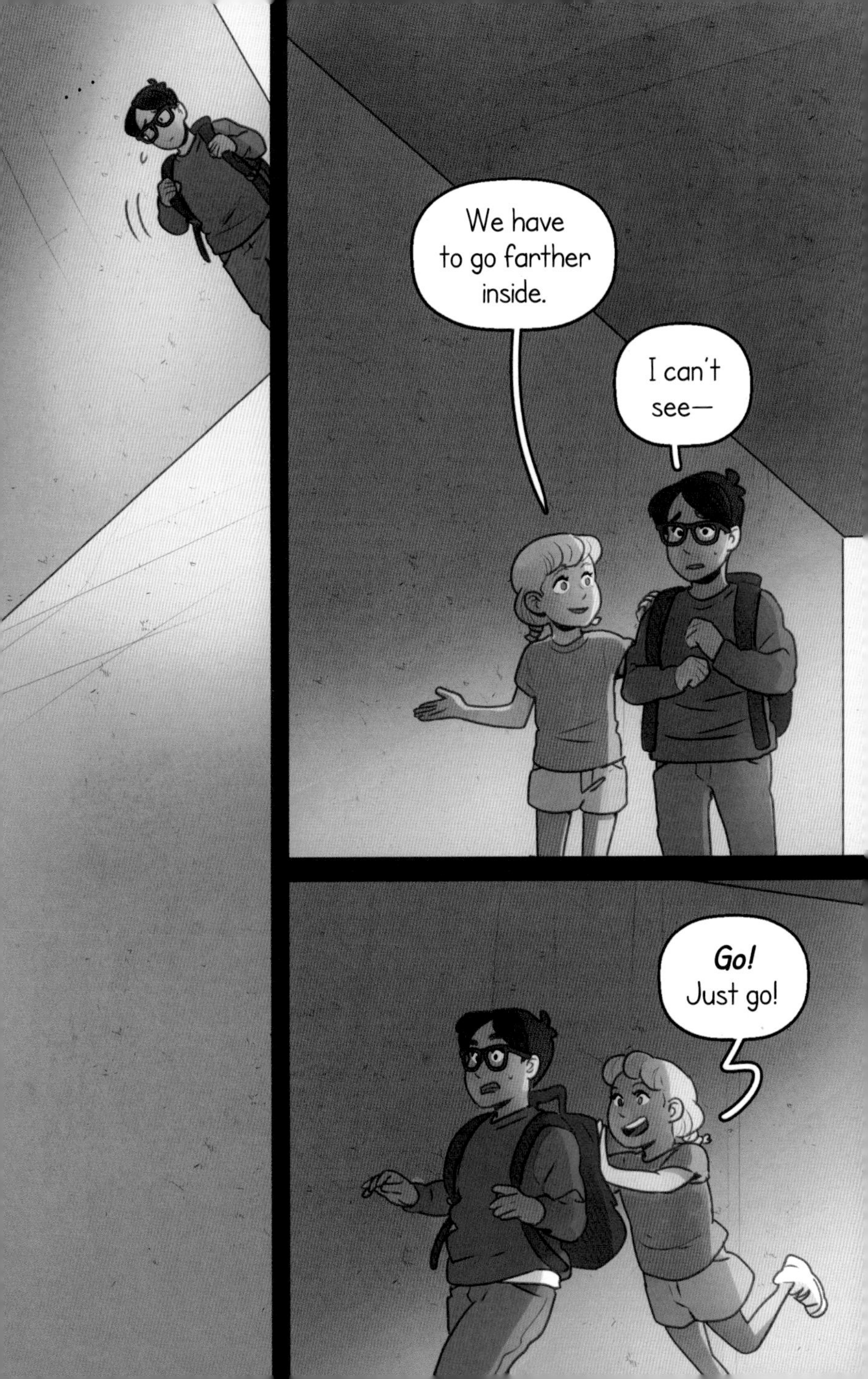
We have to go farther inside.
I can't see—
Go! Just go!

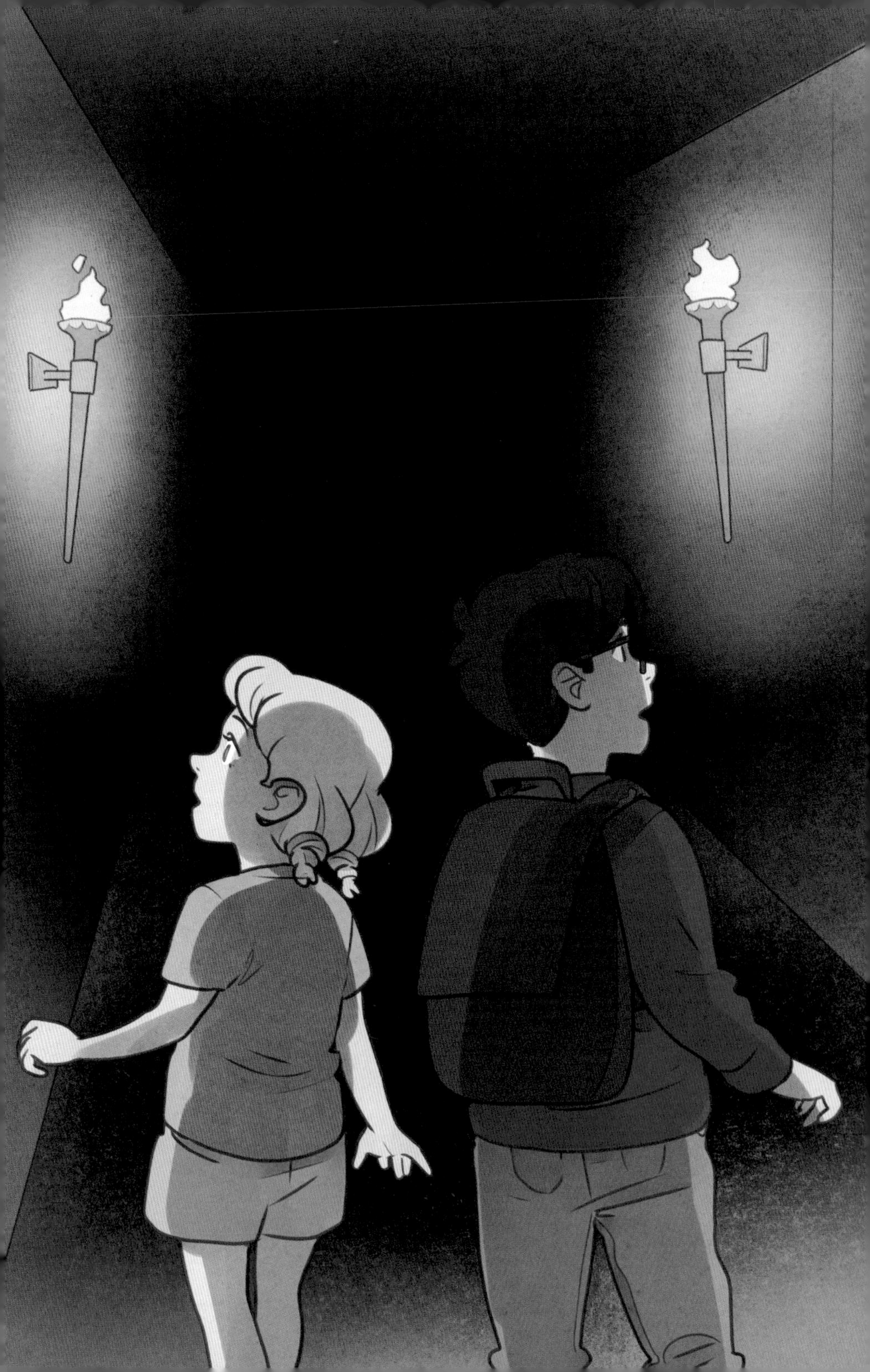

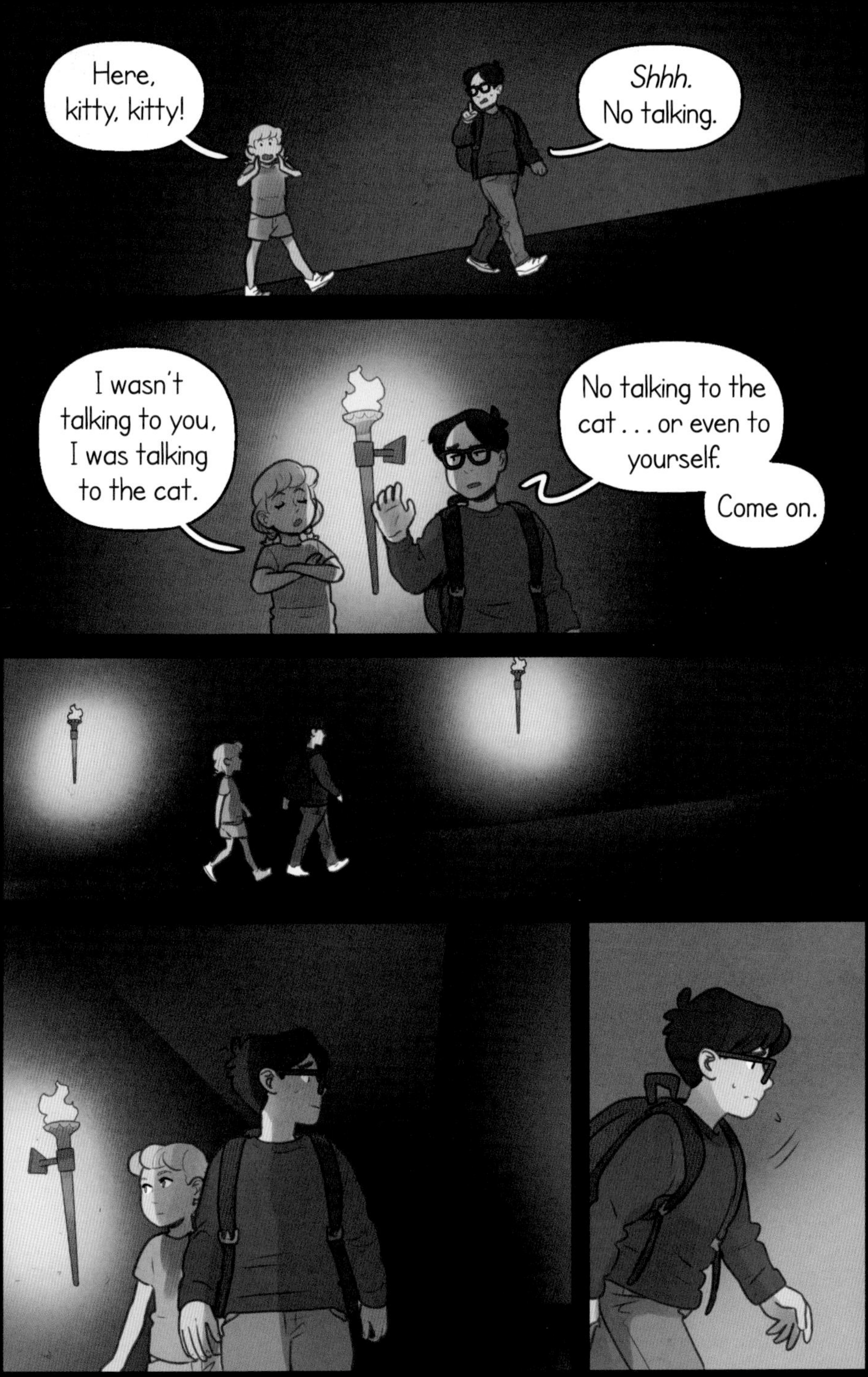
Here, kitty, kitty!
Shhh. No talking.
I wasn't talking to you, I was talking to the cat.
No talking to the cat . . . or even to yourself.
Come on.

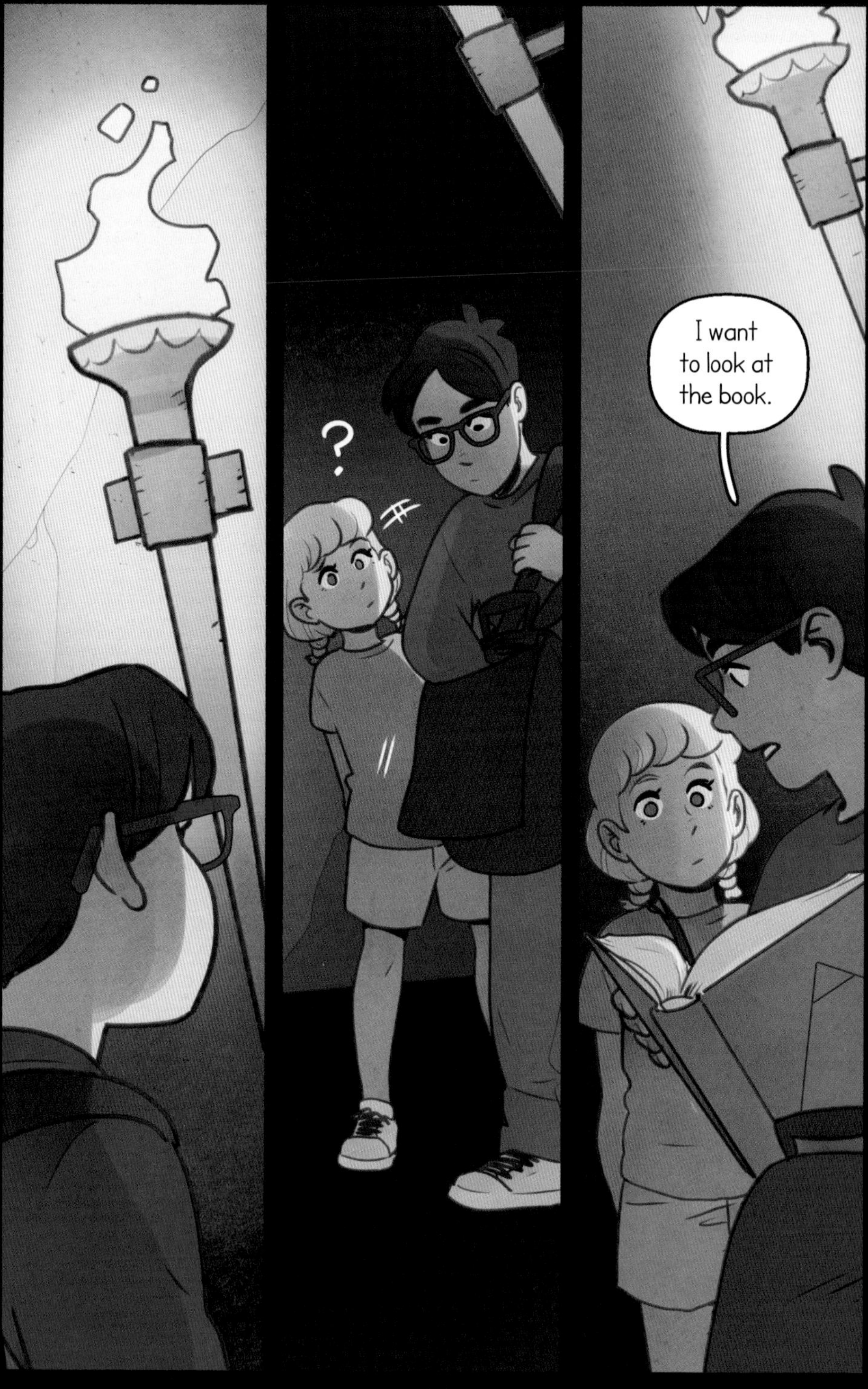
?
I want to look at the book.

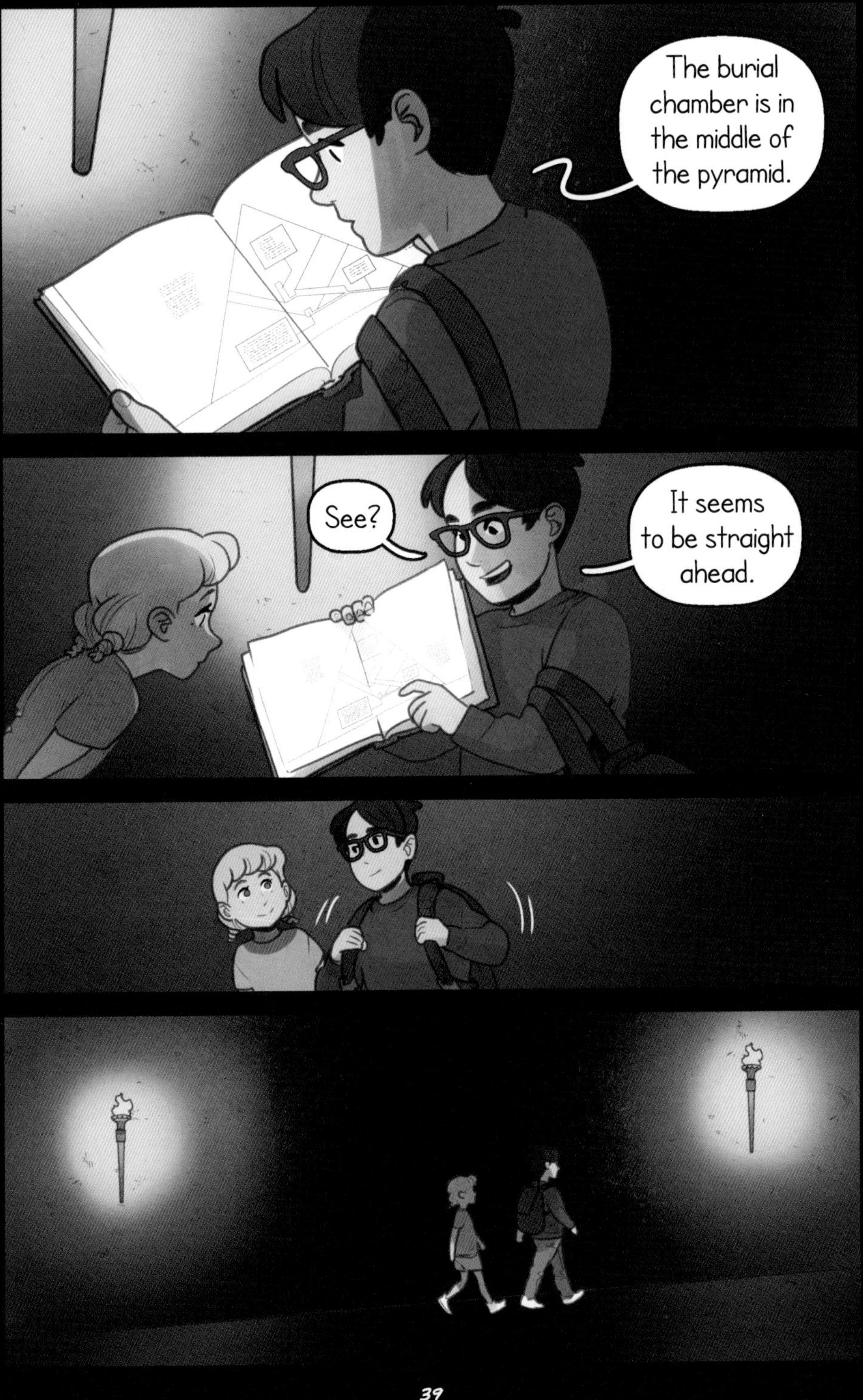
The burial chamber is in the middle of the pyramid.
See?
It seems to be straight ahead.

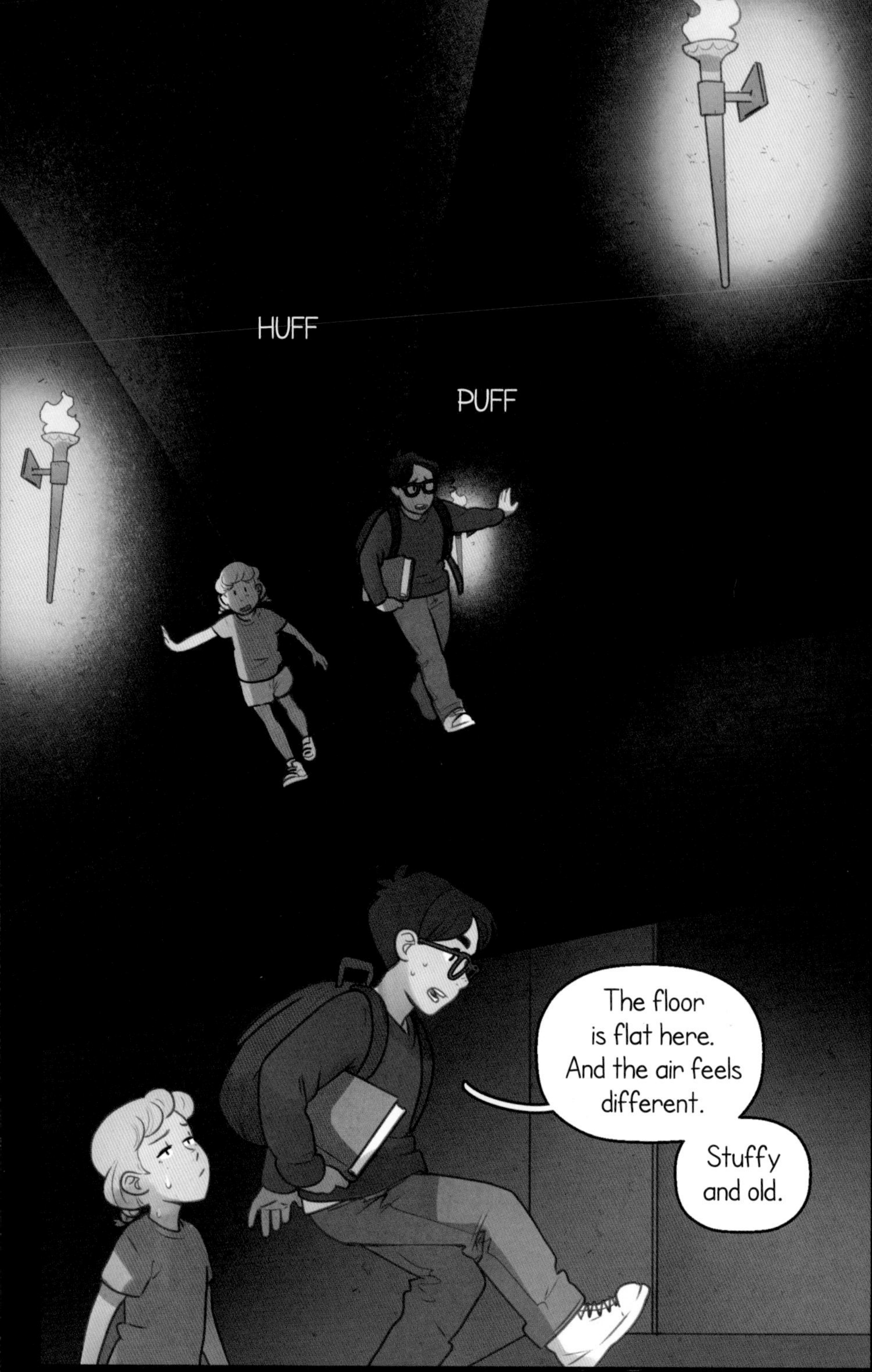
HUFF
PUFF
The floor is flat here. And the air feels different.
Stuffy and old.

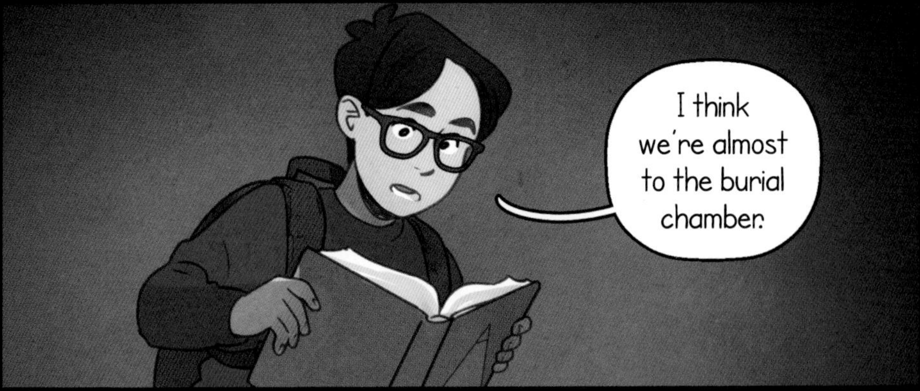
I think we're almost to the burial chamber.

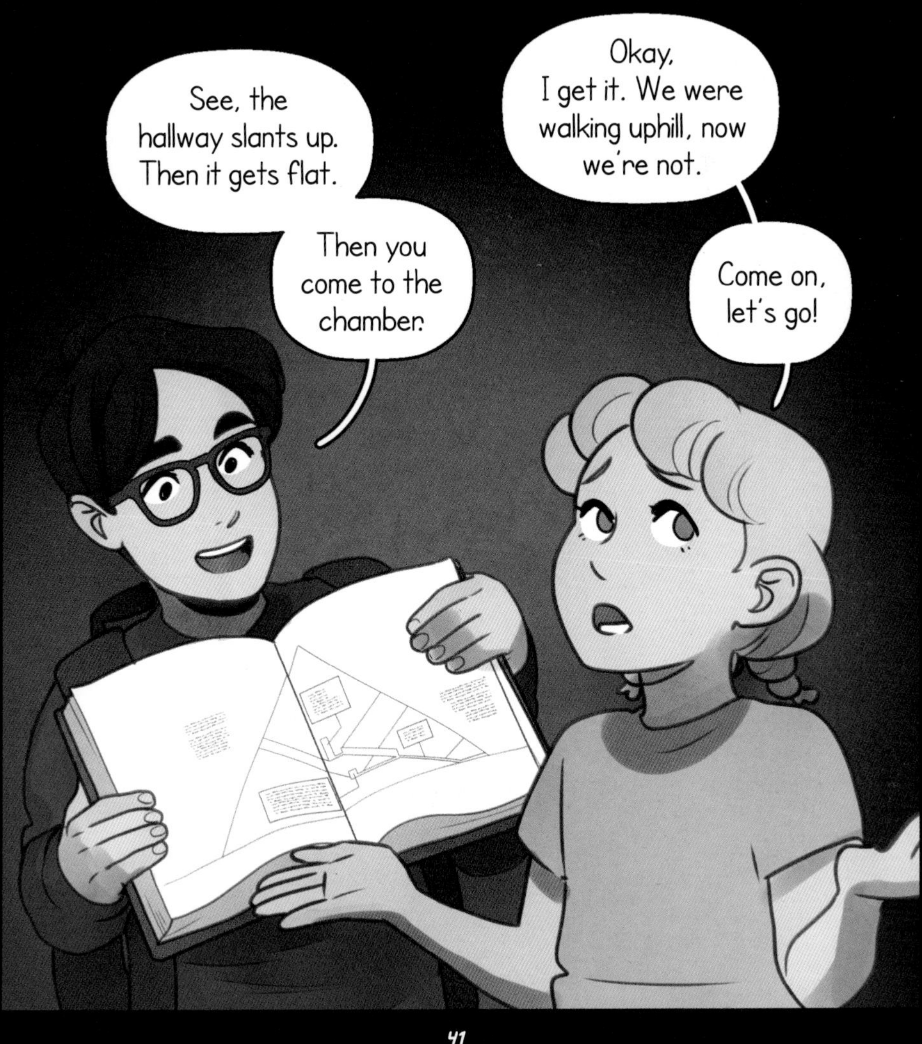
See, the hallway slants up. Then it gets flat.
Then you come to the chamber.
Okay, I get it. We were walking uphill, now we're not.
Come on, let's go!

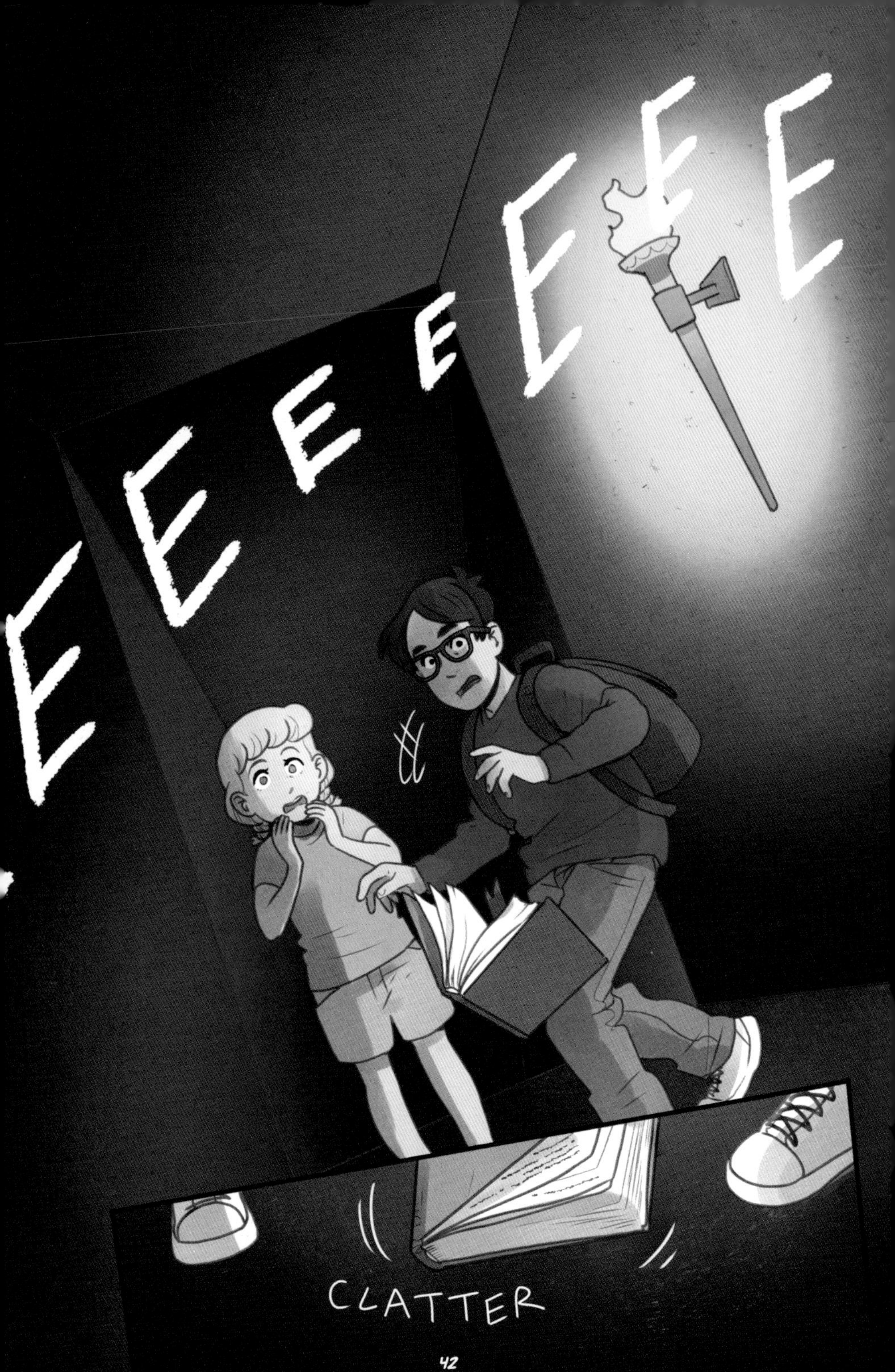
EEEEEEEE
CLATTER

CHAPTER FOUR
Back from the Dead

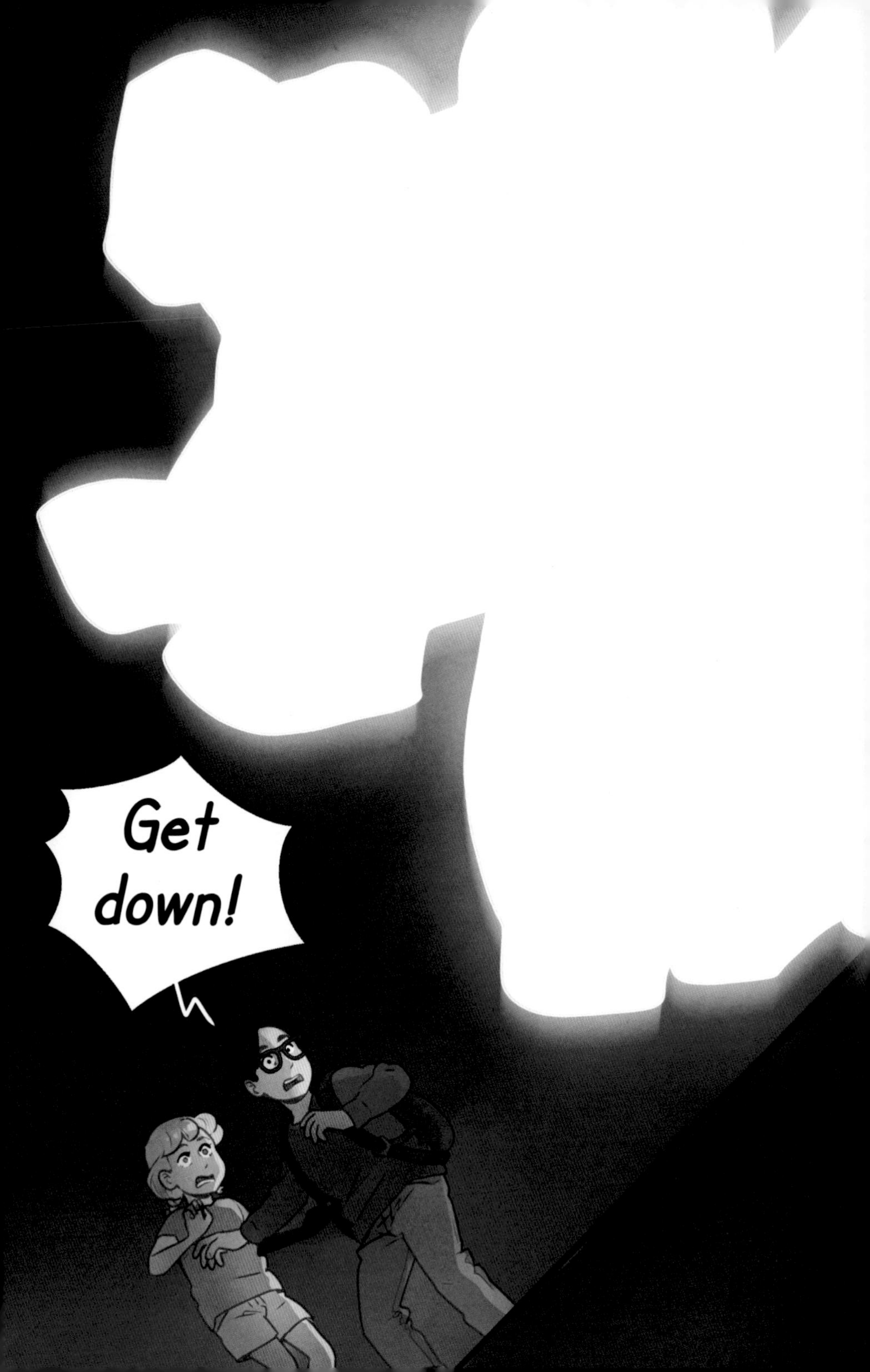
Get down!

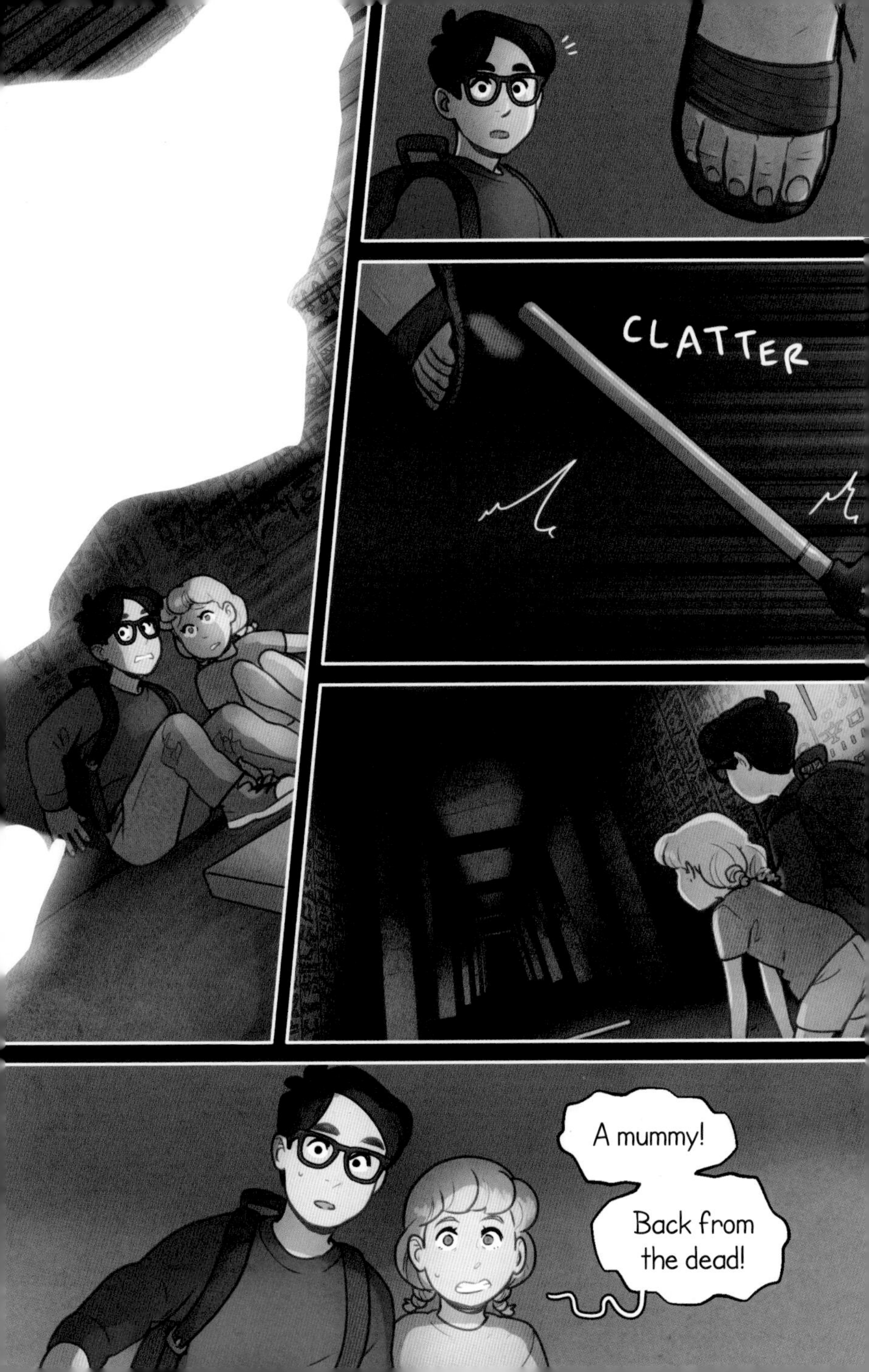

CLATTER
A mummy!
Back from the dead!

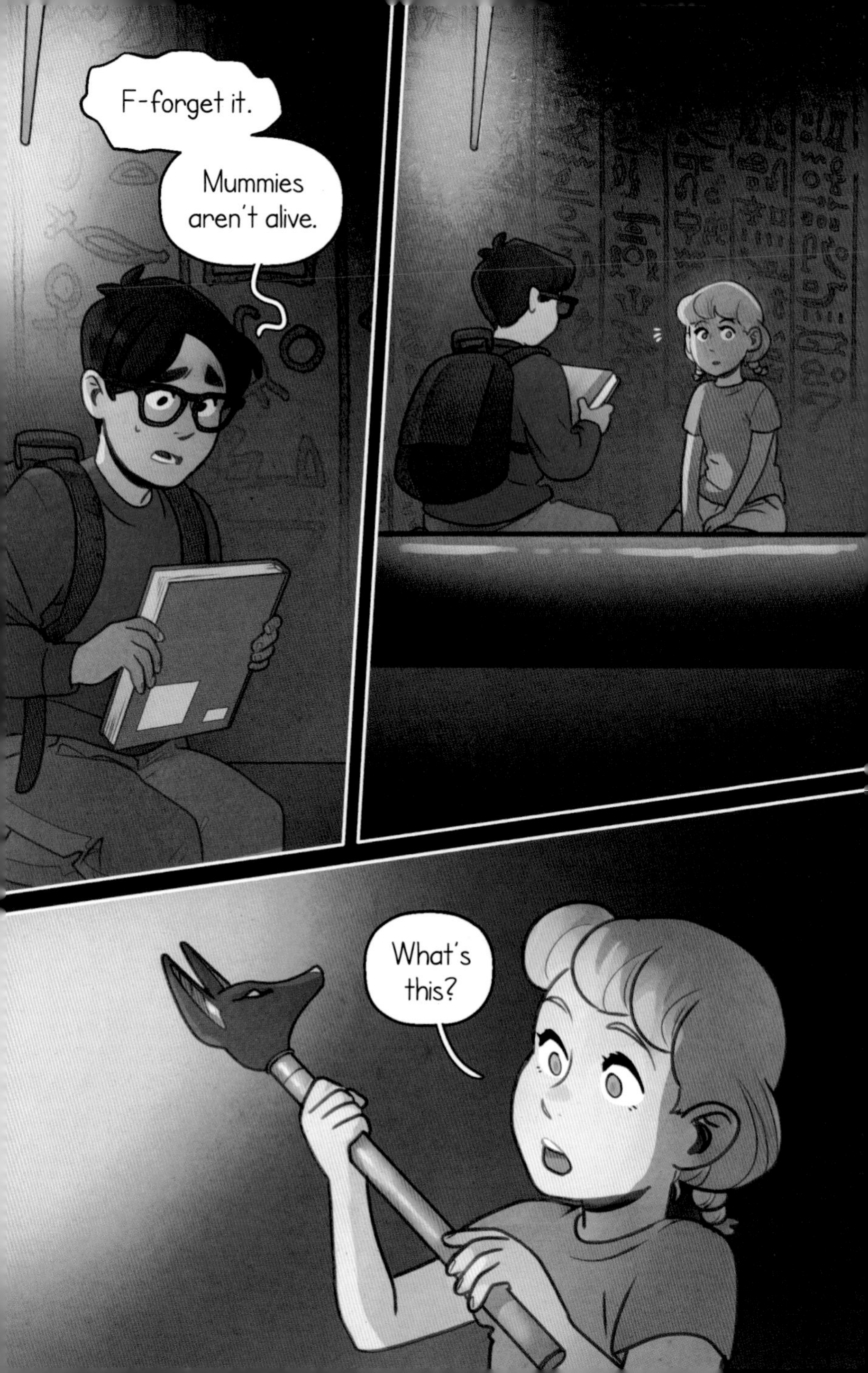
F-forget it.
Mummies aren't alive.
What's this?

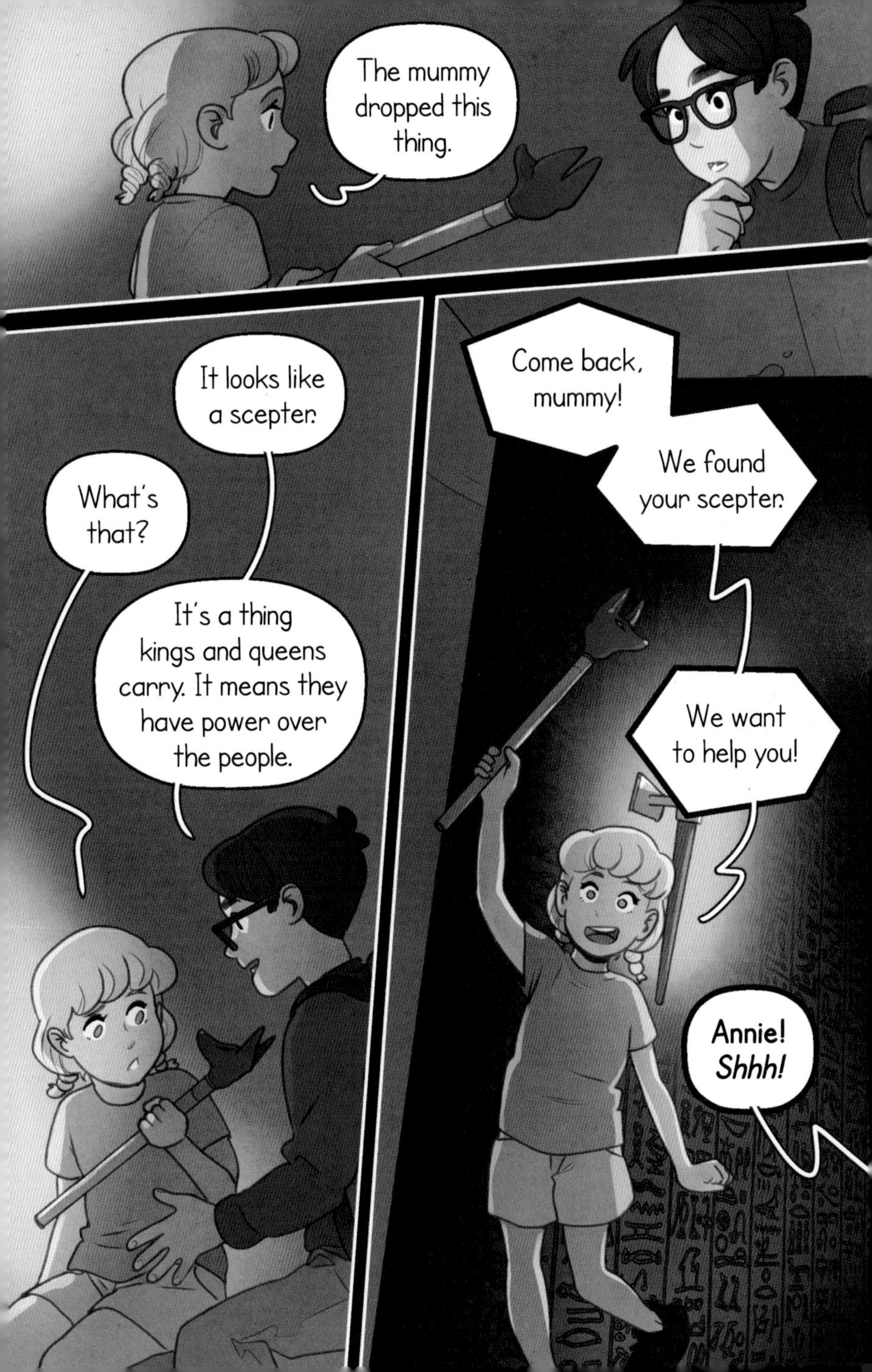
The mummy dropped this thing.
It looks like a scepter.
What's that?
It's a thing kings and queens carry. It means they have power over the people.
Come back, mummy!
We found your scepter.
We want to help you!
Annie! *Shhh!*

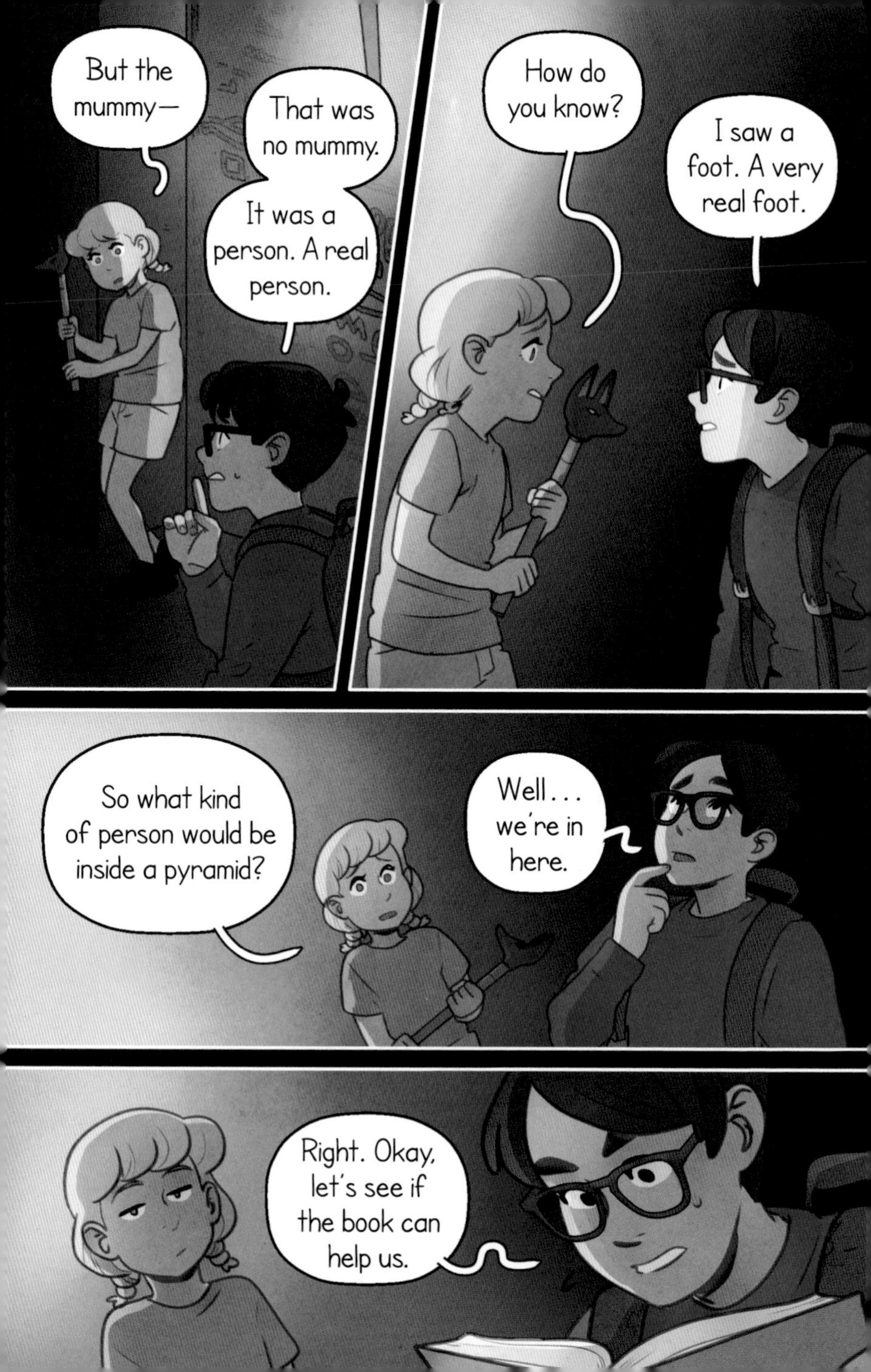
But the mummy—
That was no mummy.
It was a person. A real person.
How do you know?
I saw a foot. A very real foot.
So what kind of person would be inside a pyramid?
Well . . . we're in here.
Right. Okay, let's see if the book can help us.

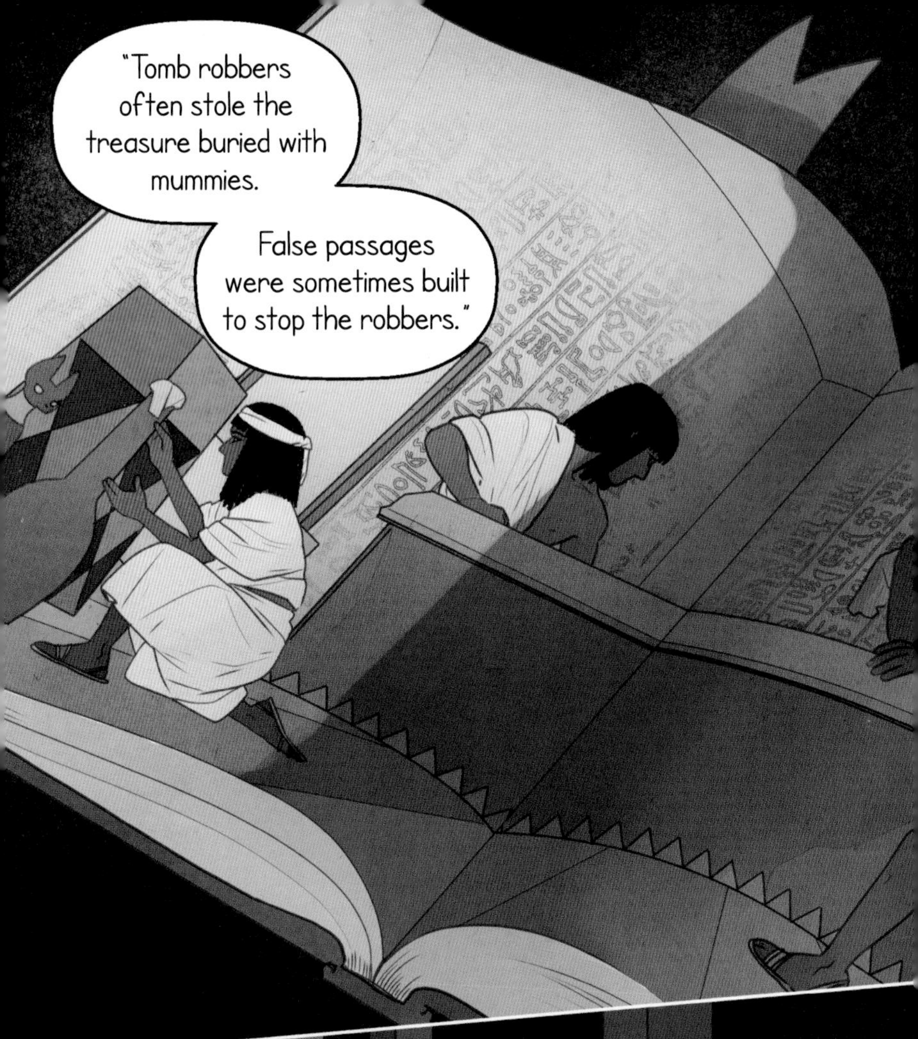
"Tomb robbers often stole the treasure buried with mummies.
False passages were sometimes built to stop the robbers."
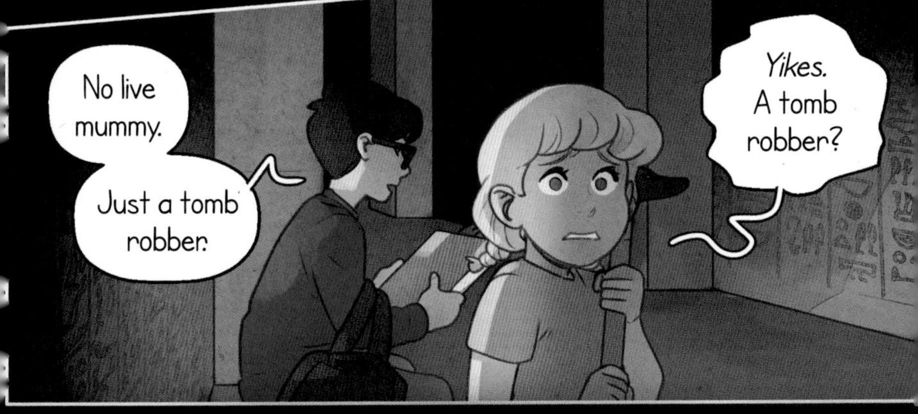
No live mummy.
Just a tomb robber.
Yikes. A tomb robber?

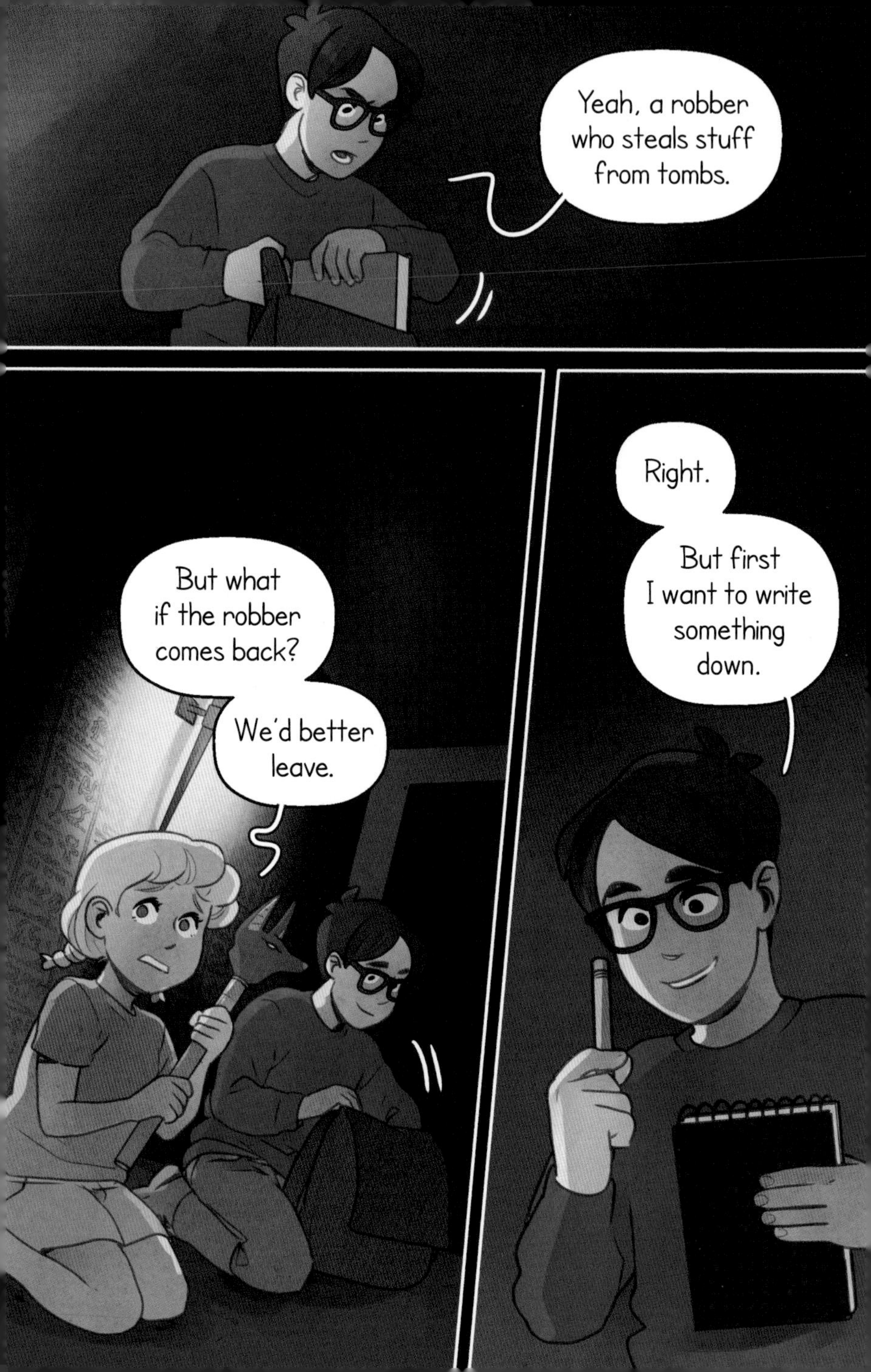
Yeah, a robber who steals stuff from tombs.
But what if the robber comes back?
We'd better leave.
Right.
But first I want to write something down.

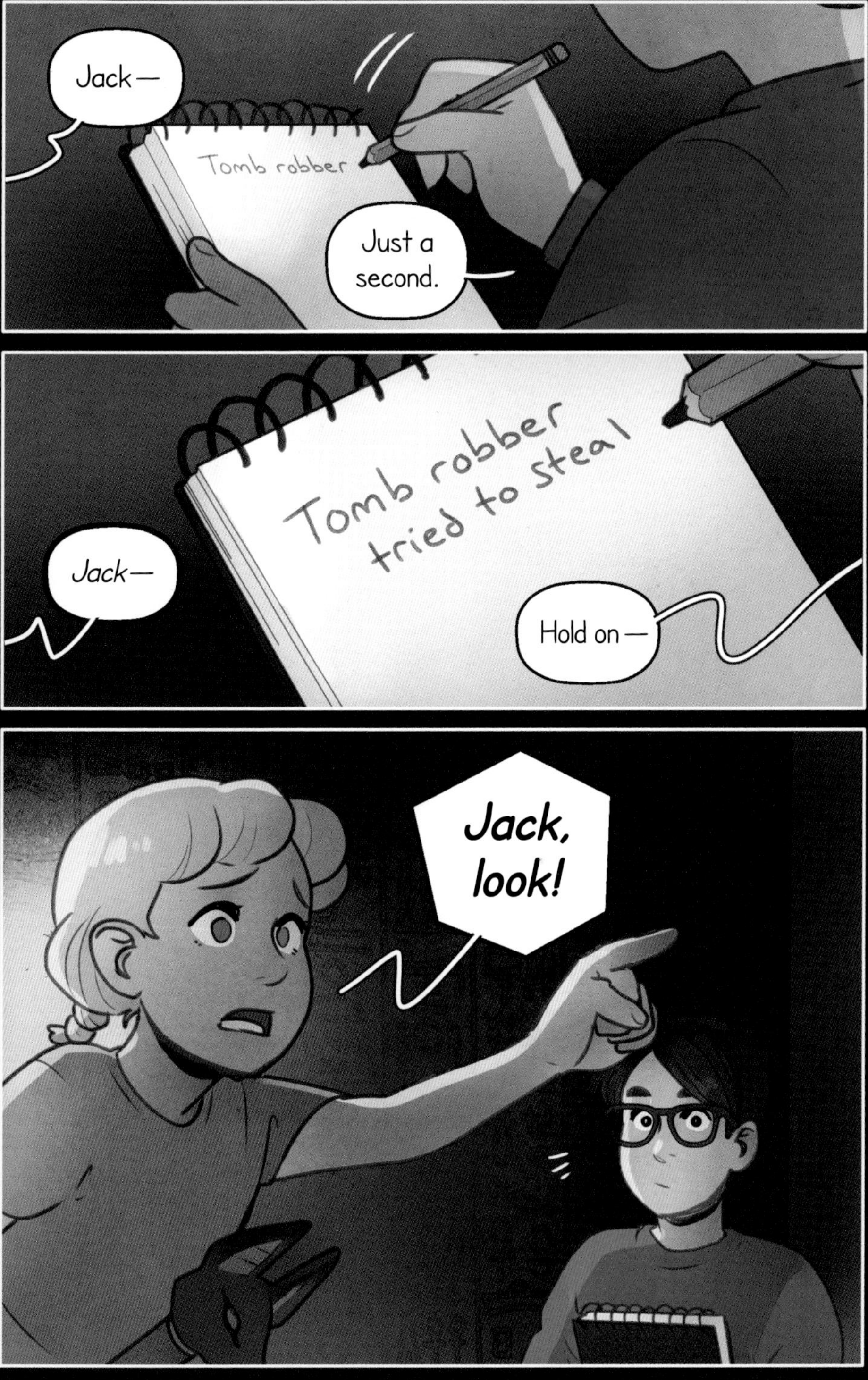
Jack—
Tomb robber
Just a second.
Tomb robber tried to steal
Jack—
Hold on—
Jack, look!

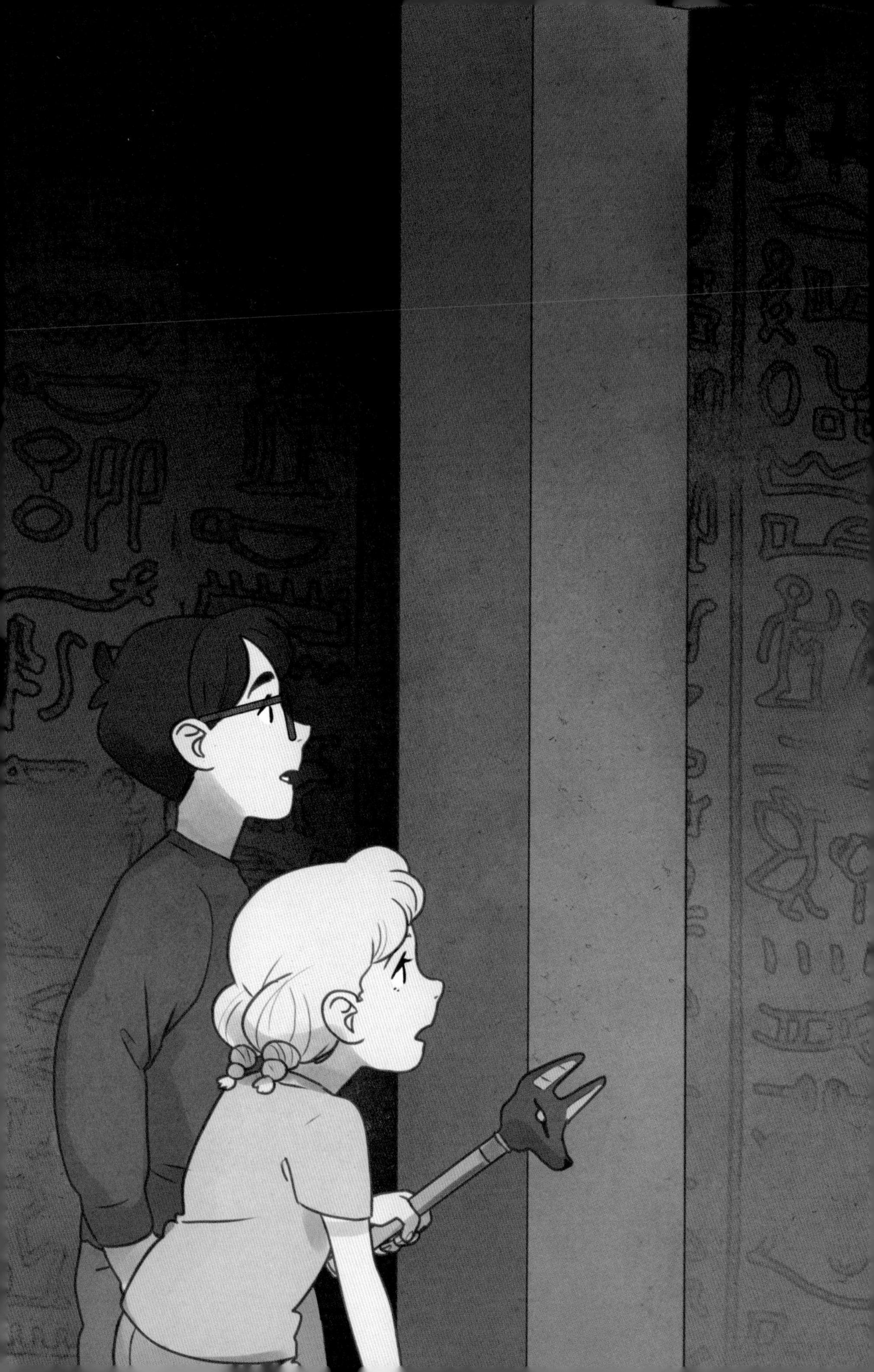

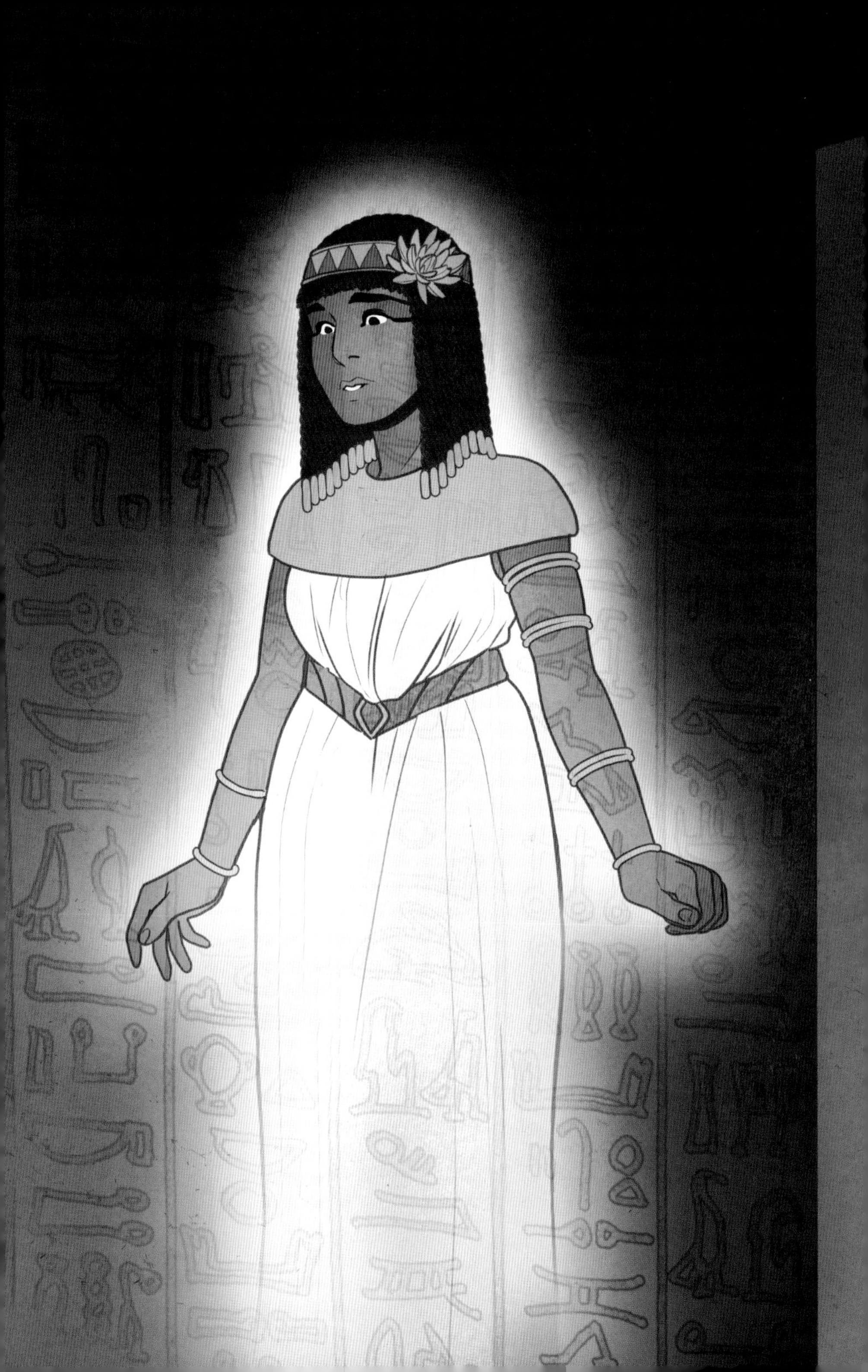

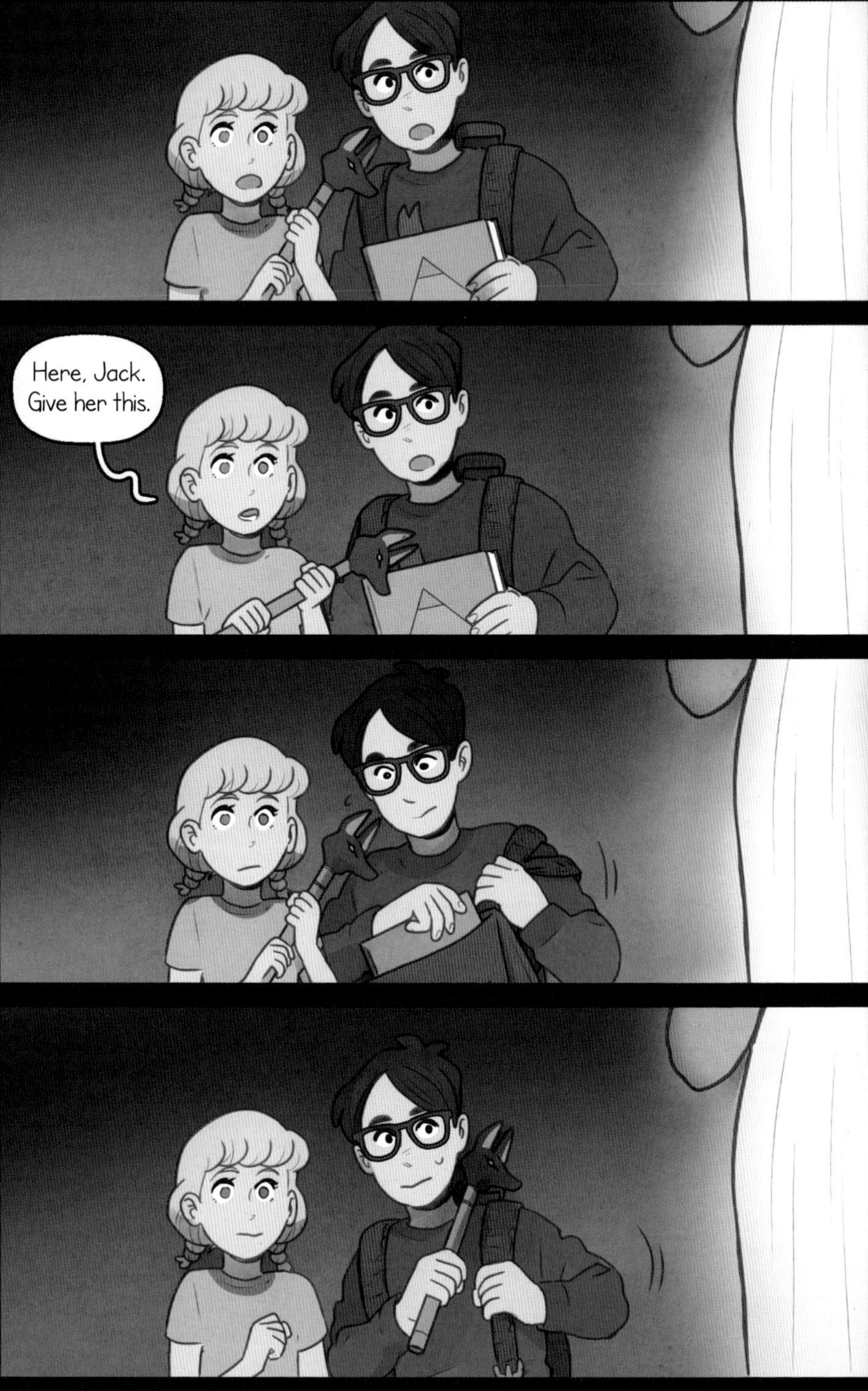
Here, Jack. Give her this.

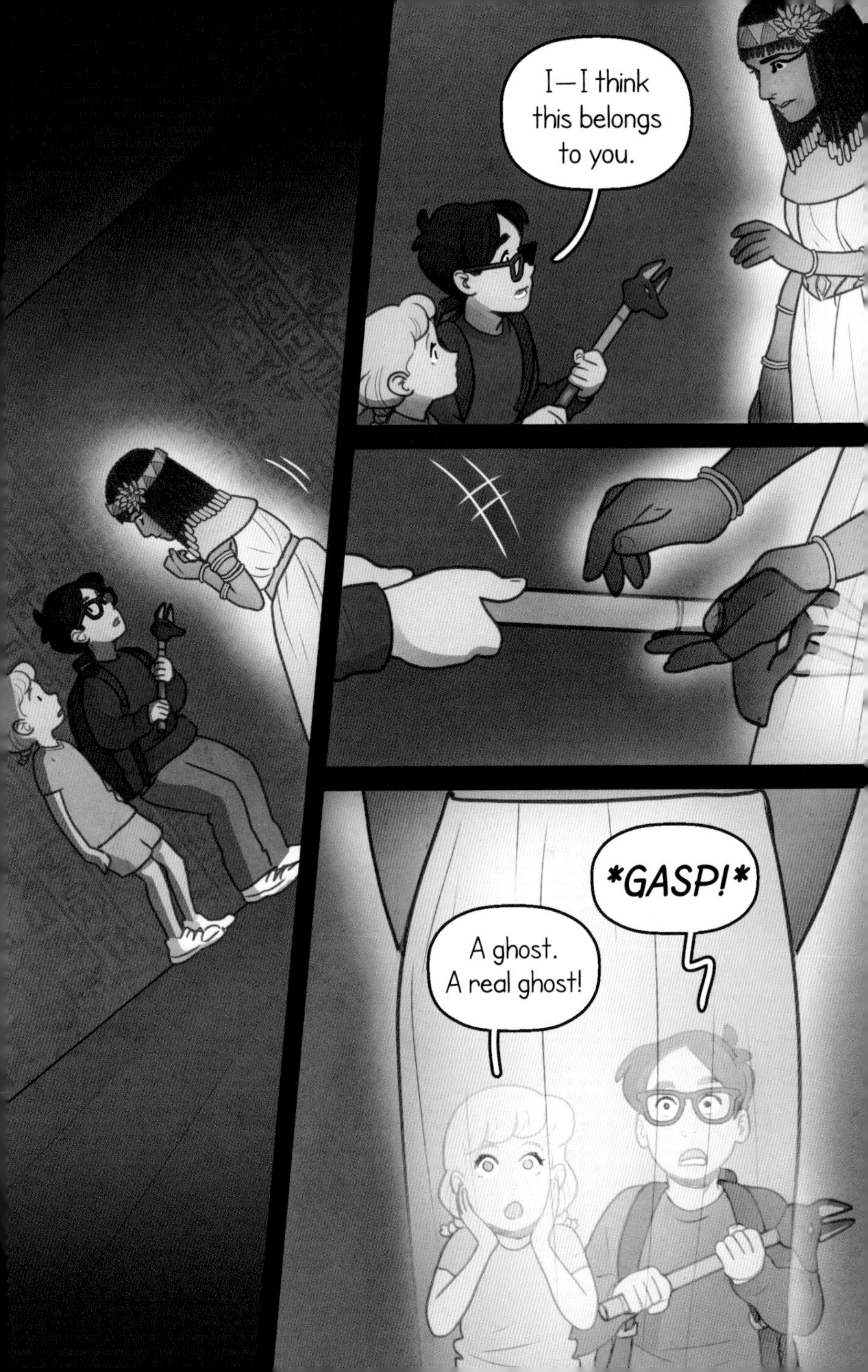
I—I think this belongs to you.
GASP!
A ghost. A real ghost!

CHAPTER FIVE
The Ghost-Queen

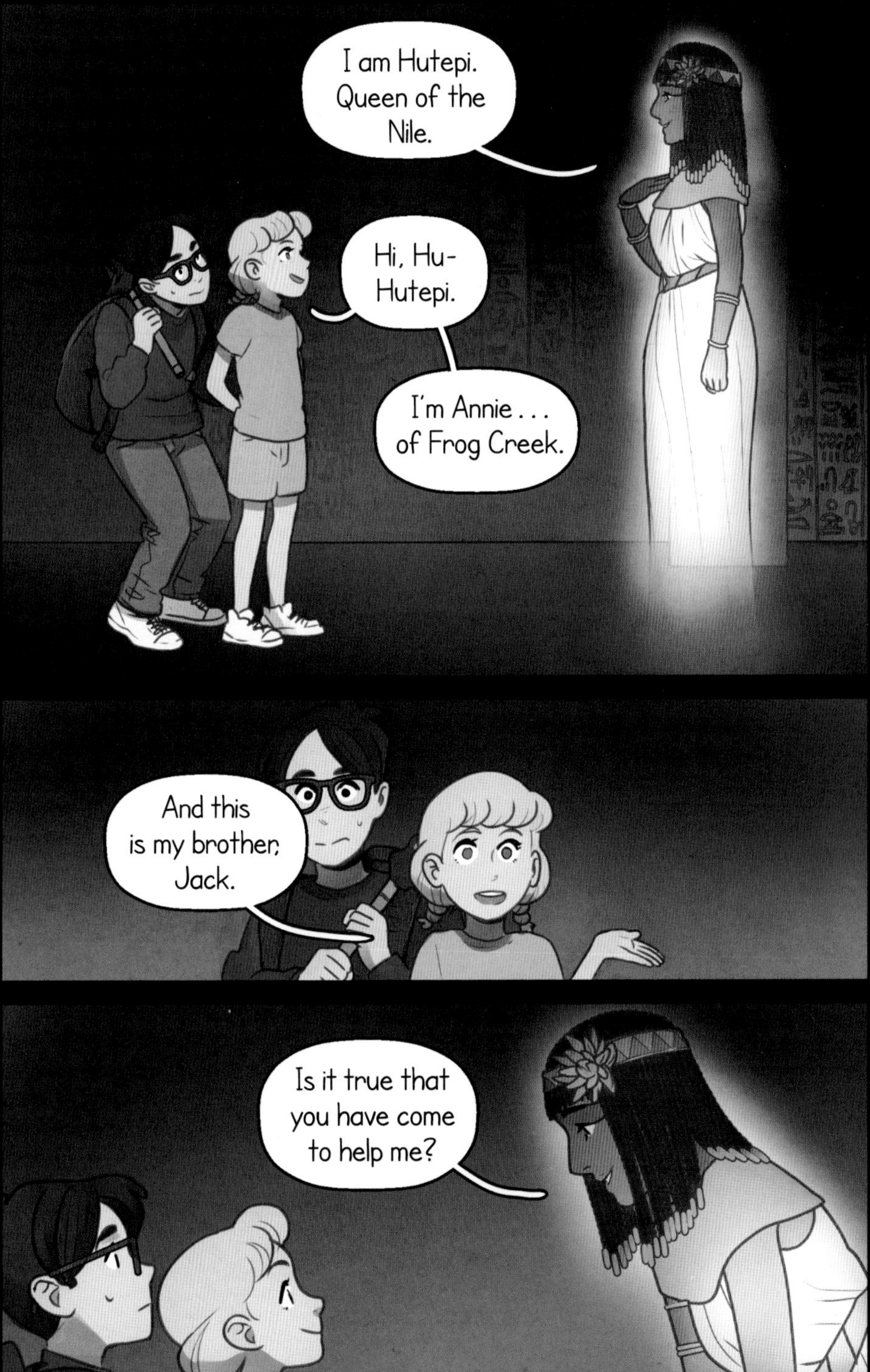
I am Hutepi. Queen of the Nile.
Hi, Hu-Hutepi.
I'm Annie . . . of Frog Creek.
And this is my brother, Jack.
Is it true that you have come to help me?

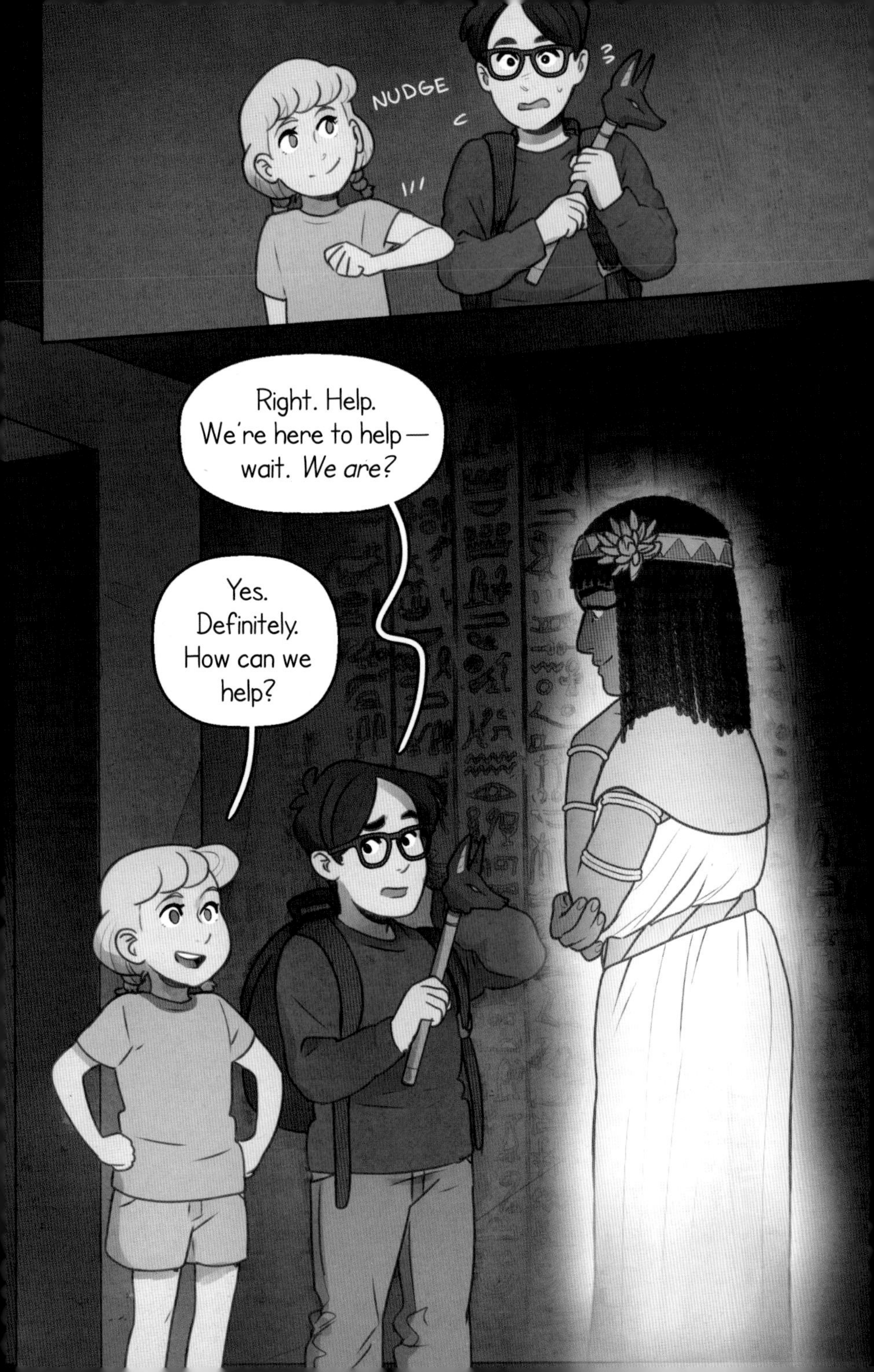
NUDGE
Right. Help. We're here to help— wait. *We are?*
Yes. Definitely. How can we help?

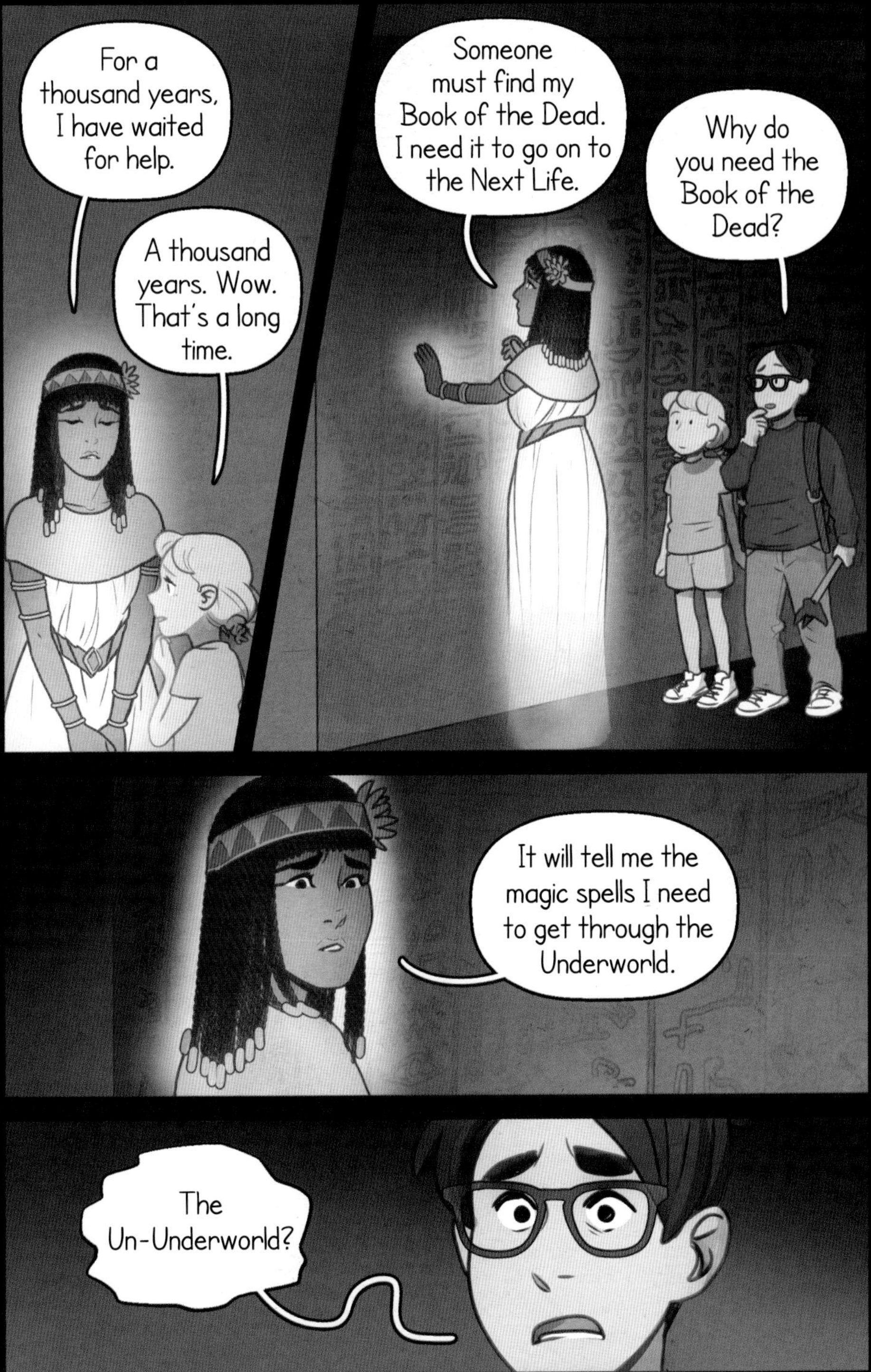

For a thousand years, I have waited for help.
A thousand years. Wow. That's a long time.
Someone must find my Book of the Dead. I need it to go on to the Next Life.
Why do you need the Book of the Dead?
It will tell me the magic spells I need to get through the Underworld.
The Un-Underworld?

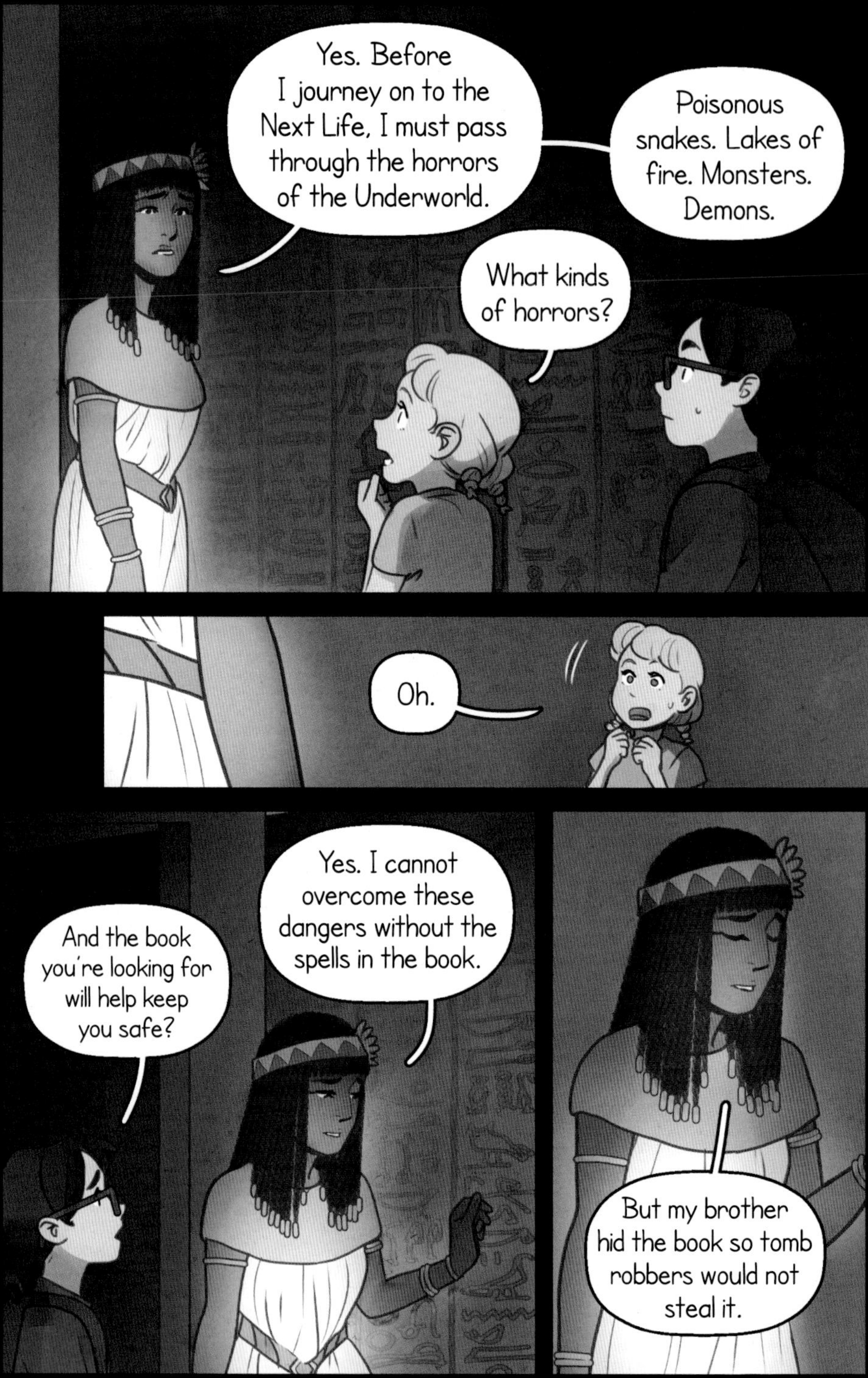
Yes. Before I journey on to the Next Life, I must pass through the horrors of the Underworld.
What kinds of horrors?
Poisonous snakes. Lakes of fire. Monsters. Demons.
Oh.
And the book you're looking for will help keep you safe?
Yes. I cannot overcome these dangers without the spells in the book.
But my brother hid the book so tomb robbers would not steal it.

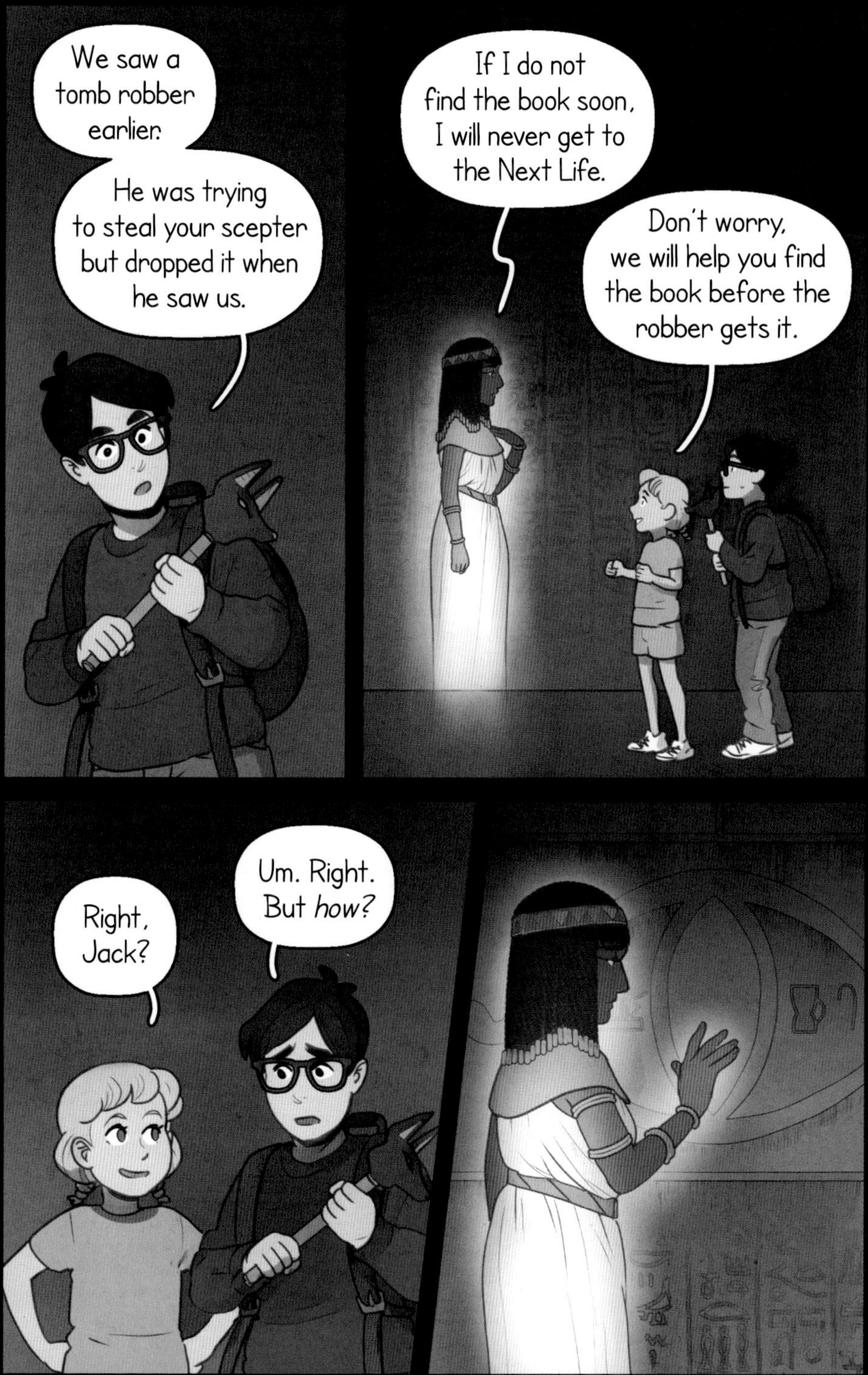
We saw a tomb robber earlier.
He was trying to steal your scepter but dropped it when he saw us.
If I do not find the book soon, I will never get to the Next Life.
Don't worry, we will help you find the book before the robber gets it.
Right, Jack?
Um. Right. But *how?*

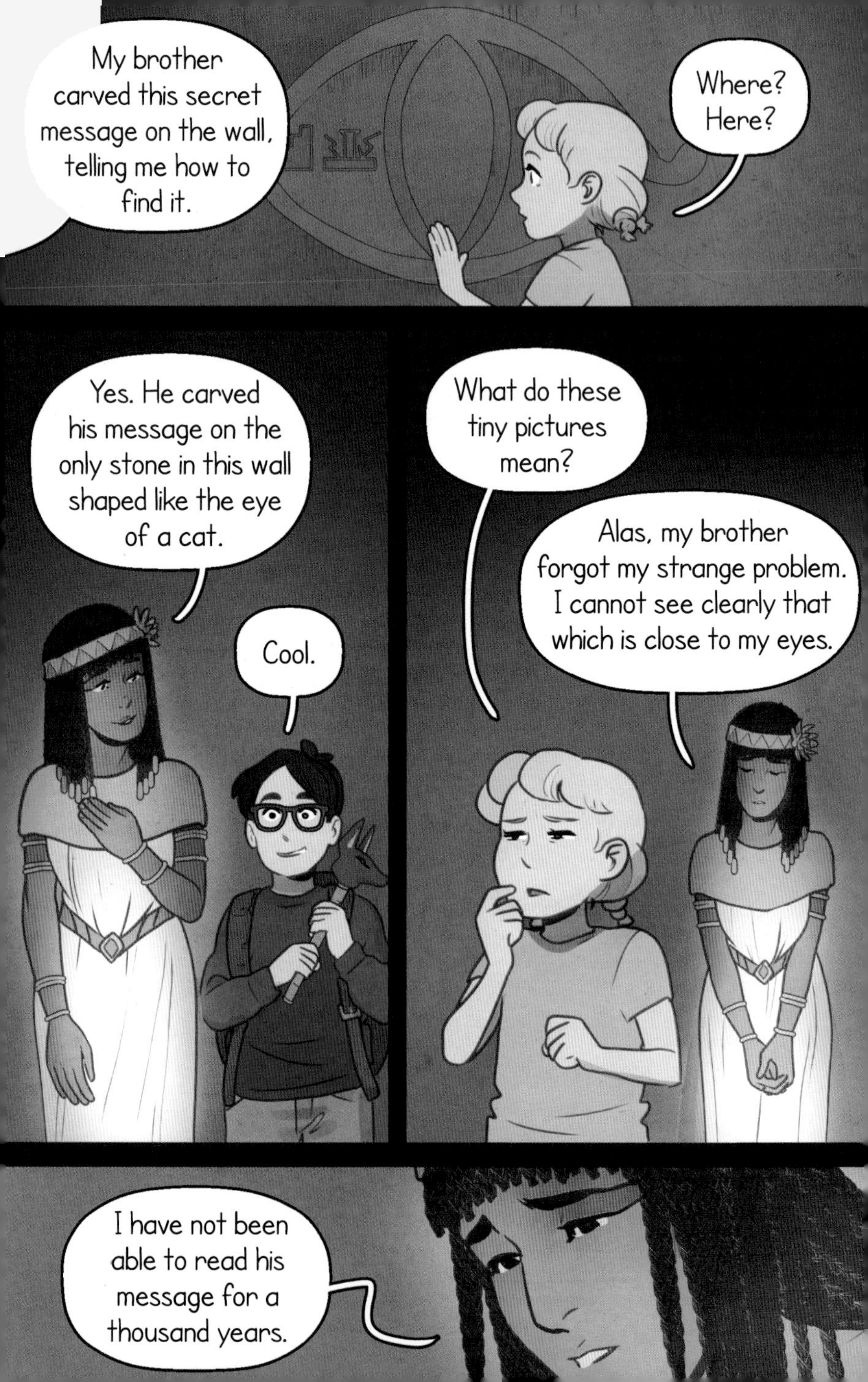

My brother carved this secret message on the wall, telling me how to find it.
Where? Here?
Yes. He carved his message on the only stone in this wall shaped like the eye of a cat.
Cool.
What do these tiny pictures mean?
Alas, my brother forgot my strange problem. I cannot see clearly that which is close to my eyes.
I have not been able to read his message for a thousand years.

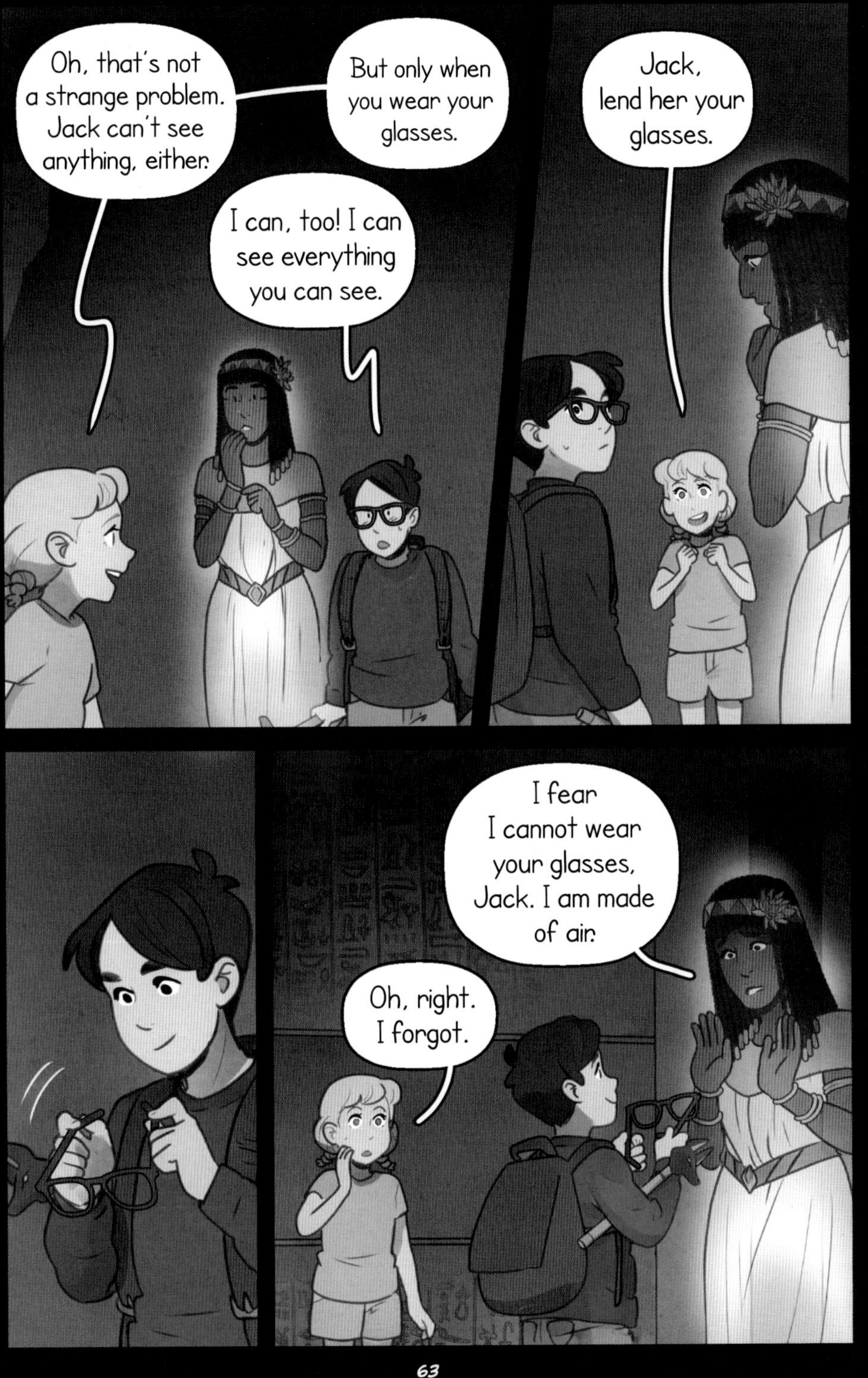
Oh, that's not a strange problem. Jack can't see anything, either.
But only when you wear your glasses.
I can, too! I can see everything you can see.
Jack, lend her your glasses.
I fear I cannot wear your glasses, Jack. I am made of air.
Oh, right. I forgot.

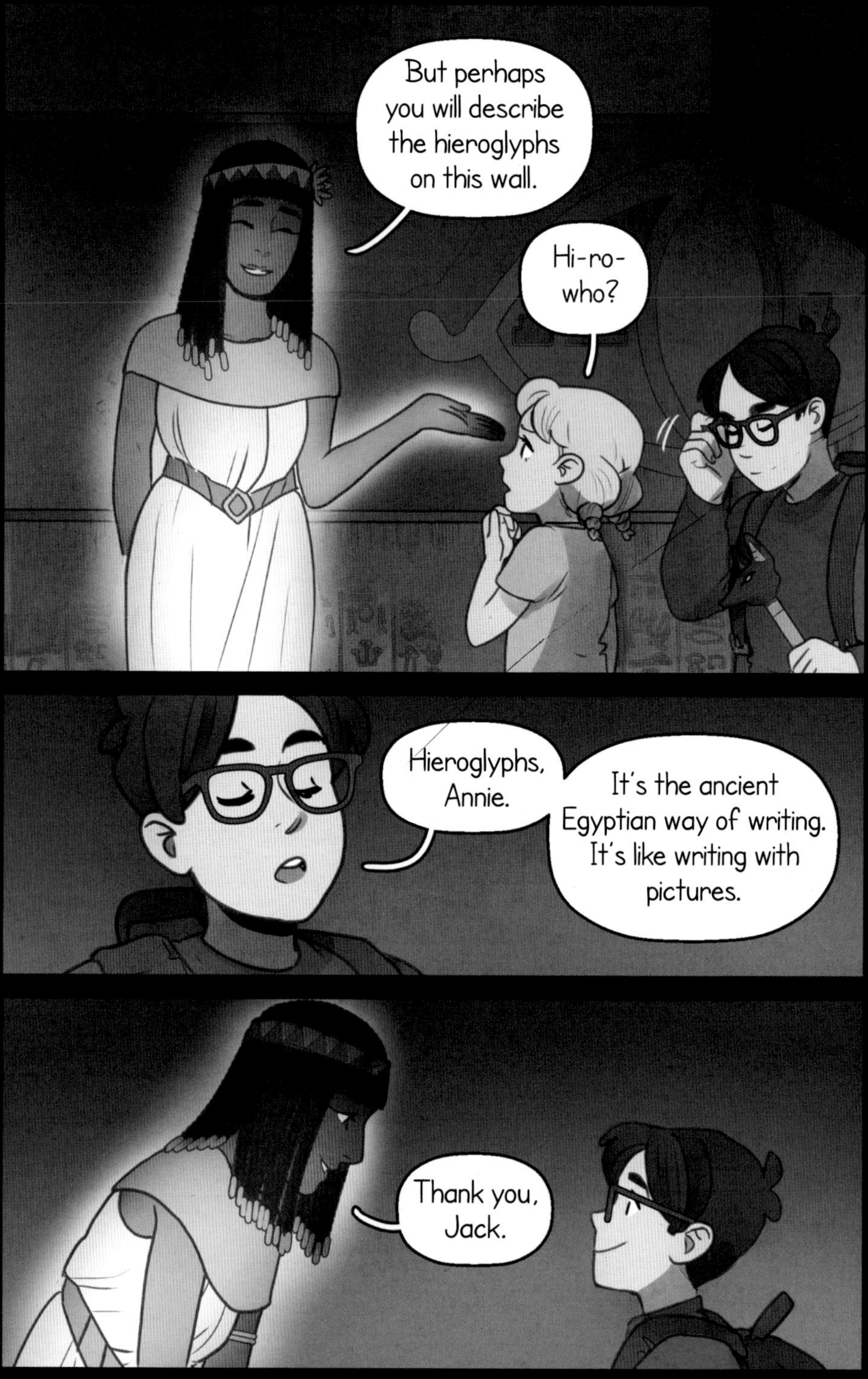
But perhaps you will describe the hieroglyphs on this wall.
Hi-ro-who?
Hieroglyphs, Annie.
It's the ancient Egyptian way of writing. It's like writing with pictures.
Thank you, Jack.

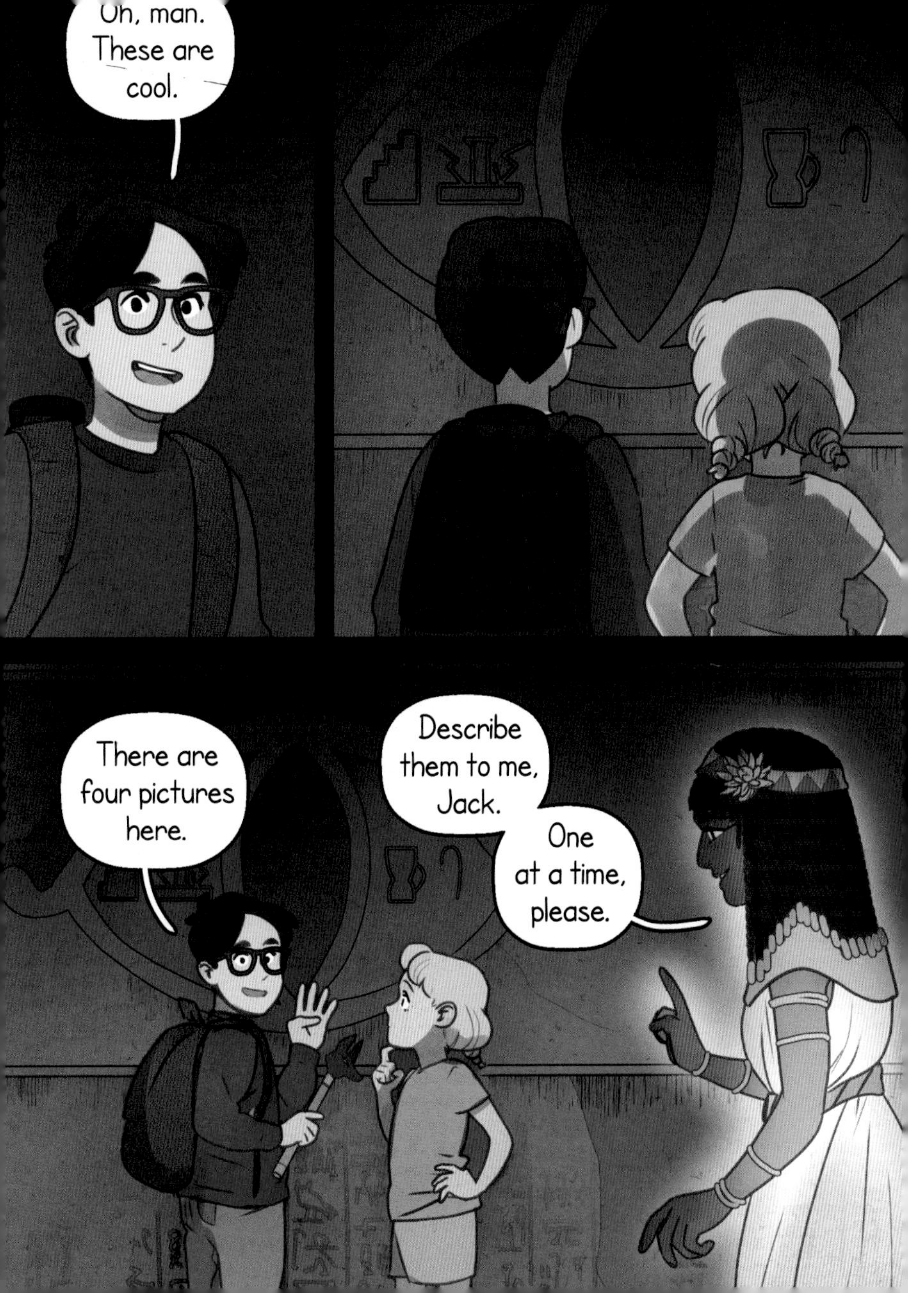
Oh, man. These are cool.
There are four pictures here.
Describe them to me, Jack.
One at a time, please.

CHAPTER SIX
The Writing on the Wall

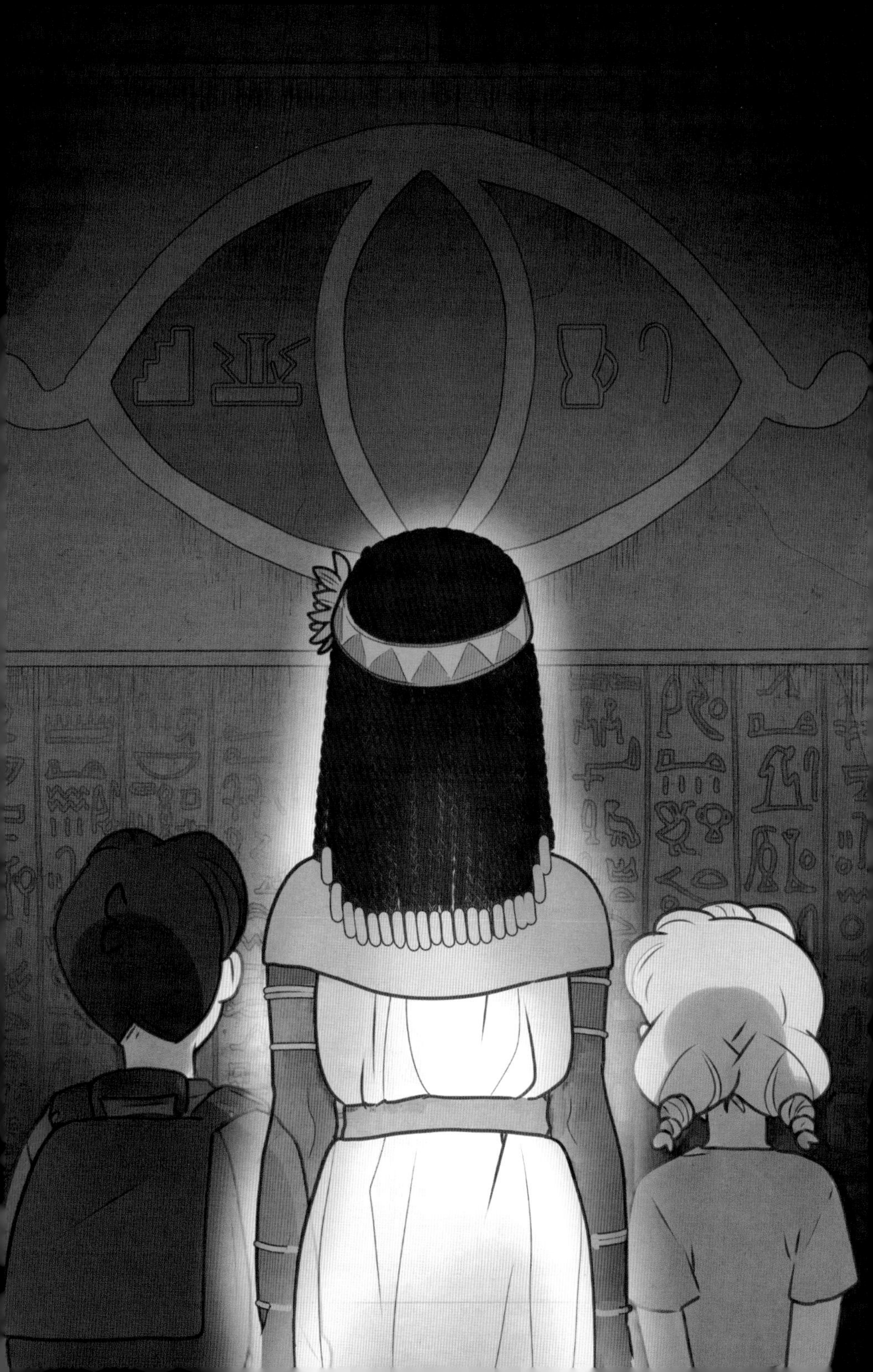

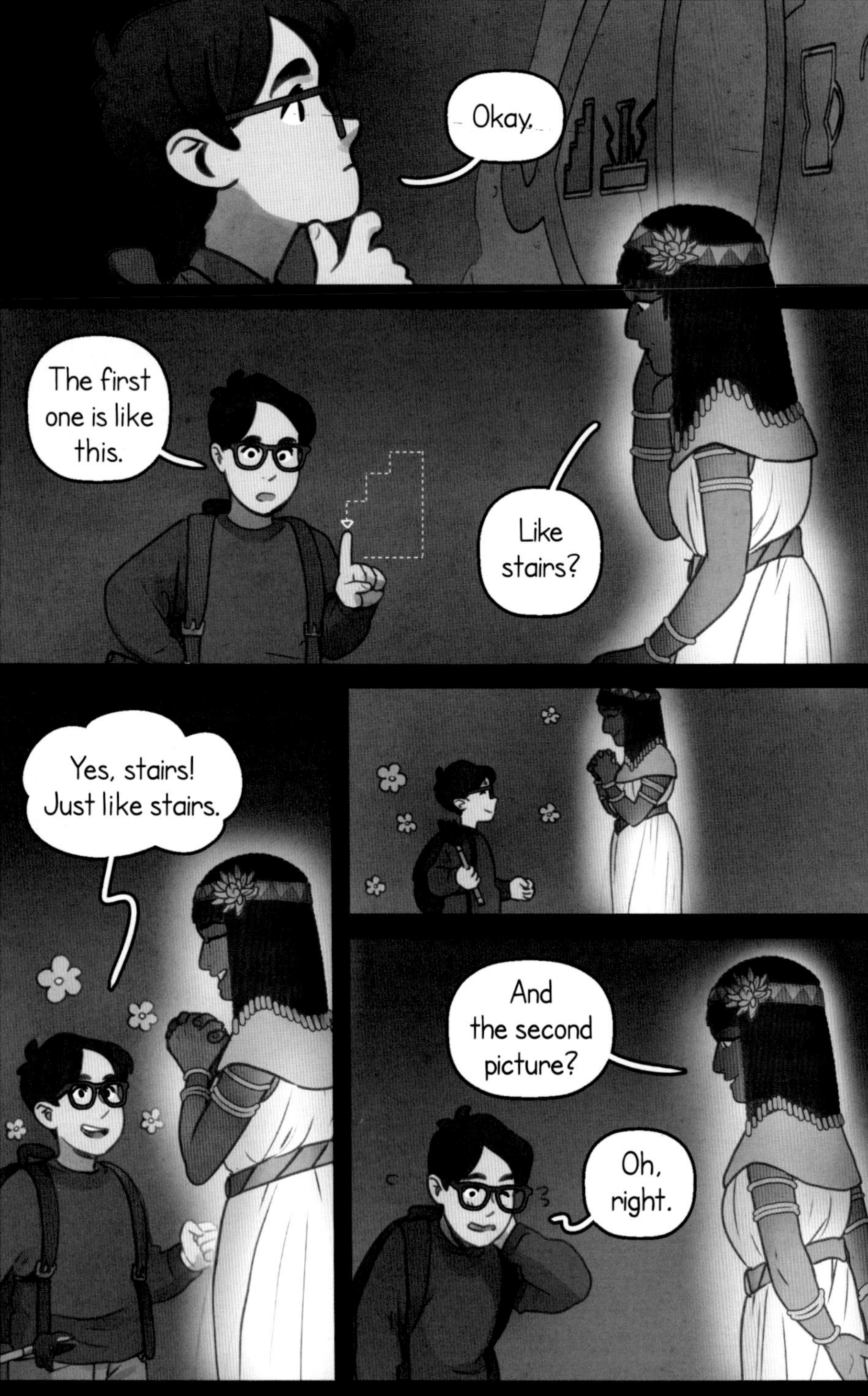
Okay.
The first one is like this.
Like stairs?
Yes, stairs! Just like stairs.
And the second picture?
Oh, right.

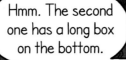

Hmm. The second one has a long box on the bottom.

With shapes on top of the box.

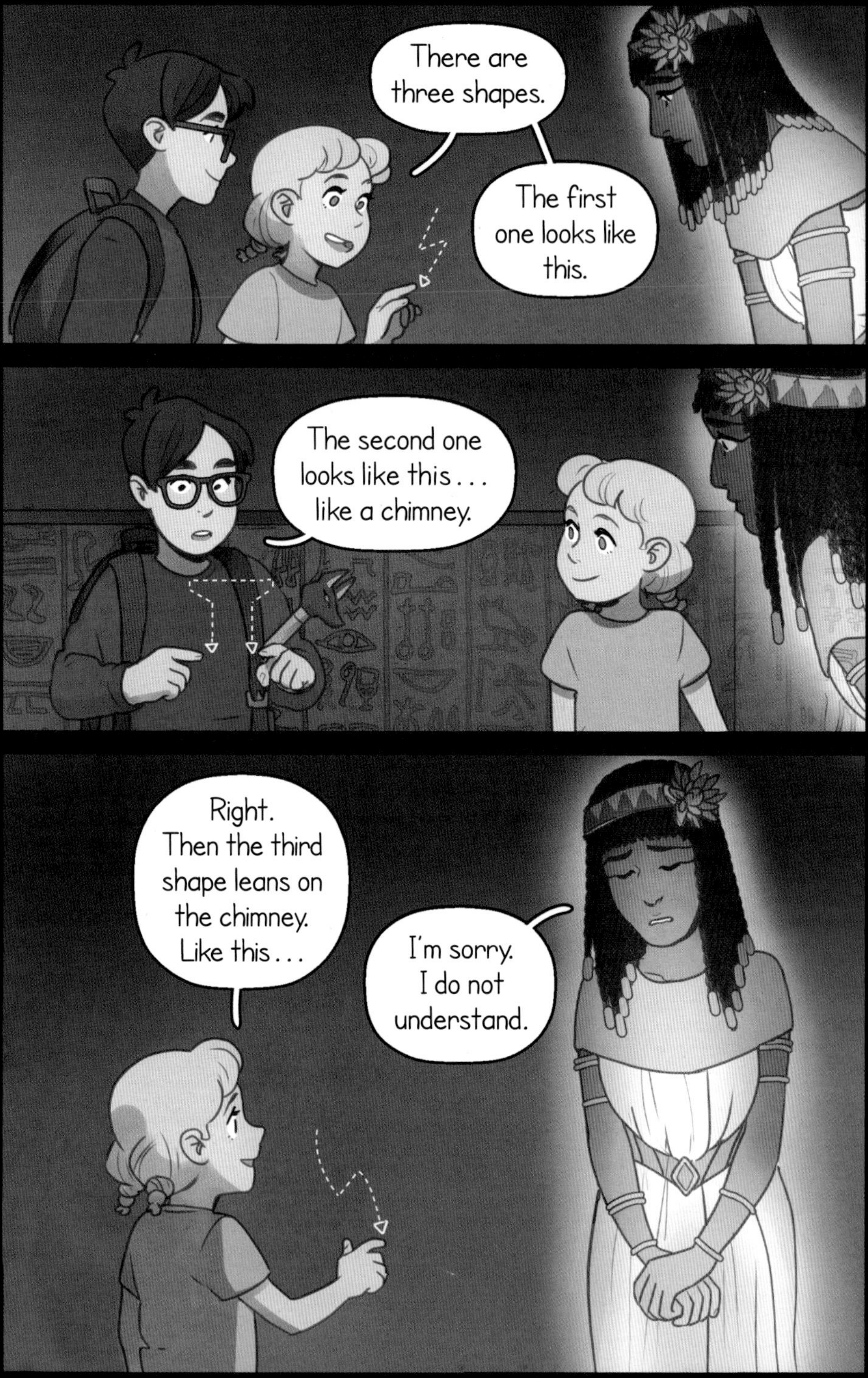
There are three shapes.
The first one looks like this.
The second one looks like this . . . like a chimney.
Right. Then the third shape leans on the chimney. Like this . . .
I'm sorry. I do not understand.

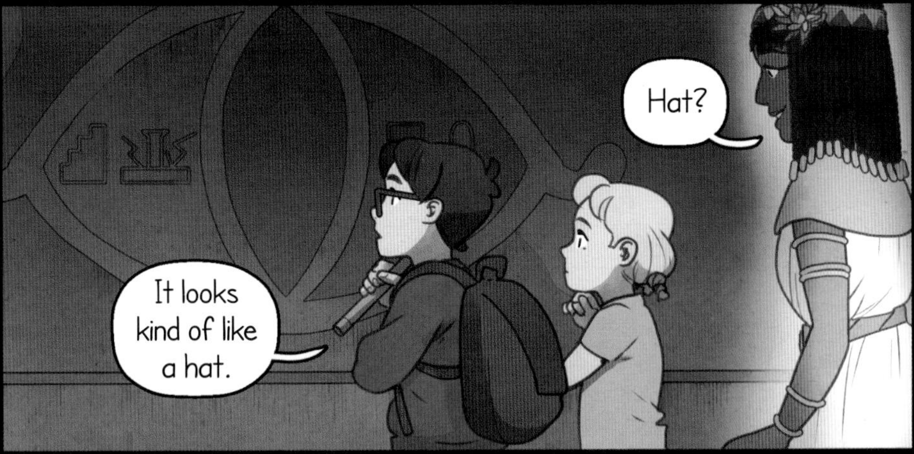
Hat?
It looks kind of like a hat.

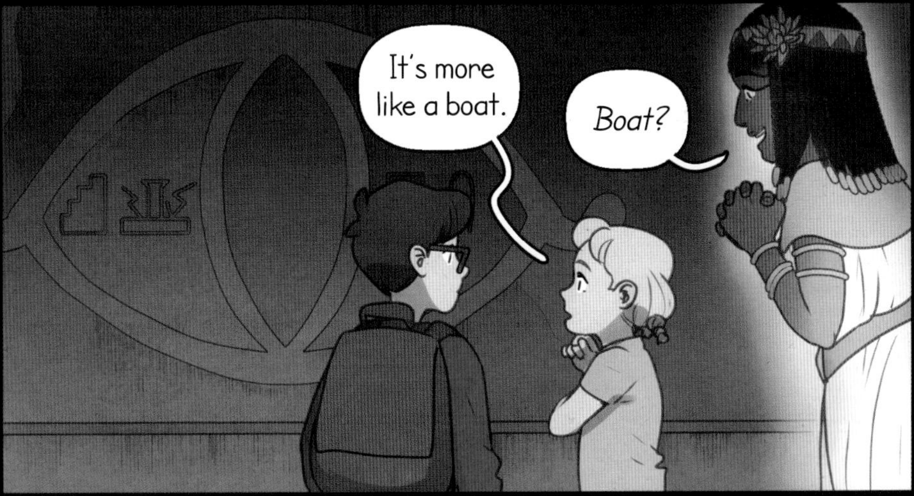
It's more like a boat.
Boat?

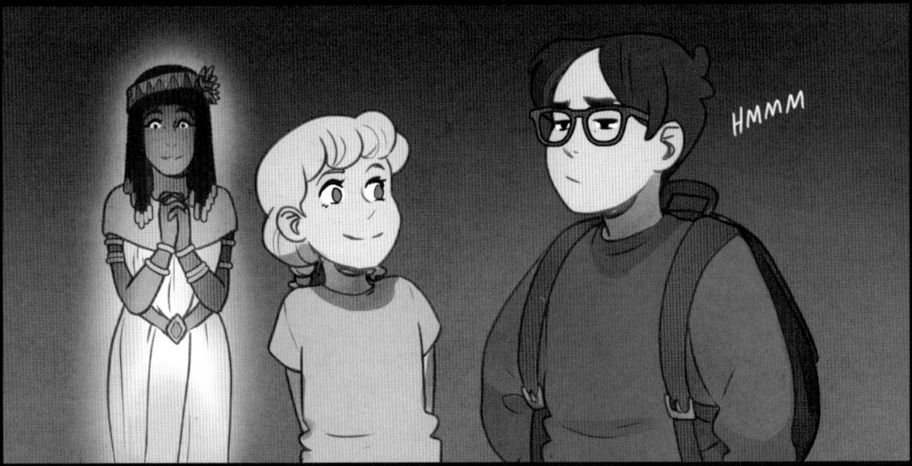
HMMM

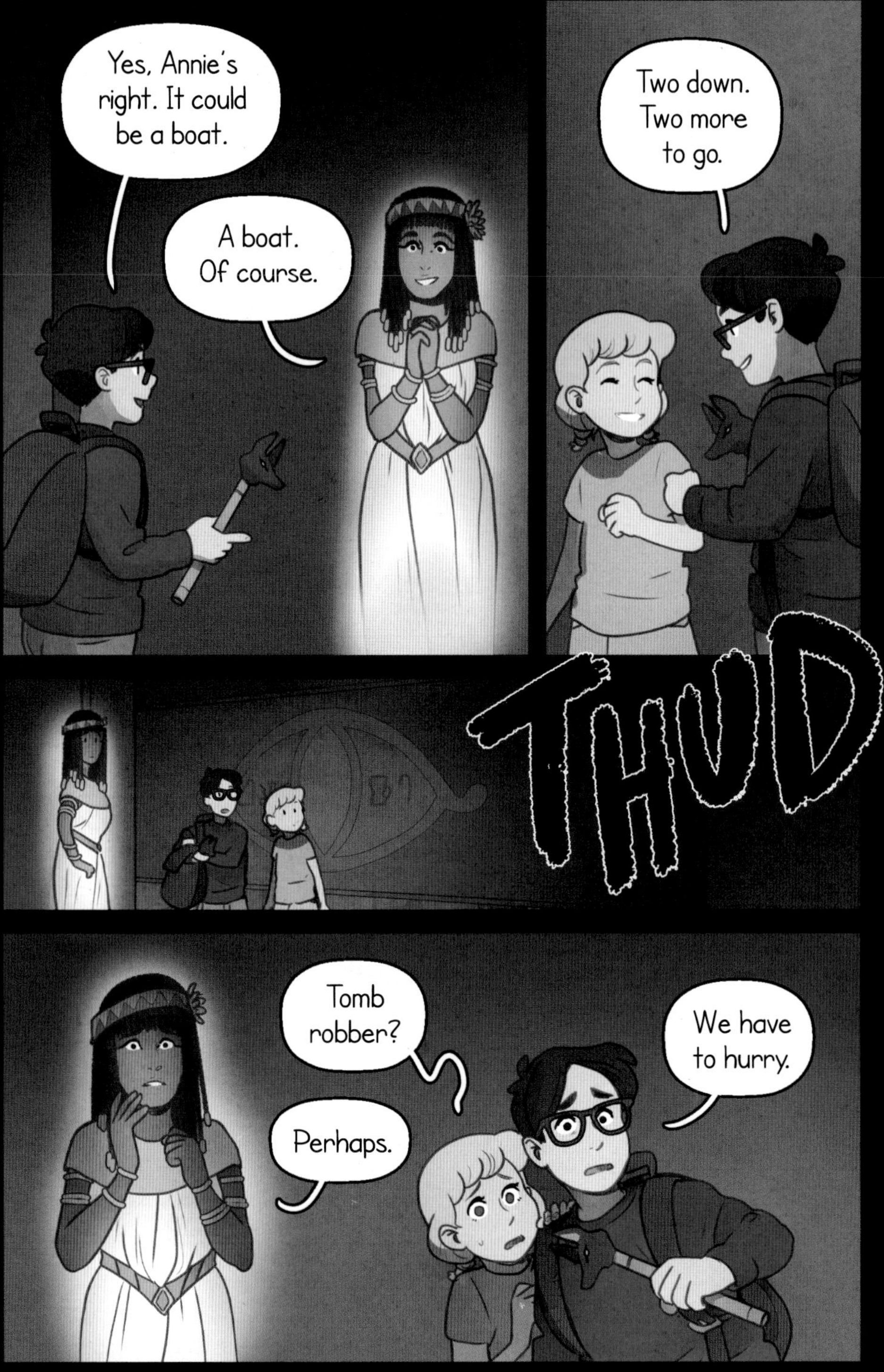
Yes, Annie's right. It could be a boat.
A boat. Of course.
Two down. Two more to go.
THUD
Tomb robber?
Perhaps.
We have to hurry.

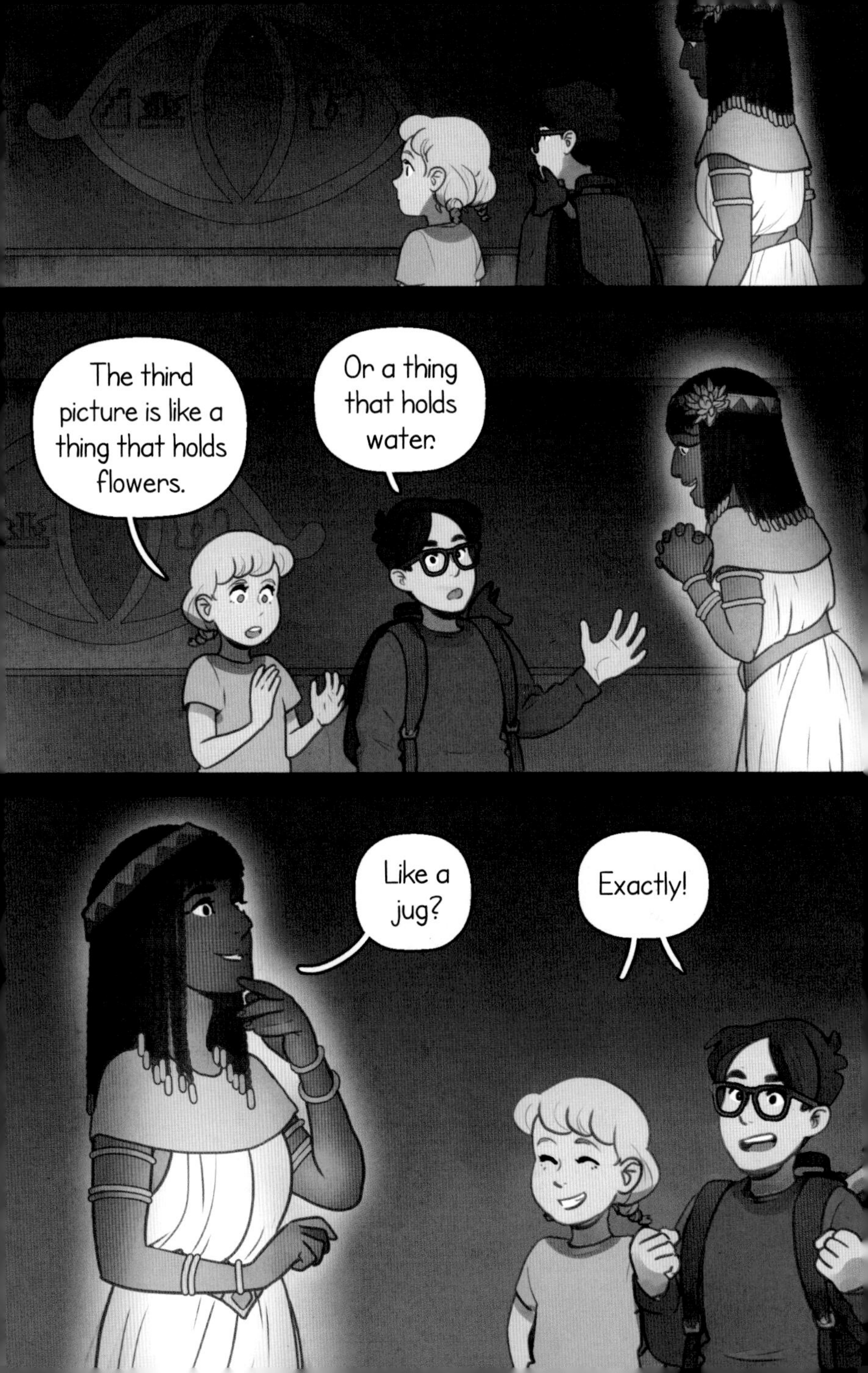
The third picture is like a thing that holds flowers.
Or a thing that holds water.
Like a jug?
Exactly!

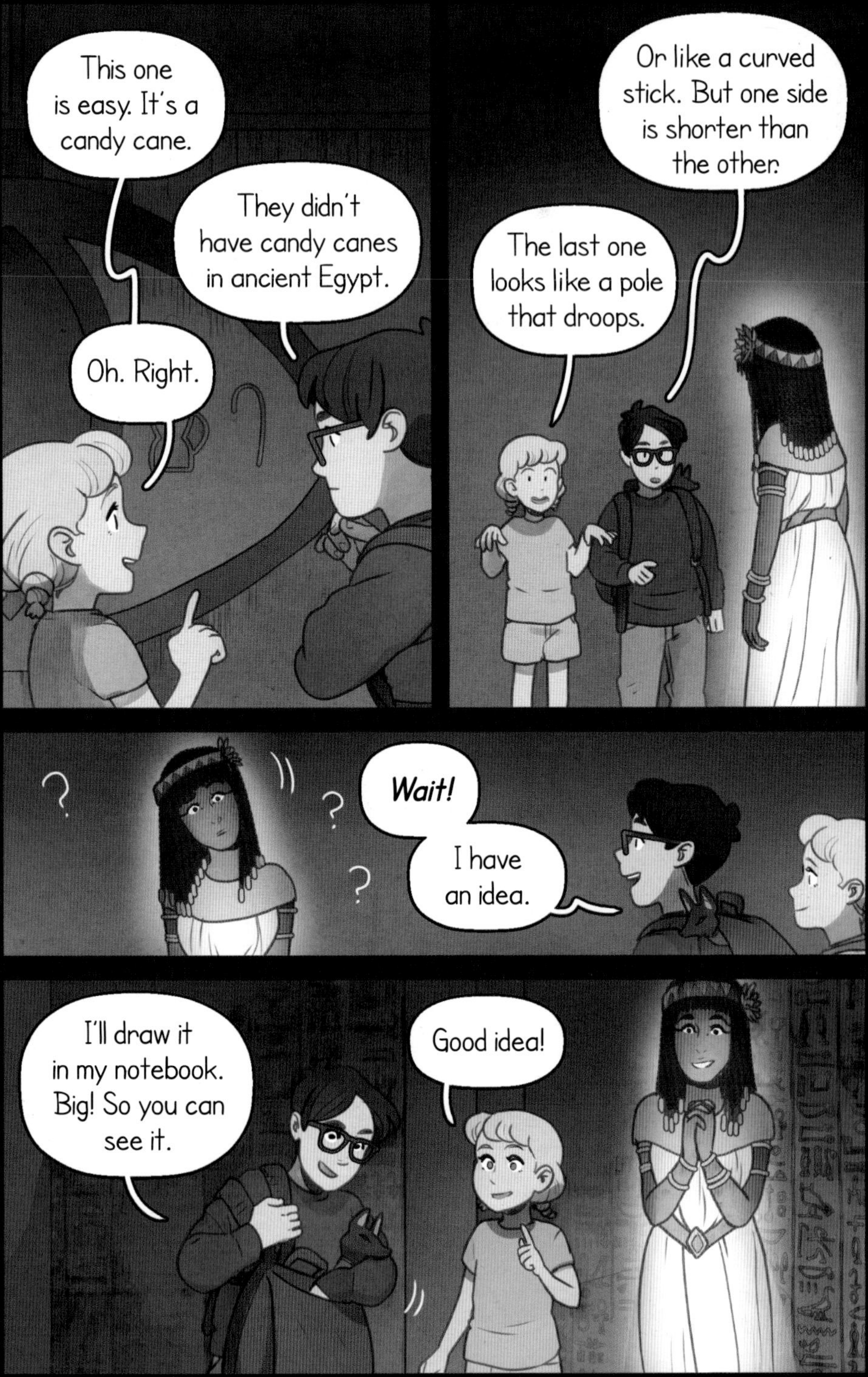
This one is easy. It's a candy cane.
They didn't have candy canes in ancient Egypt.
Oh. Right.
Or like a curved stick. But one side is shorter than the other.
The last one looks like a pole that droops.
? ? ?
Wait!
I have an idea.
I'll draw it in my notebook. Big! So you can see it.
Good idea!

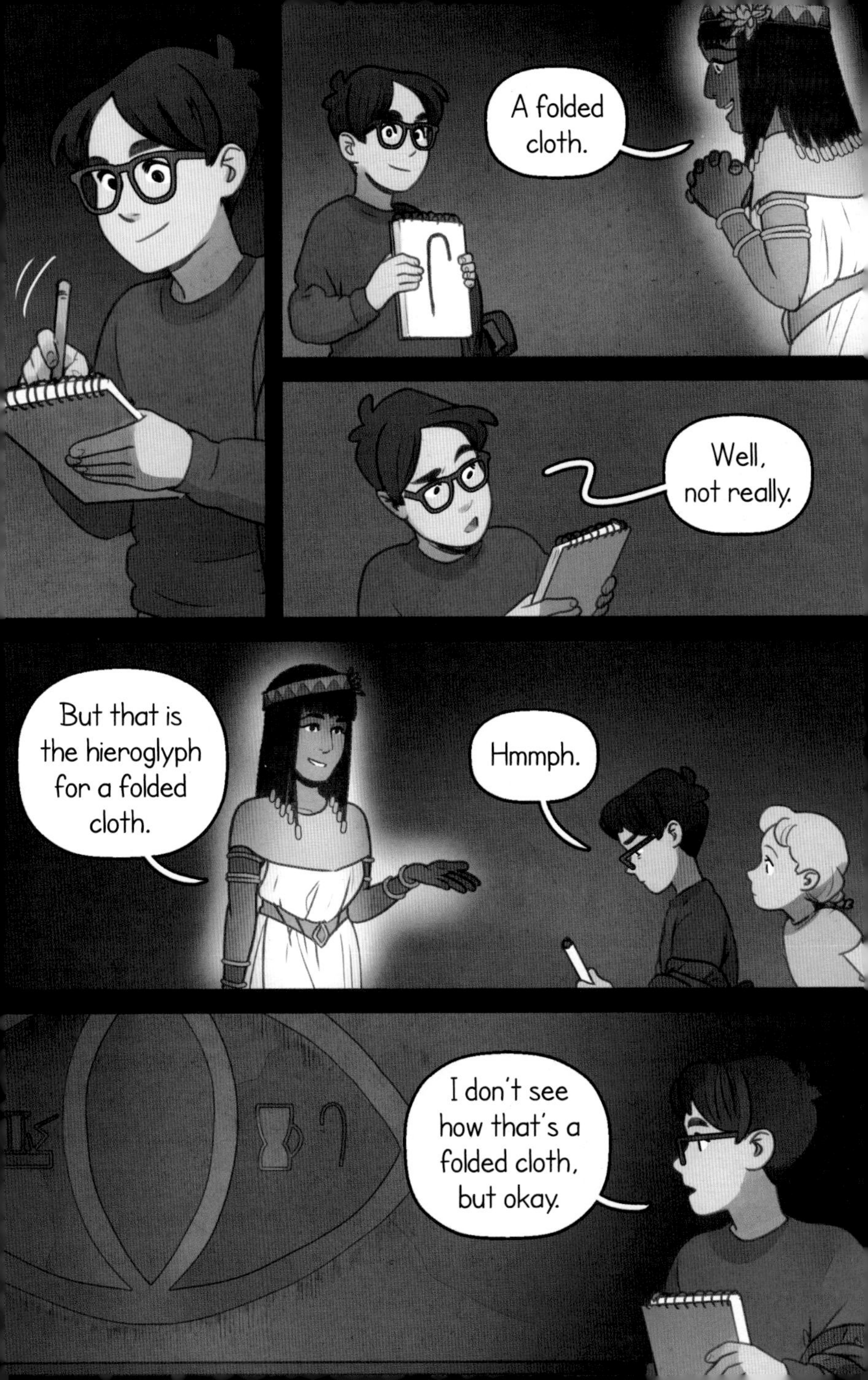
A folded cloth.
Well, not really.
But that is the hieroglyph for a folded cloth.
Hmmph.
I don't see how that's a folded cloth, but okay.

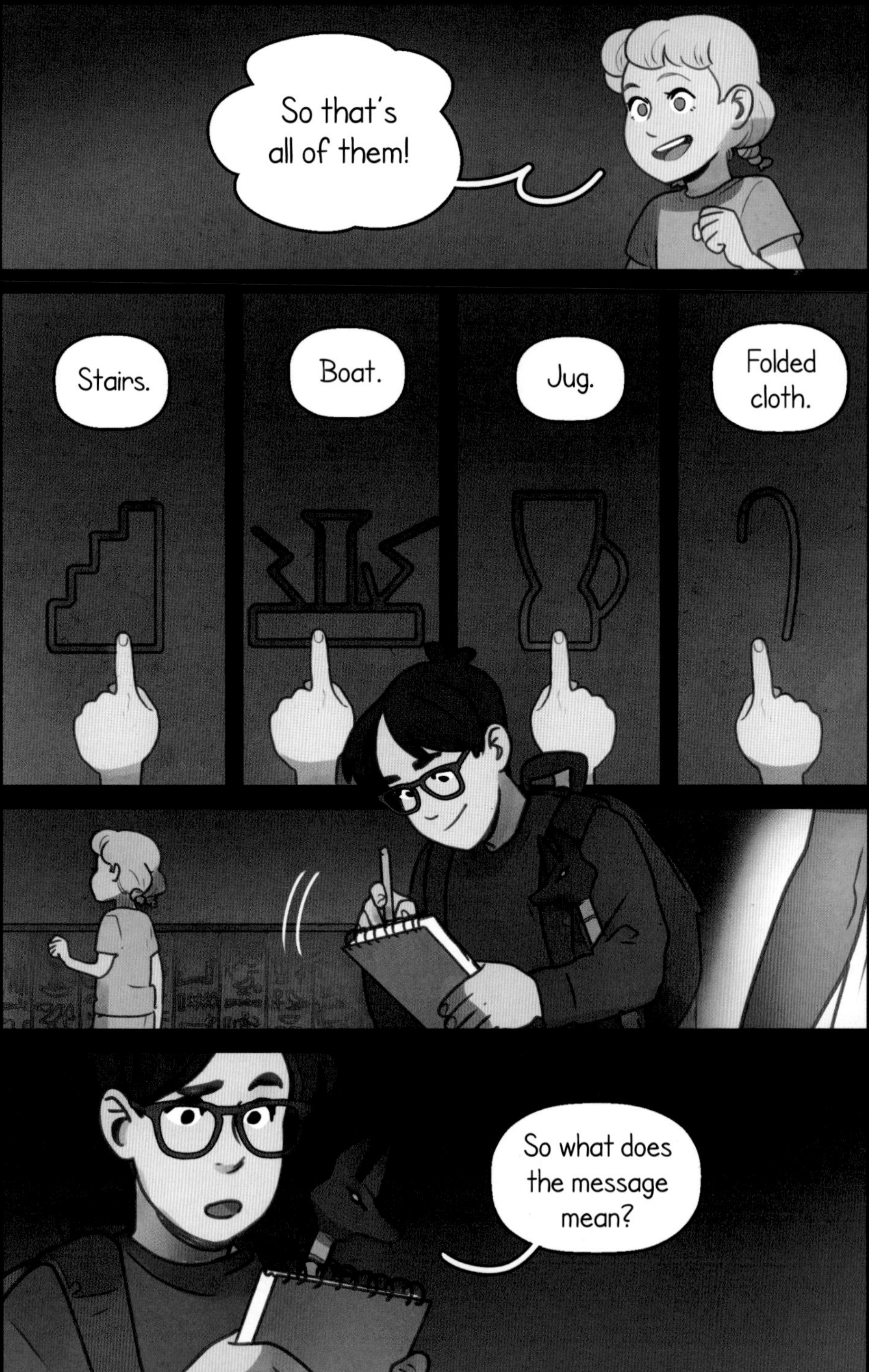
So that's all of them!
Stairs.
Boat.
Jug.
Folded cloth.
So what does the message mean?

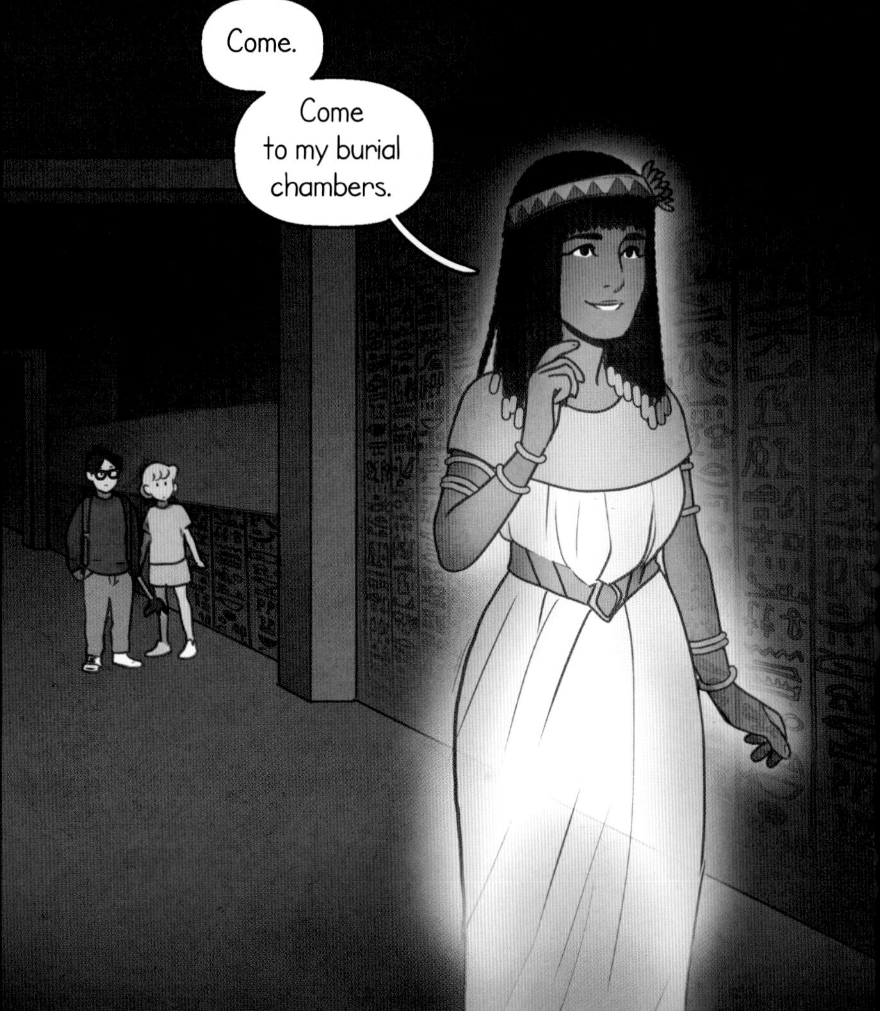
Come.
Come to my burial chambers.

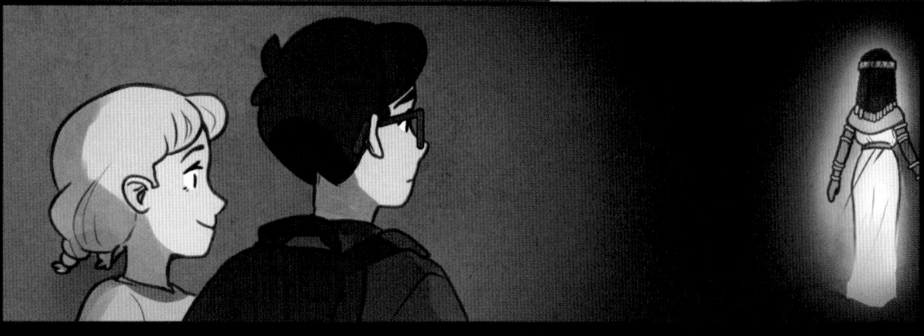

CHAPTER SEVEN
The Scroll

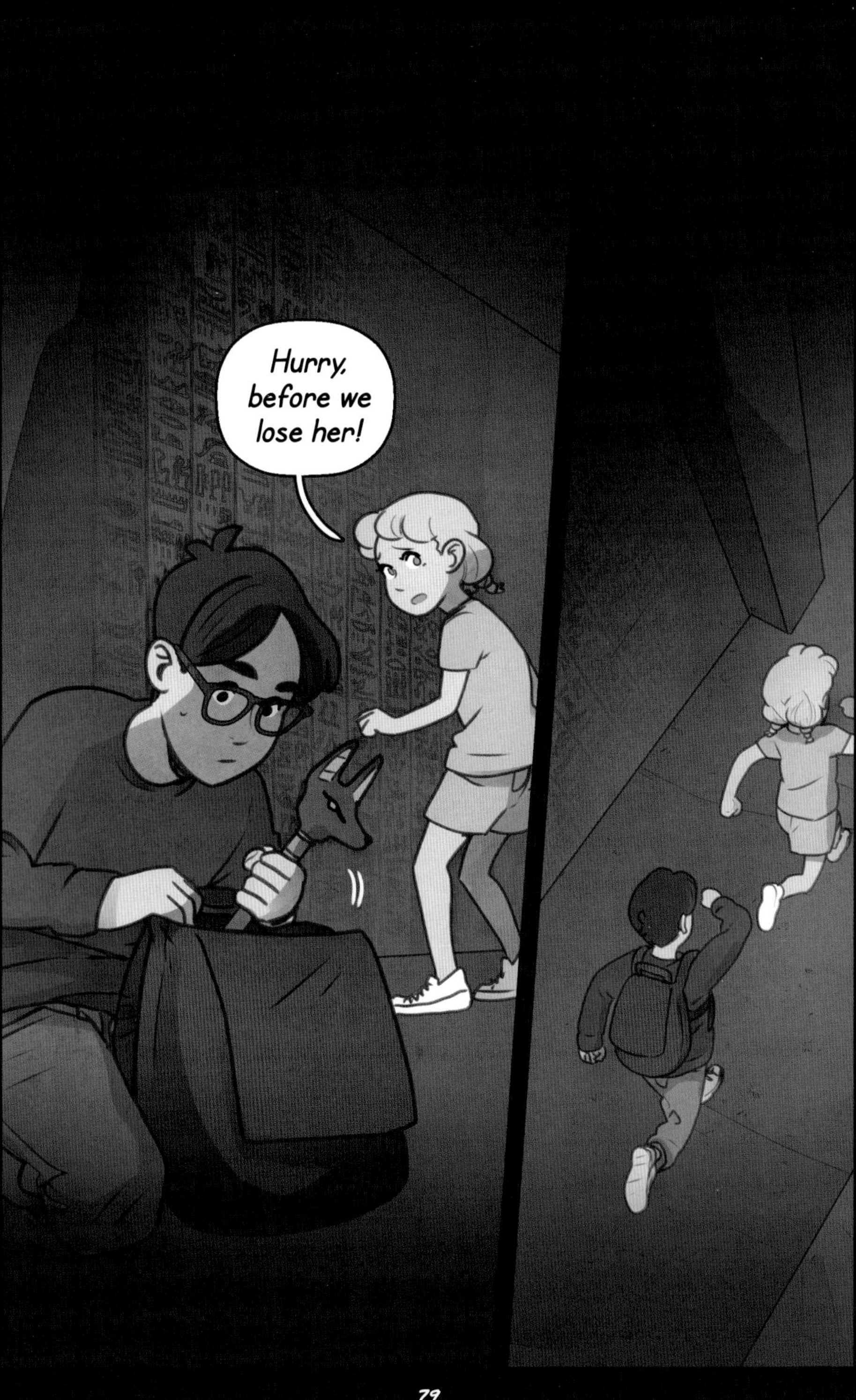
Hurry, before we lose her!

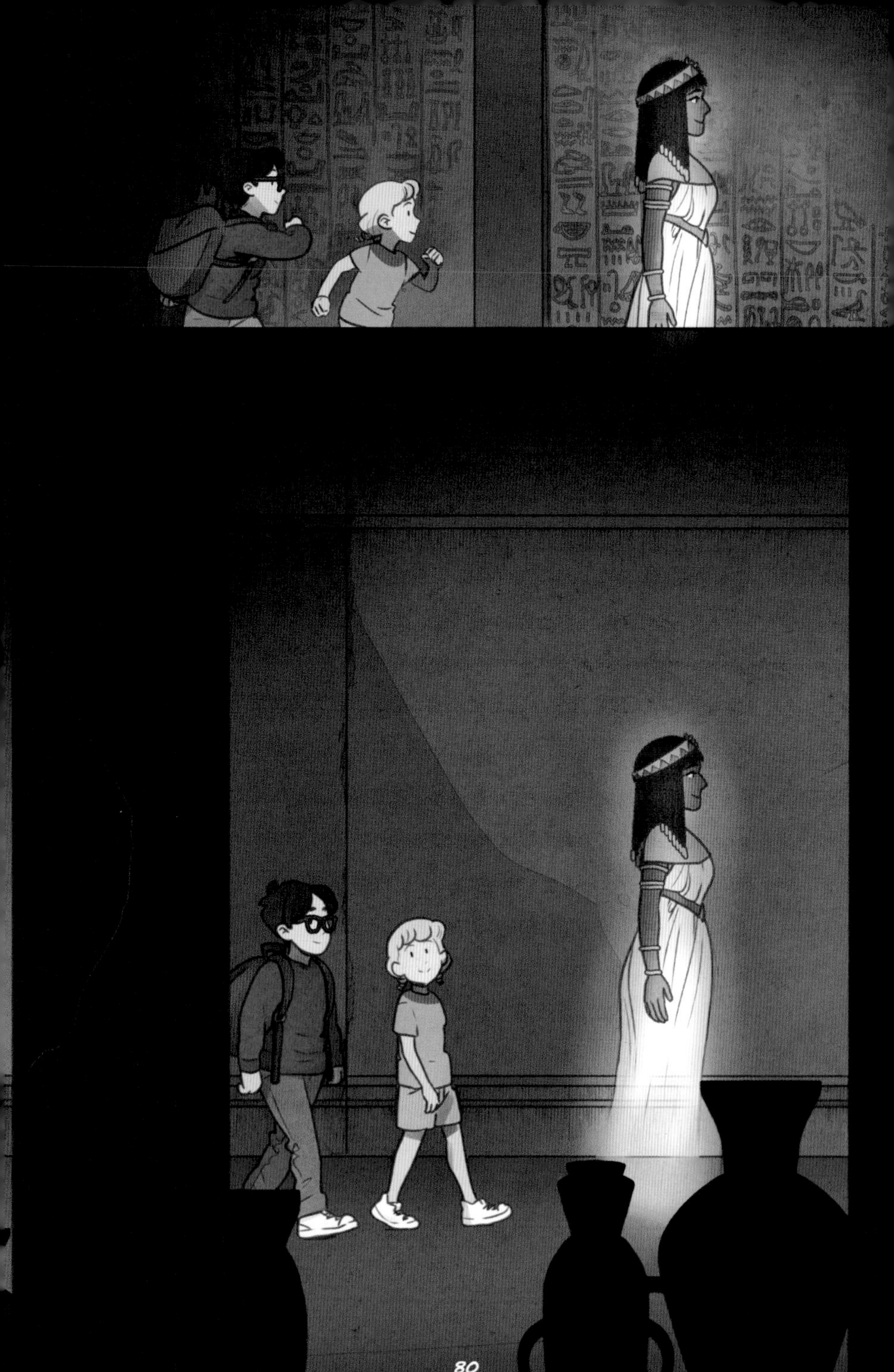

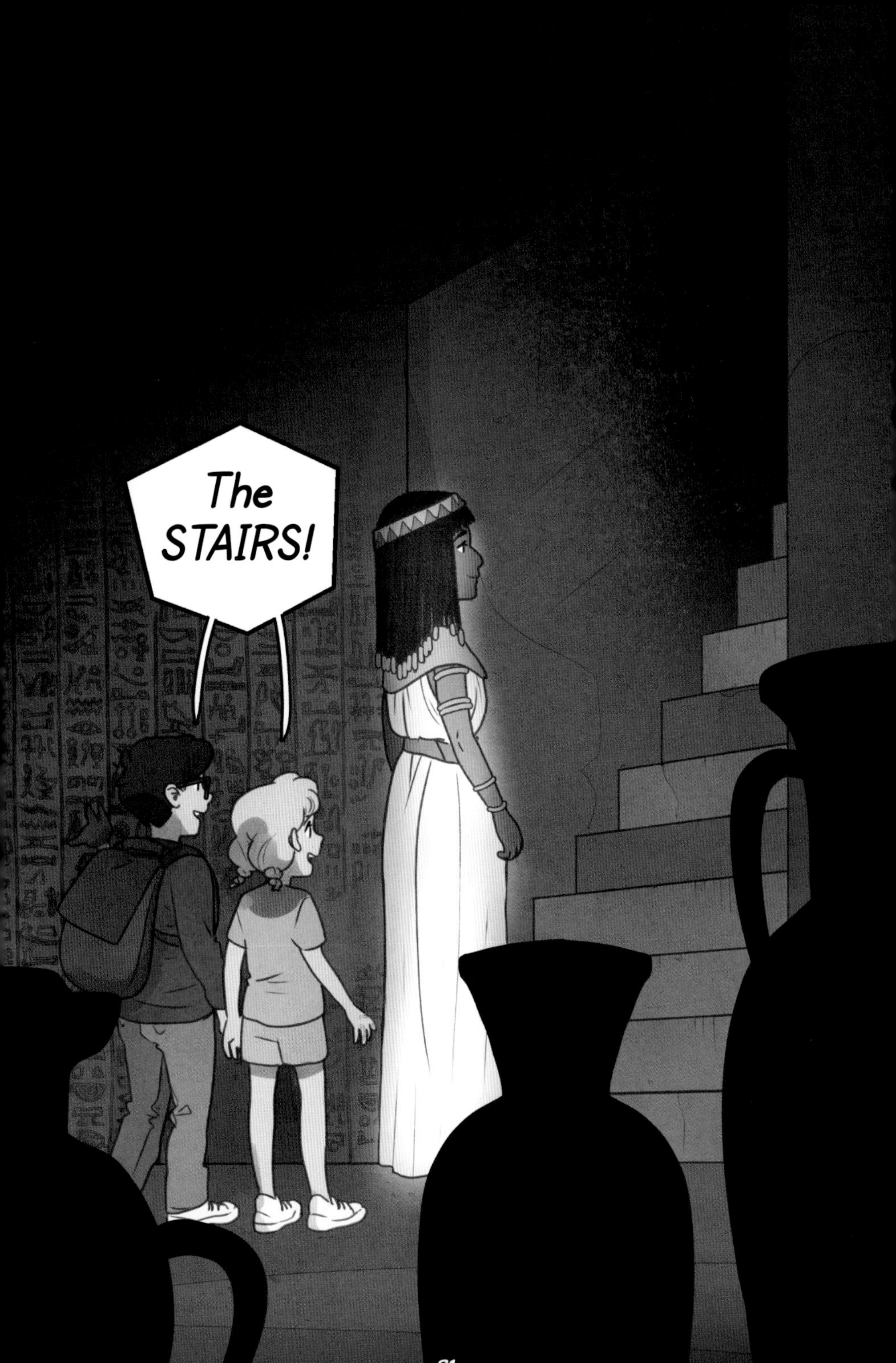
The STAIRS!

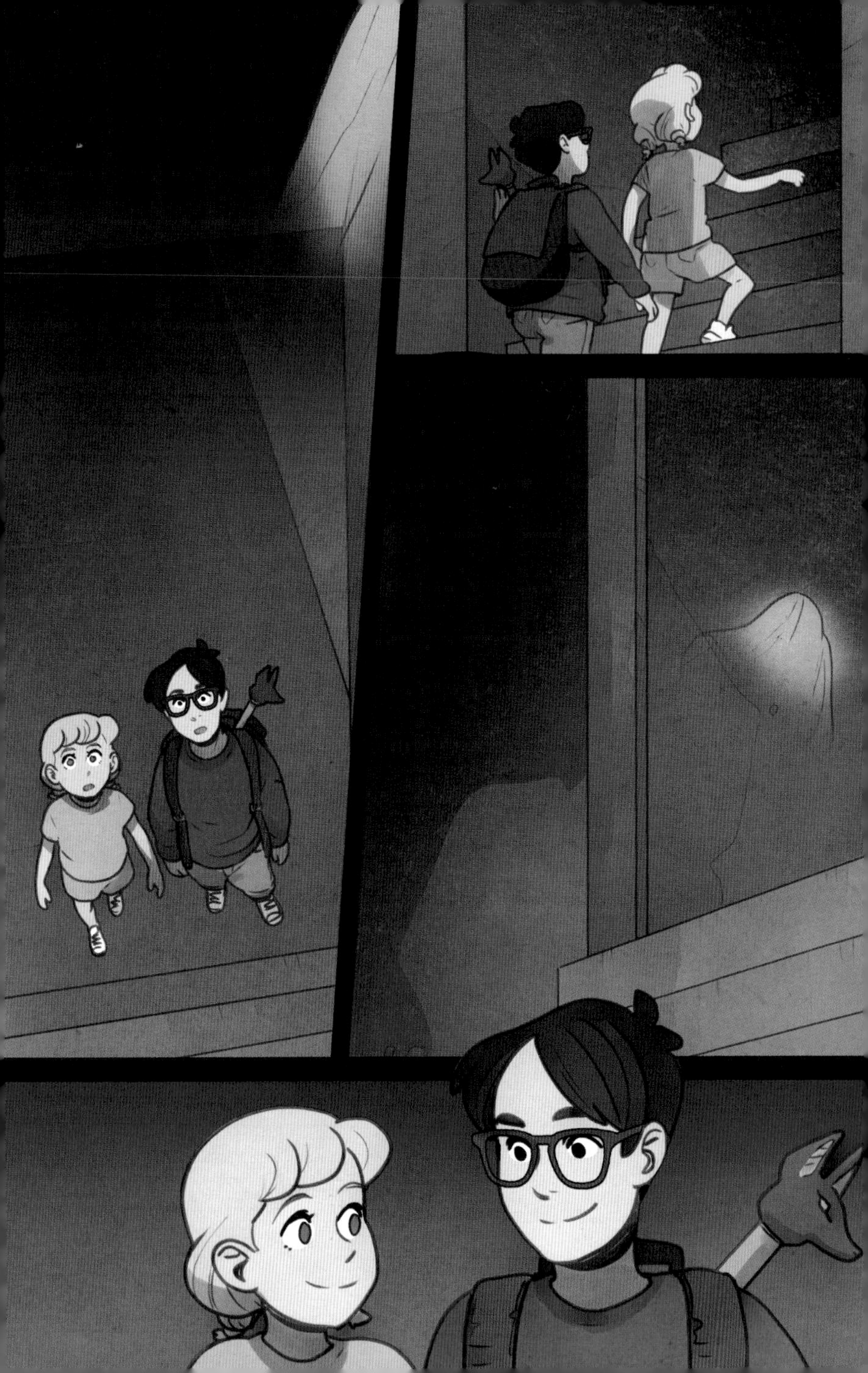

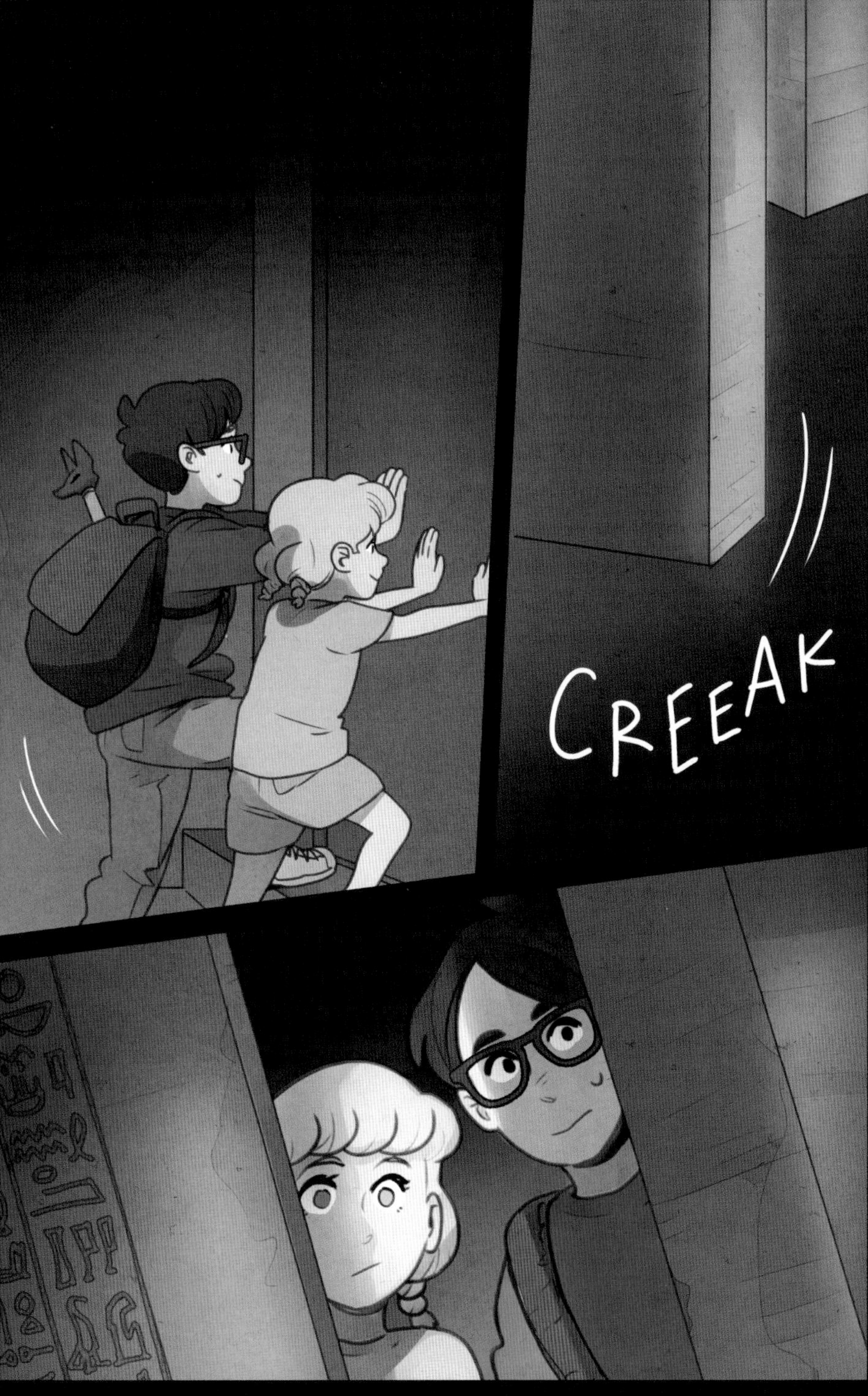
CREEAK

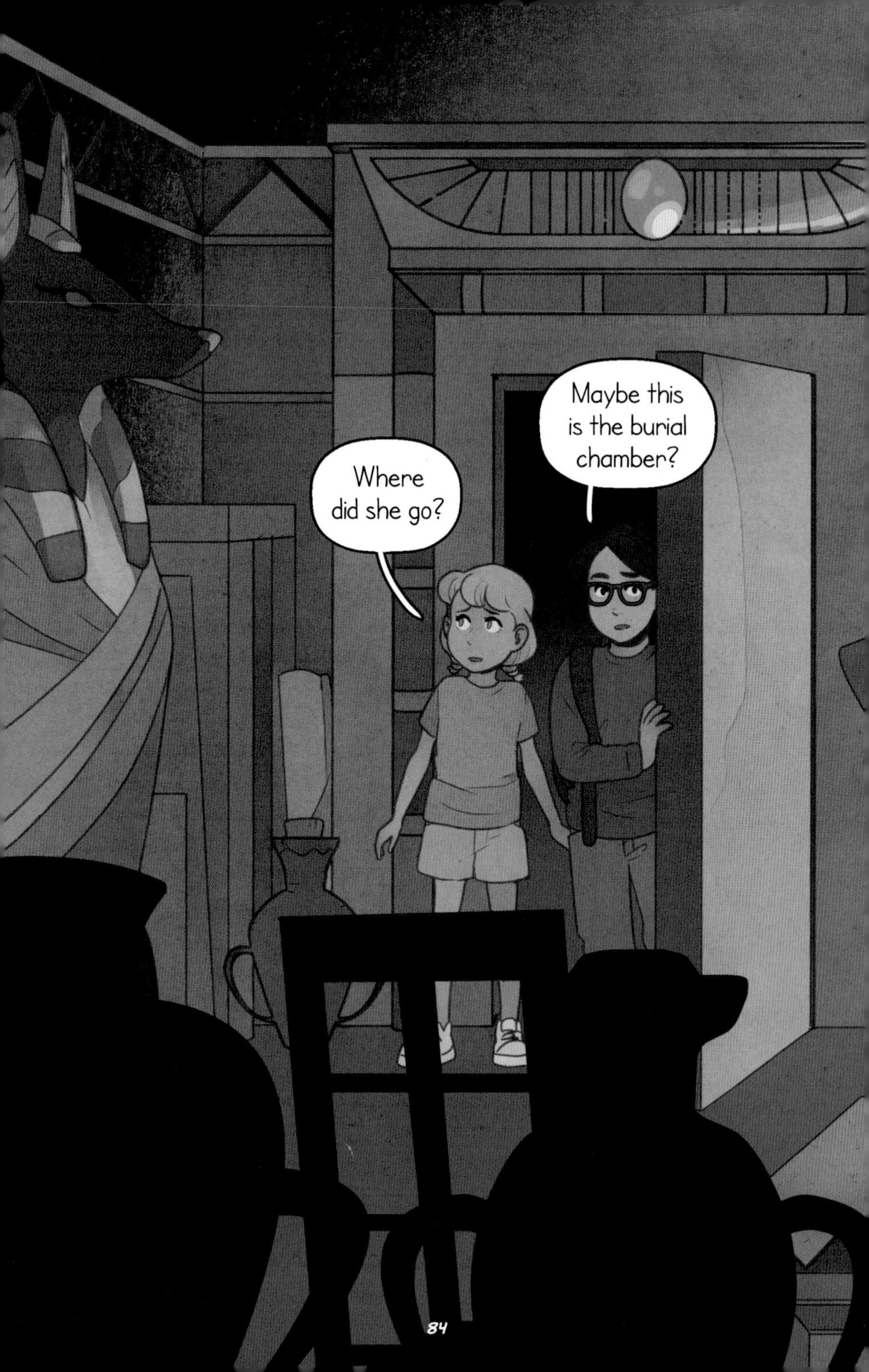
Where did she go?
Maybe this is the burial chamber?

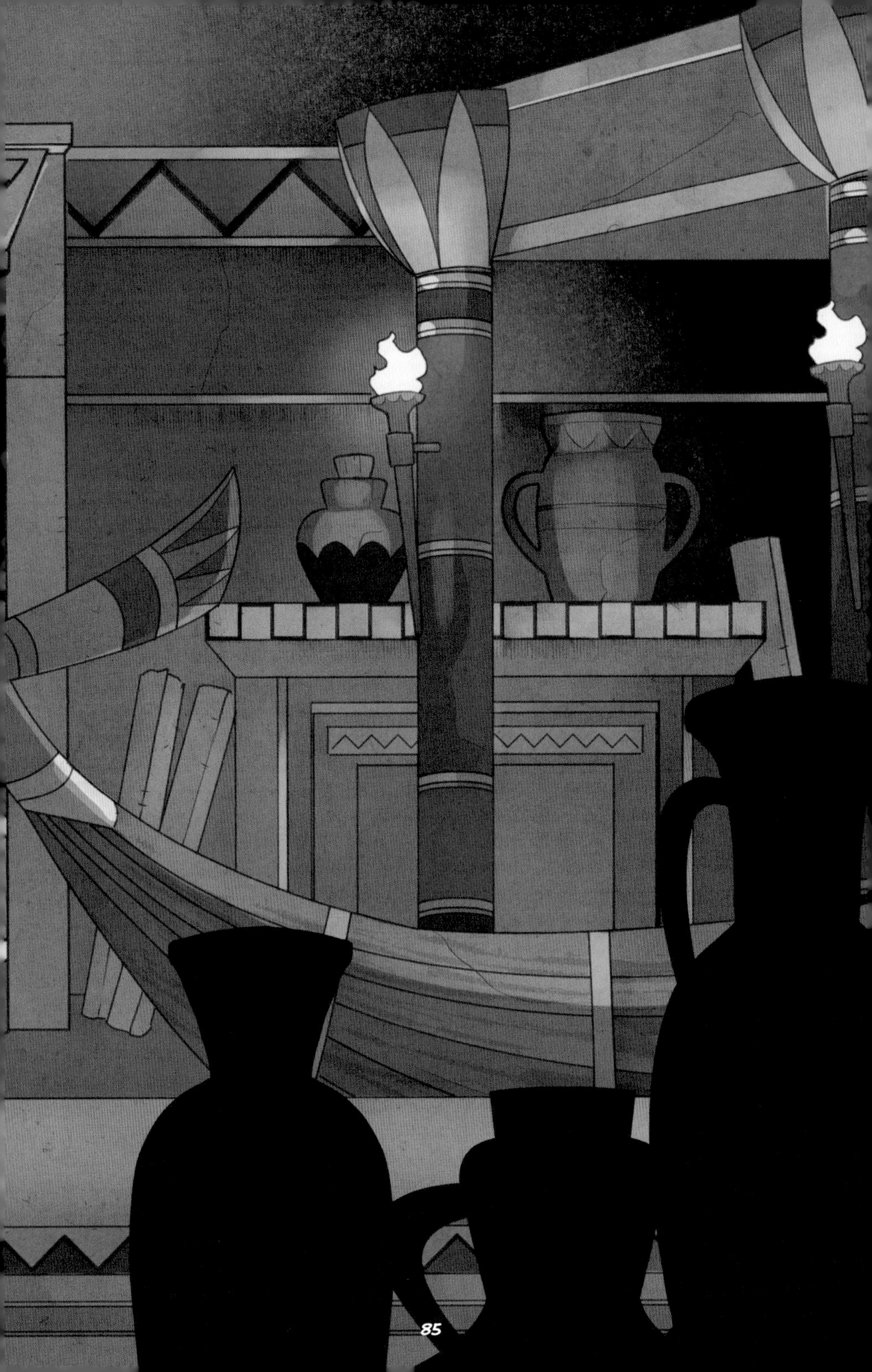

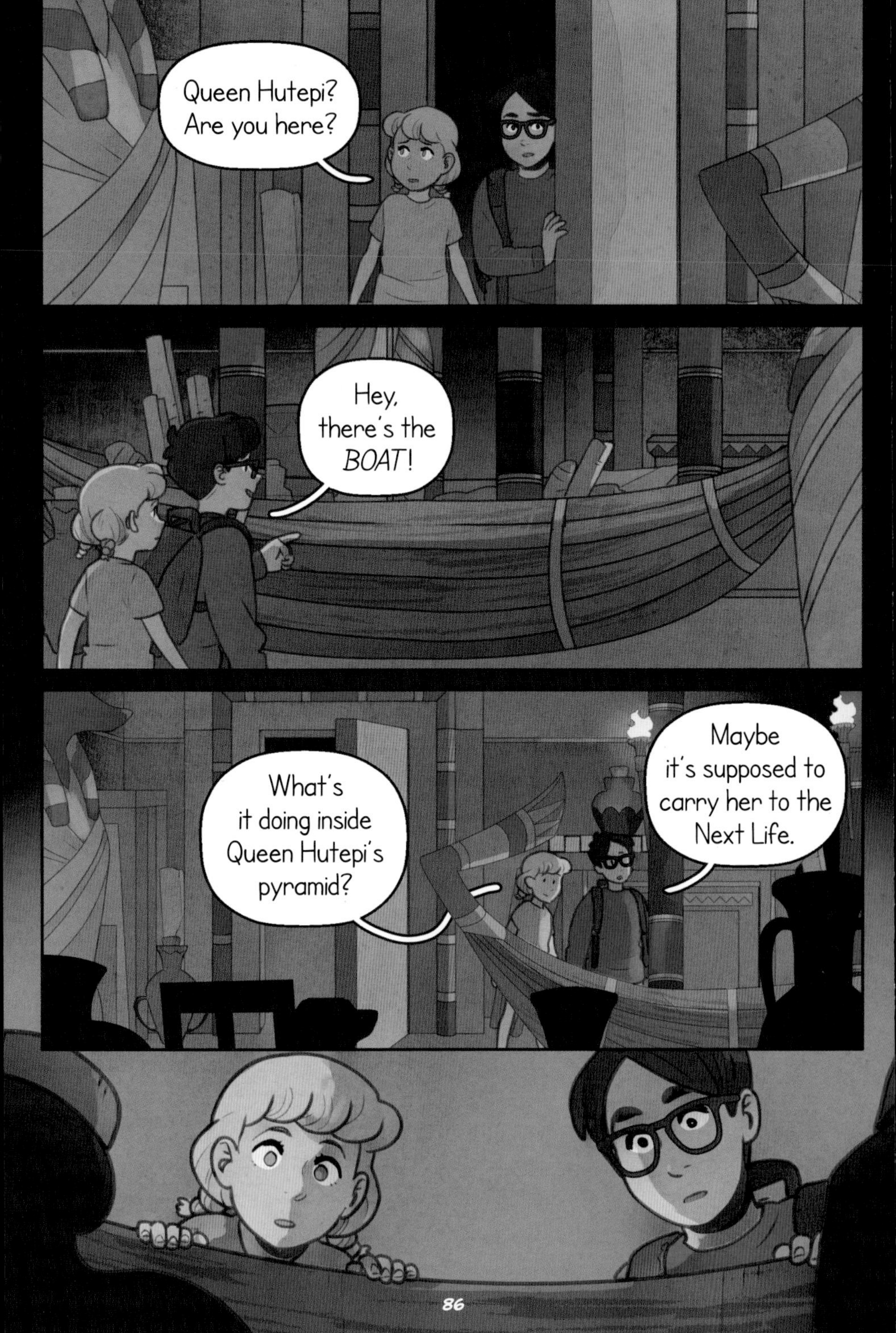
Queen Hutepi? Are you here?
Hey, there's the *BOAT*!
What's it doing inside Queen Hutepi's pyramid?
Maybe it's supposed to carry her to the Next Life.

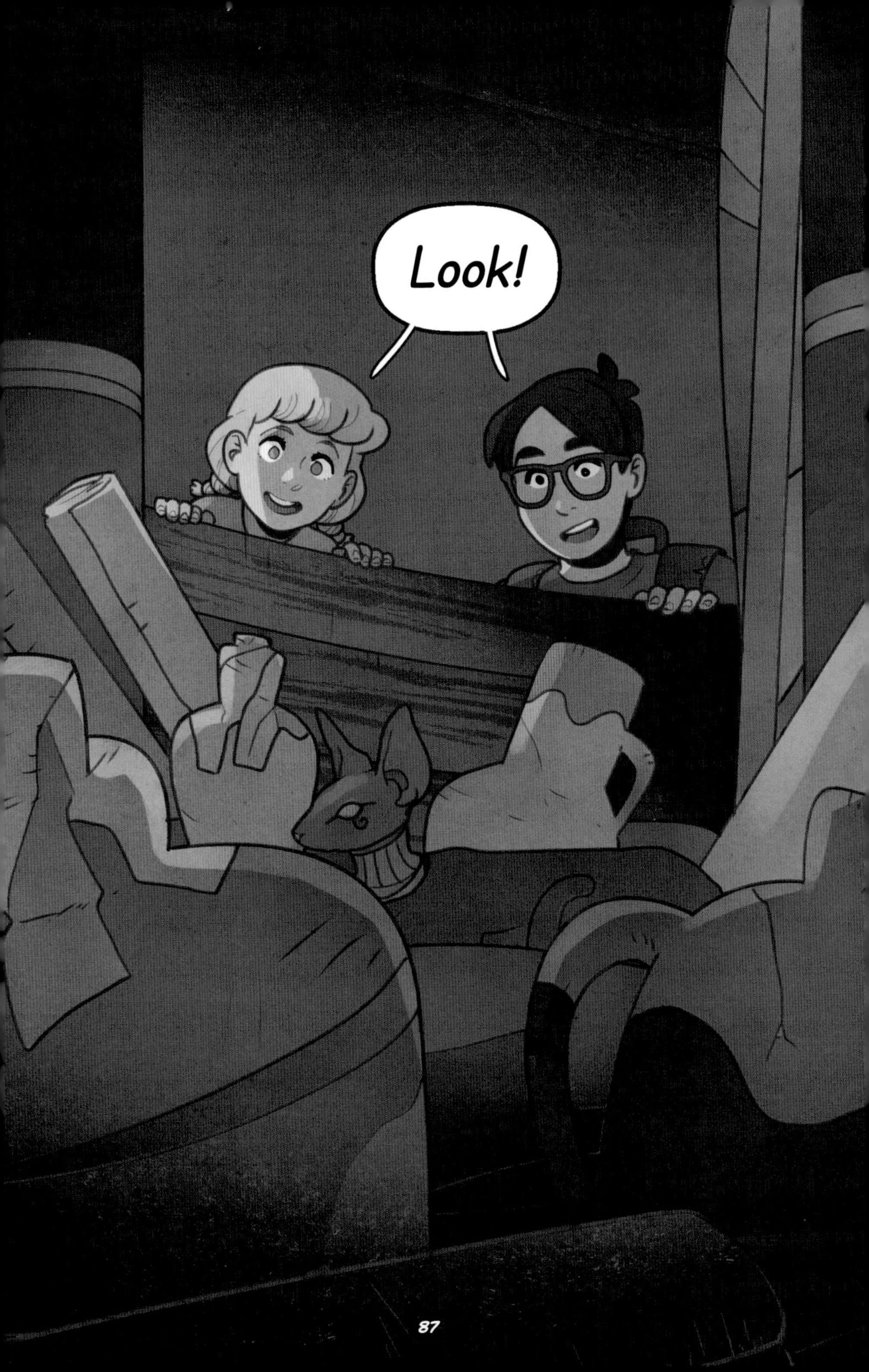
Look!

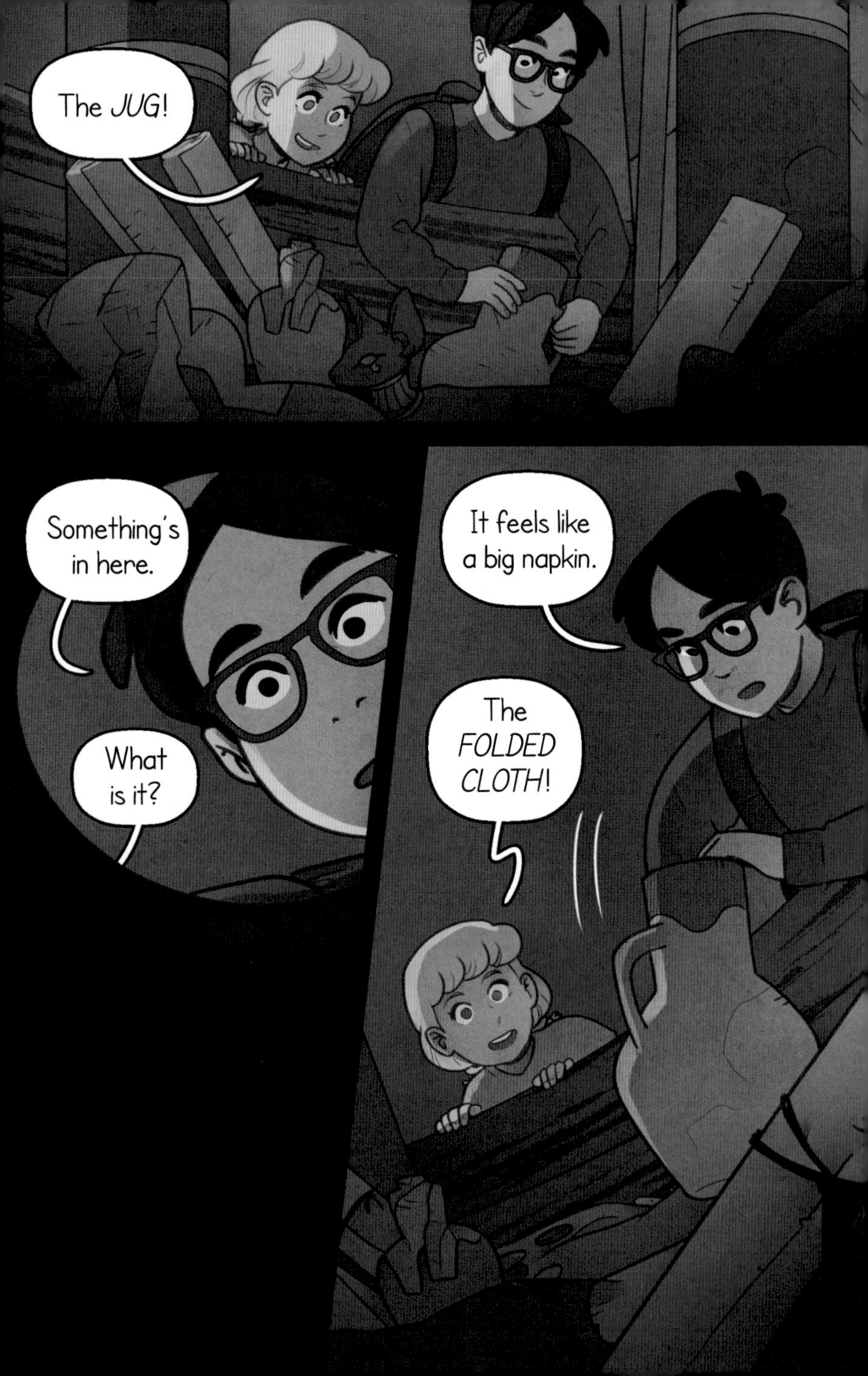
The *JUG*!
Something's in here.
What is it?
It feels like a big napkin.
The *FOLDED CLOTH*!

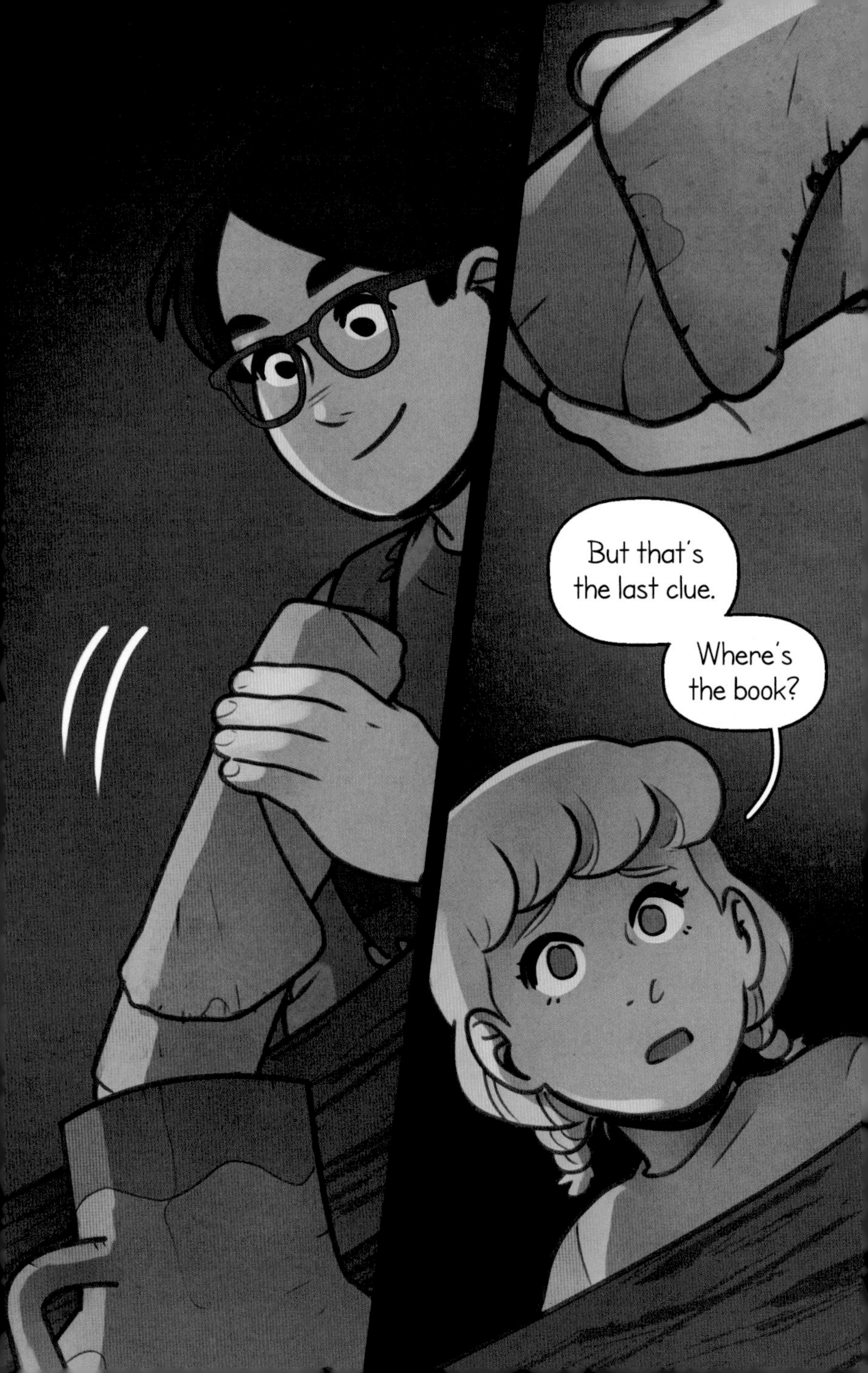
But that's the last clue.
Where's the book?

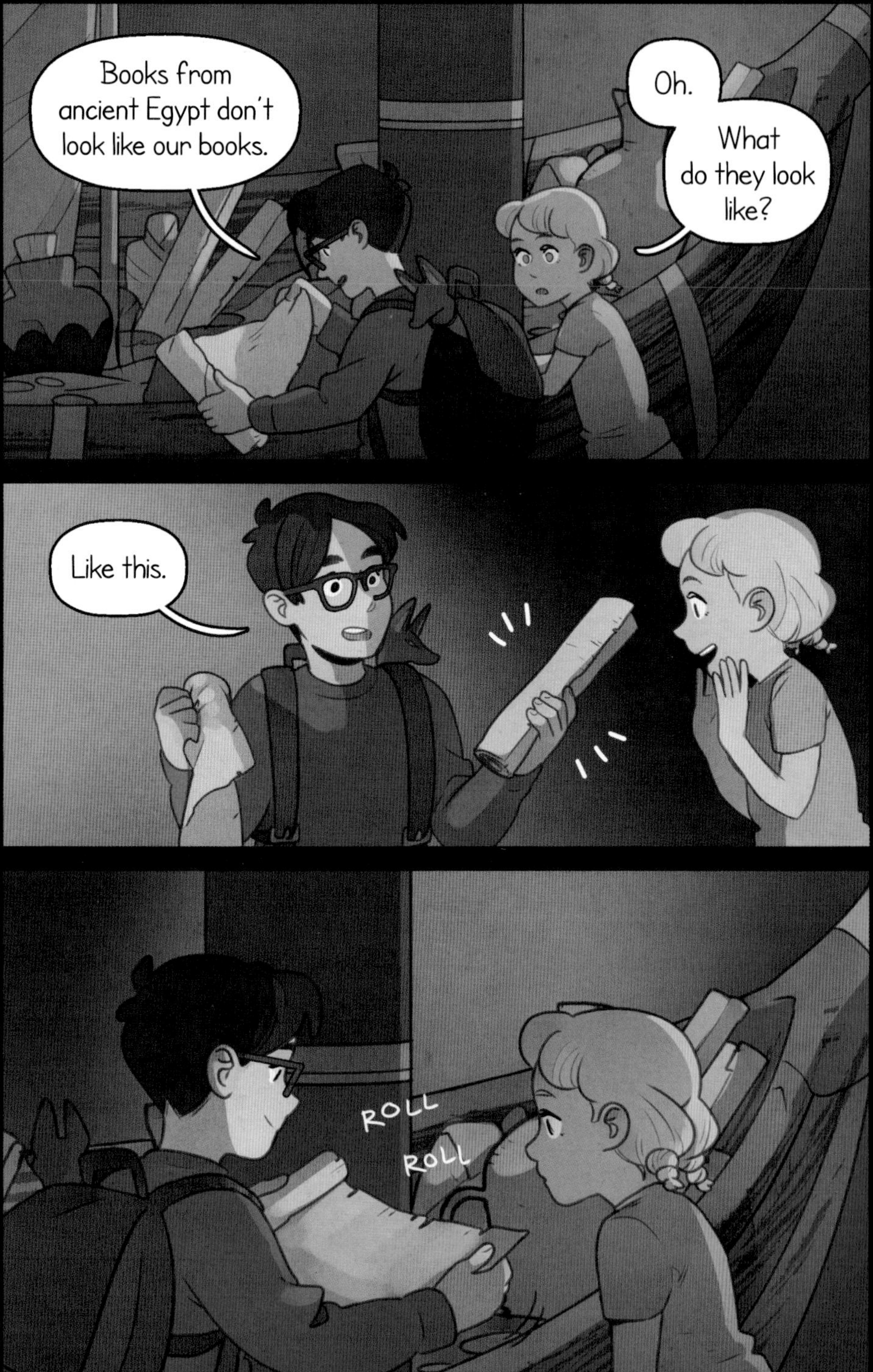
Books from ancient Egypt don't look like our books.
Oh.
What do they look like?
Like this.
ROLL
ROLL

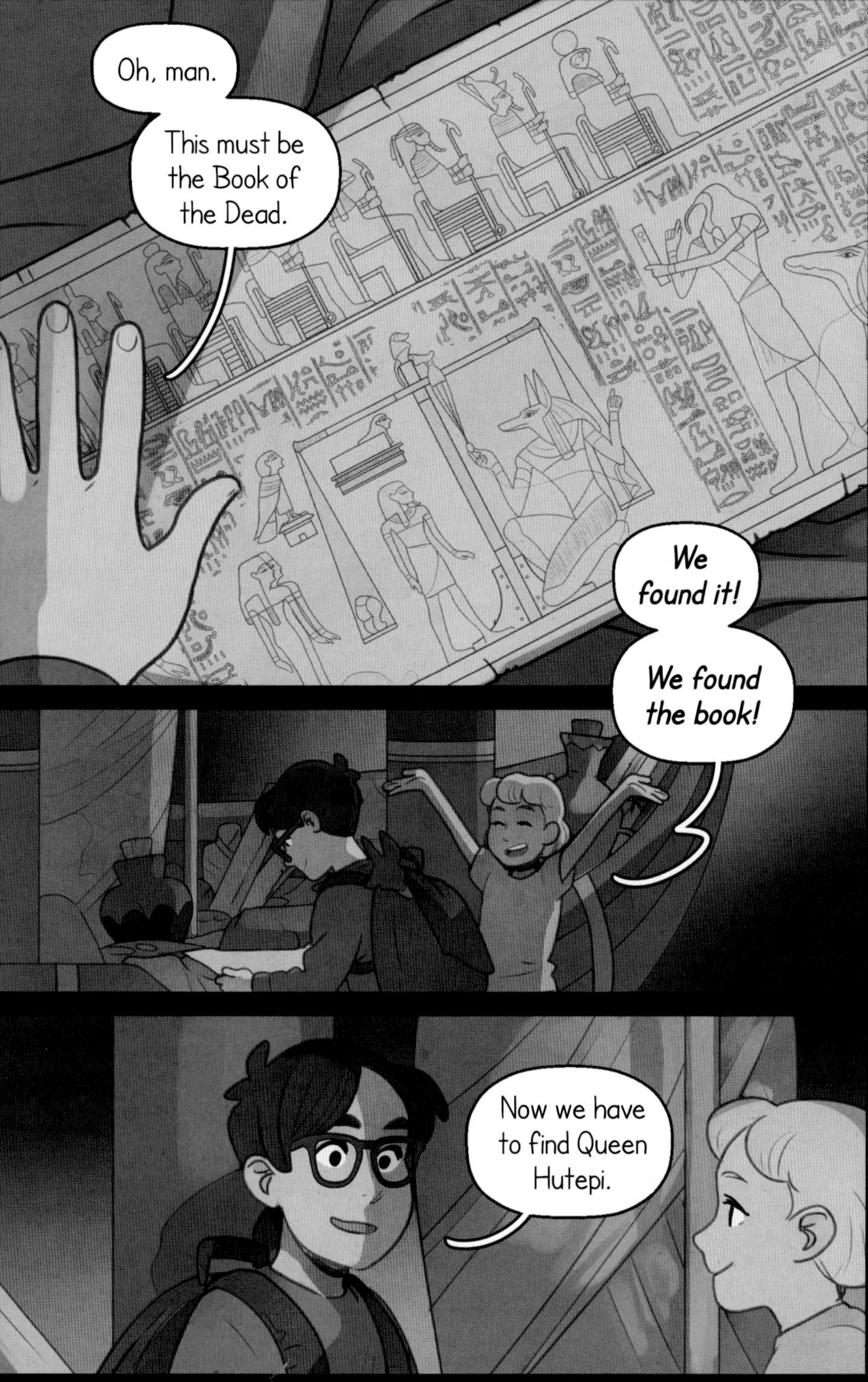
Oh, man.
This must be the Book of the Dead.
We found it!
We found the book!
Now we have to find Queen Hutepi.

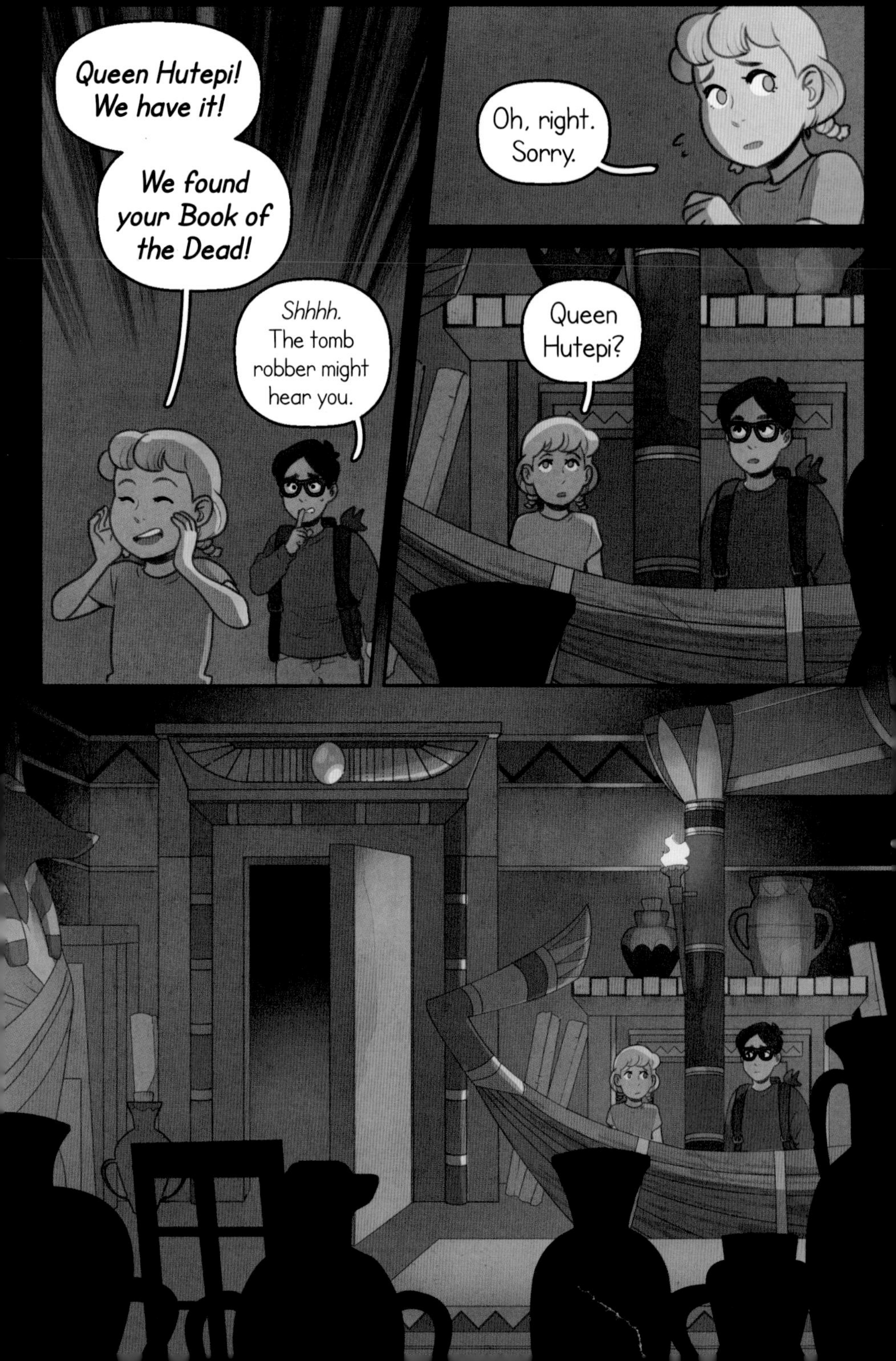
Queen Hutepi! We have it!
We found your Book of the Dead!
Shhhh. The tomb robber might hear you.
Oh, right. Sorry.
Queen Hutepi?

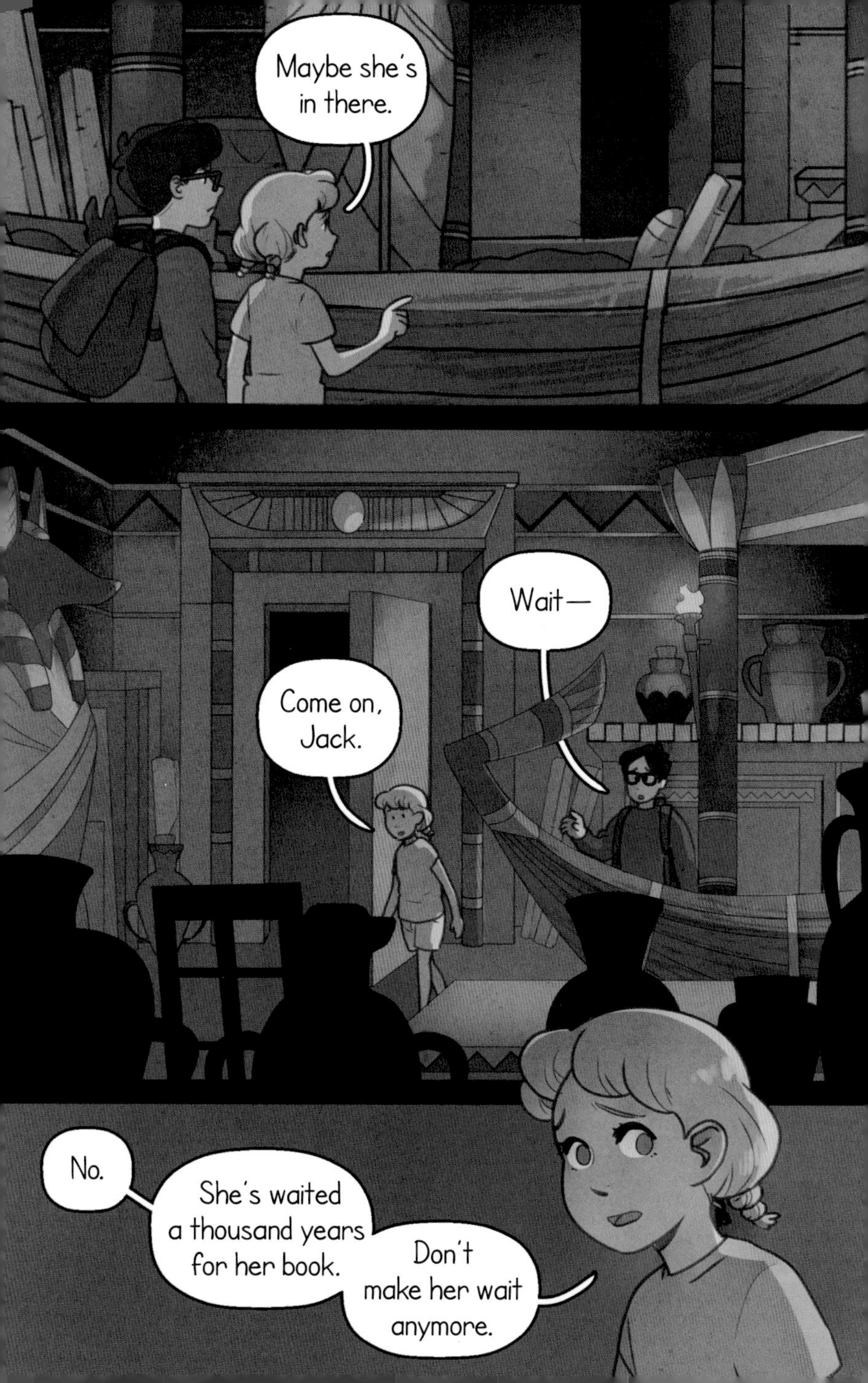
Maybe she's in there.
Wait—
Come on, Jack.
No.
She's waited a thousand years for her book.
Don't make her wait anymore.

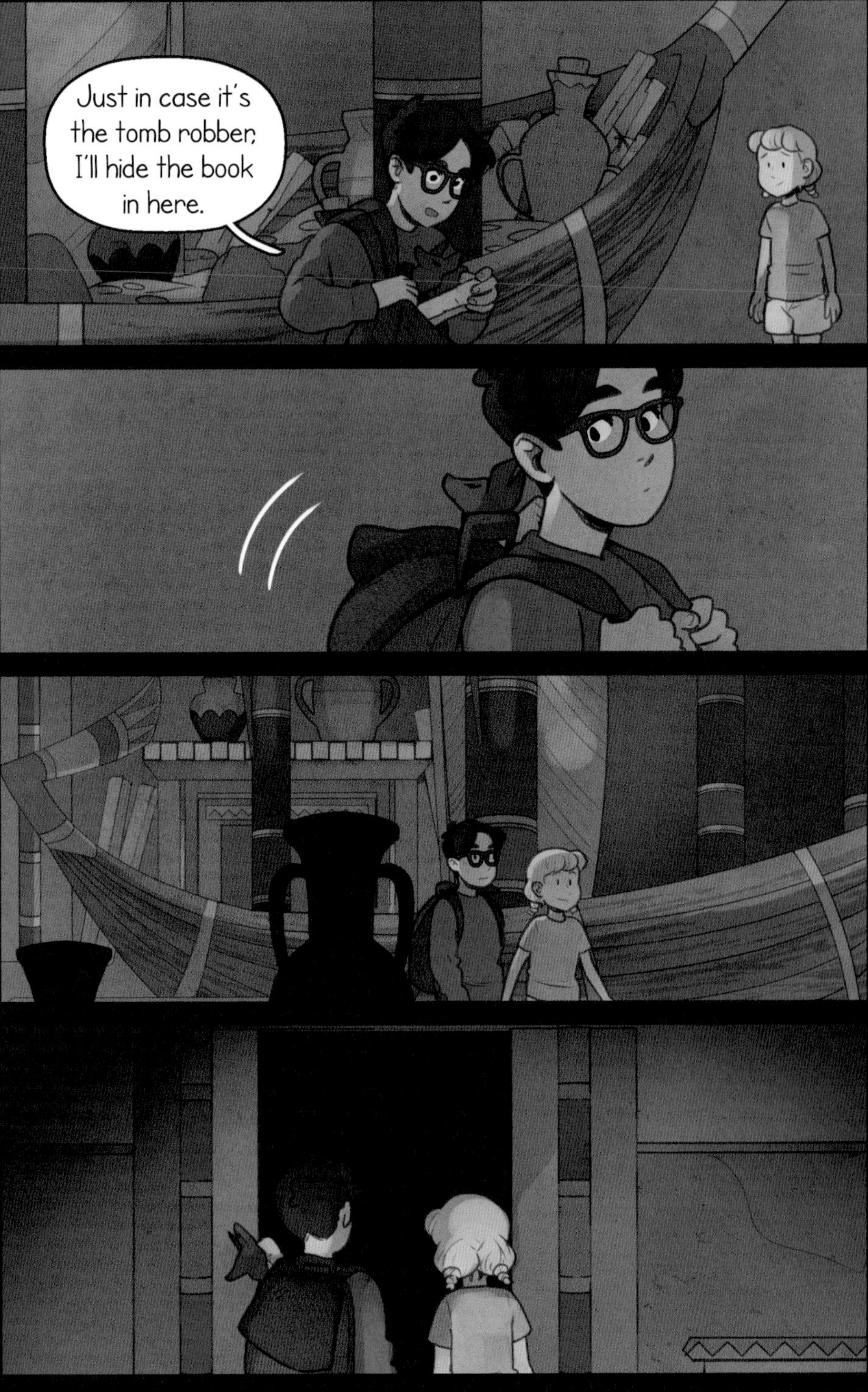
Just in case it's the tomb robber, I'll hide the book in here.

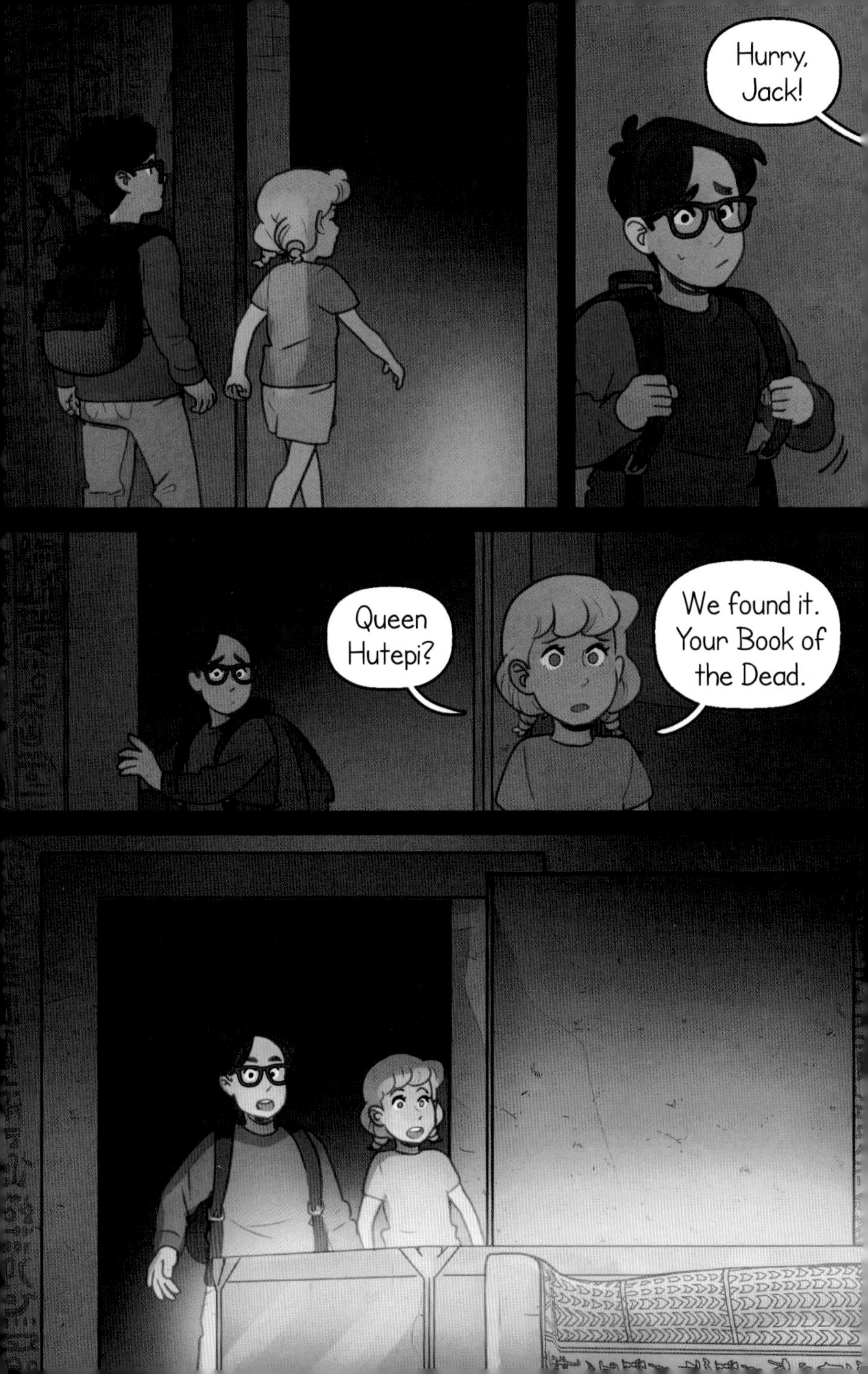
Hurry, Jack!
Queen Hutepi?
We found it. Your Book of the Dead.

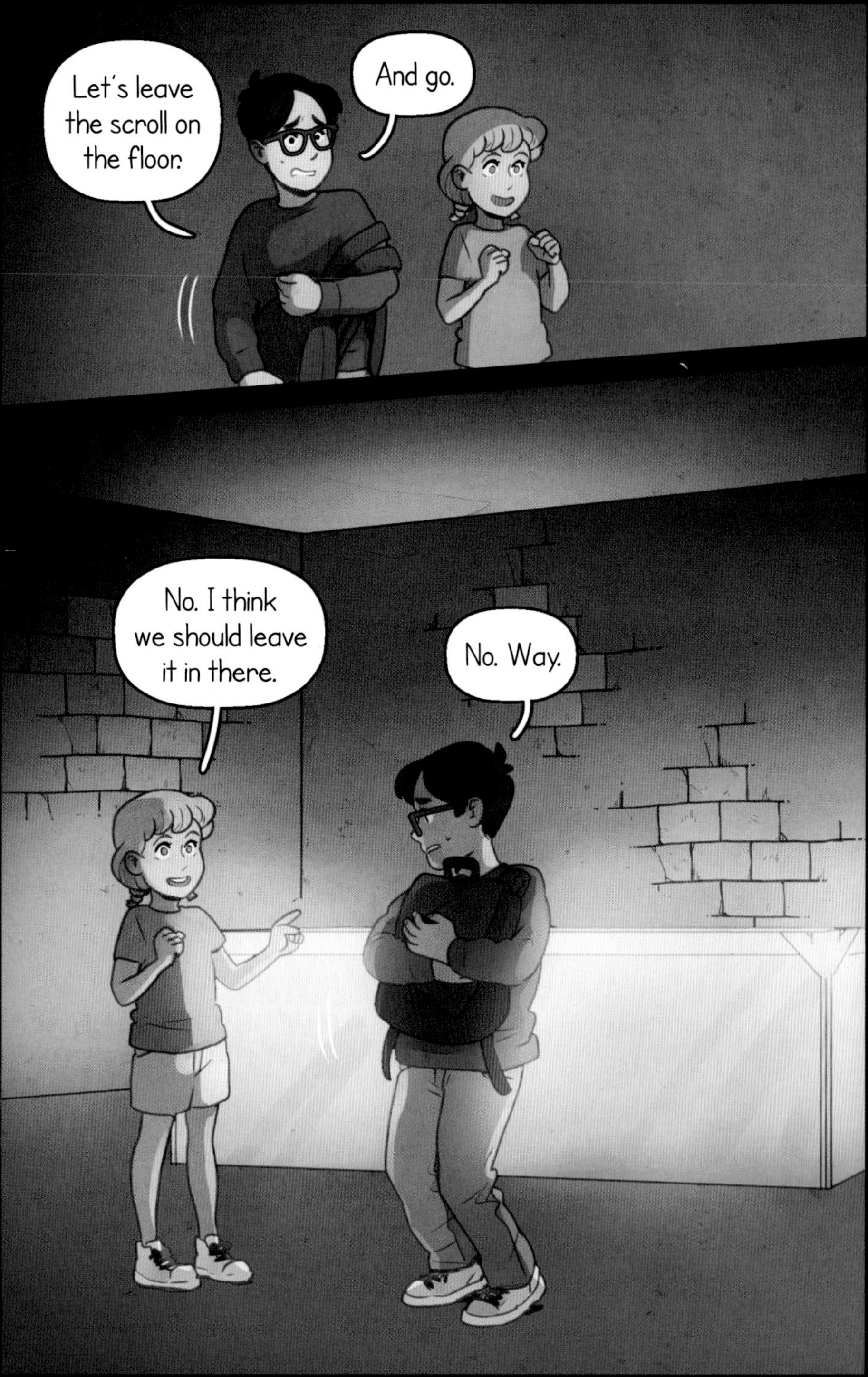
Let's leave the scroll on the floor.
And go.
No. I think we should leave it in there.
No. Way.

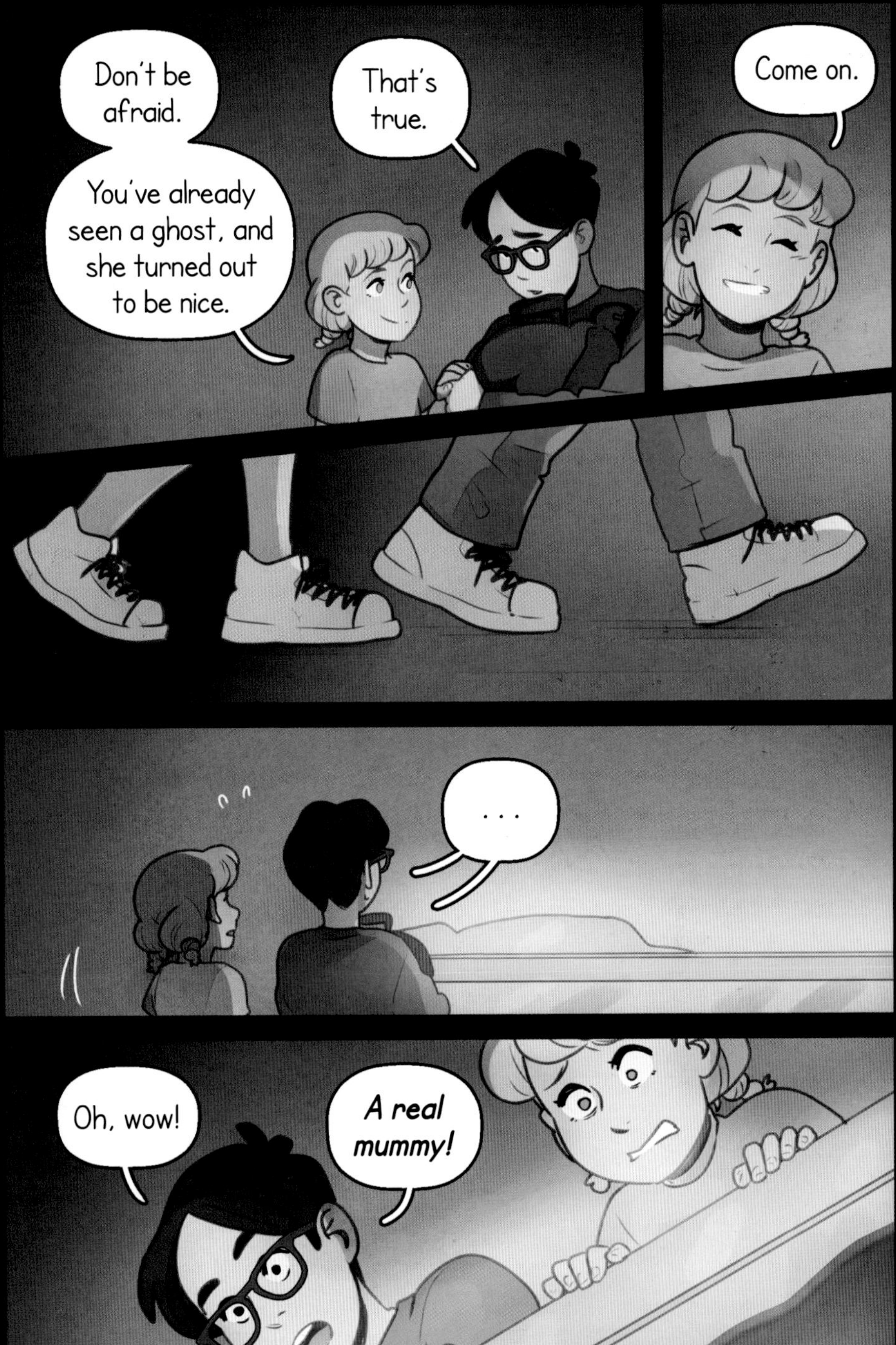
Don't be afraid.
You've already seen a ghost, and she turned out to be nice.
That's true.
Come on.
. . .
Oh, wow!
A real mummy!

CHAPTER EIGHT
The Mummy

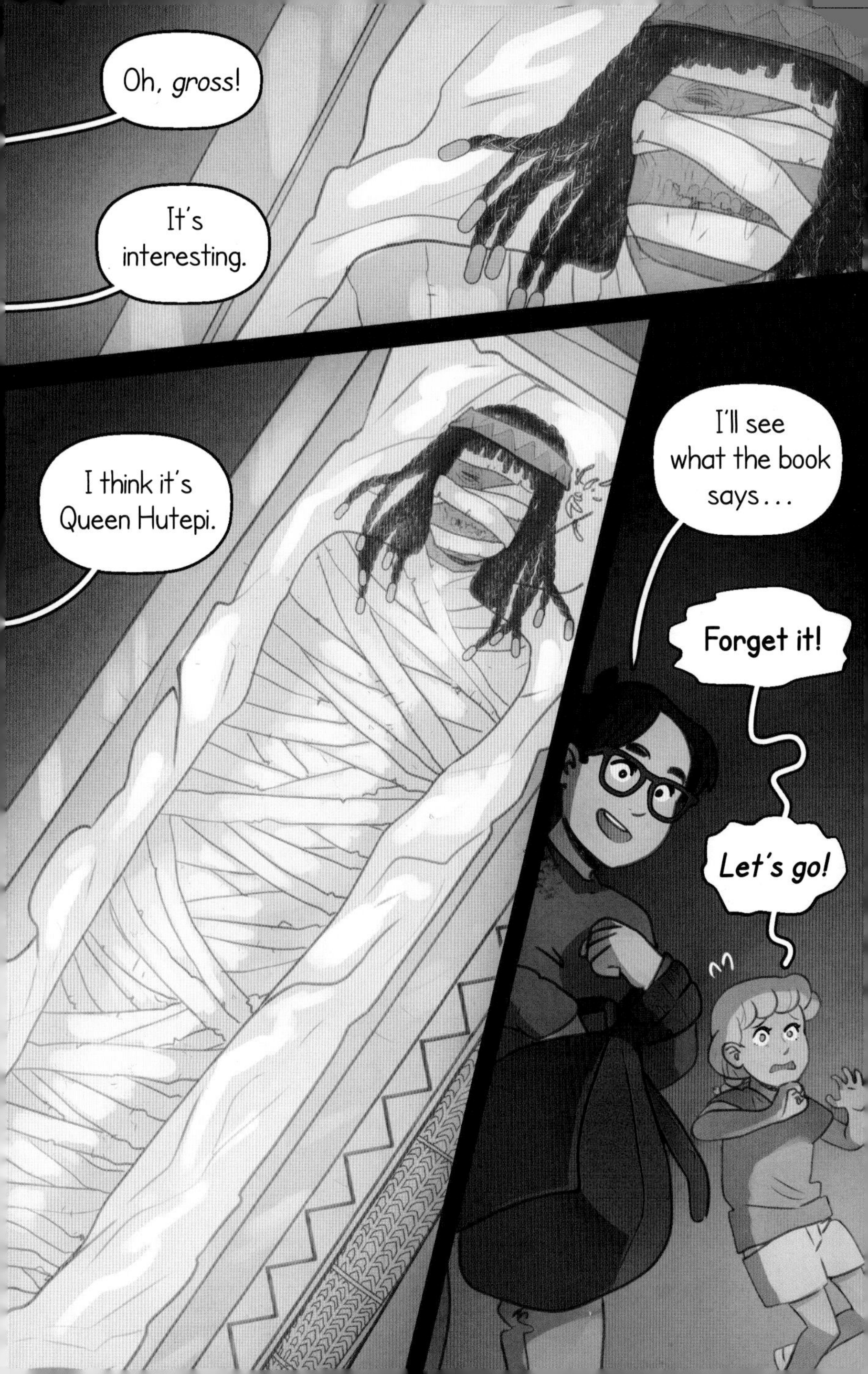
Oh, *gross*!
It's interesting.
I think it's Queen Hutepi.
I'll see what the book says...
Forget it!
Let's go!

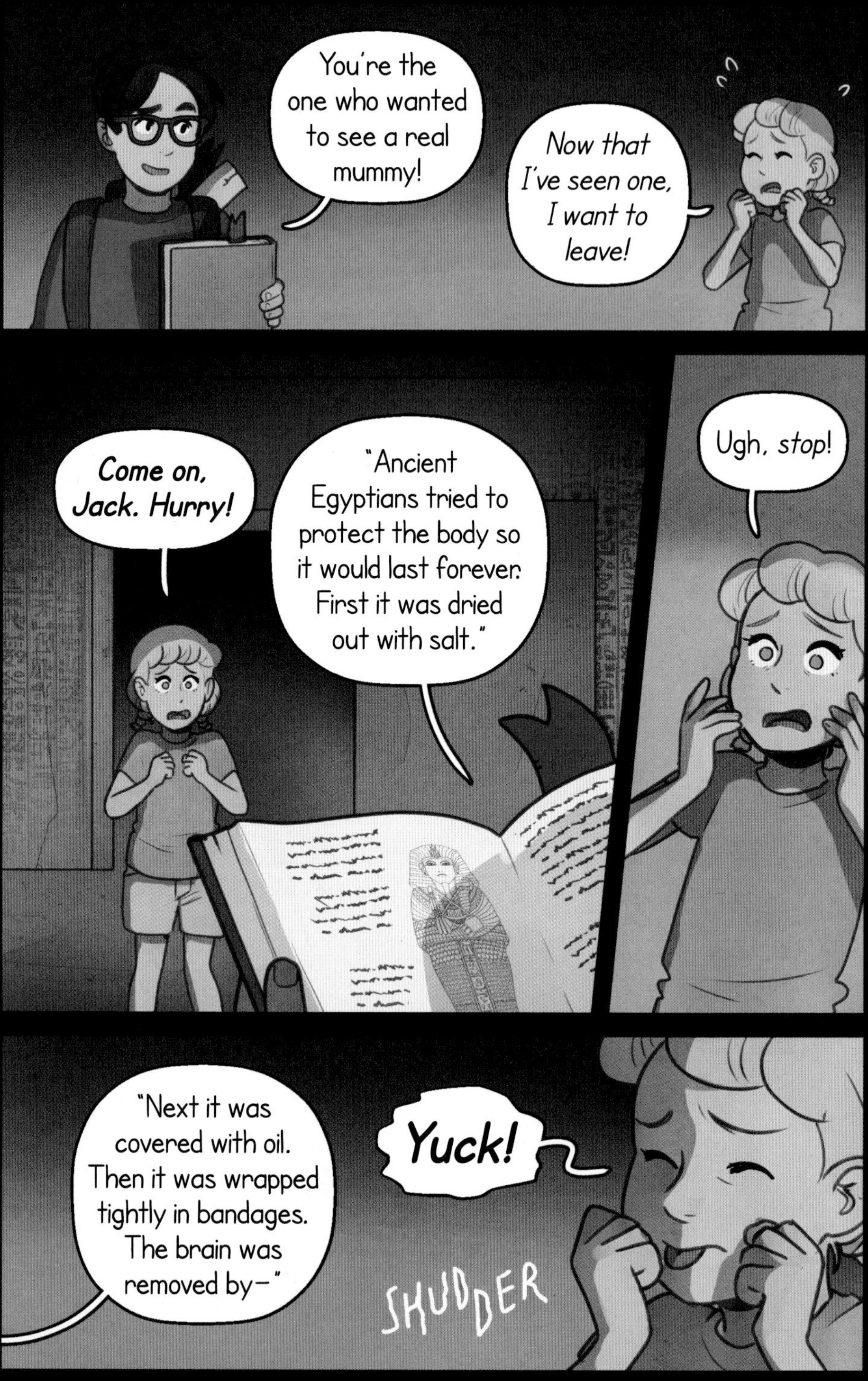

You're the one who wanted to see a real mummy!
Now that I've seen one, I want to leave!
Come on, Jack. Hurry!
"Ancient Egyptians tried to protect the body so it would last forever. First it was dried out with salt."
Ugh, *stop*!
"Next it was covered with oil. Then it was wrapped tightly in bandages. The brain was removed by—"
Yuck!
SHUDDER

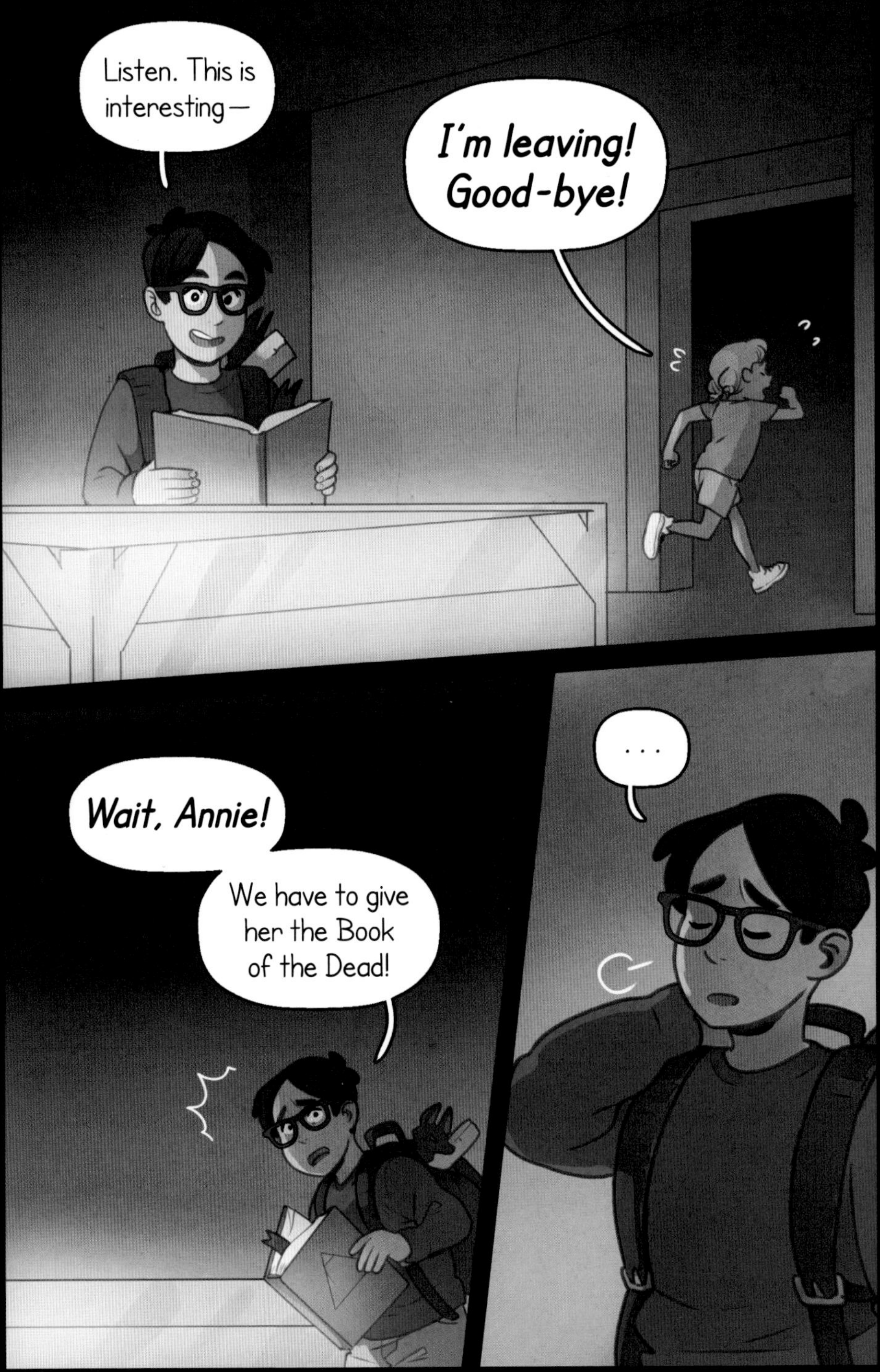
Listen. This is interesting—
I'm leaving! Good-bye!
Wait, Annie!
We have to give her the Book of the Dead!
. . .

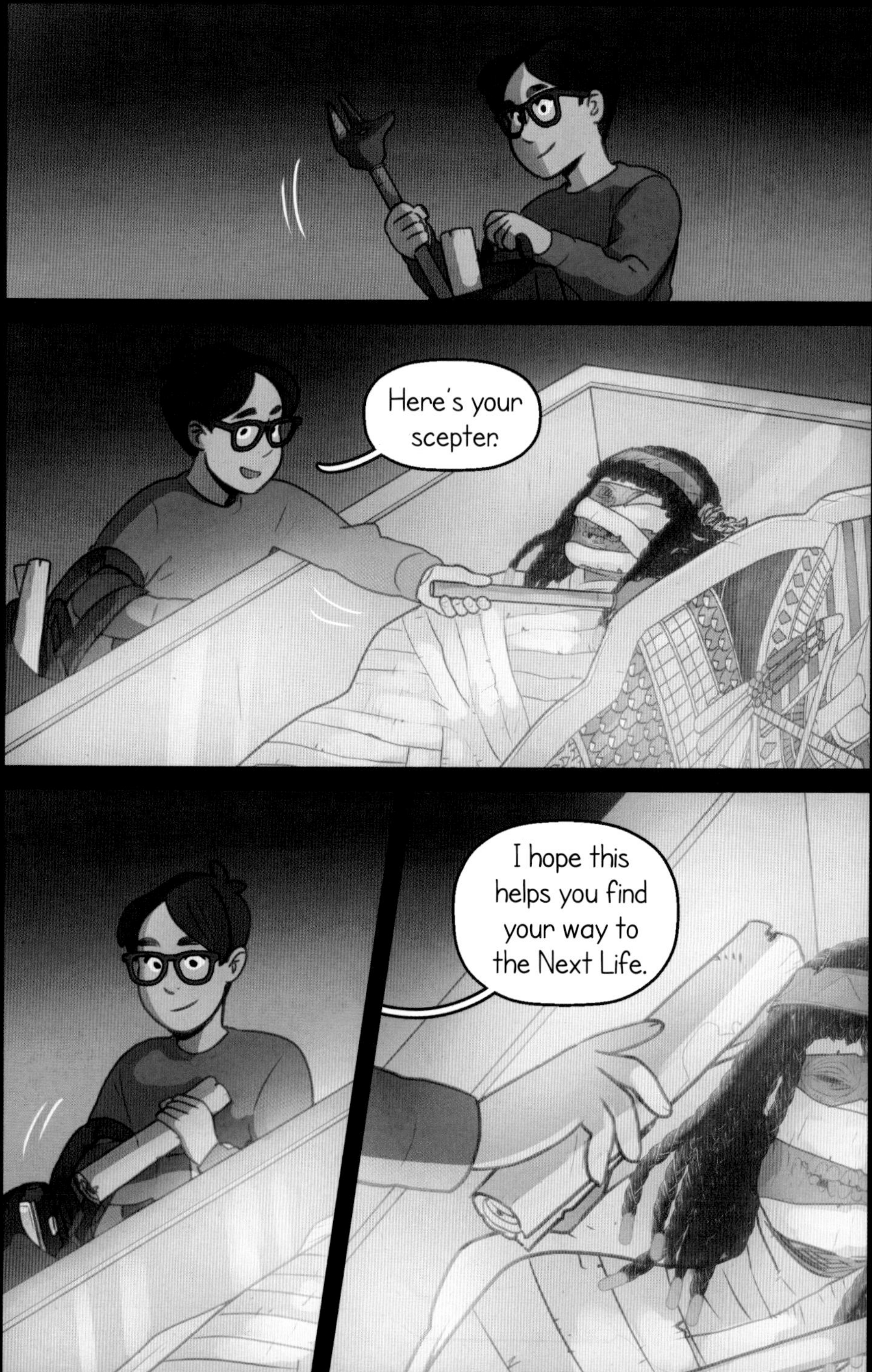
Here's your scepter.
I hope this helps you find your way to the Next Life.

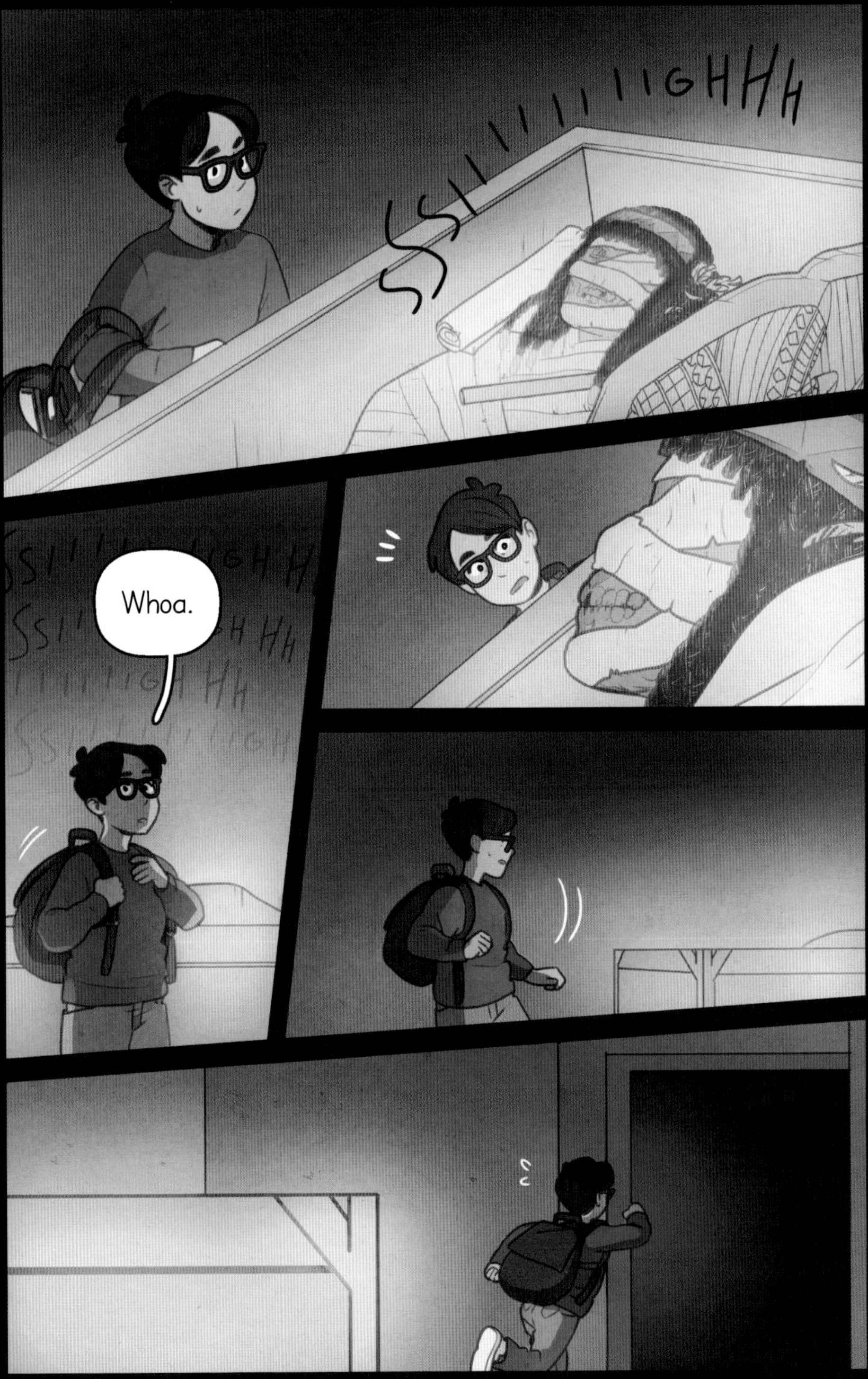
SSIIIIIIIIGHHHH
Whoa.

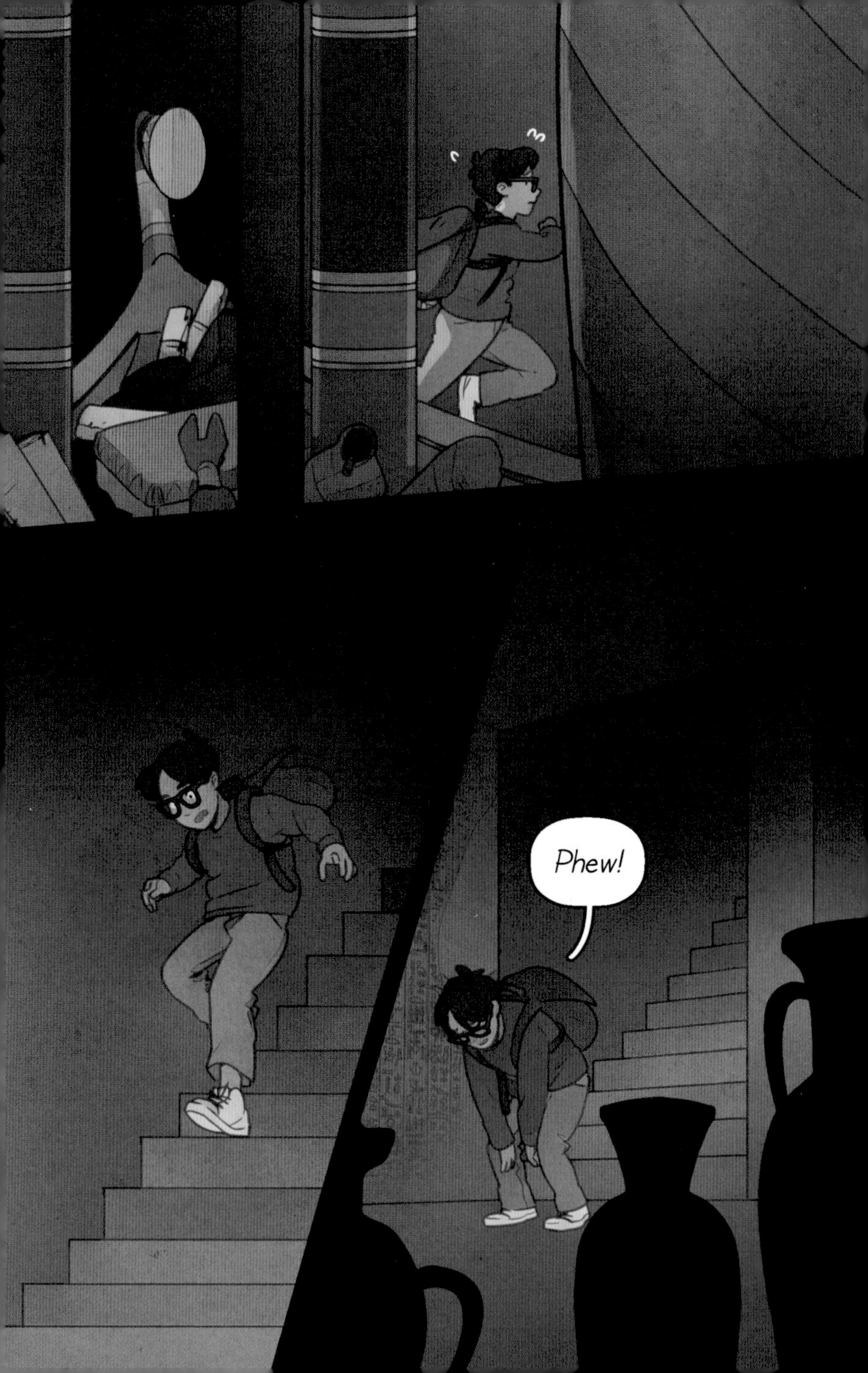
Phew!

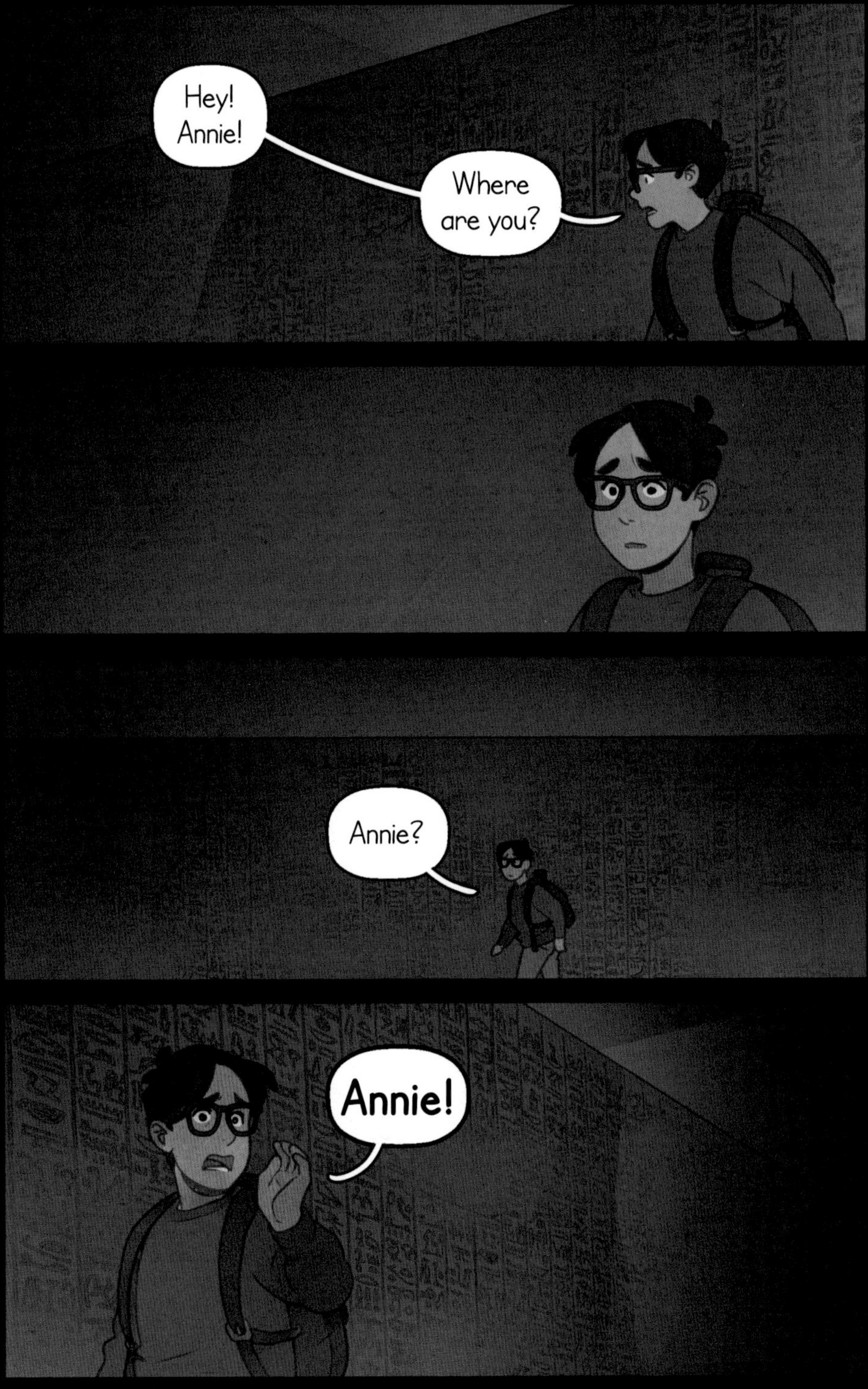
Hey! Annie!
Where are you?
Annie?
Annie!

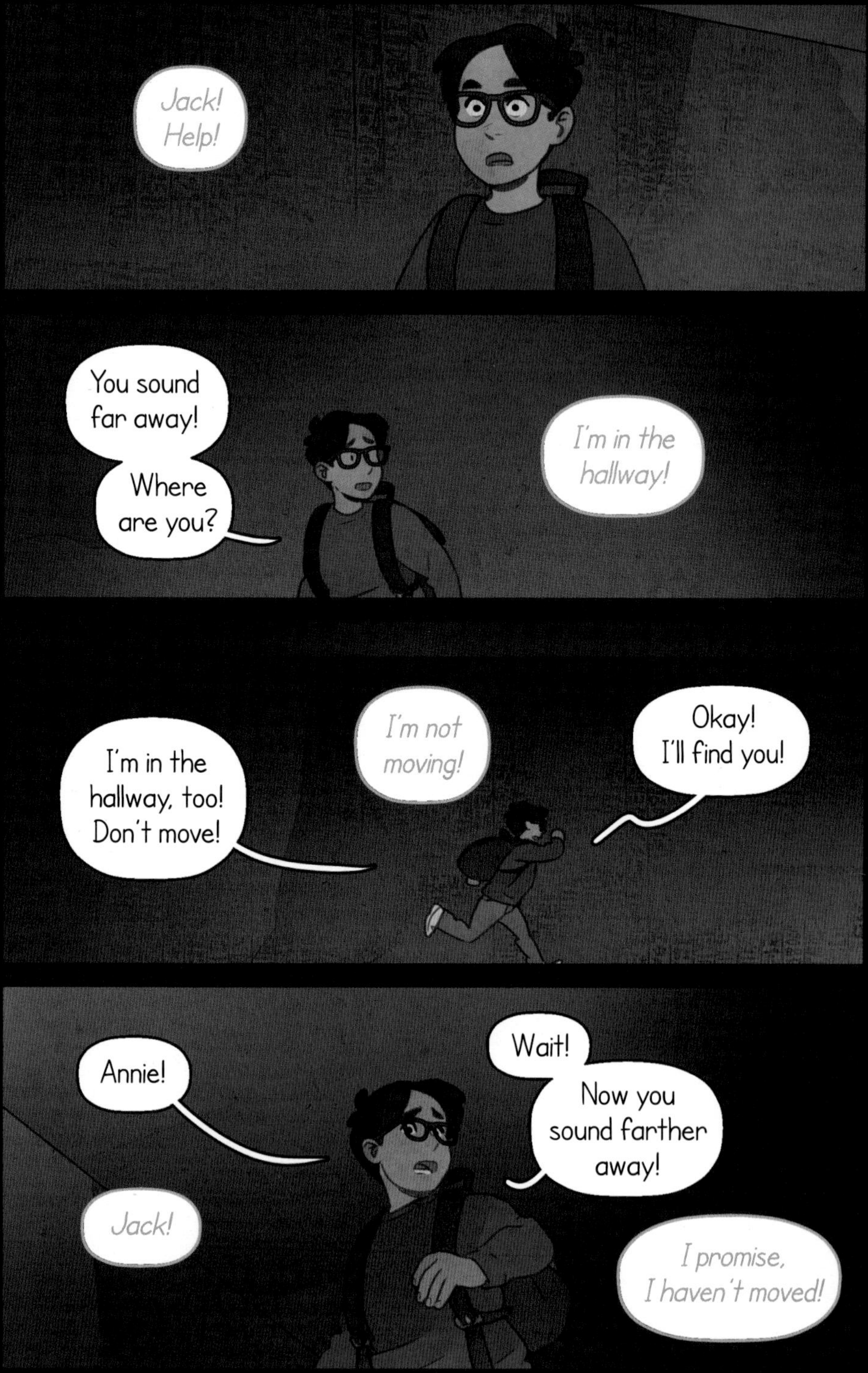
Jack! Help!
You sound far away!
Where are you?
I'm in the hallway!
I'm in the hallway, too! Don't move!
I'm not moving!
Okay! I'll find you!
Annie!
Wait!
Now you sound farther away!
Jack!
I promise, I haven't moved!

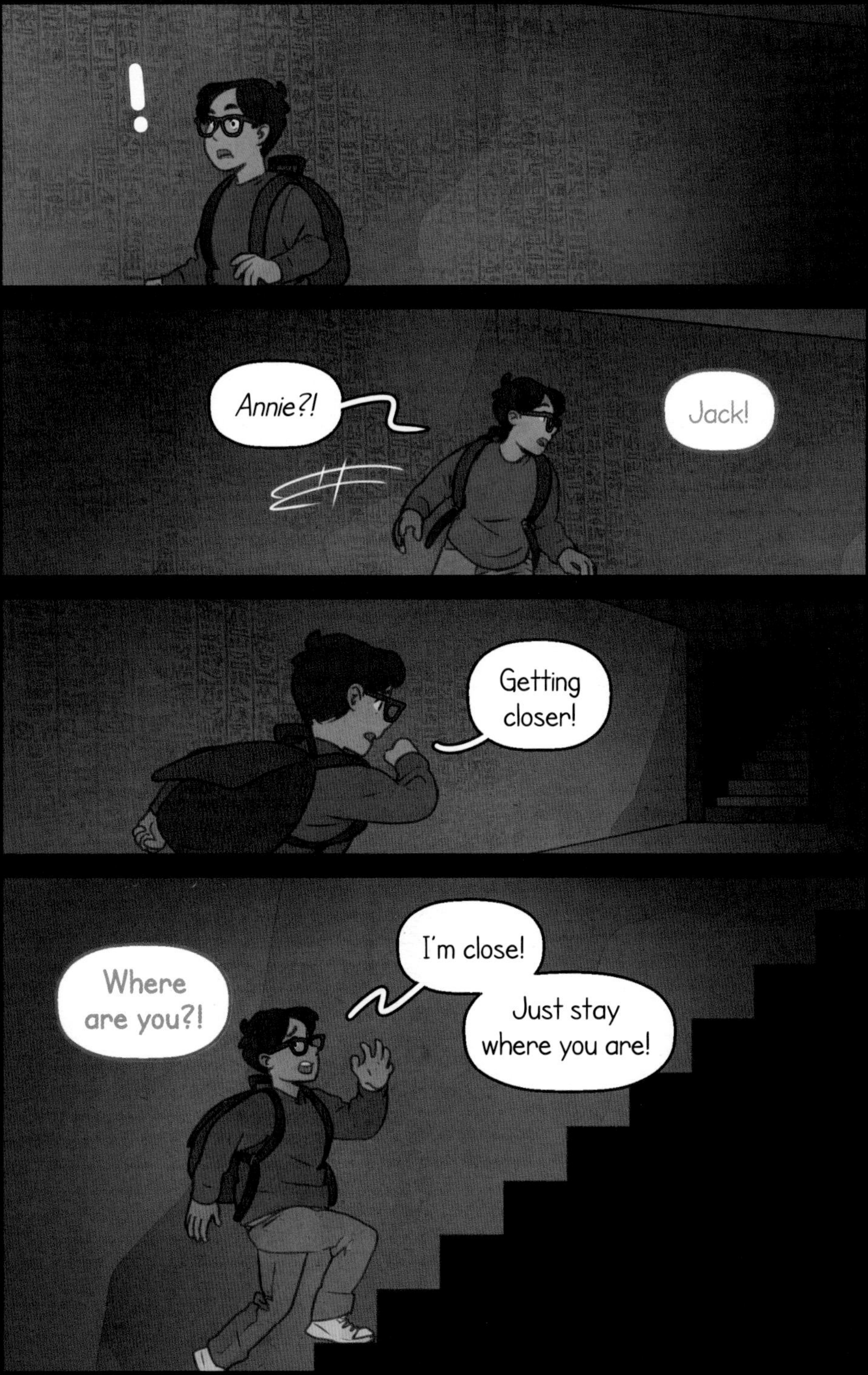
!
Annie?!
Jack!
Getting closer!
Where are you?!
I'm close!
Just stay where you are!

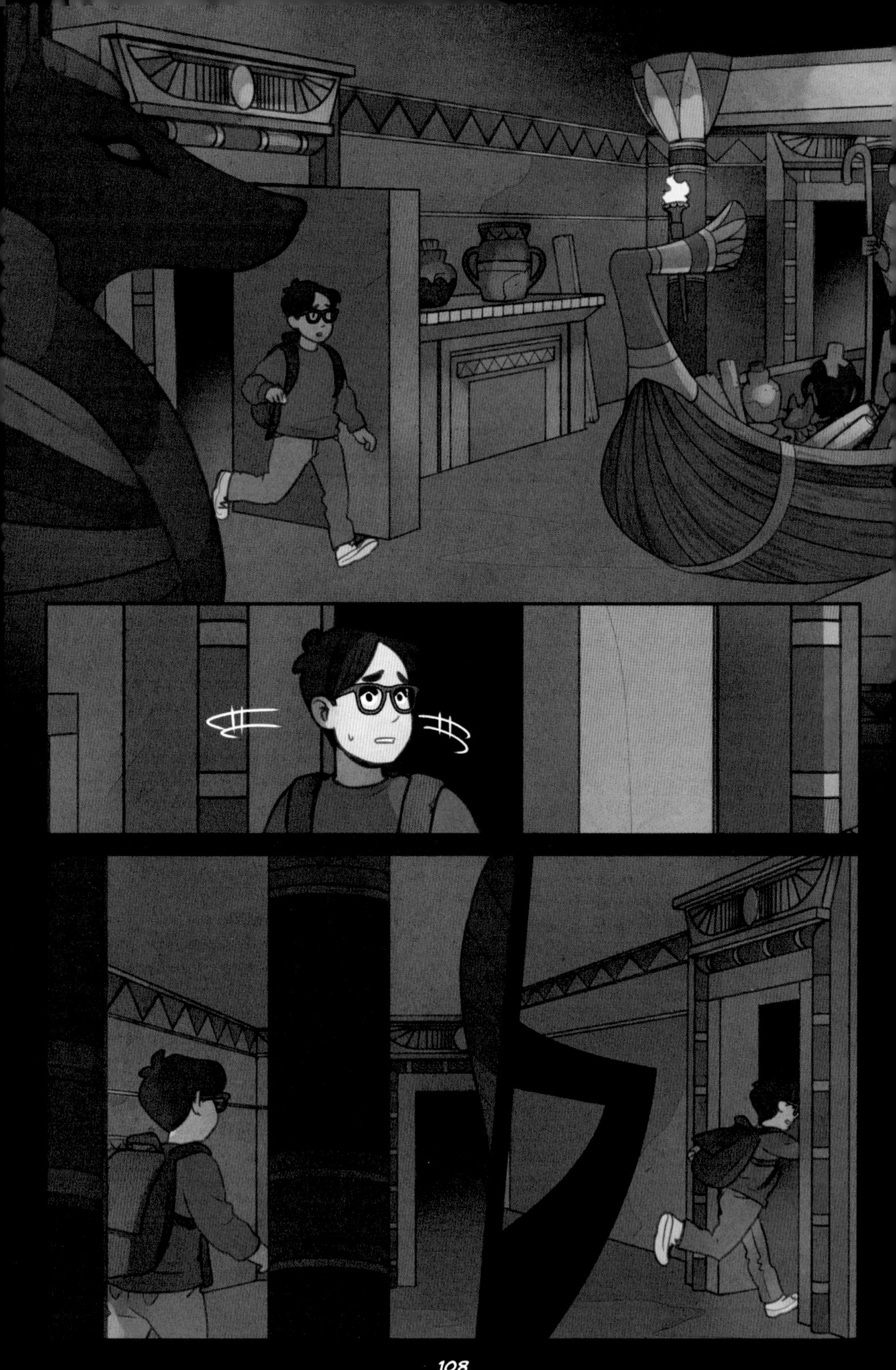

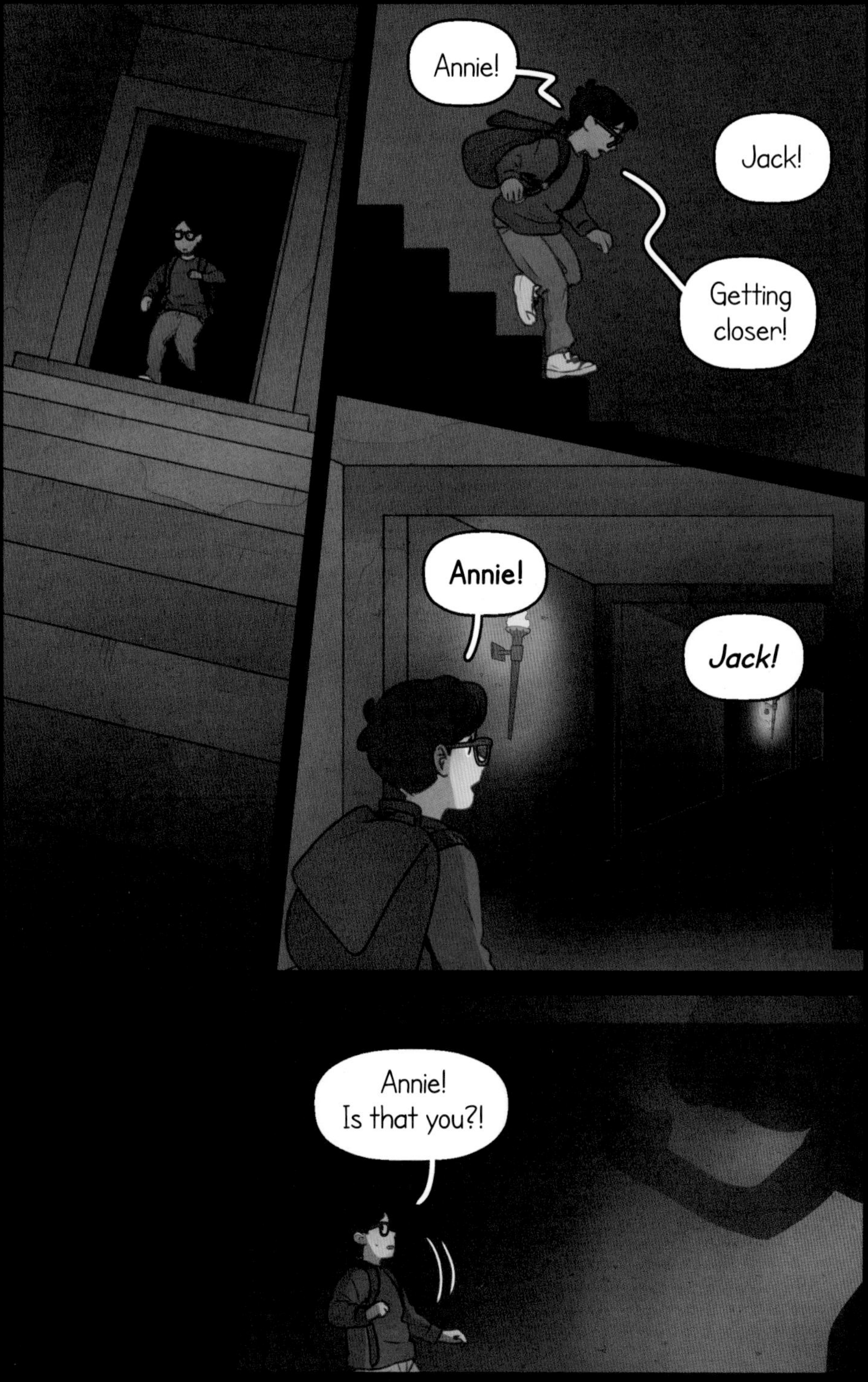
Annie!
Jack!
Getting closer!
Annie!
Jack!
Annie!
Is that you?!

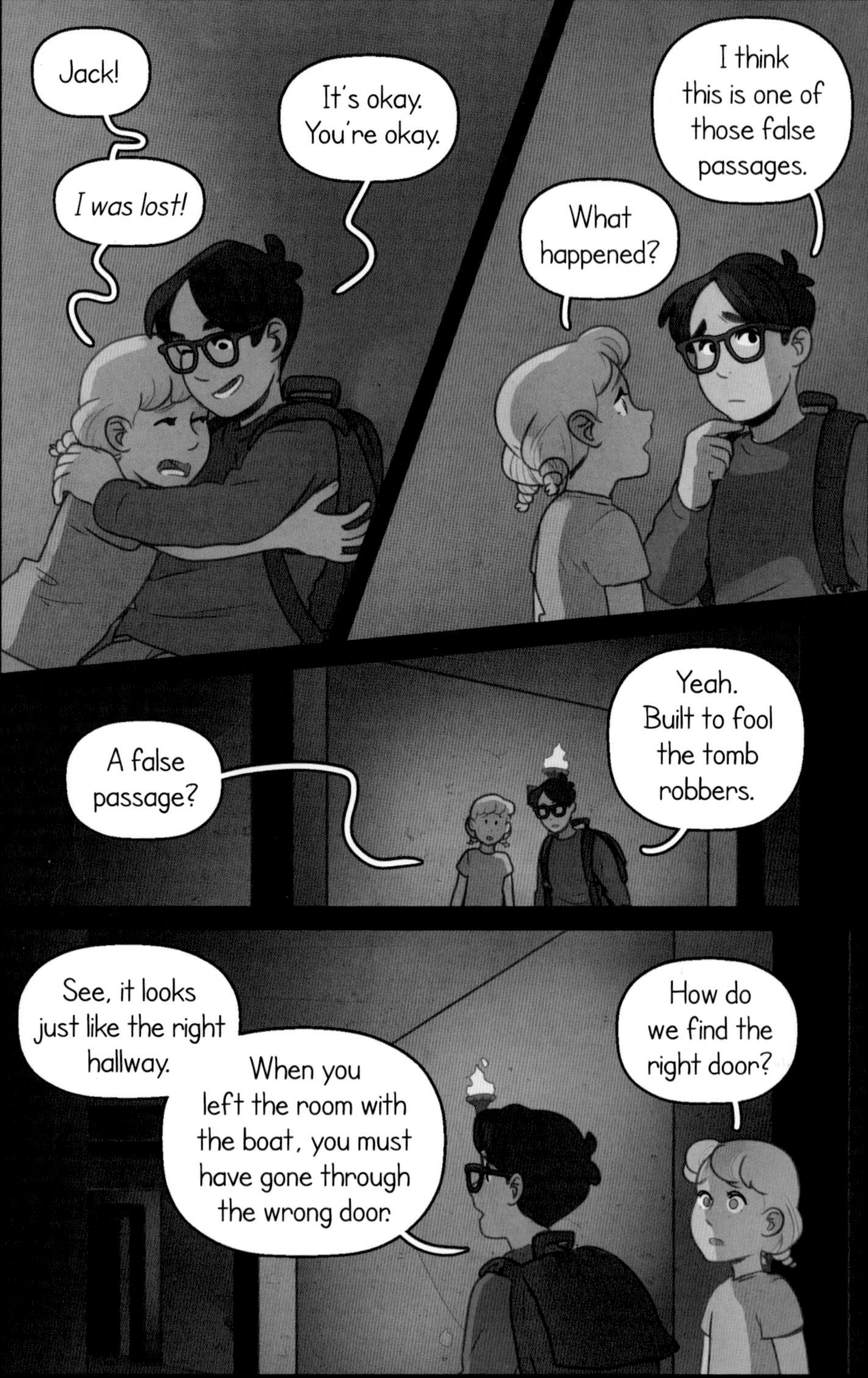
Jack!
I was lost!
It's okay. You're okay.
What happened?
I think this is one of those false passages.
A false passage?
Yeah. Built to fool the tomb robbers.
See, it looks just like the right hallway.
When you left the room with the boat, you must have gone through the wrong door.
How do we find the right door?

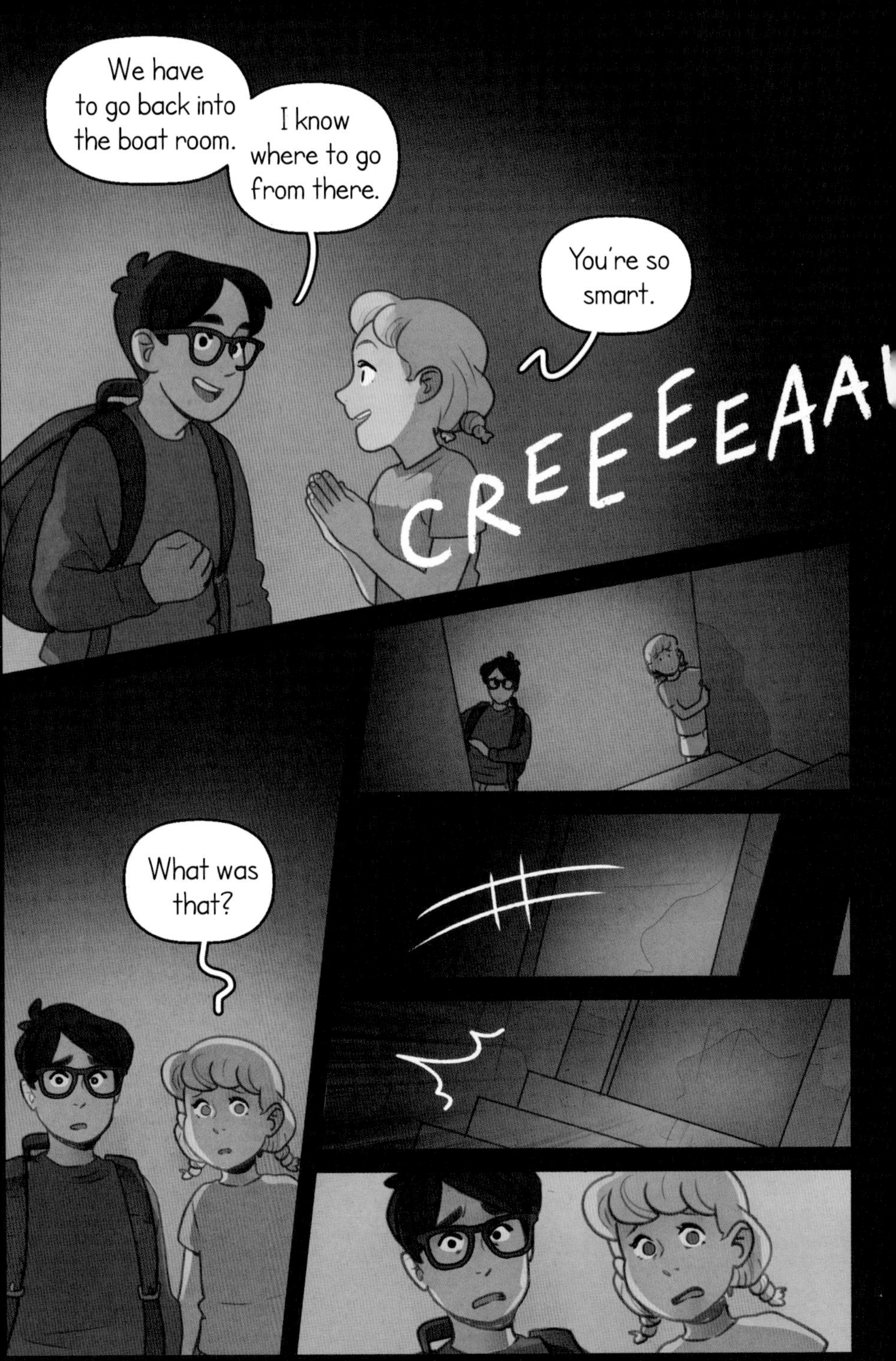
We have to go back into the boat room.
I know where to go from there.
You're so smart.
CREEEEAA
What was that?

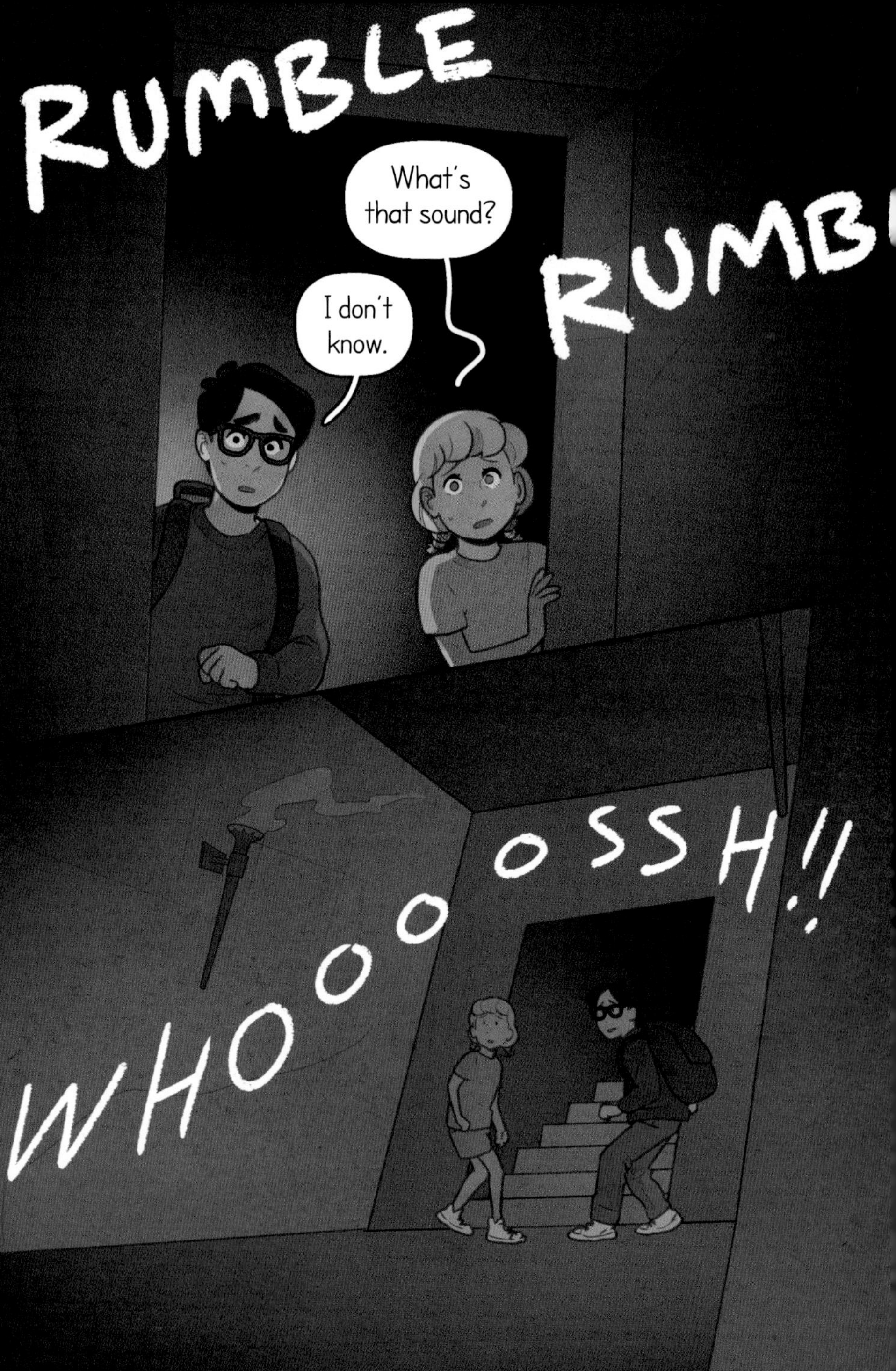
RUMBLE
What's that sound?
I don't know.
RUMBL
WHOOOOSSH!!

CHAPTER NINE
Follow the Leader

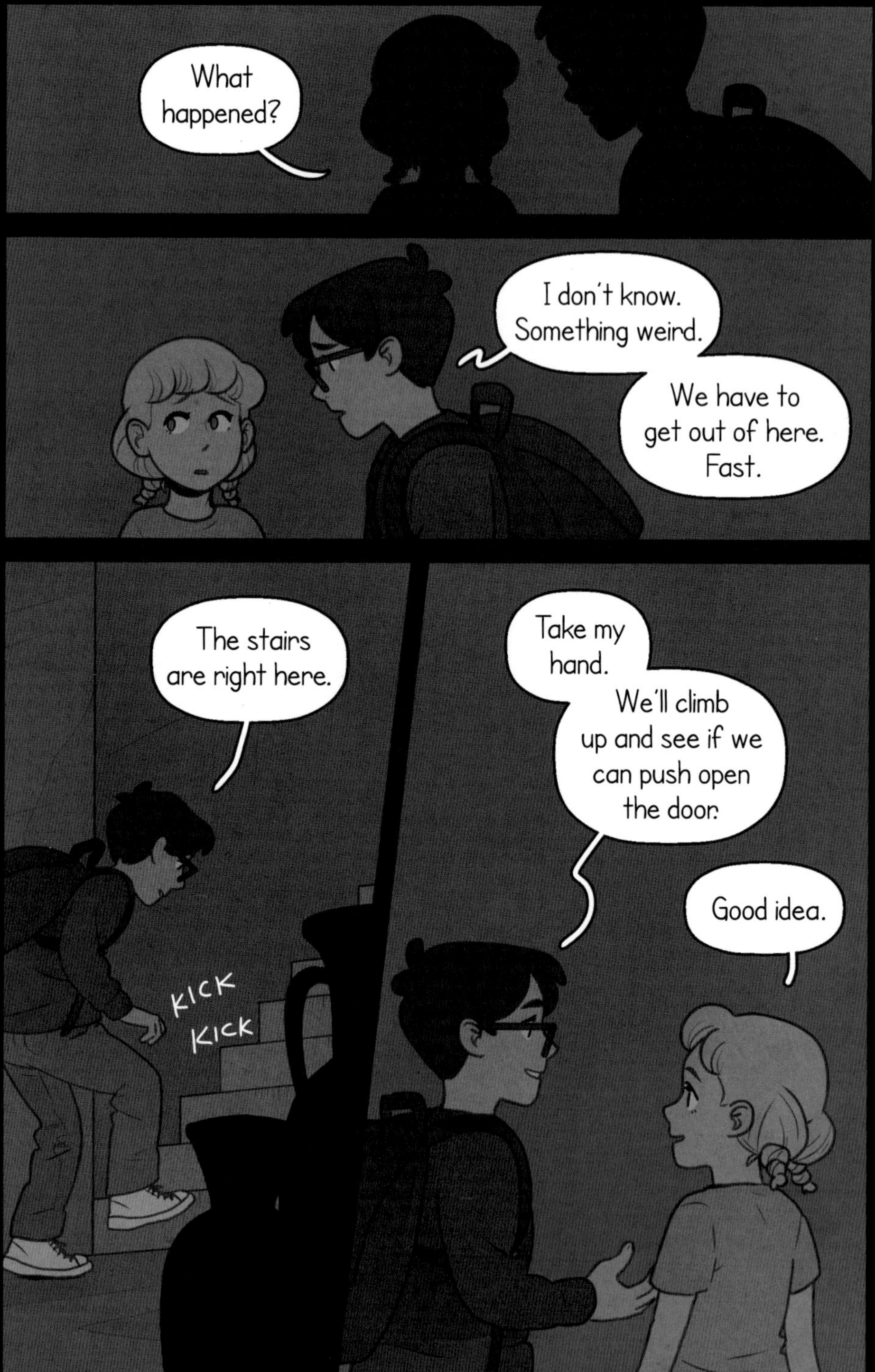
What happened?
I don't know. Something weird.
We have to get out of here. Fast.
The stairs are right here.
KICK KICK
Take my hand.
We'll climb up and see if we can push open the door.
Good idea.

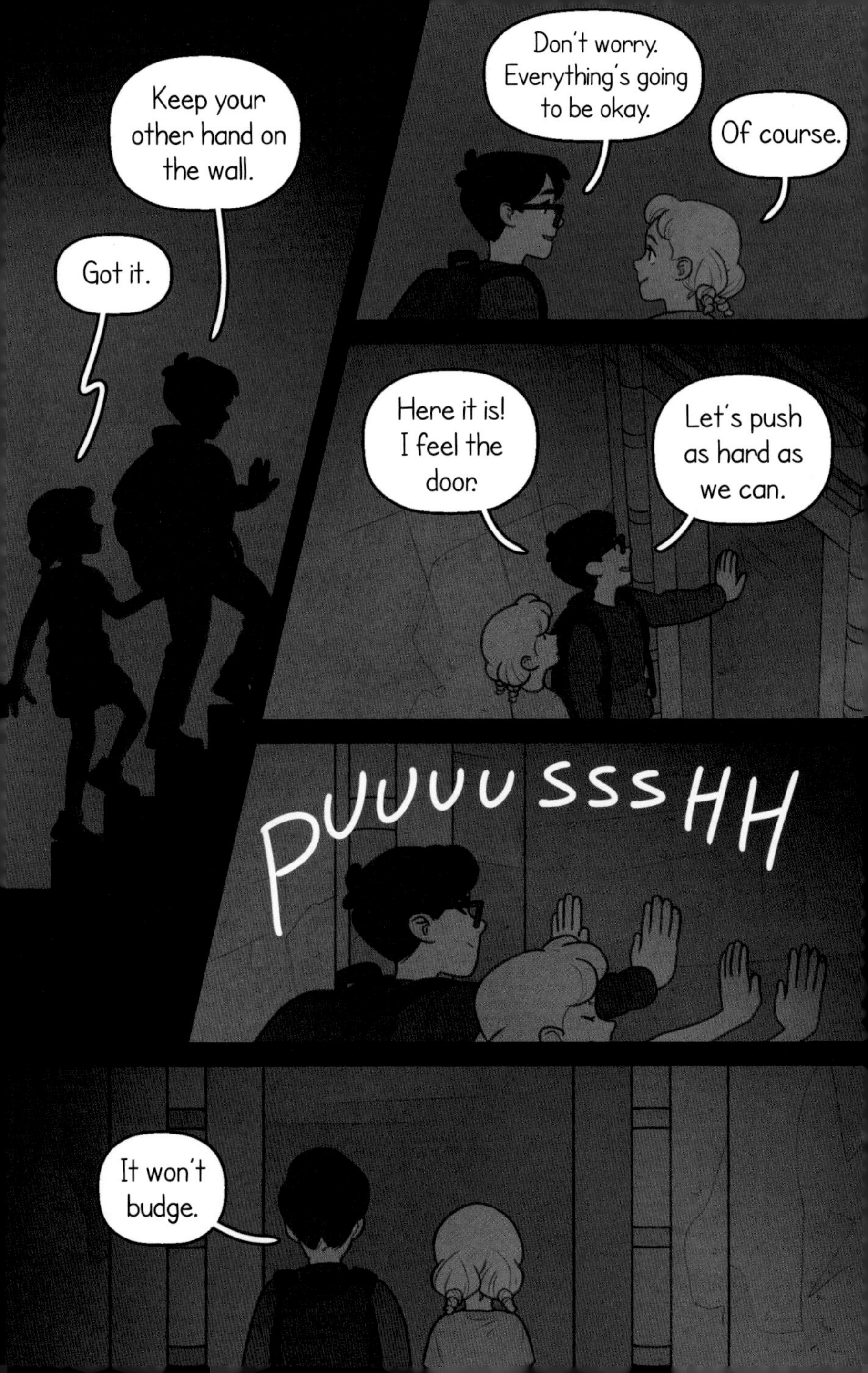
Keep your other hand on the wall.
Got it.
Don't worry. Everything's going to be okay.
Of course.
Here it is! I feel the door.
Let's push as hard as we can.
PUUUUSSSHH
It won't budge.

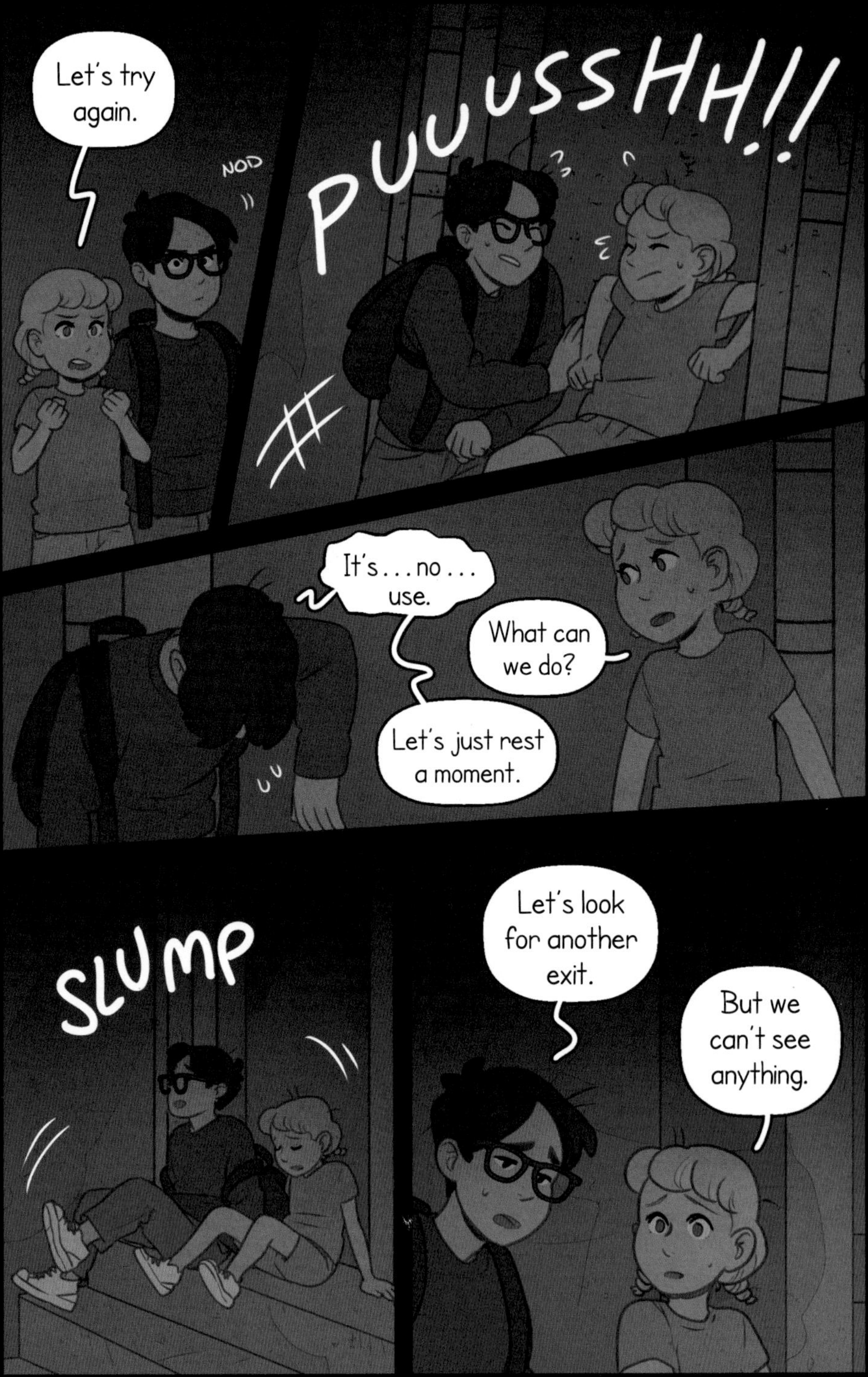
Let's try again.
NOD
PUUUSSHH!!
It's... no... use.
What can we do?
Let's just rest a moment.
SLUMP
Let's look for another exit.
But we can't see anything.

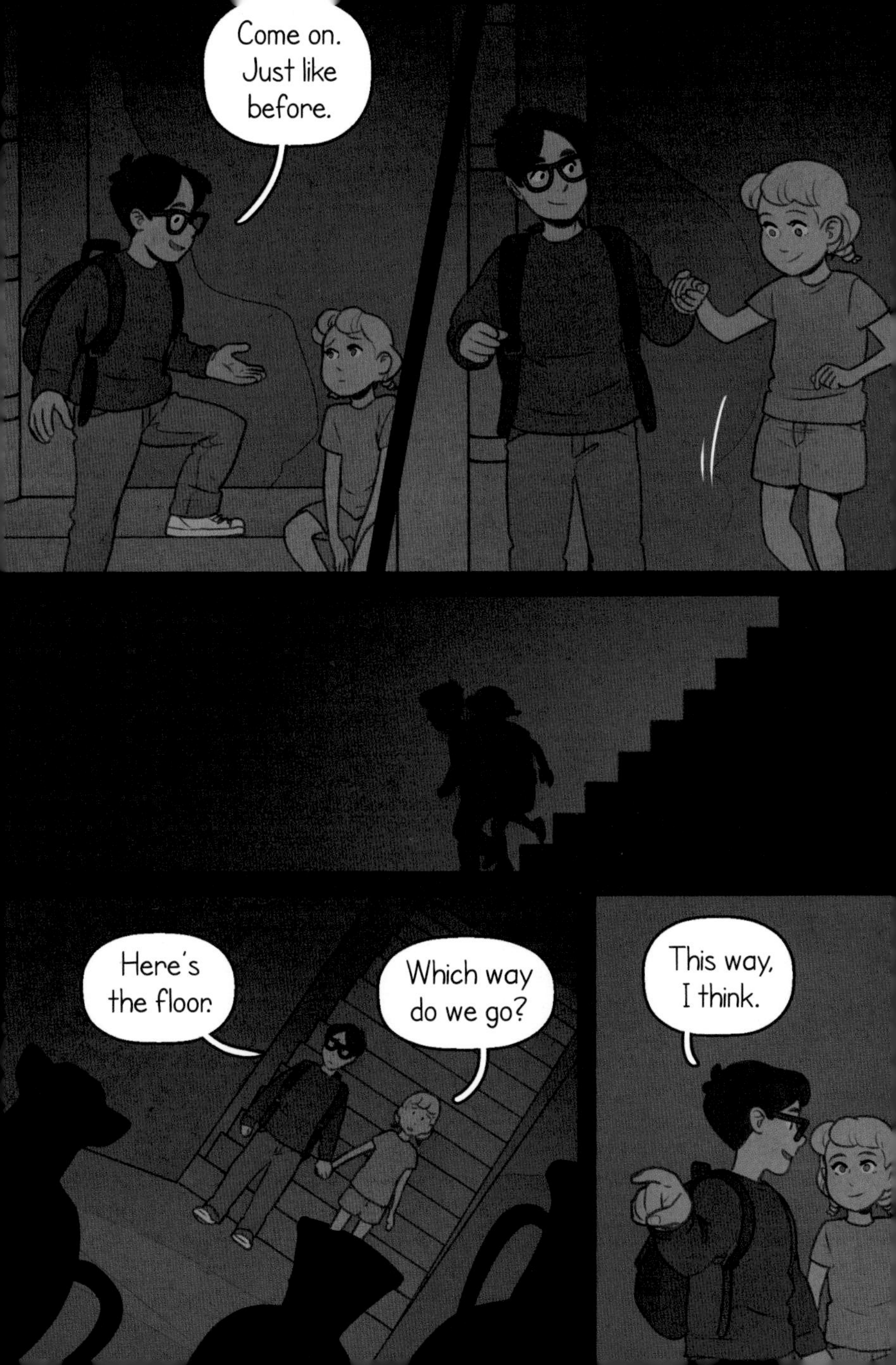
Come on. Just like before.
Here's the floor.
Which way do we go?
This way, I think.

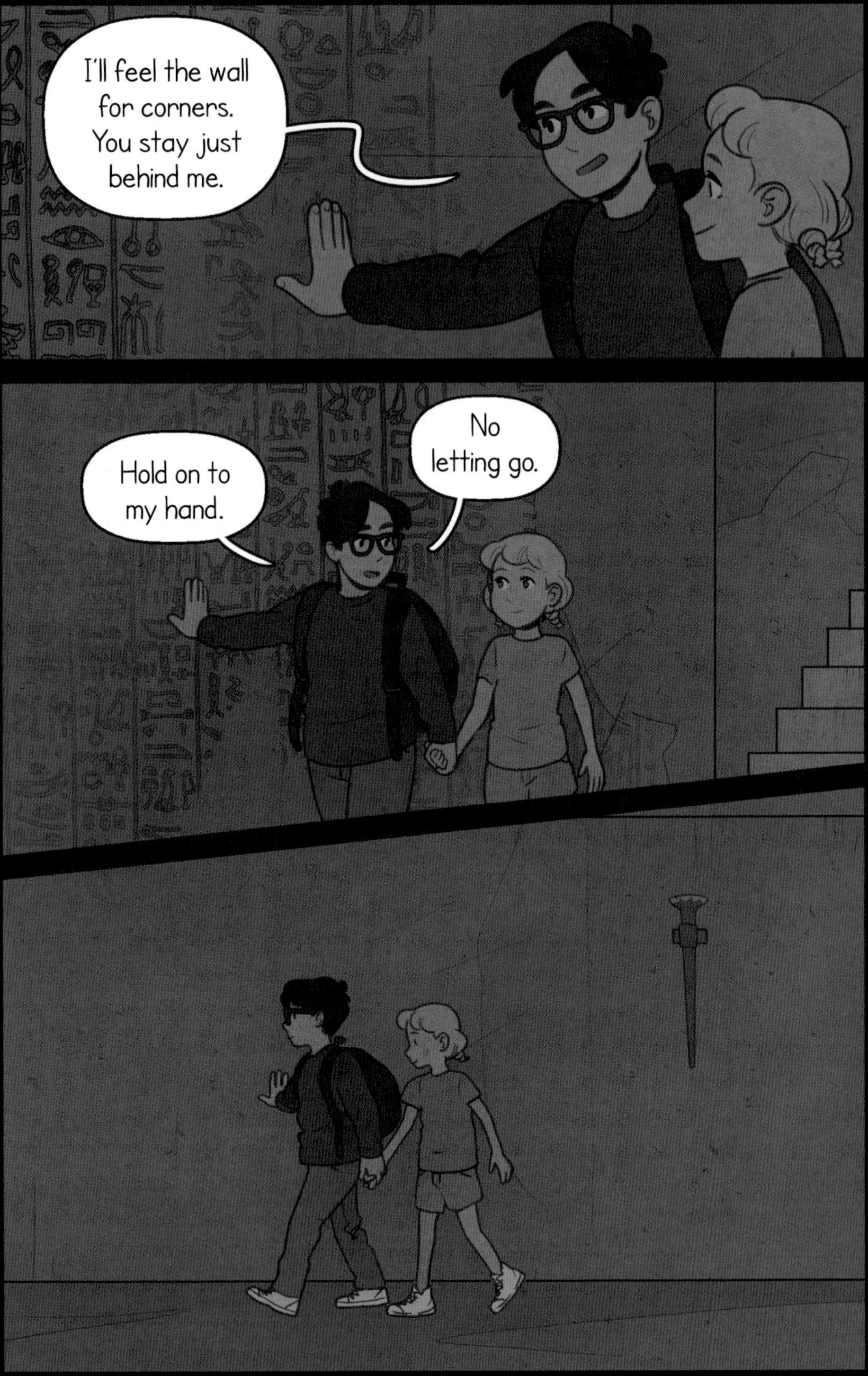
I'll feel the wall for corners. You stay just behind me.
Hold on to my hand.
No letting go.

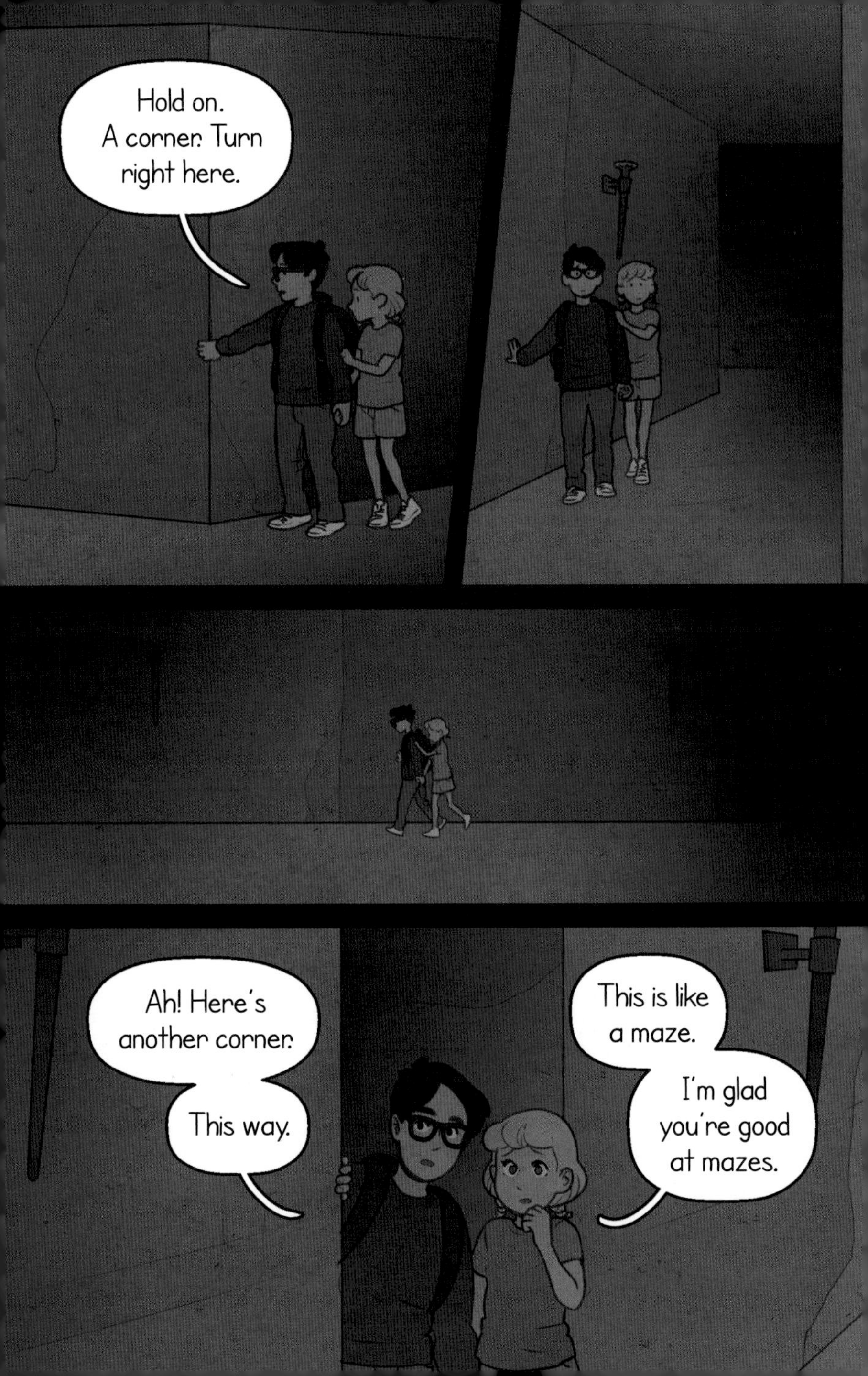
Hold on. A corner. Turn right here.
Ah! Here's another corner.
This way.
This is like a maze.
I'm glad you're good at mazes.

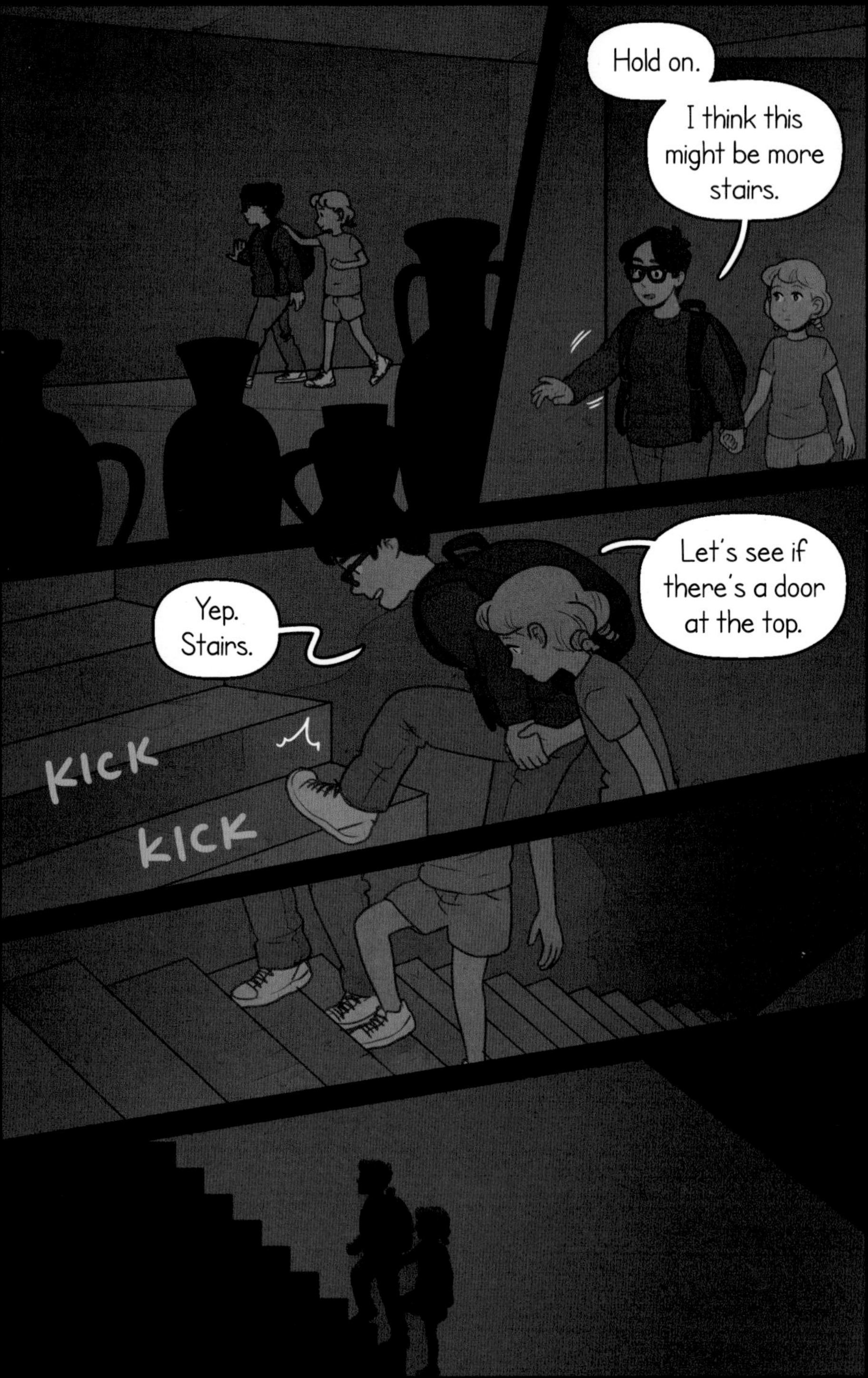
Hold on.
I think this might be more stairs.
Let's see if there's a door at the top.
Yep. Stairs.
KICK
KICK

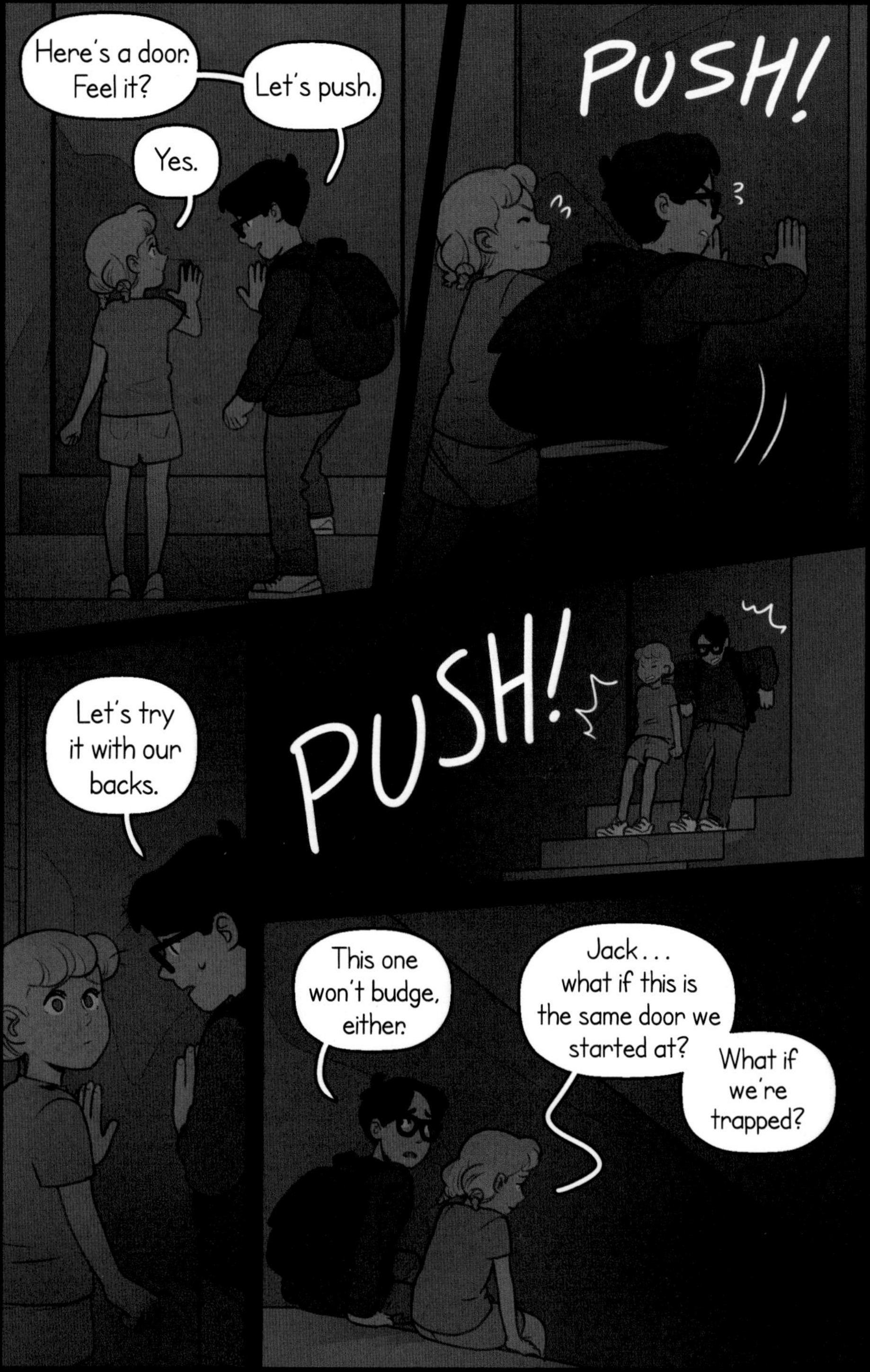
Here's a door. Feel it?
Let's push.
Yes.
PUSH!
Let's try it with our backs.
PUSH!
This one won't budge, either.
Jack... what if this is the same door we started at?
What if we're trapped?

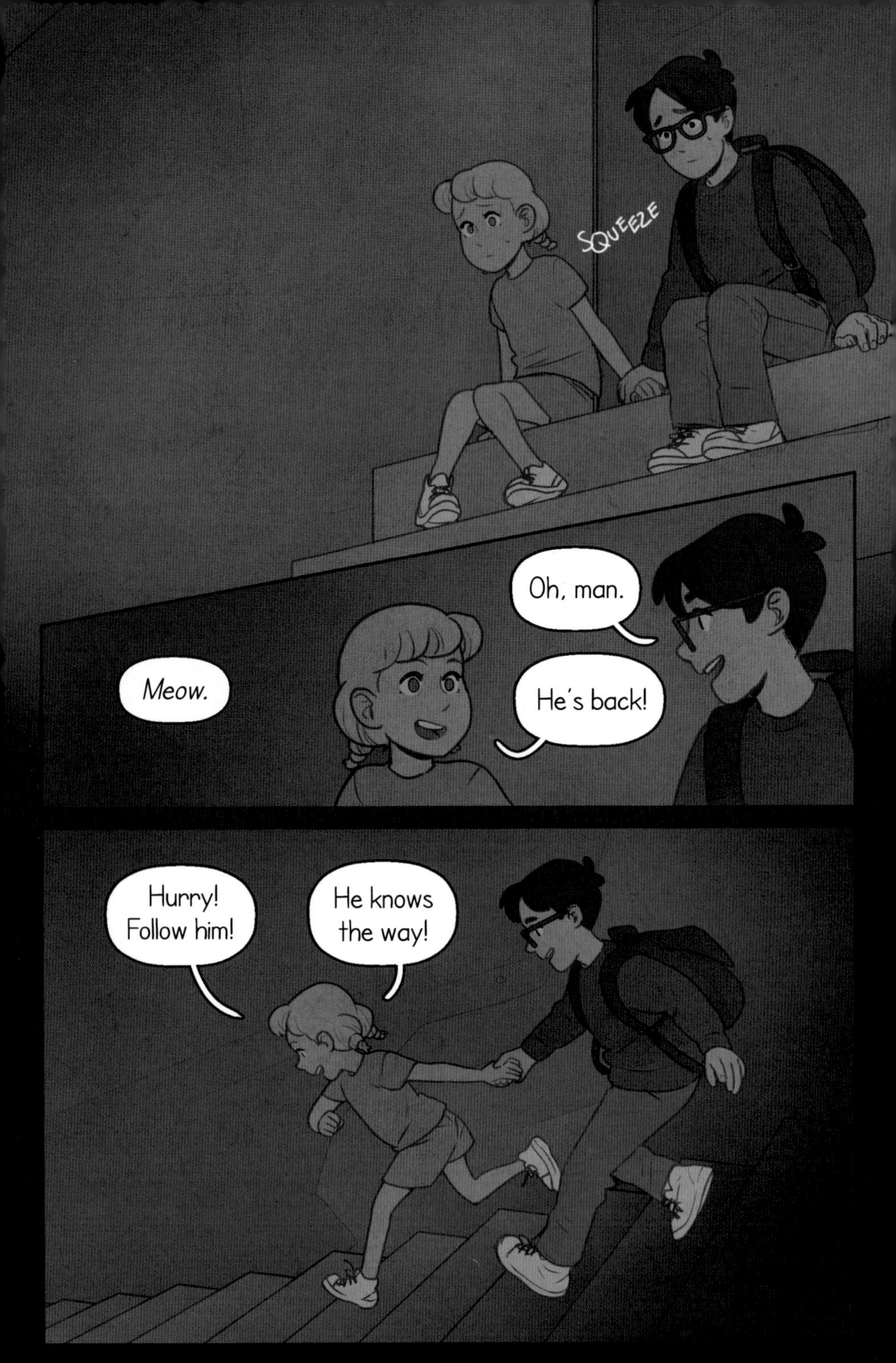
SQUEEZE
Oh, man.
Meow.
He's back!
Hurry! Follow him!
He knows the way!

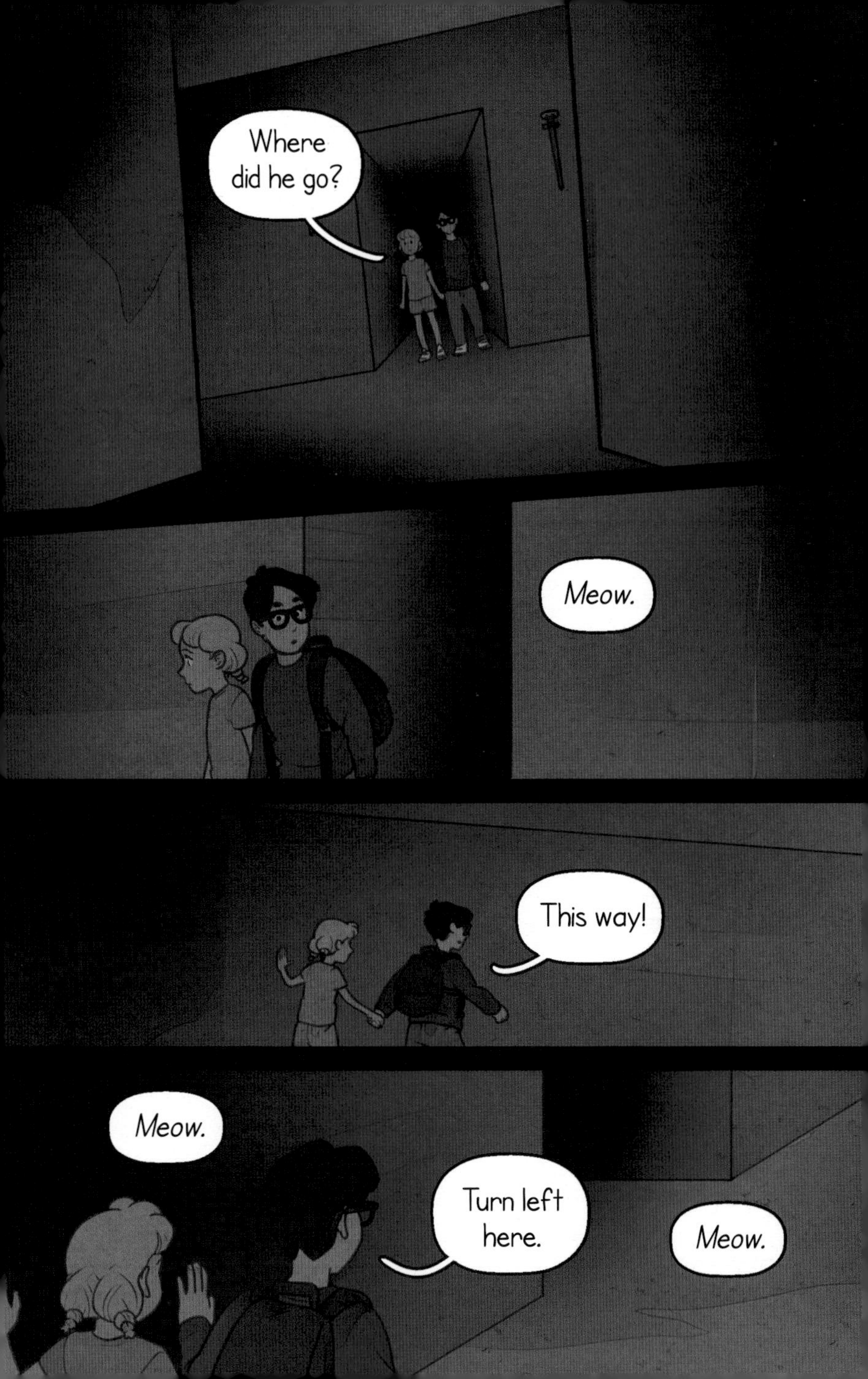
Where did he go?
Meow.
This way!
Meow.
Turn left here.
Meow.

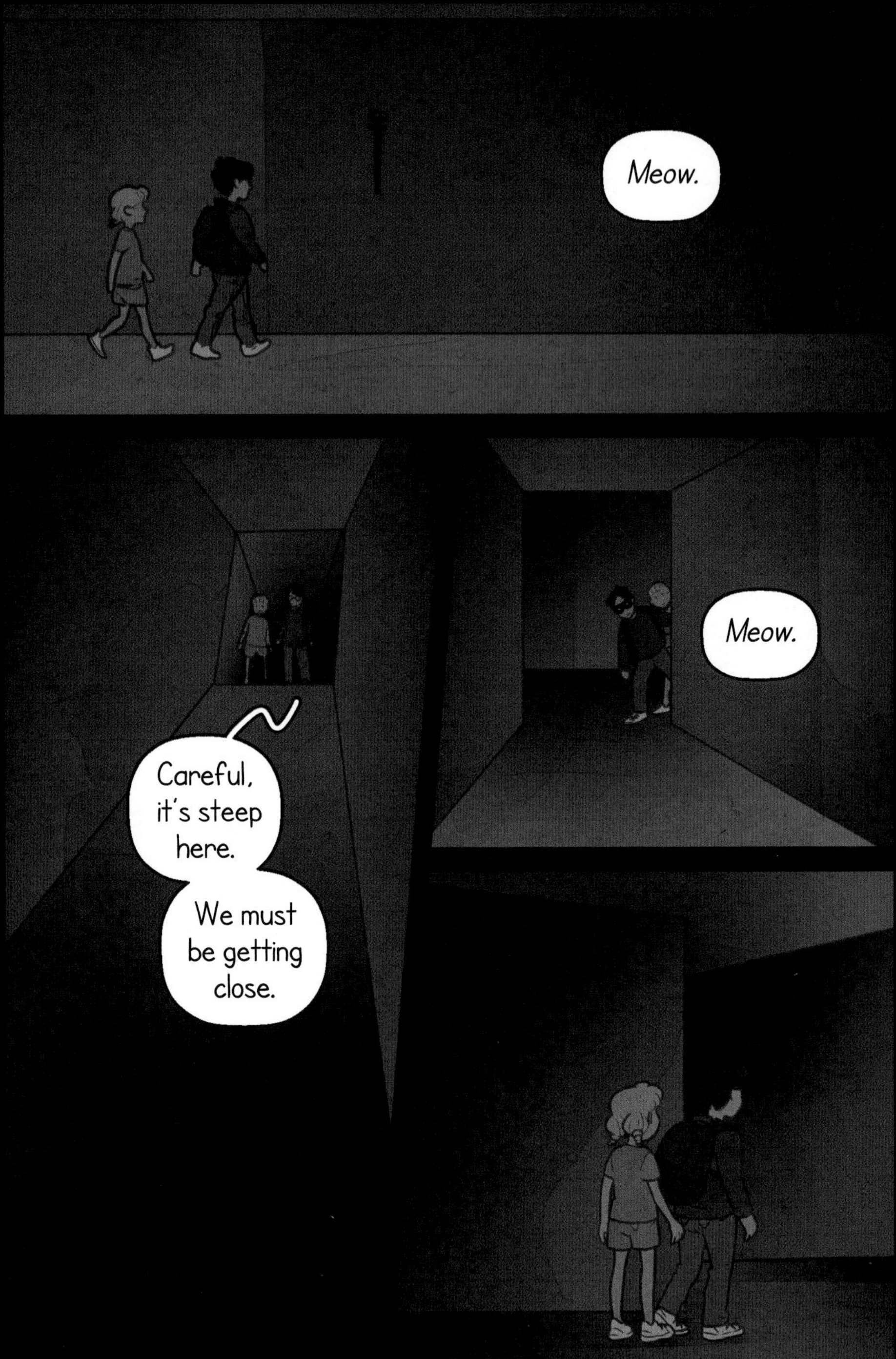
Meow.
Meow.
Careful, it's steep here.
We must be getting close.

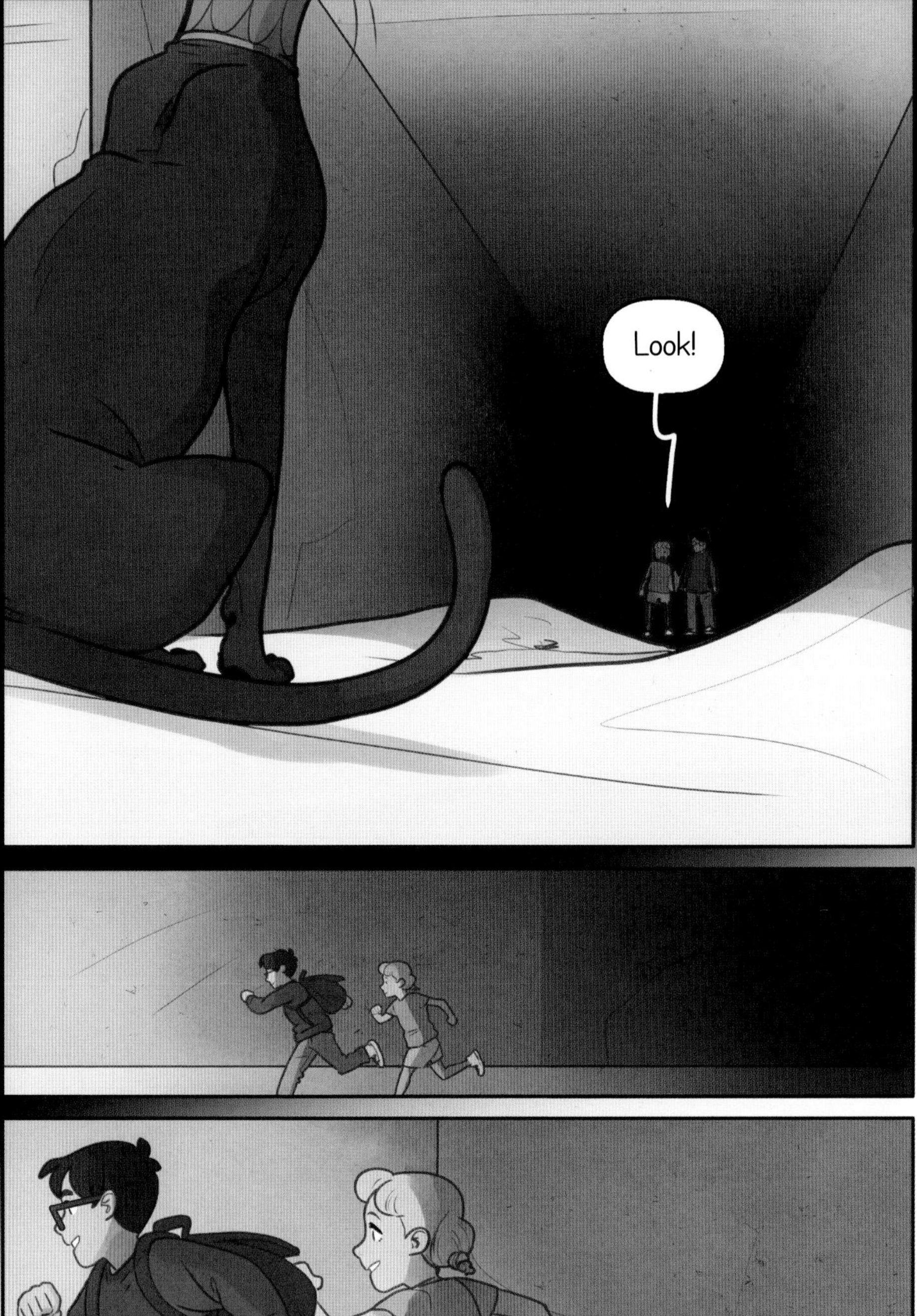
Look!

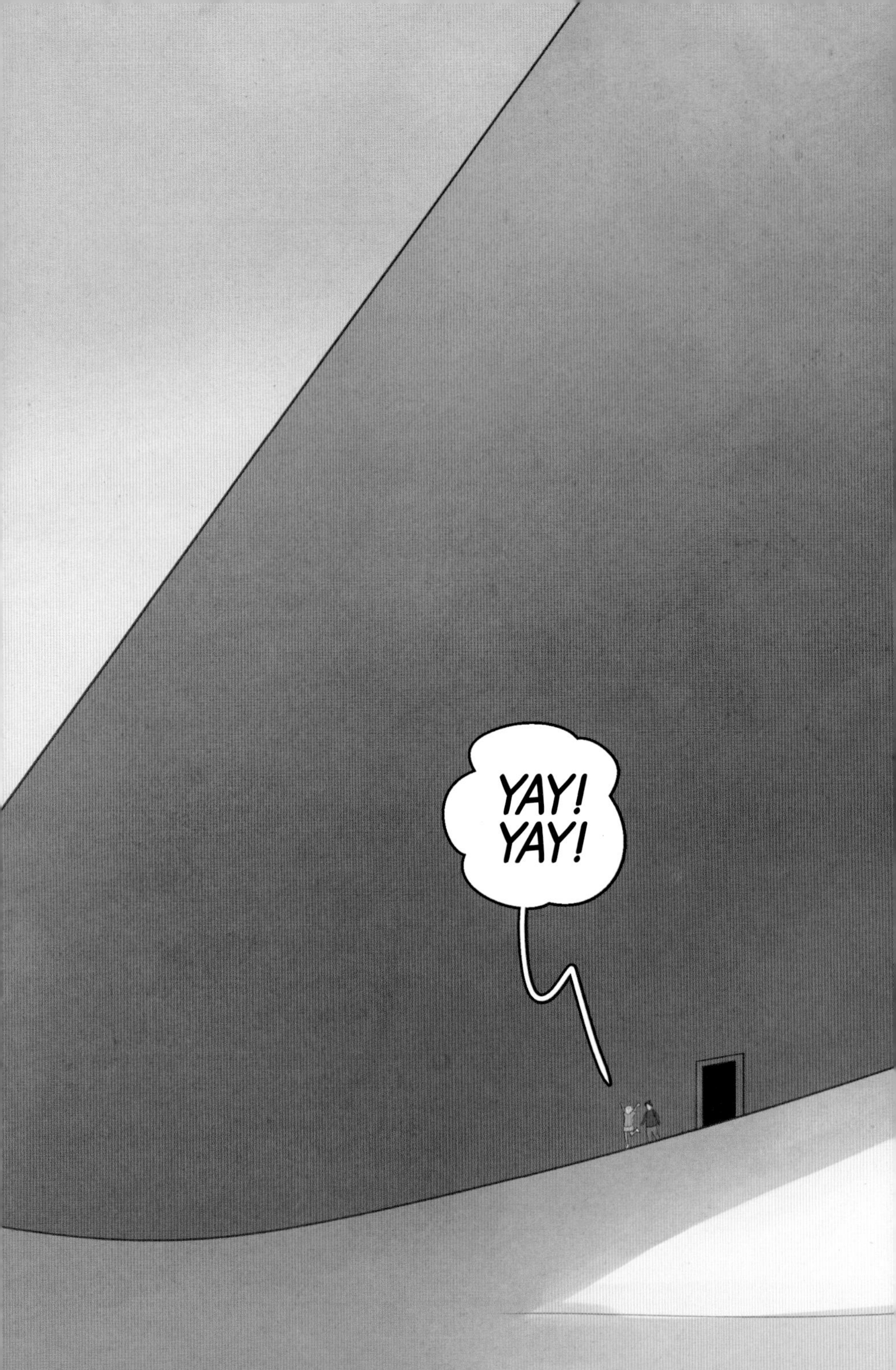
YAY! YAY!

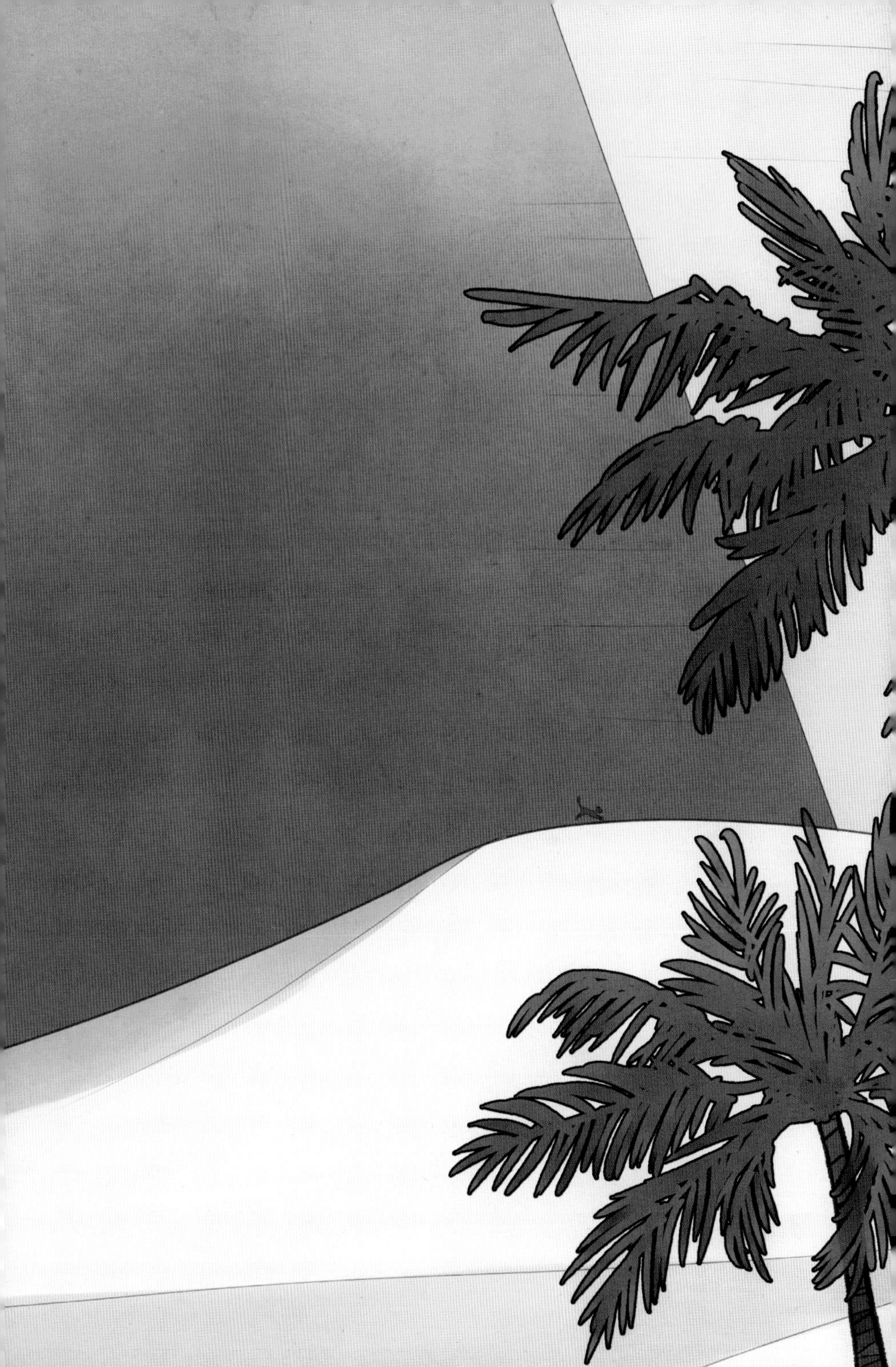

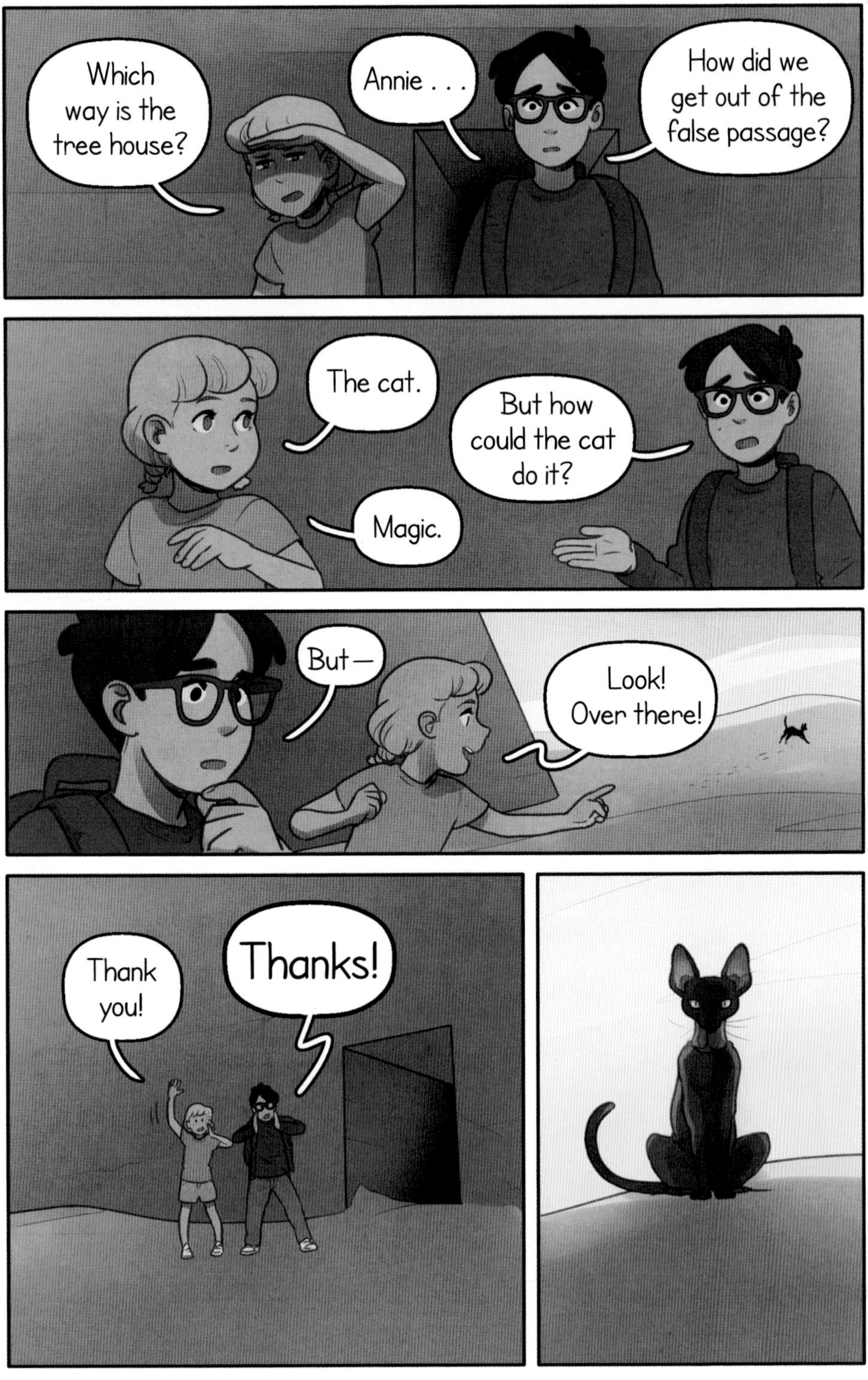
Which way is the tree house?
Annie . . .
How did we get out of the false passage?
The cat.
But how could the cat do it?
Magic.
But—
Look! Over there!
Thank you!
Thanks!

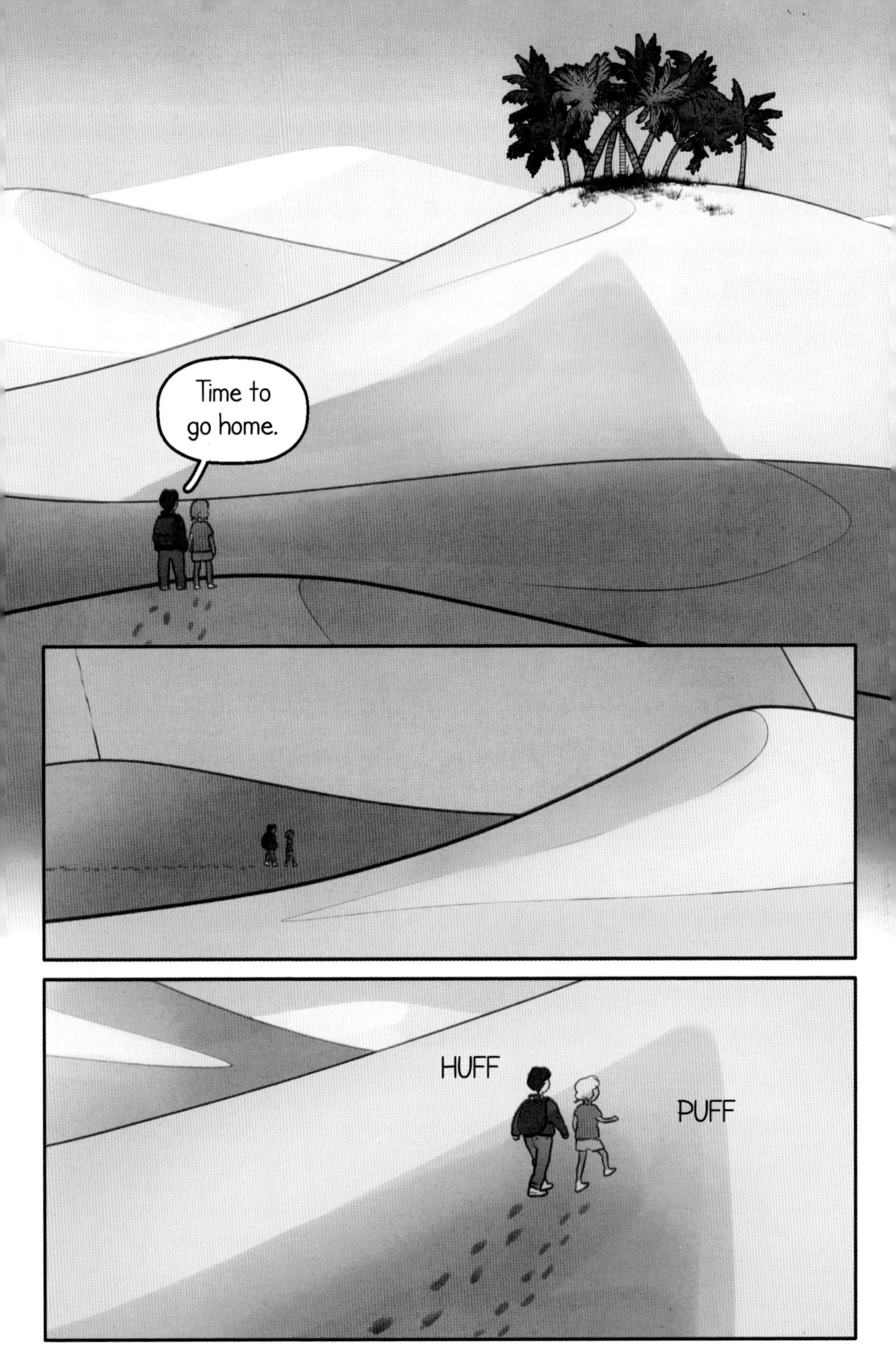
Time to go home.
HUFF
PUFF

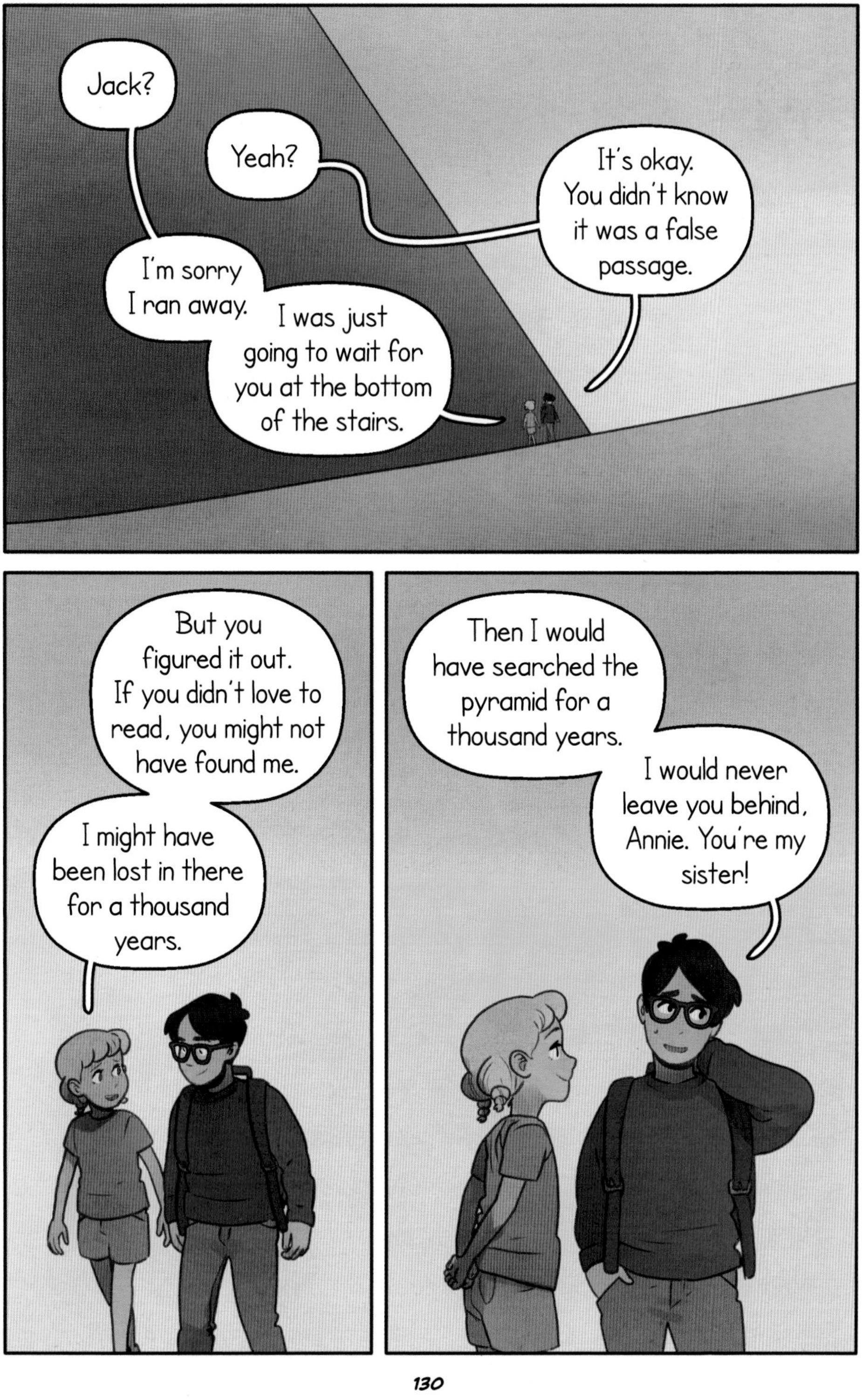
Jack?
Yeah?
I'm sorry I ran away.
I was just going to wait for you at the bottom of the stairs.
It's okay. You didn't know it was a false passage.
But you figured it out. If you didn't love to read, you might not have found me.
I might have been lost in there for a thousand years.
Then I would have searched the pyramid for a thousand years.
I would never leave you behind, Annie. You're my sister!

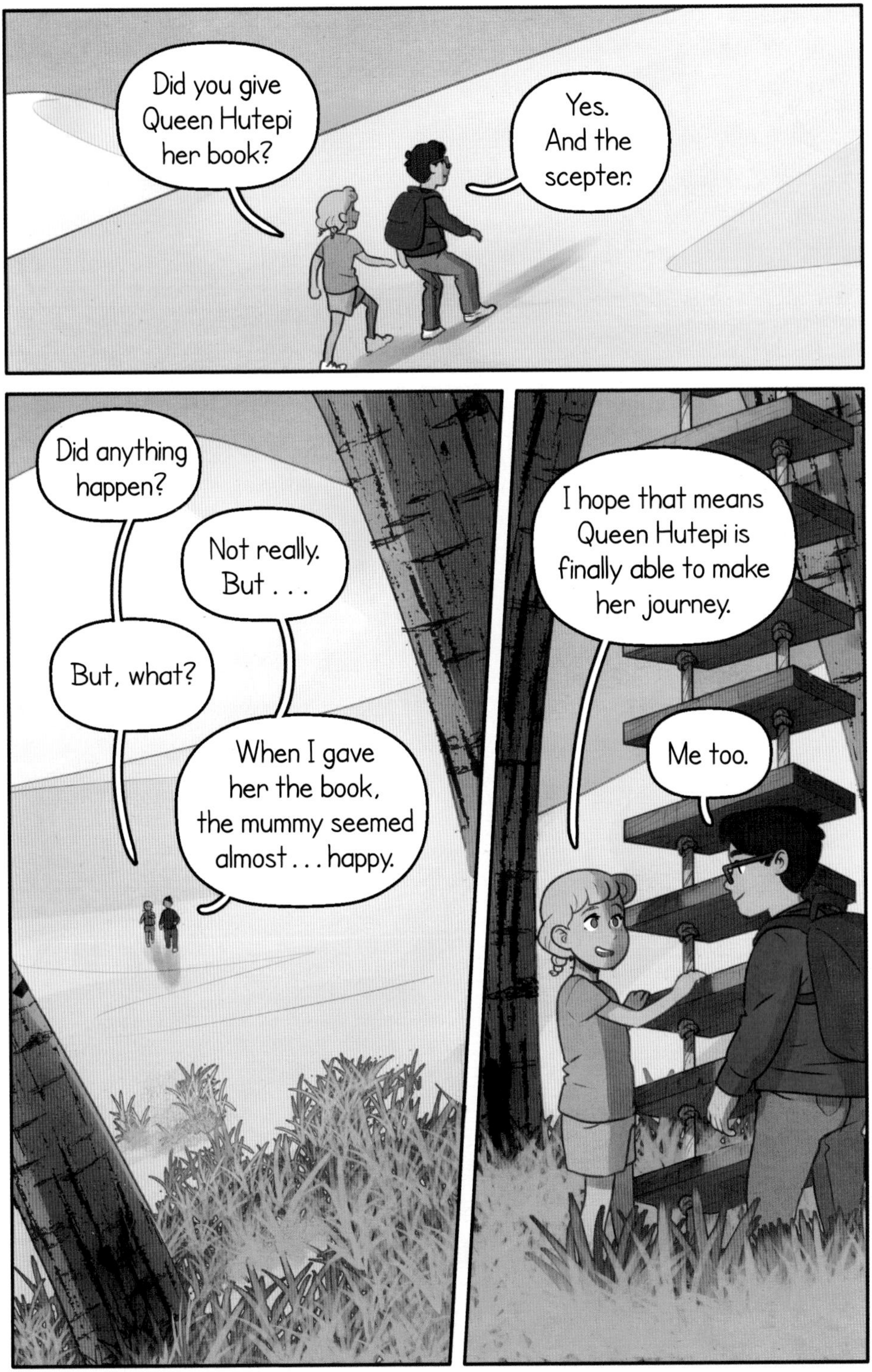
Did you give Queen Hutepi her book?
Yes. And the scepter.
Did anything happen?
Not really. But . . .
But, what?
When I gave her the book, the mummy seemed almost . . . happy.
I hope that means Queen Hutepi is finally able to make her journey.
Me too.

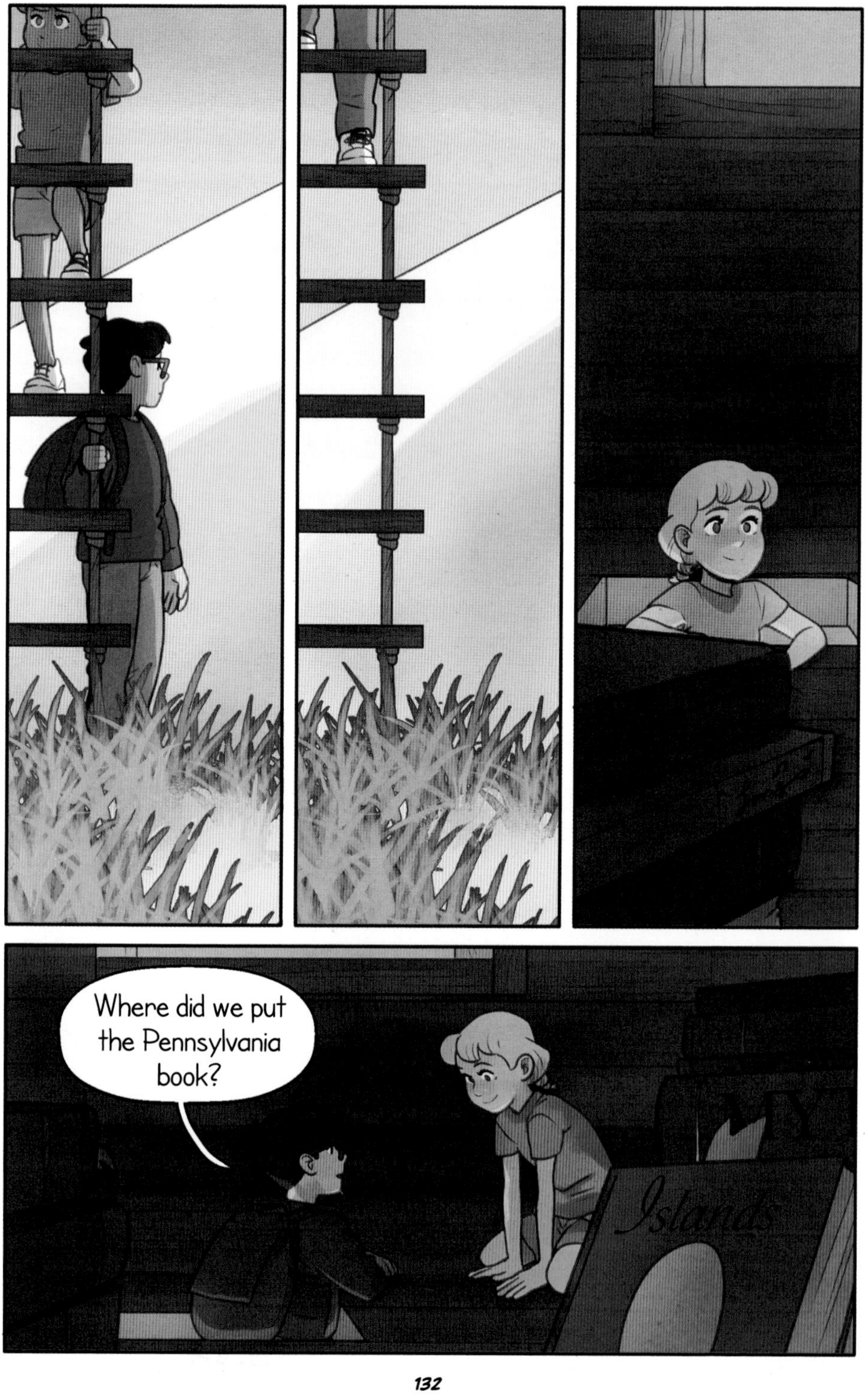
Where did we put the Pennsylvania book?
Islands

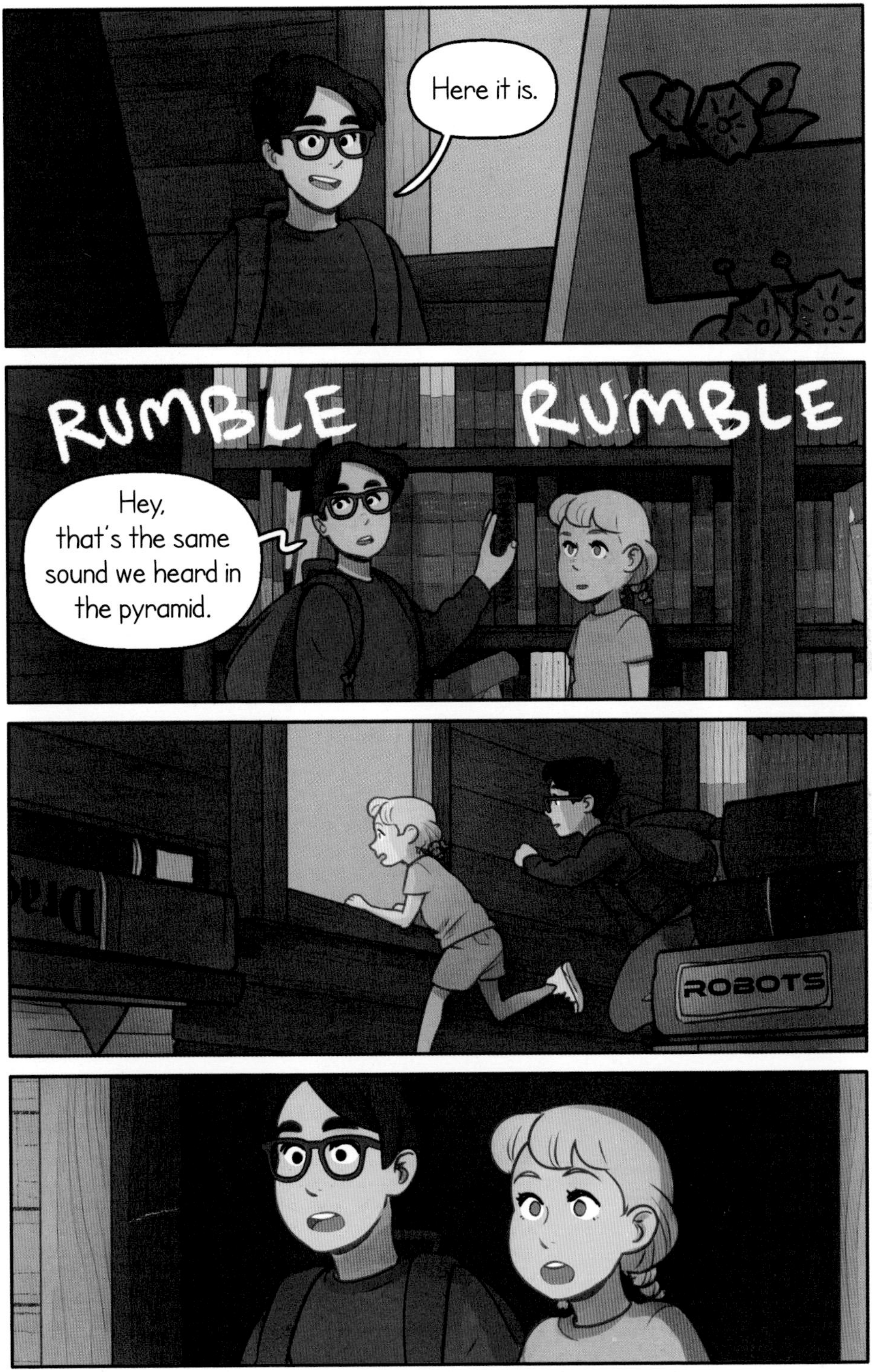
Here it is.
RUMBLE RUMBLE
Hey, that's the same sound we heard in the pyramid.
ROBOTS

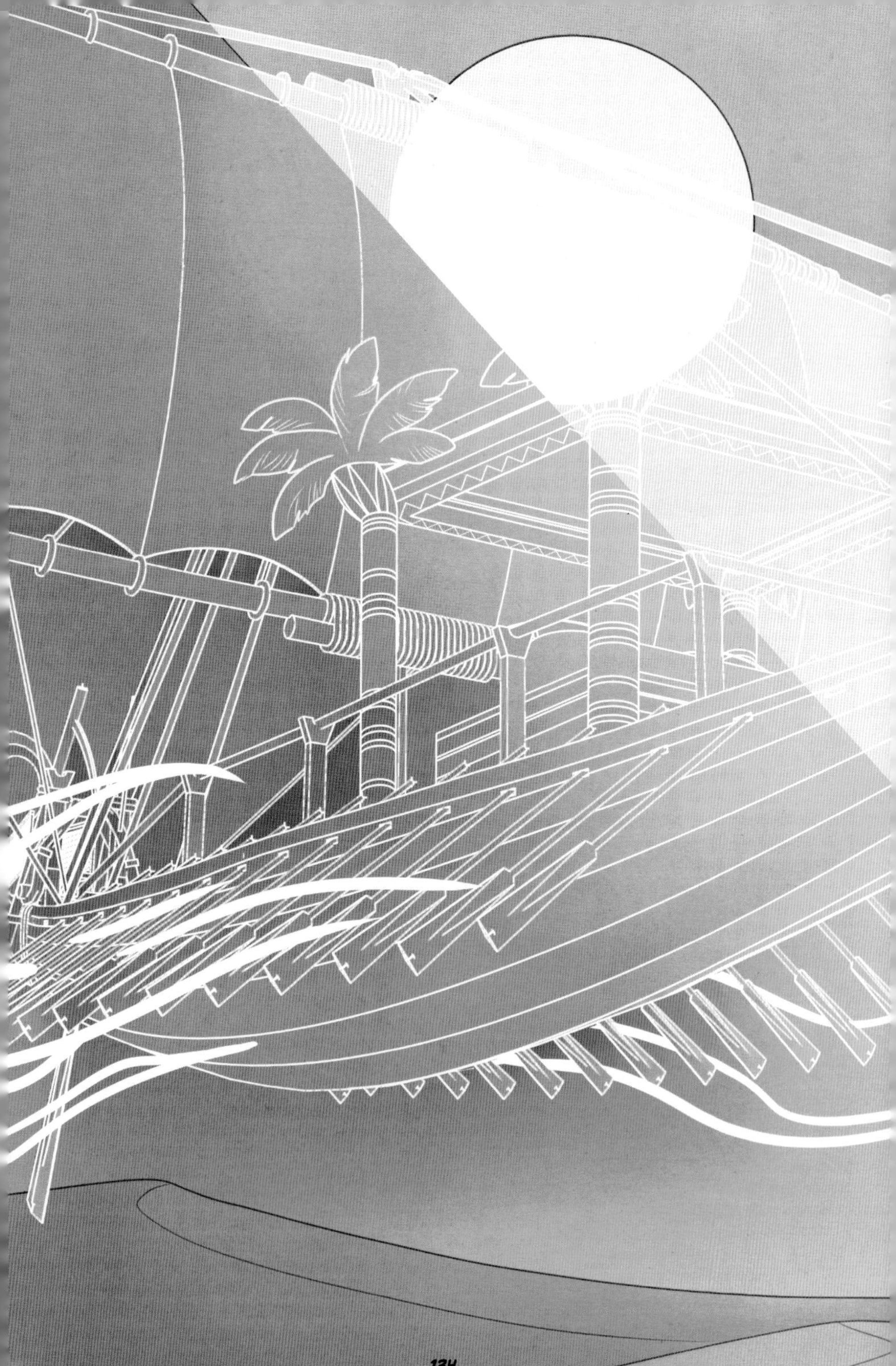

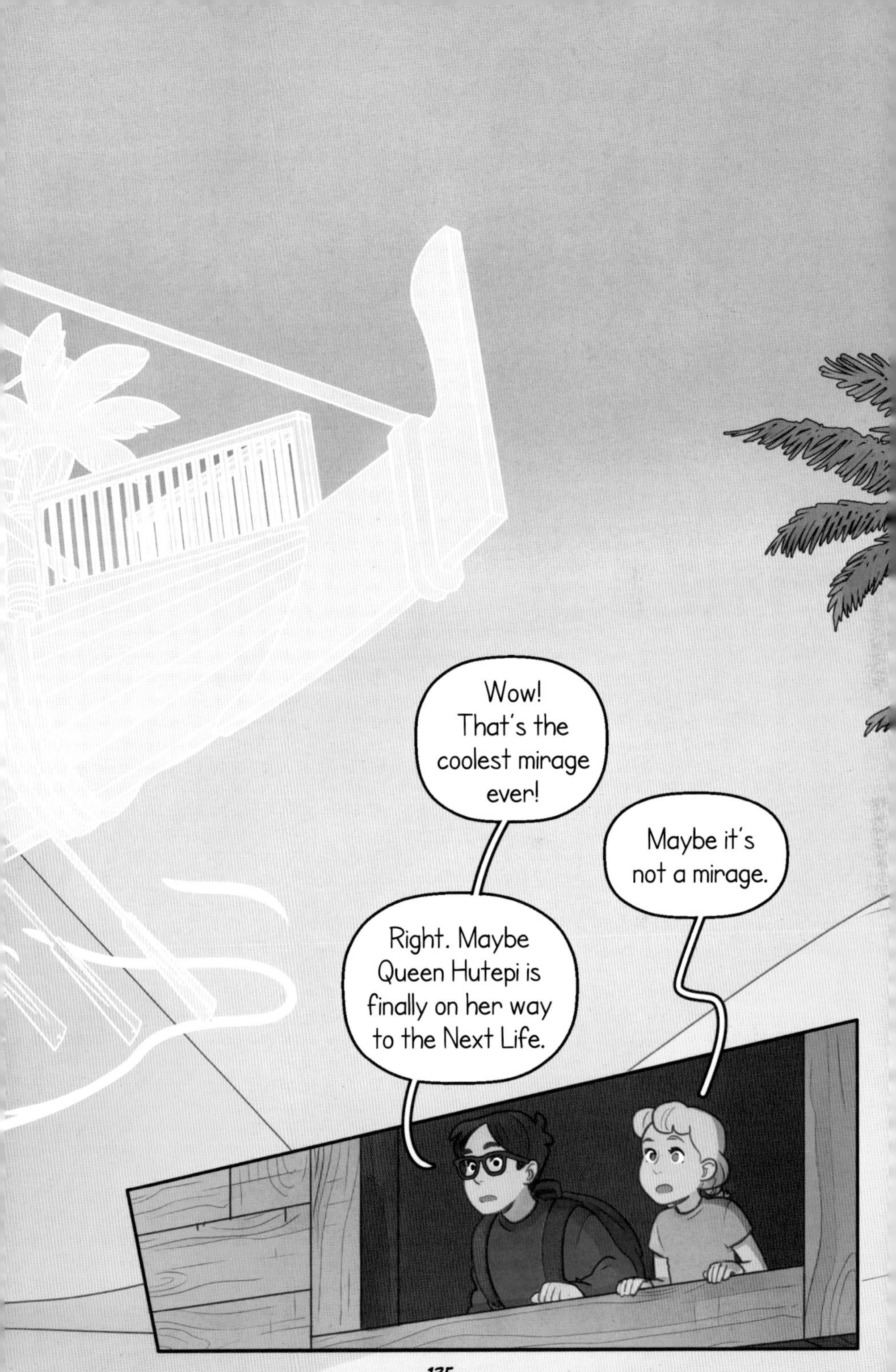
Wow! That's the coolest mirage ever!
Maybe it's not a mirage.
Right. Maybe Queen Hutepi is finally on her way to the Next Life.

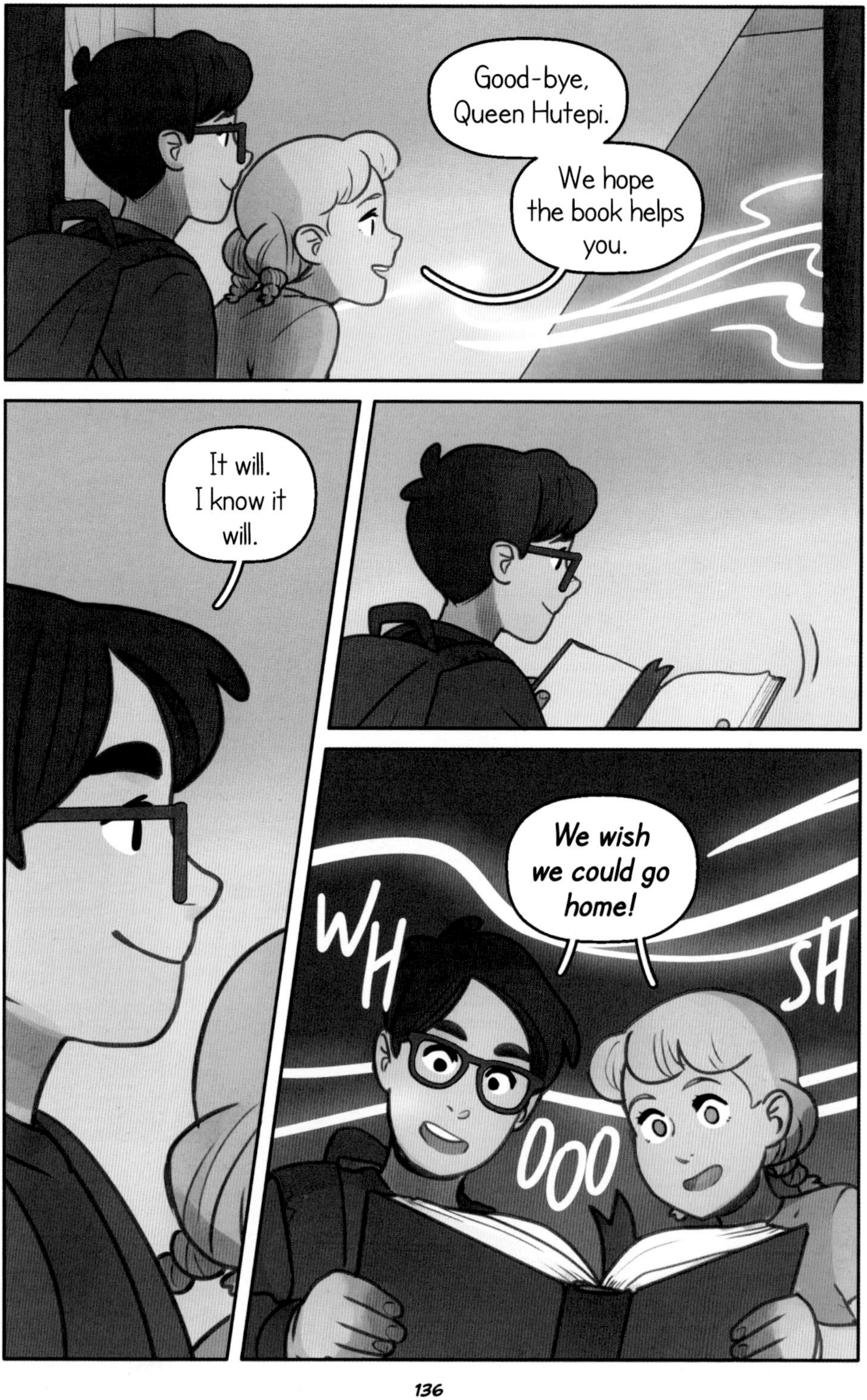
Good-bye, Queen Hutepi.
We hope the book helps you.
It will. I know it will.
We wish we could go home!
WHOOOOSH

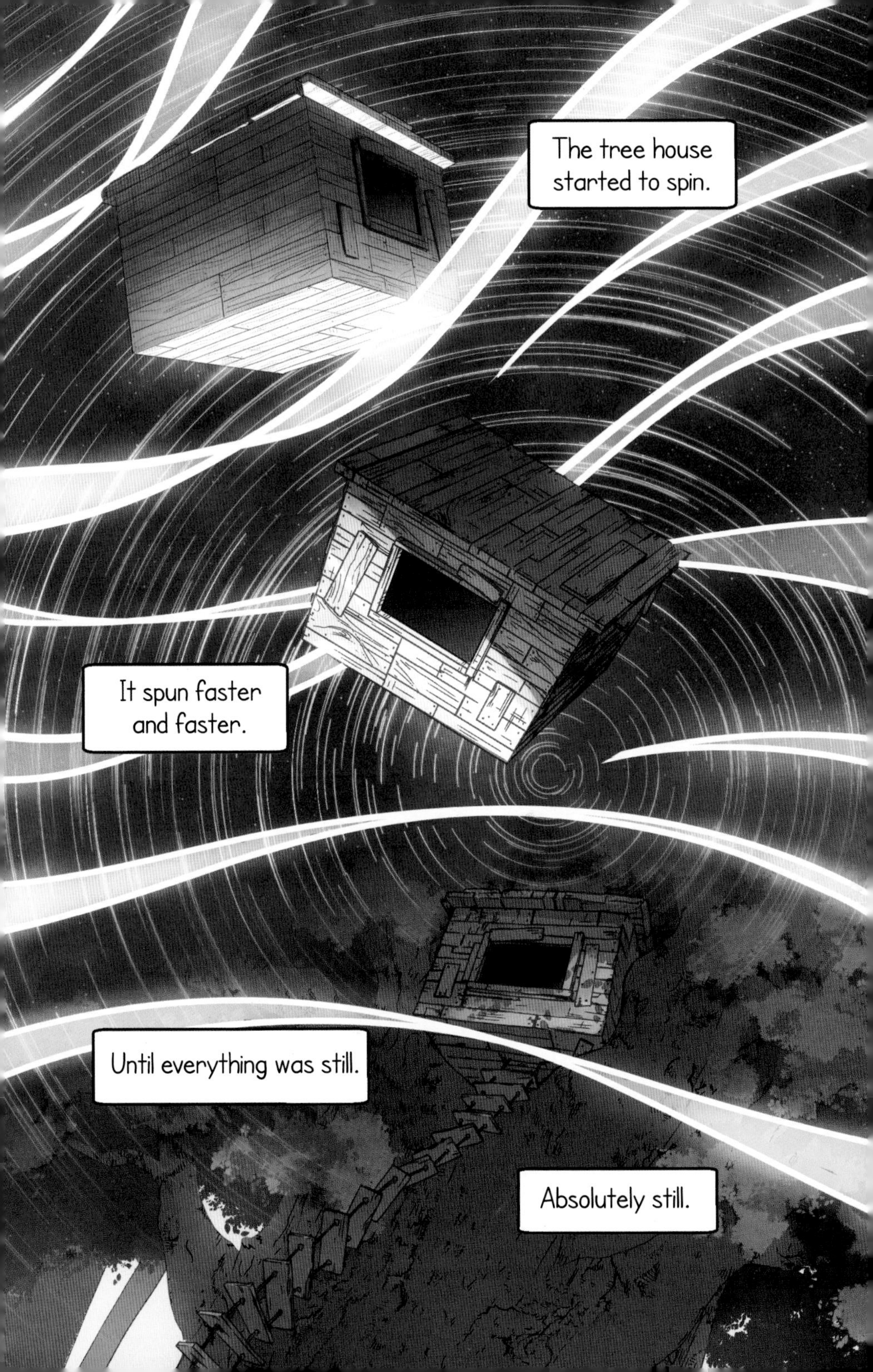
The tree house started to spin.
It spun faster and faster.
Until everything was still.
Absolutely still.

CHAPTER TEN

Another Clue

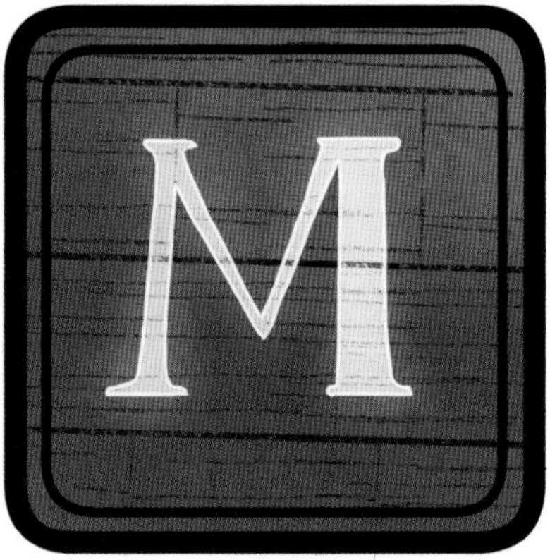
M

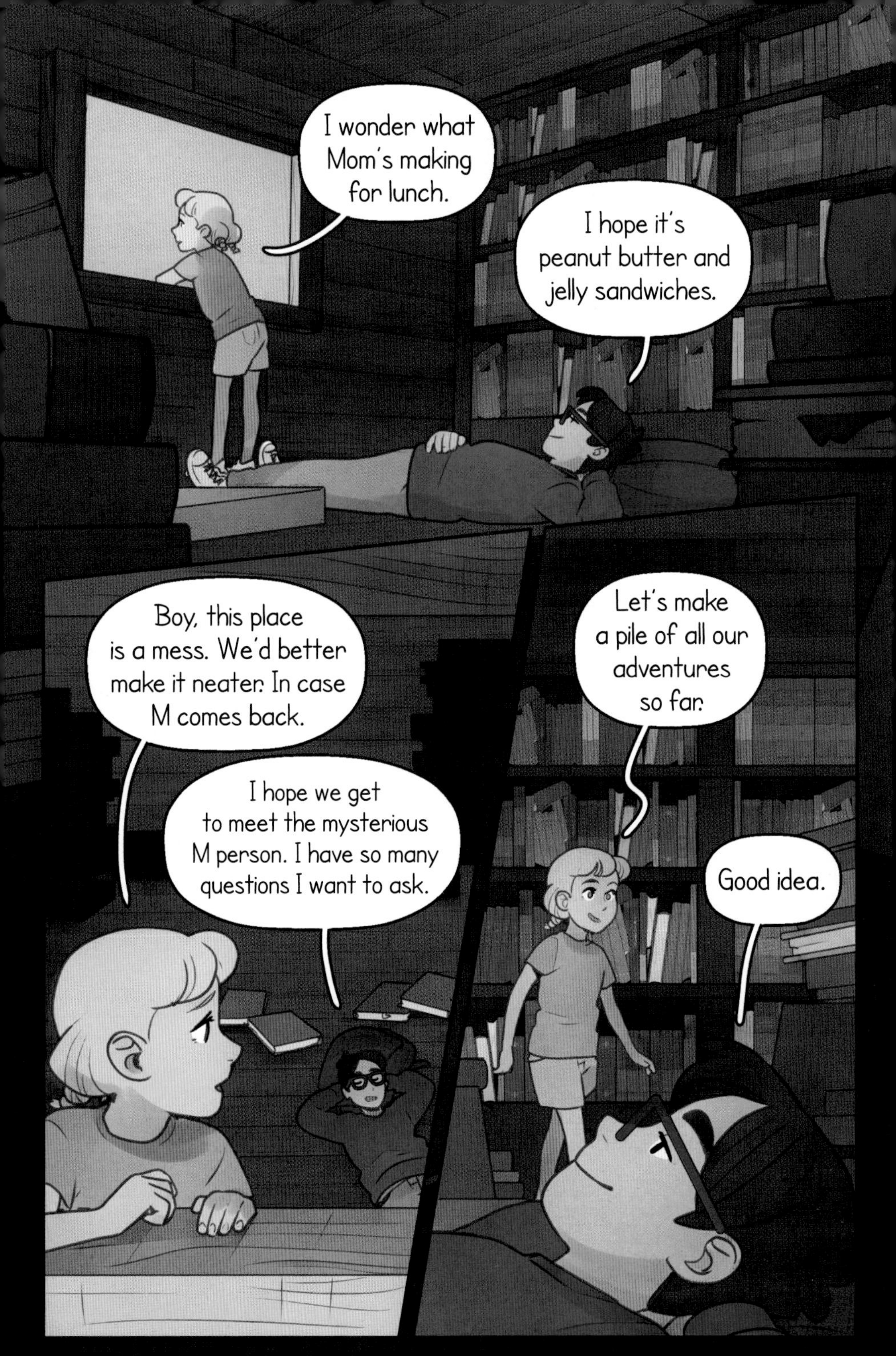
I wonder what Mom's making for lunch.
I hope it's peanut butter and jelly sandwiches.
Boy, this place is a mess. We'd better make it neater. In case M comes back.
I hope we get to meet the mysterious M person. I have so many questions I want to ask.
Let's make a pile of all our adventures so far.
Good idea.

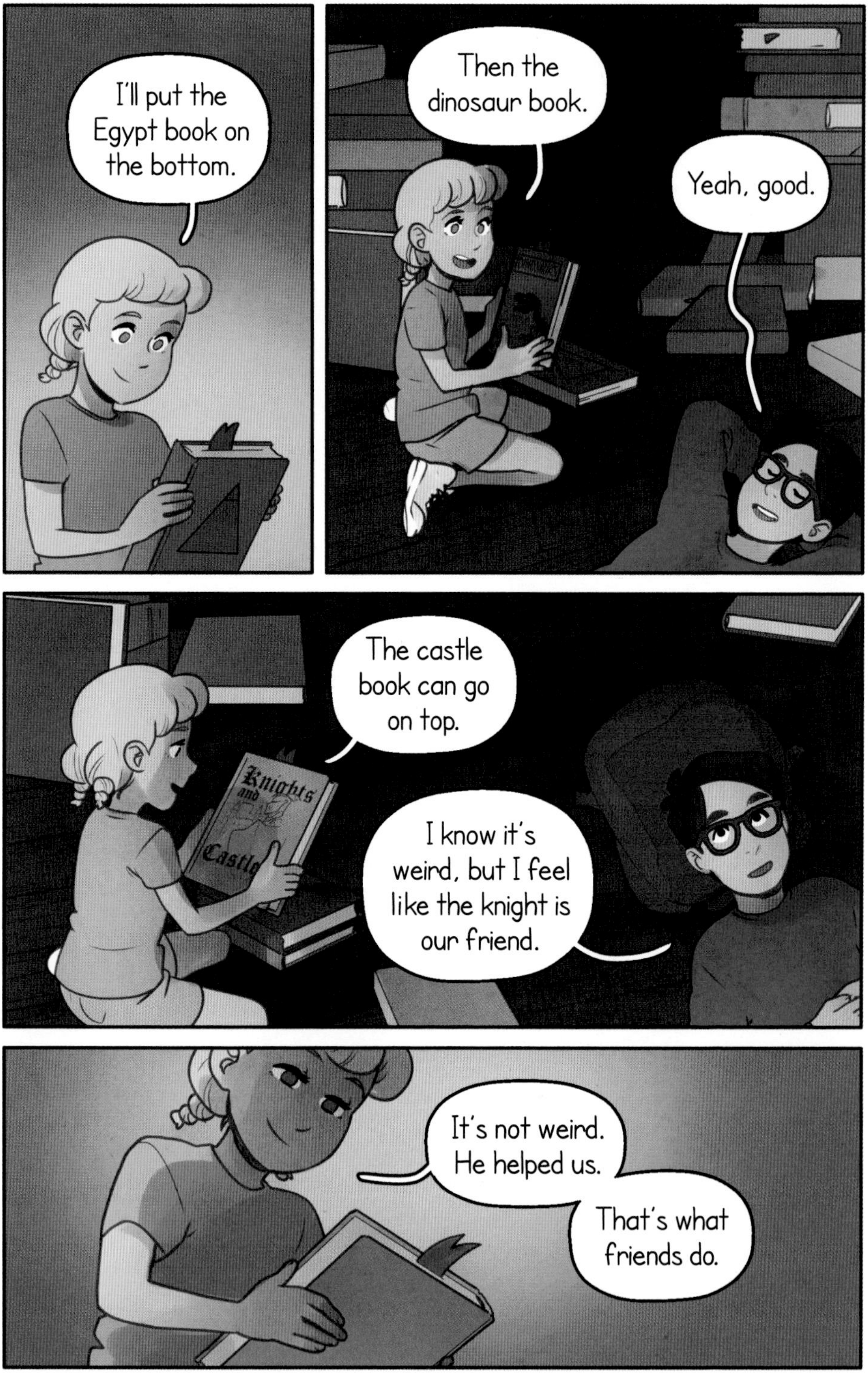
I'll put the Egypt book on the bottom.
Then the dinosaur book.
Yeah, good.
The castle book can go on top.
Knights and Castles
I know it's weird, but I feel like the knight is our friend.
It's not weird. He helped us.
That's what friends do.

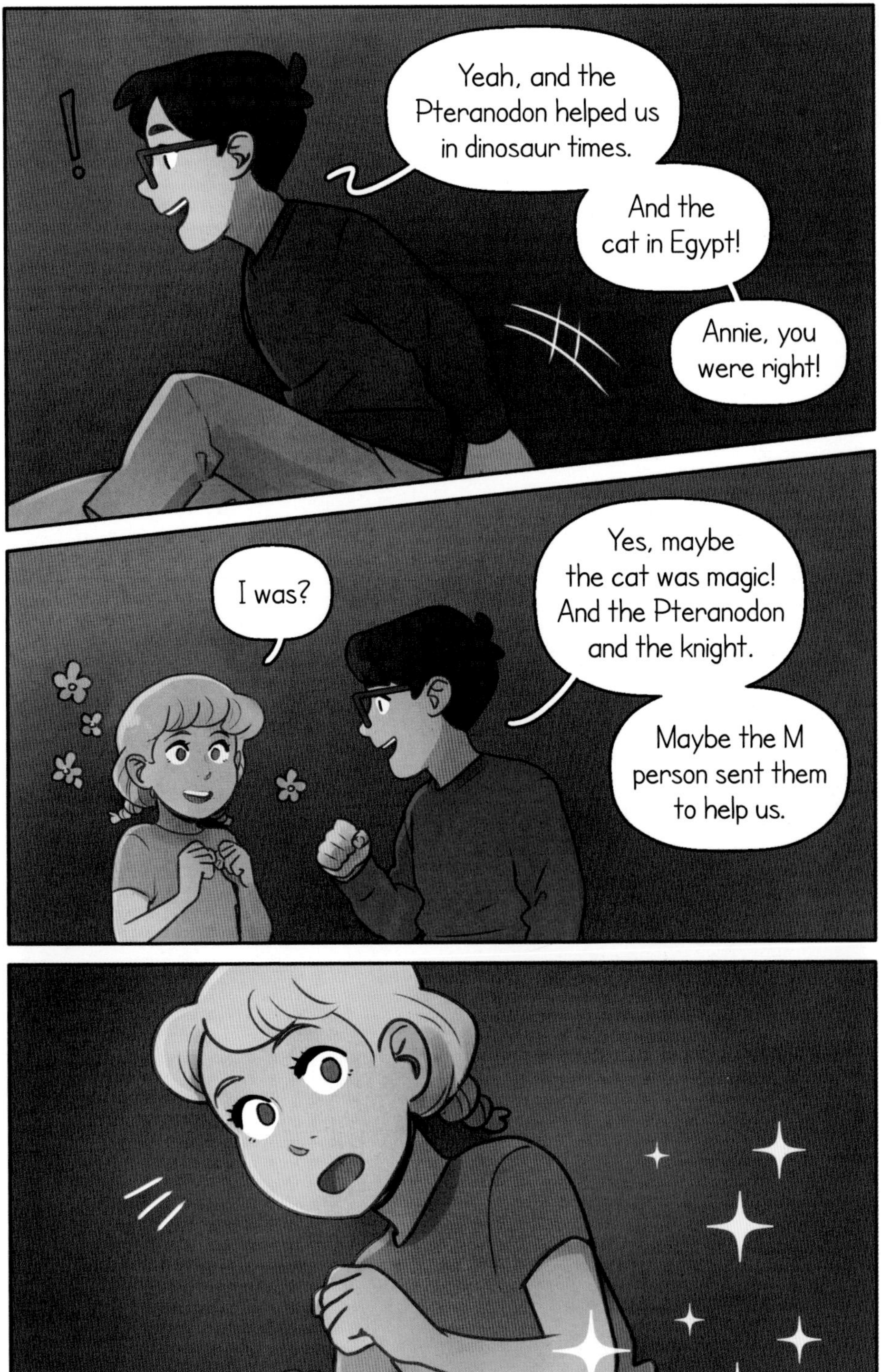

!
Yeah, and the Pteranodon helped us in dinosaur times.
And the cat in Egypt!
Annie, you were right!
I was?
Yes, maybe the cat was magic! And the Pteranodon and the knight.
Maybe the M person sent them to help us.

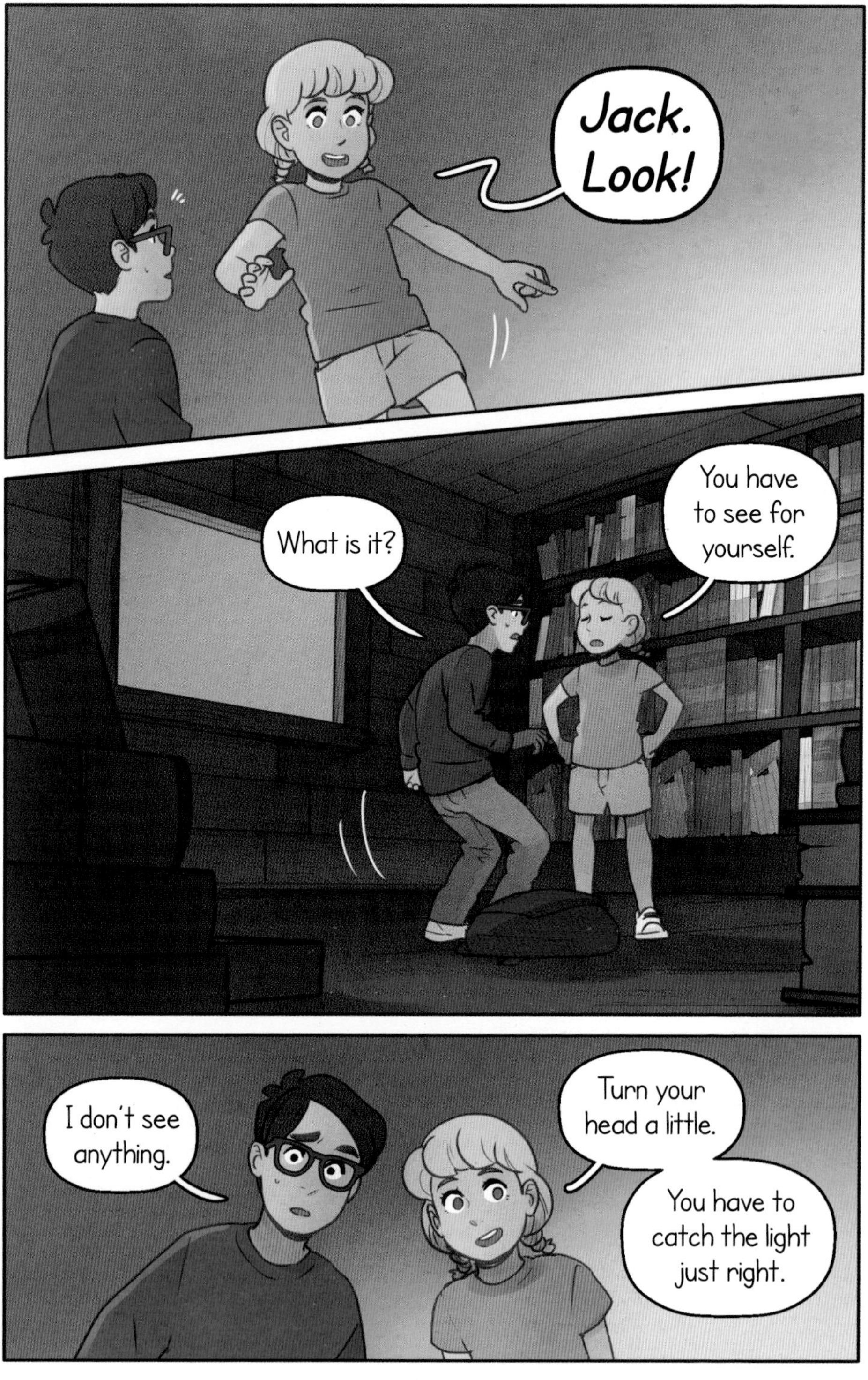
Jack. Look!
What is it?
You have to see for yourself.
I don't see anything.
Turn your head a little.
You have to catch the light just right.

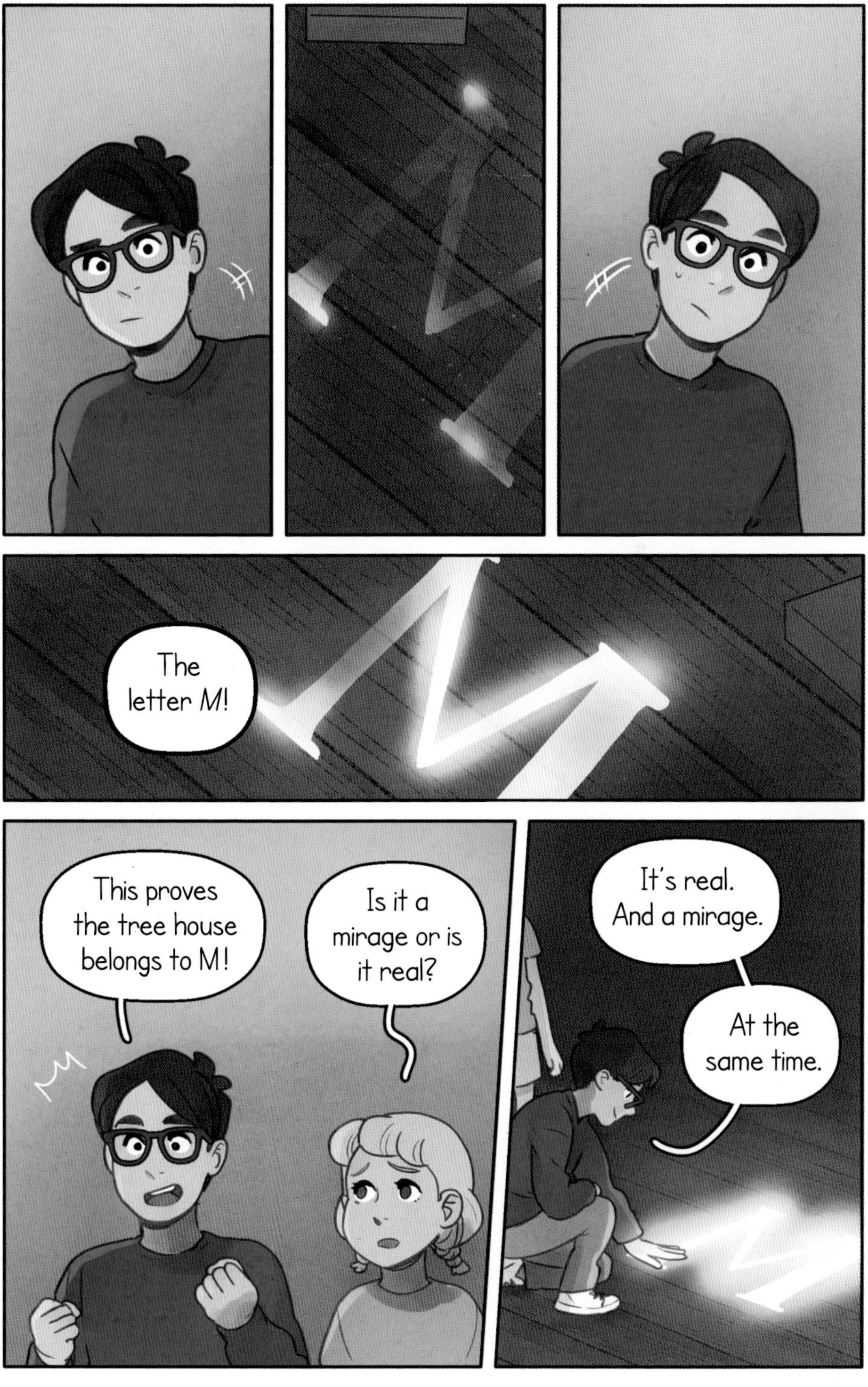

The letter M!
This proves the tree house belongs to M!
Is it a mirage or is it real?
It's real. And a mirage.
At the same time.

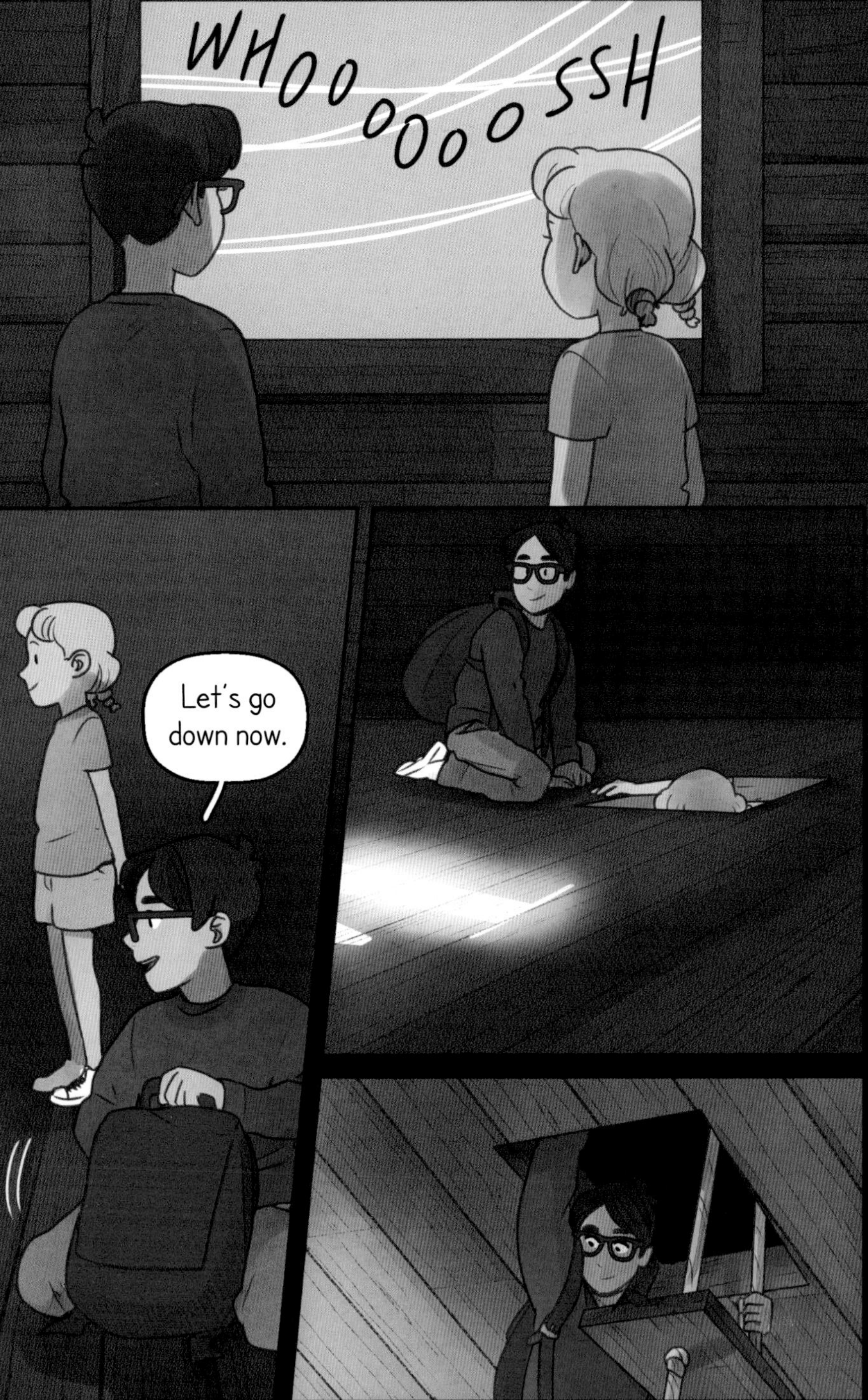
WHOOOOOOOSSH
Let's go down now.

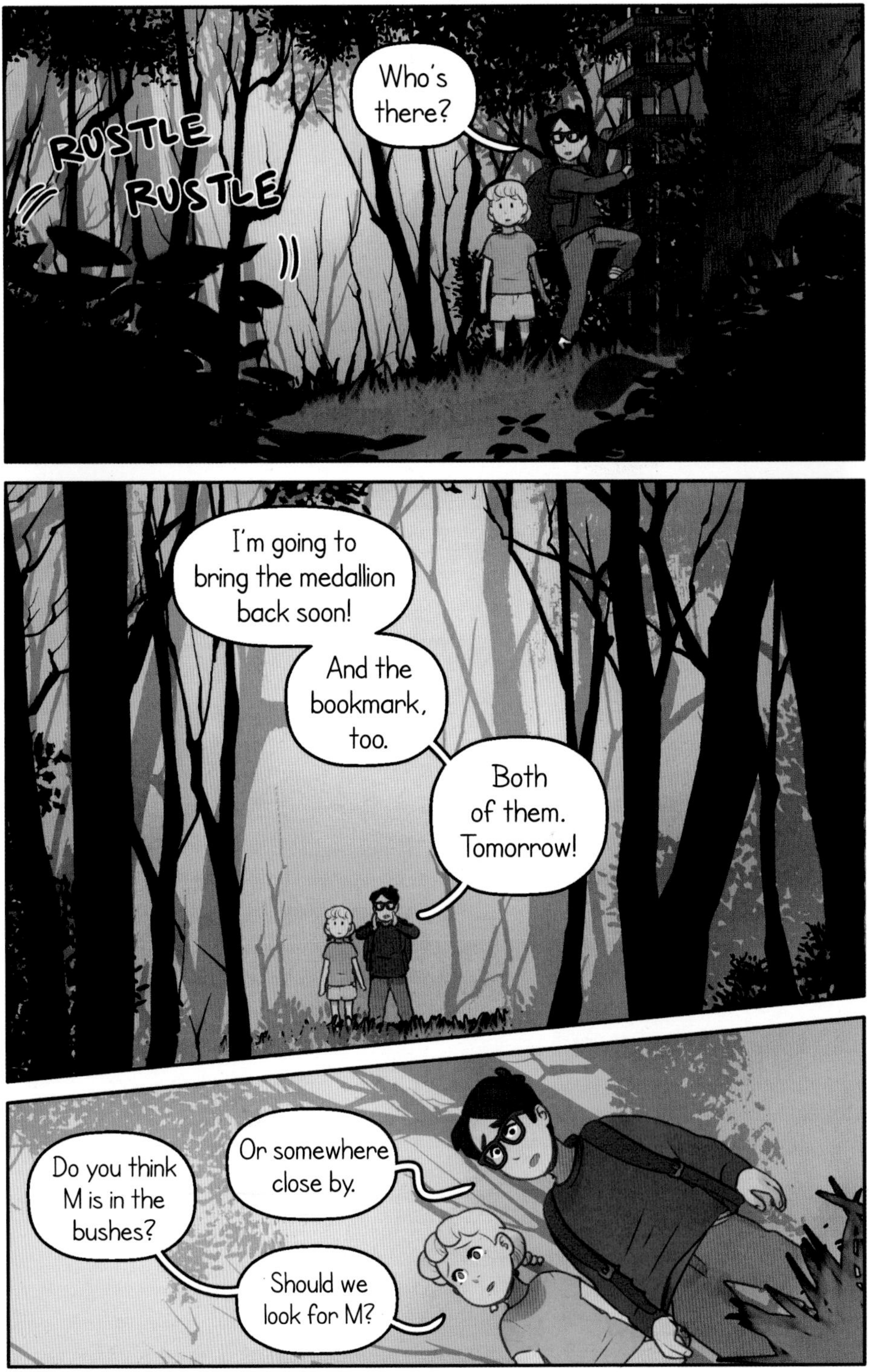
Who's there?
RUSTLE
RUSTLE
I'm going to bring the medallion back soon!
And the bookmark, too.
Both of them. Tomorrow!
Do you think M is in the bushes?
Or somewhere close by.
Should we look for M?

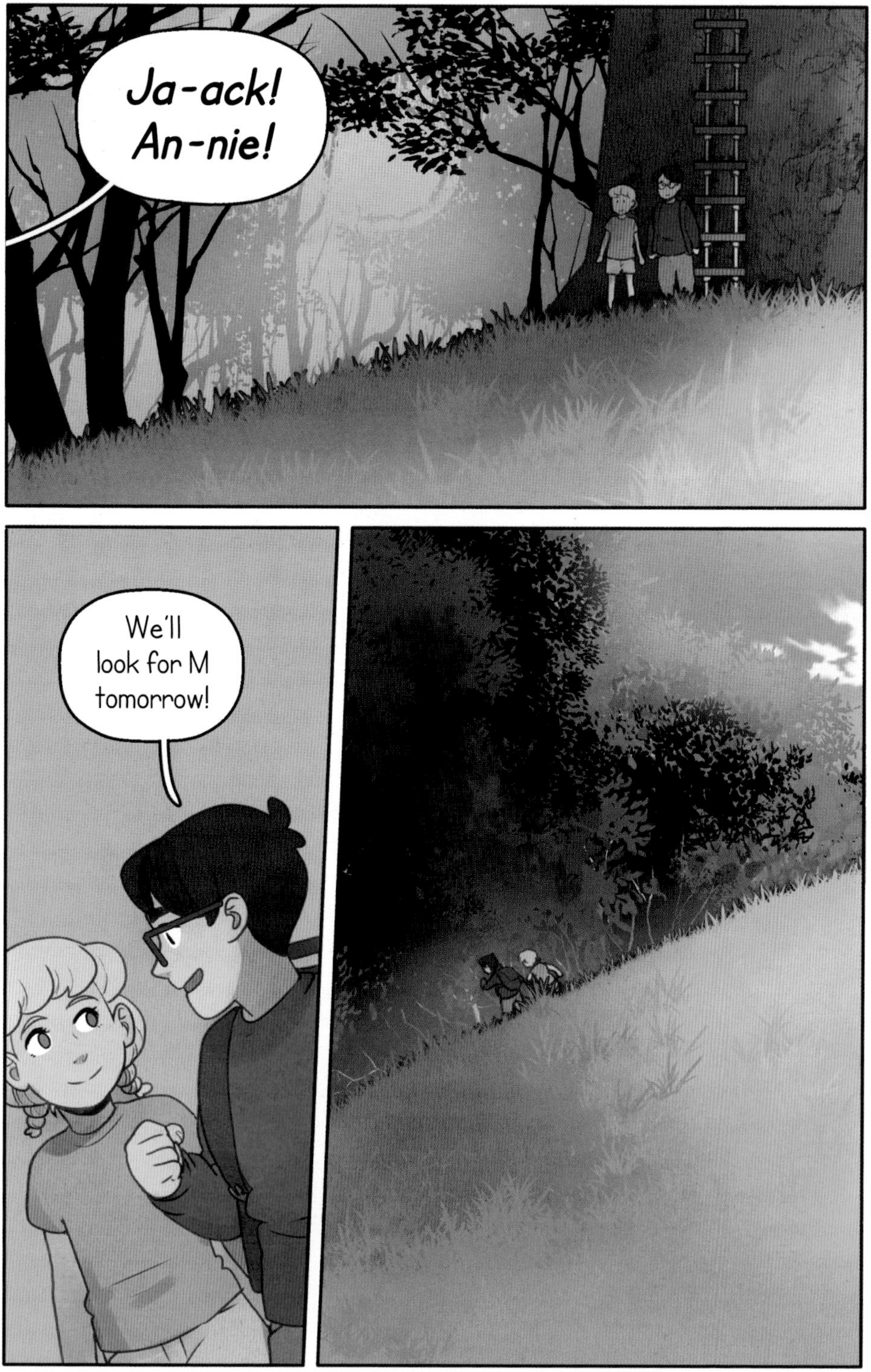
Ja-ack!
An-nie!
We'll look for M tomorrow!

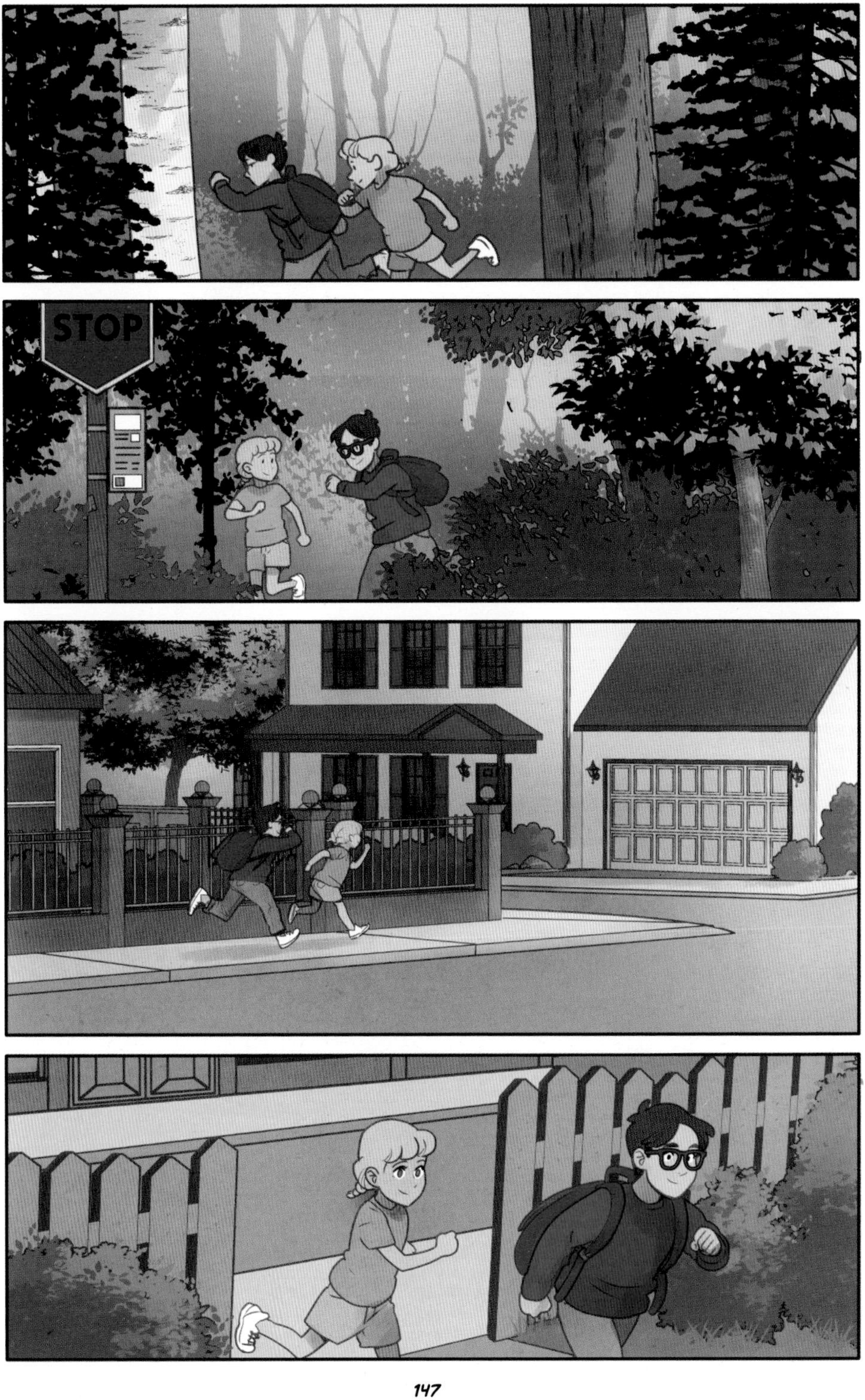
STOP

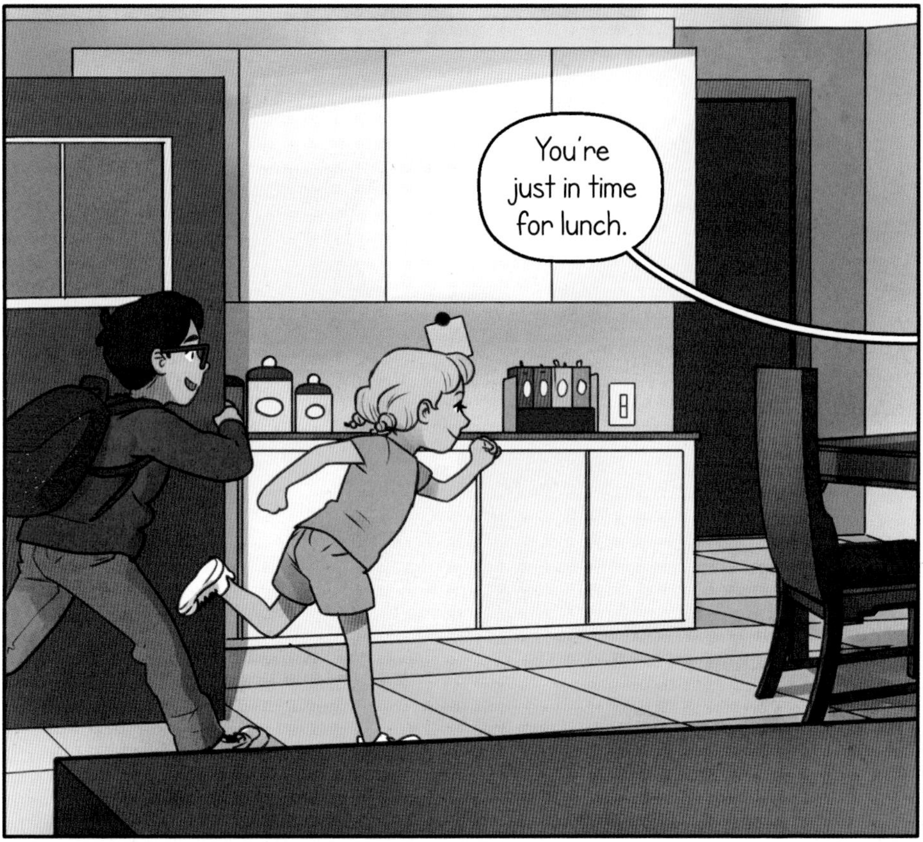
You're just in time for lunch.

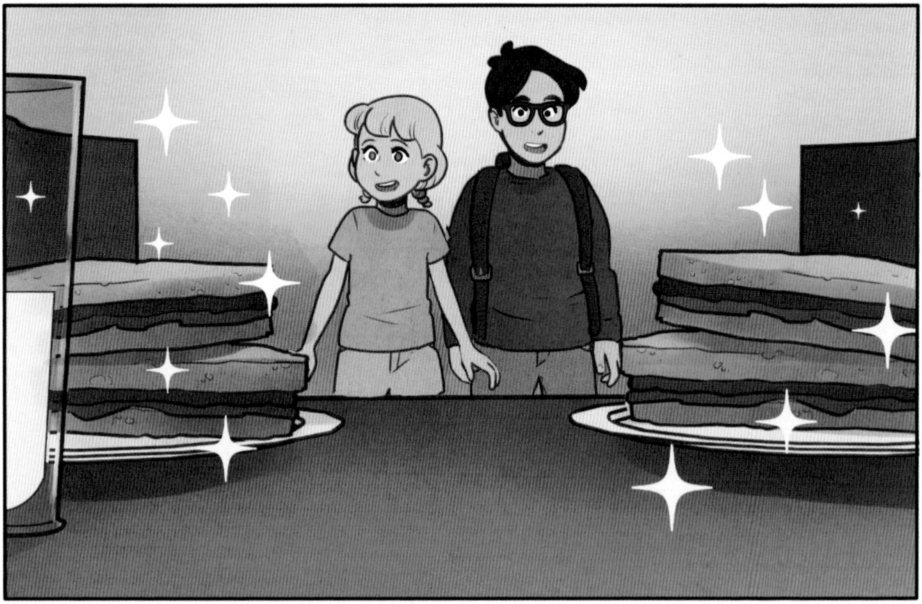

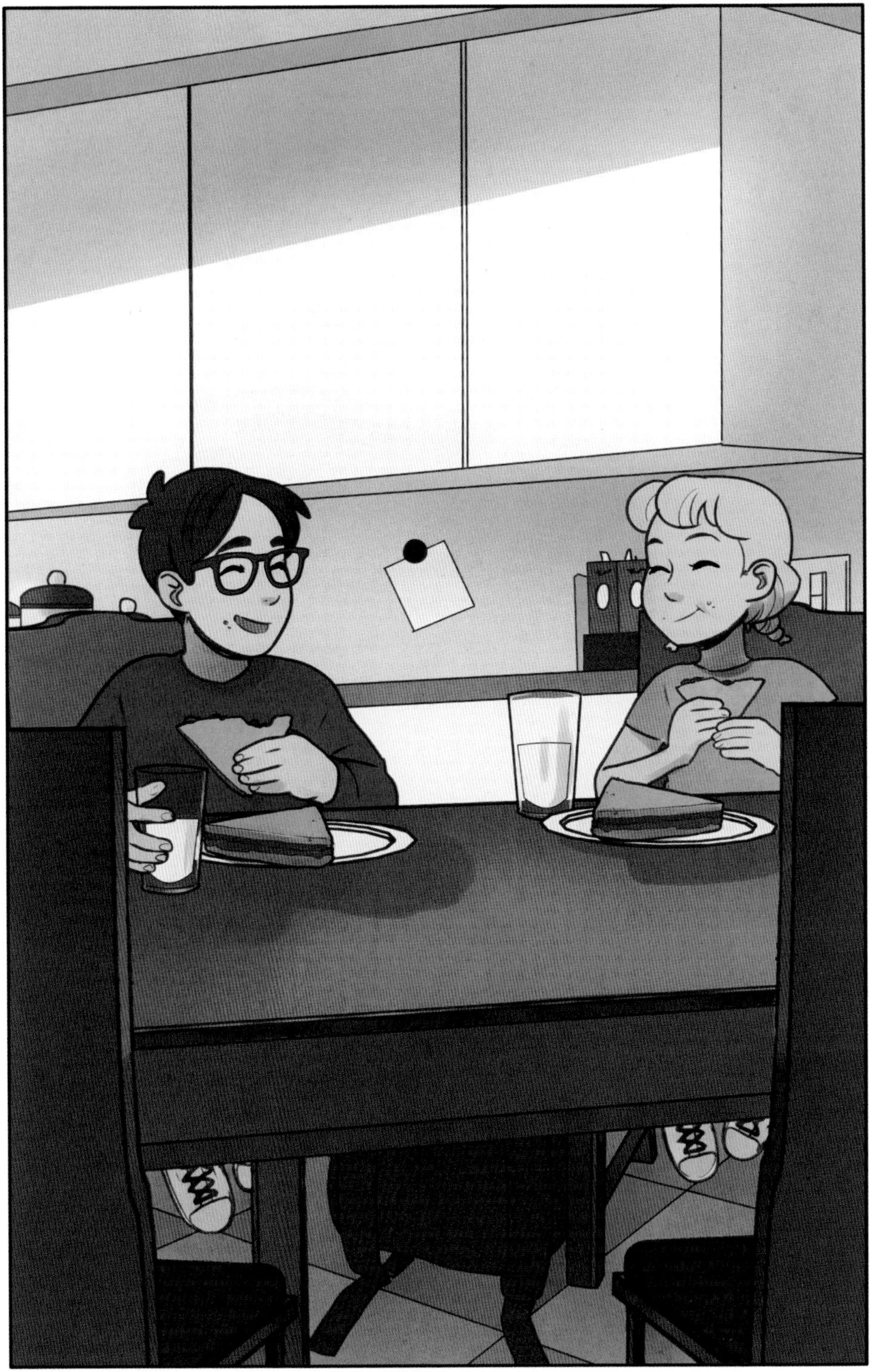

Missed the first adventure? Get whisked back to the time of dinosaurs with Jack and Annie in . . .

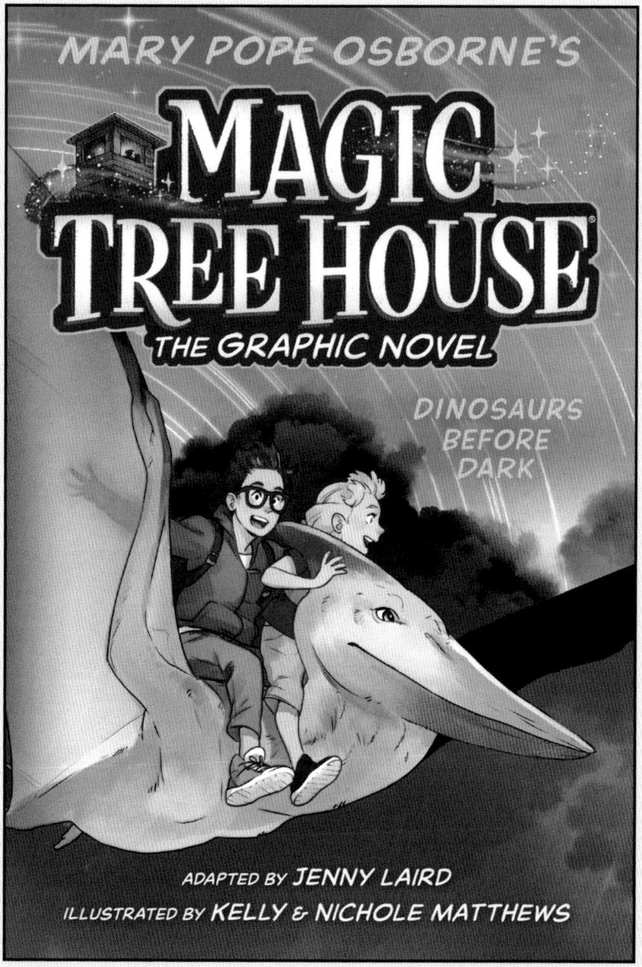
MARY POPE OSBORNE'S
MAGIC TREE HOUSE
THE GRAPHIC NOVEL
DINOSAURS BEFORE DARK
ADAPTED BY JENNY LAIRD
ILLUSTRATED BY KELLY & NICHOLE MATTHEWS

Where Is Here?

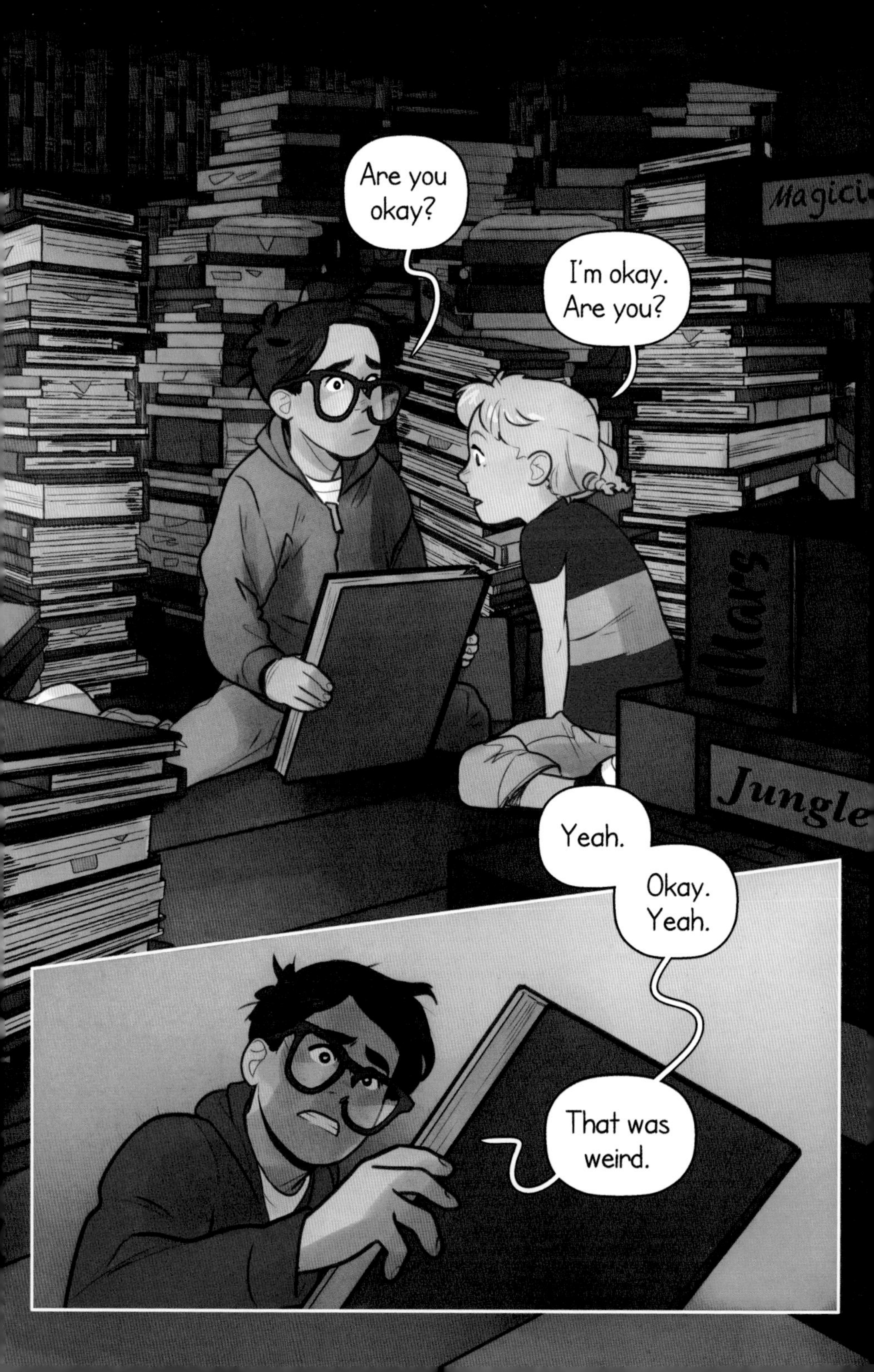
Are you okay?
I'm okay. Are you?
Magici
Wars
Jungle
Yeah.
Okay. Yeah.
That was weird.

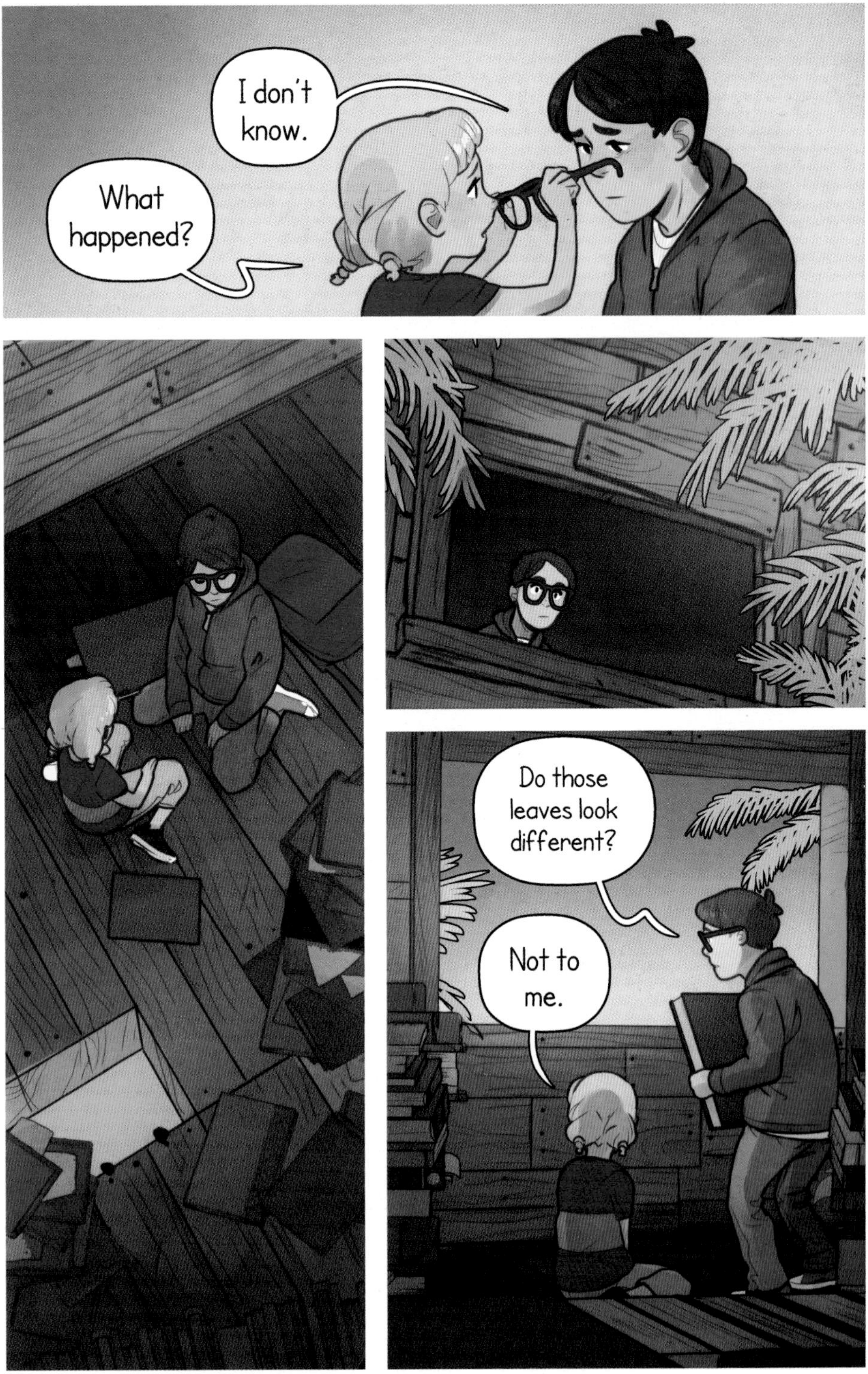
What happened?
I don't know.
Do those leaves look different?
Not to me.

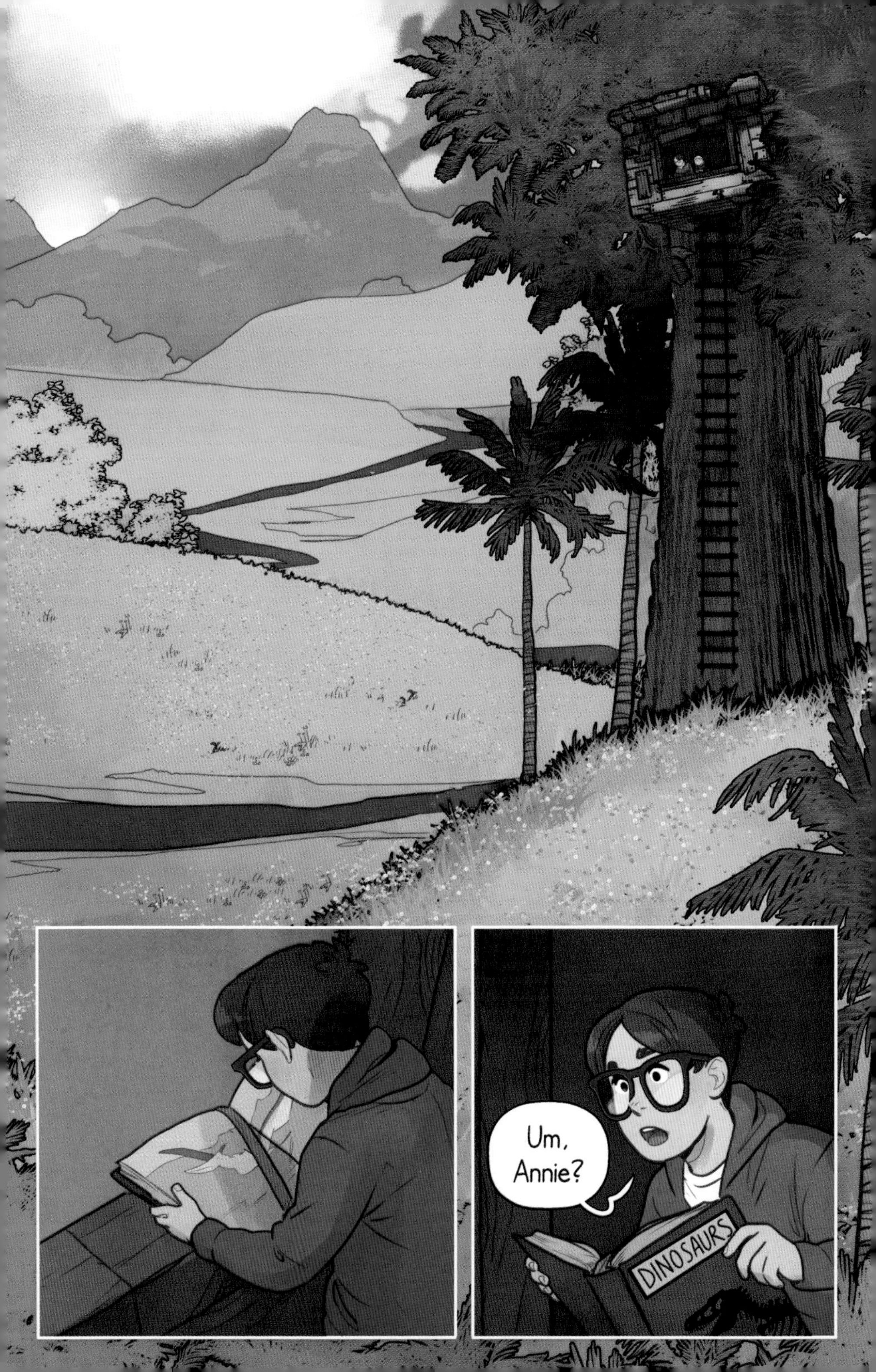
Um, Annie?
DINOSAURS

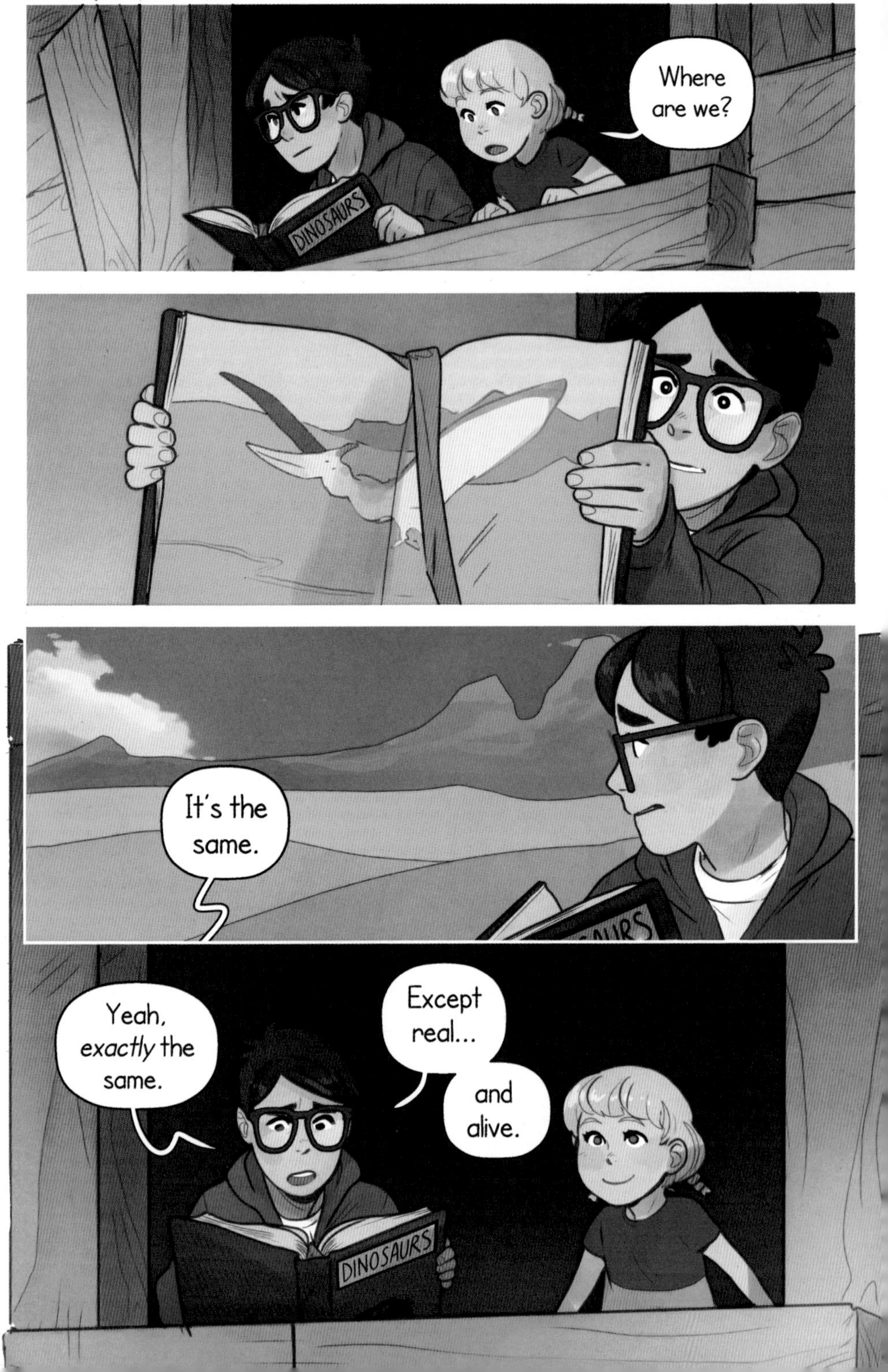
Where are we?
DINOSAURS
It's the same.
Yeah, *exactly* the same.
Except real...
and alive.
DINOSAURS

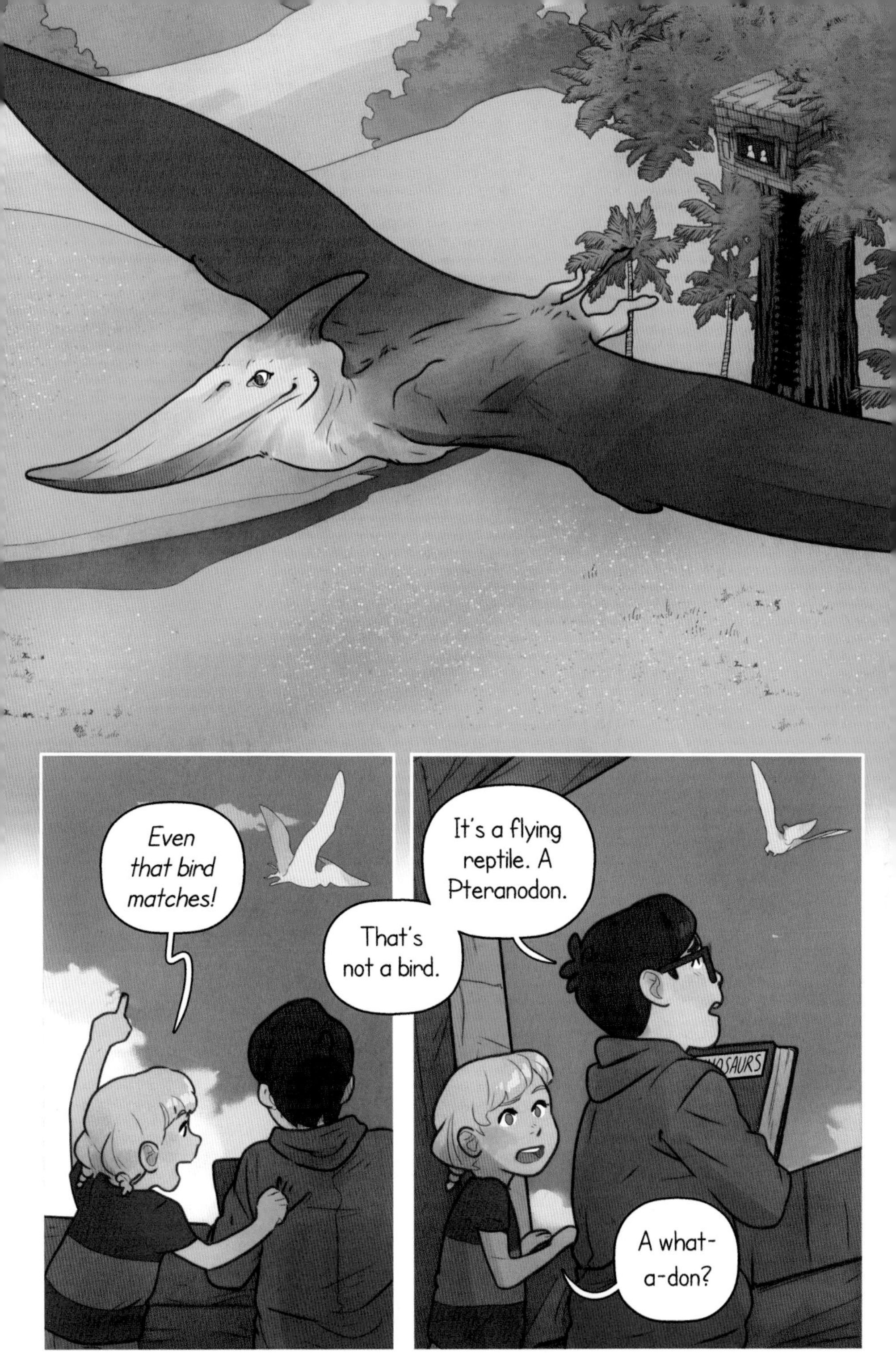
Even that bird matches!
It's a flying reptile. A Pteranodon.
That's not a bird.
A what-a-don?

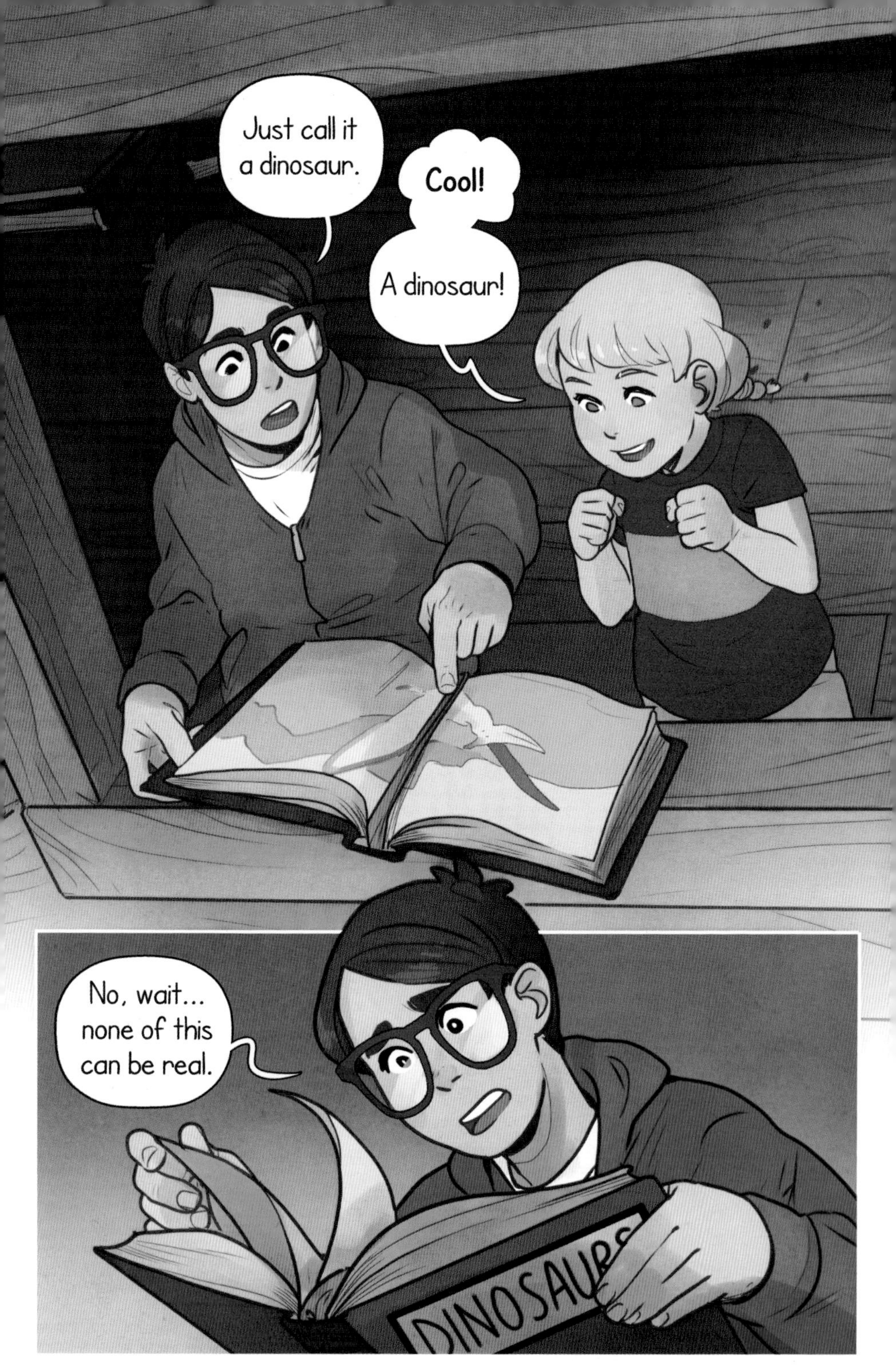
Just call it a dinosaur.
Cool!
A dinosaur!
No, wait... none of this can be real.
DINOSAURS

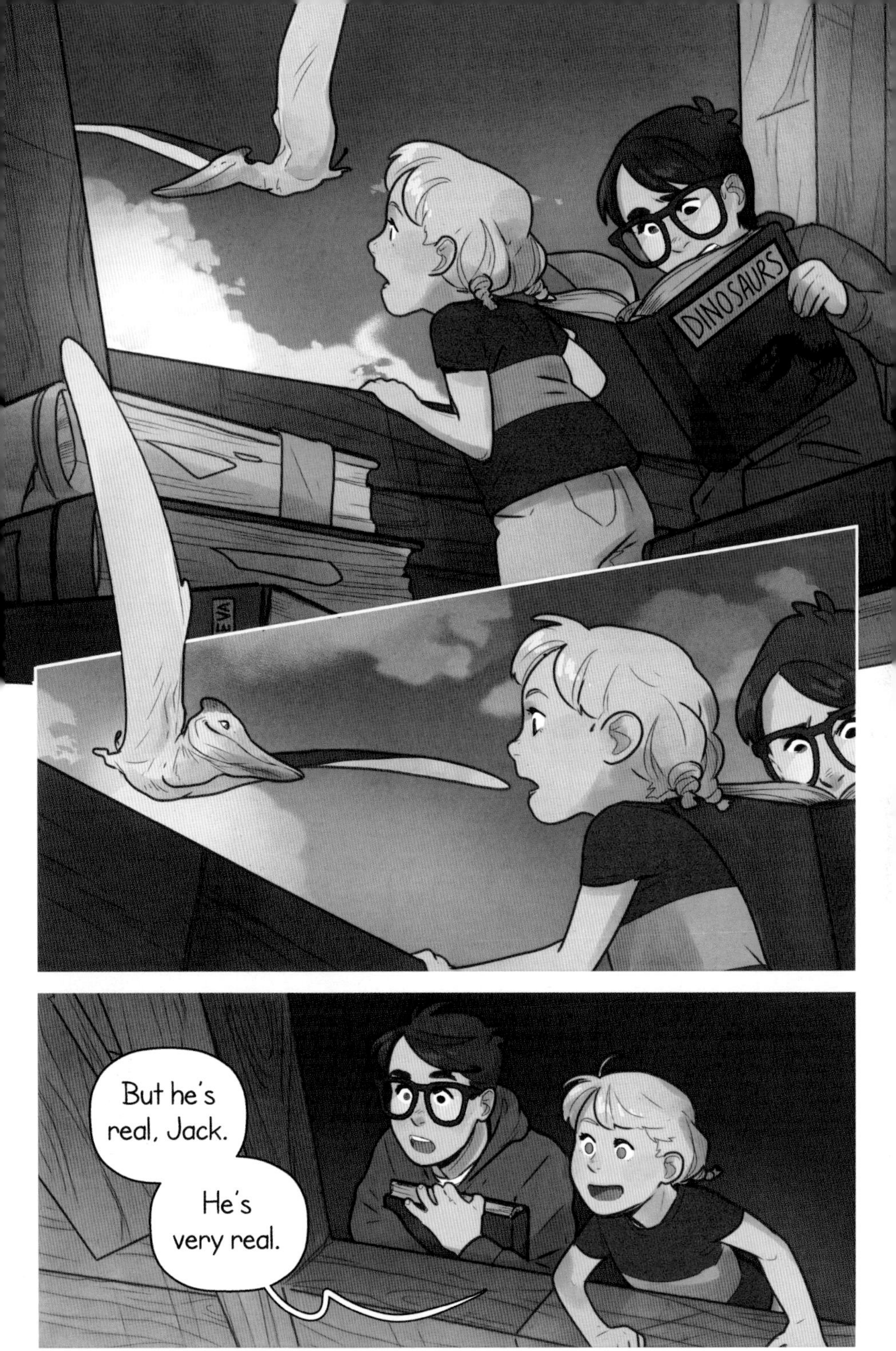
DINOSAURS
EVA
But he's real, Jack.
He's very real.

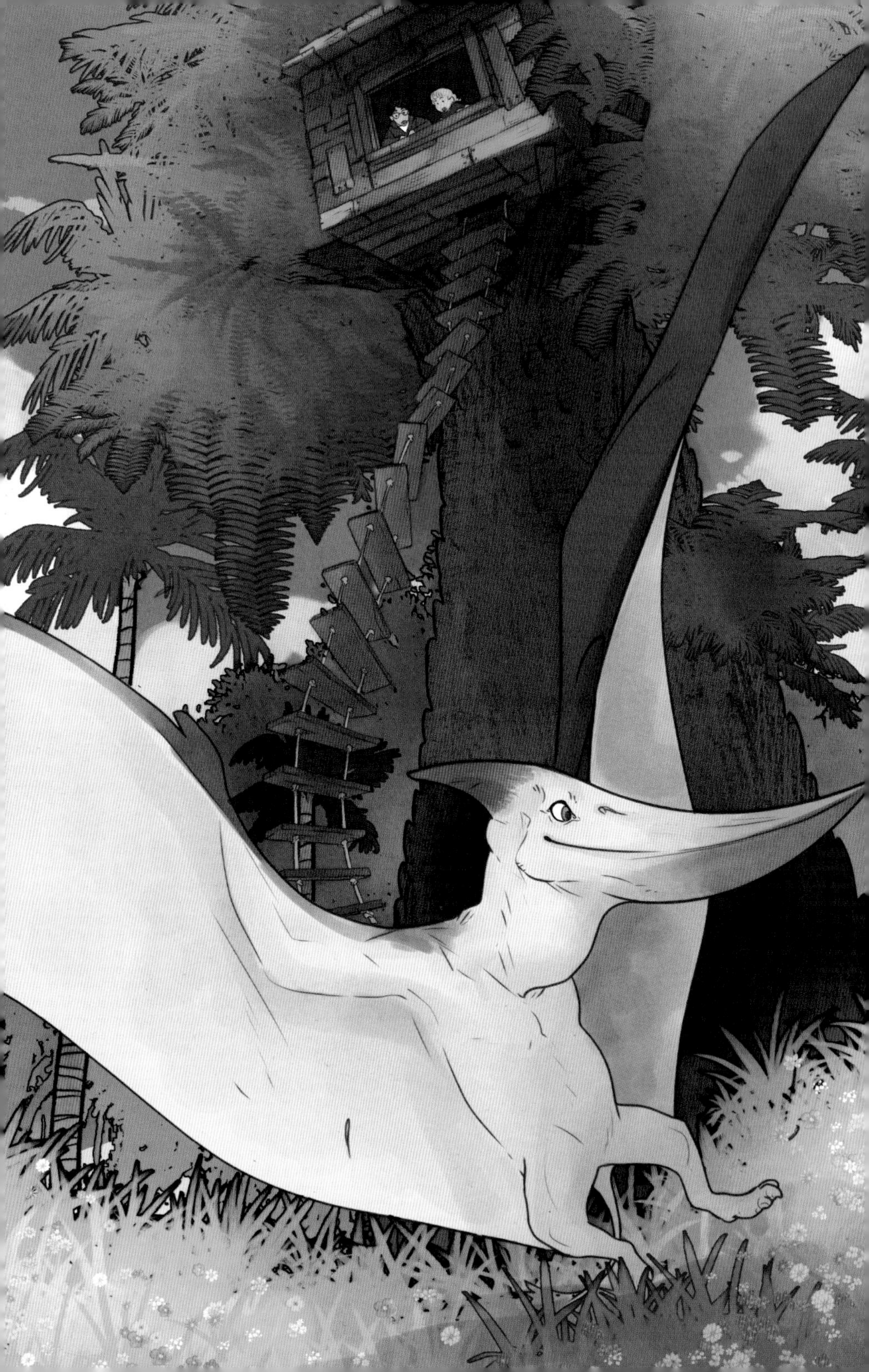

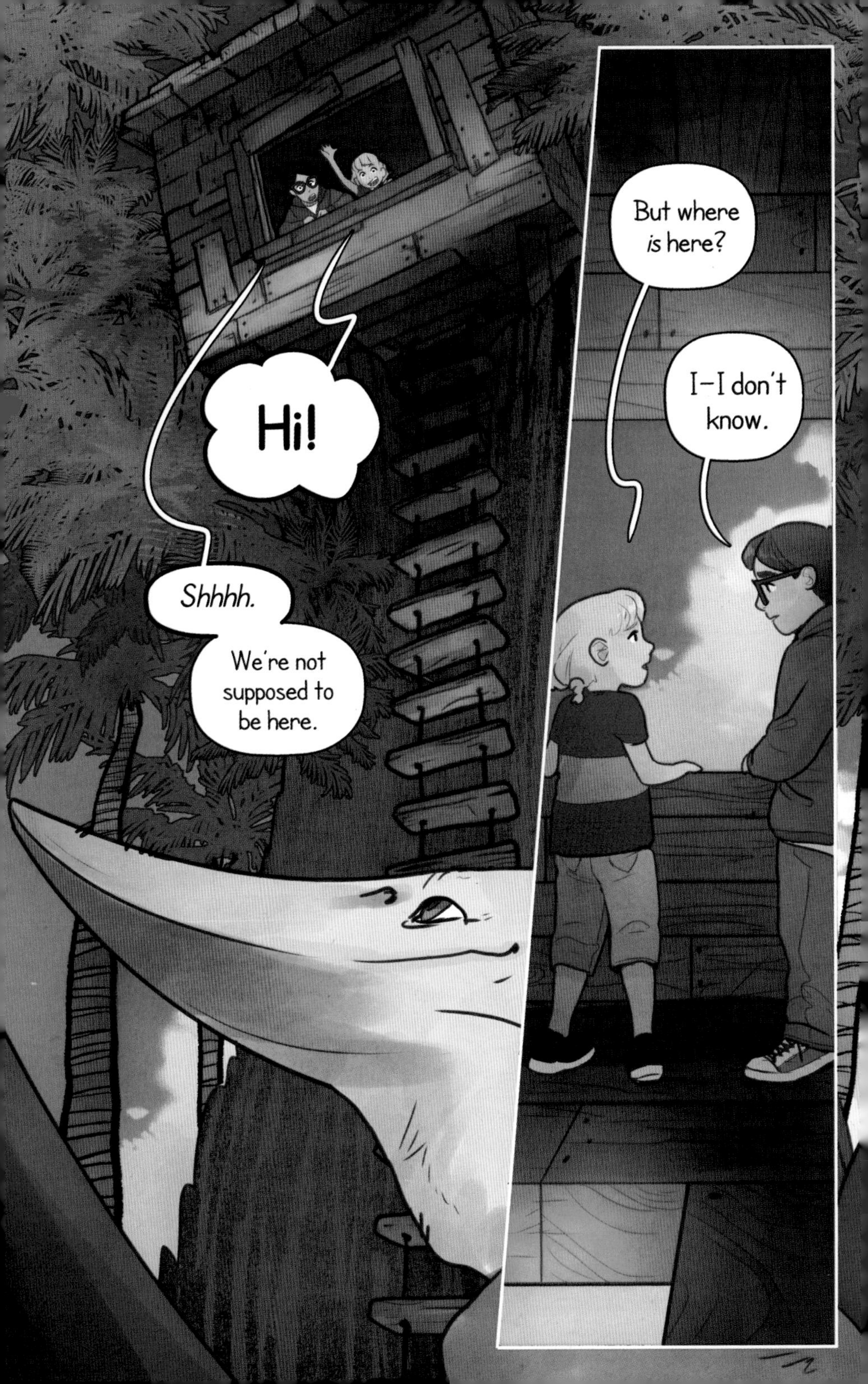
Hi!
Shhhh.
We're not supposed to be here.
But where is here?
I—I don't know.

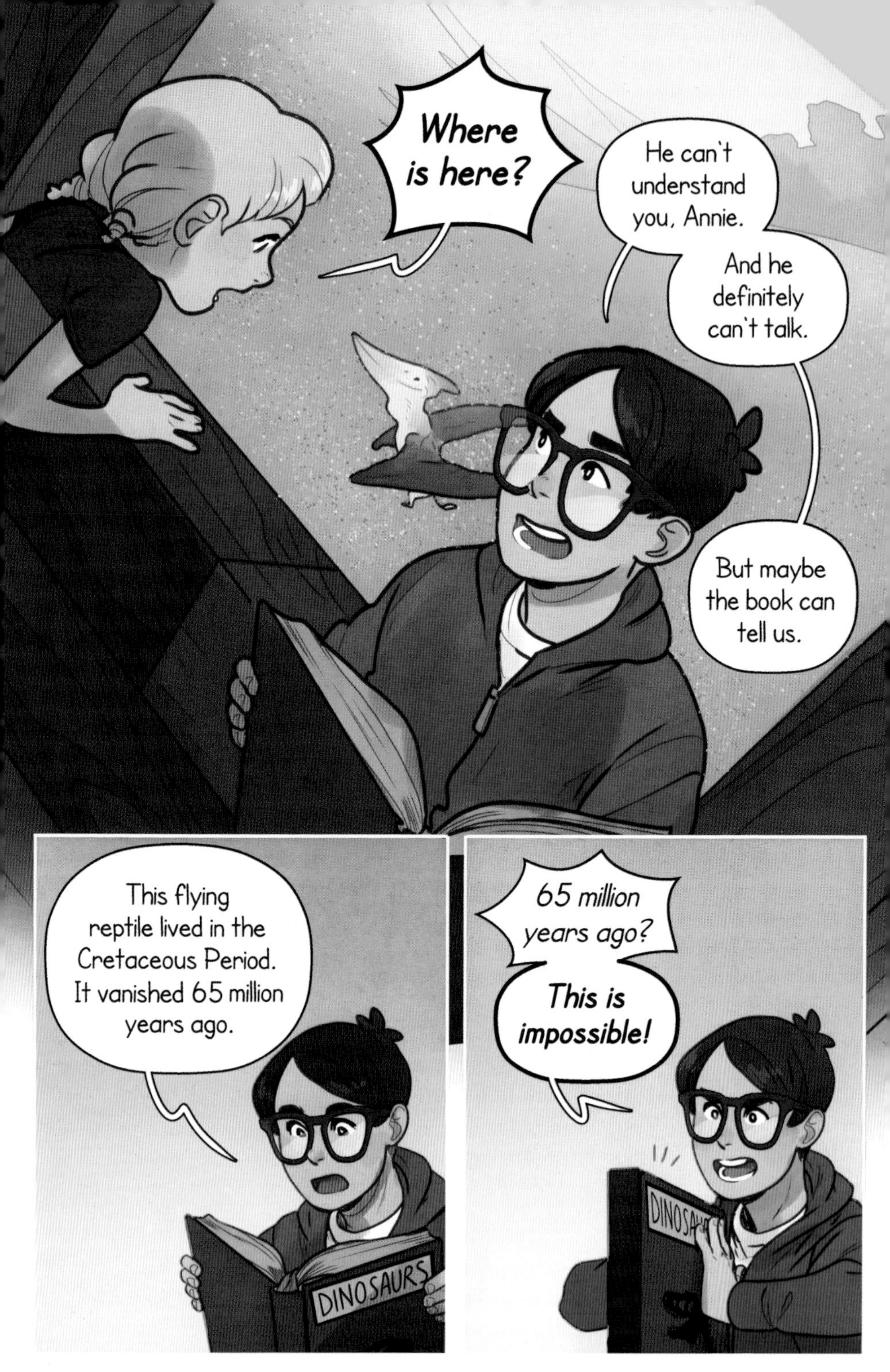
Where is here?
He can't understand you, Annie.
And he definitely can't talk.
But maybe the book can tell us.
This flying reptile lived in the Cretaceous Period. It vanished 65 million years ago.
DINOSAURS
65 million years ago?
This is impossible!

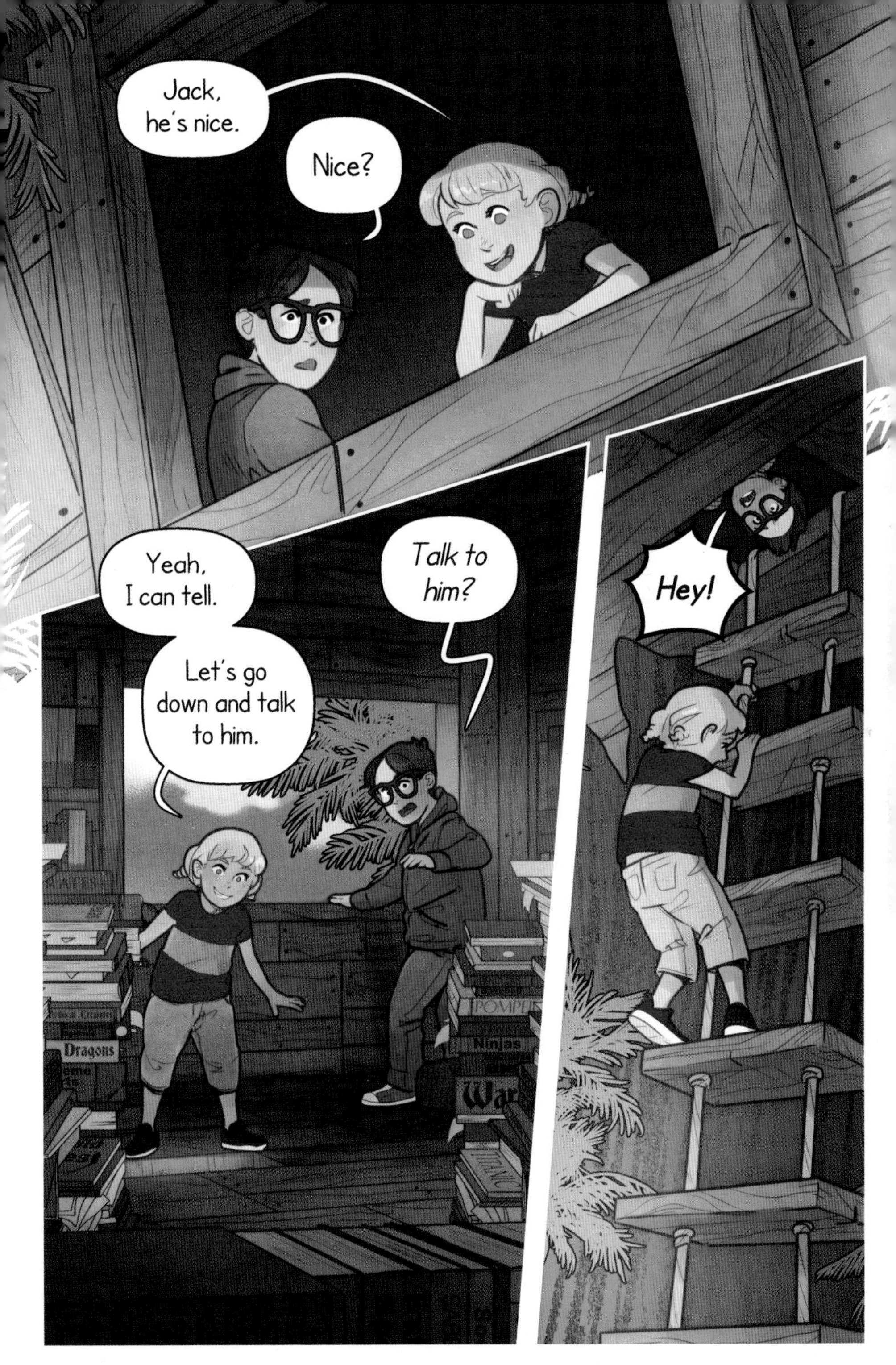
Jack,
he's nice.
Nice?
Yeah,
I can tell.
Let's go
down and talk
to him.
Talk to
him?
Hey!
Dragons
Ninjas
War

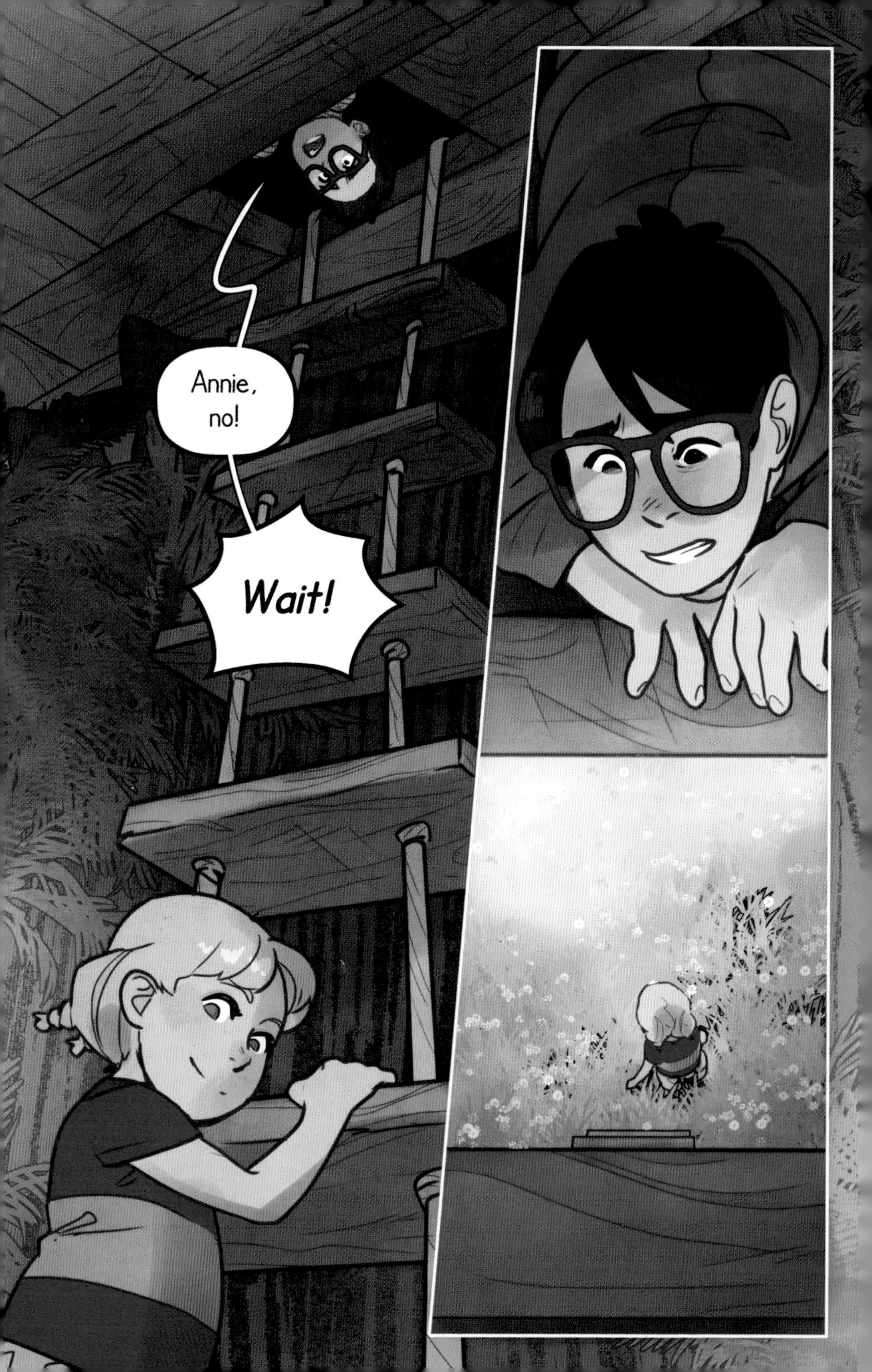
Annie, no!
Wait!

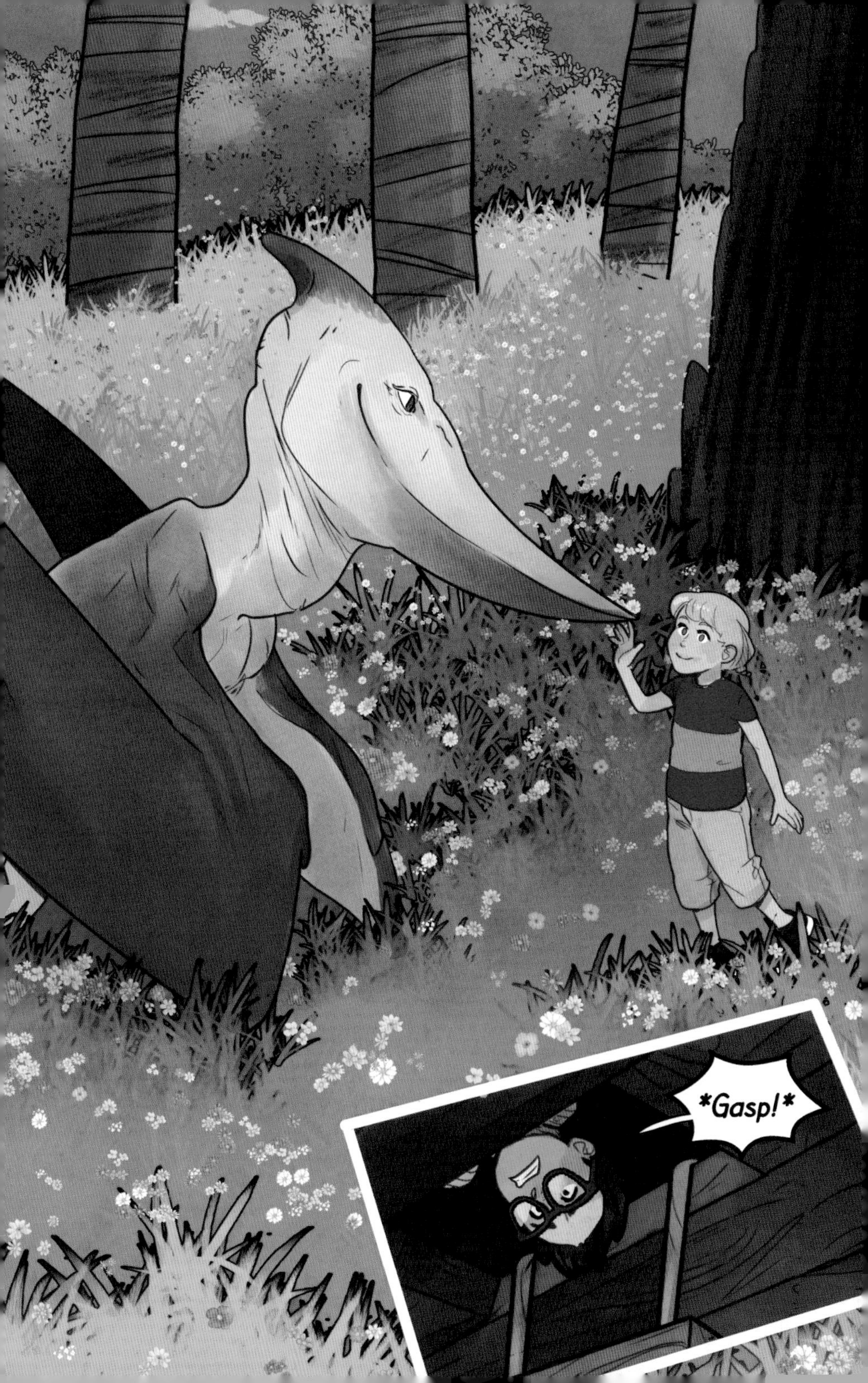
Gasp!

LET THE MAGIC TREE HOUSE® WHISK YOU AWAY!

MARY POPE OSBORNE
MAGIC TREE HOUSE
#1 Dinosaurs Before Dark
#1 NEW YORK TIMES BESTSELLING SERIES

MARY POPE OSBORNE
MAGIC TREE HOUSE
#2 The Knight at Dawn
#1 NEW YORK TIMES BESTSELLING SERIES

MARY POPE OSBORNE
MAGIC TREE HOUSE
#3 Mummies in the Morning
#1 NEW YORK TIMES BESTSELLING SERIES

MARY POPE OSBORNE
MAGIC TREE HOUSE
#4 Pirates Past Noon
#1 NEW YORK TIMES BESTSELLING SERIES

MARY POPE OSBORNE
MAGIC TREE HOUSE
#5 Night of the Ninjas
#1 NEW YORK TIMES BESTSELLING SERIES

MARY POPE OSBORNE
MAGIC TREE HOUSE
#6 Afternoon on the Amazon
#1 NEW YORK TIMES BESTSELLING SERIES

MARY POPE OSBORNE
MAGIC TREE HOUSE
#7 Sunset of the Sabertooth
#1 NEW YORK TIMES BESTSELLING SERIES

MARY POPE OSBORNE
MAGIC TREE HOUSE
#8 Midnight on the Moon
#1 NEW YORK TIMES BESTSELLING SERIES

MARY POPE OSBORNE
MAGIC TREE HOUSE
#9 Dolphins at Daybreak
#1 NEW YORK TIMES BESTSELLING SERIES

MARY POPE OSBORNE
MAGIC TREE HOUSE
#10 Ghost Town at Sundown
#1 NEW YORK TIMES BESTSELLING SERIES

MARY POPE OSBORNE
MAGIC TREE HOUSE
#11 Lions at Lunchtime
#1 NEW YORK TIMES BESTSELLING SERIES

MARY POPE OSBORNE
MAGIC TREE HOUSE
#12 Polar Bears Past Bedtime
#1 NEW YORK TIMES BESTSELLING SERIES

MARY POPE OSBORNE
MAGIC TREE HOUSE
#13 Vacation Under the Volcano
#1 NEW YORK TIMES BESTSELLING SERIES

MARY POPE OSBORNE
MAGIC TREE HOUSE
#14 Day of the Dragon King
#1 NEW YORK TIMES BESTSELLING SERIES

MARY POPE OSBORNE
MAGIC TREE HOUSE
#15 Viking Ships at Sunrise
#1 NEW YORK TIMES BESTSELLING SERIES

MARY POPE OSBORNE
MAGIC TREE HOUSE
#16 Hour of the Olympics
#1 NEW YORK TIMES BESTSELLING SERIES

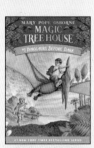

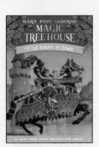

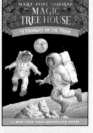

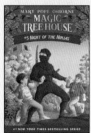

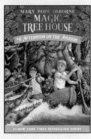

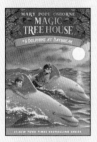

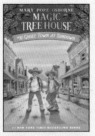

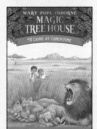

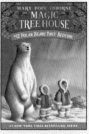

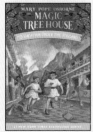

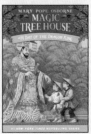

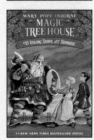

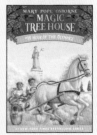

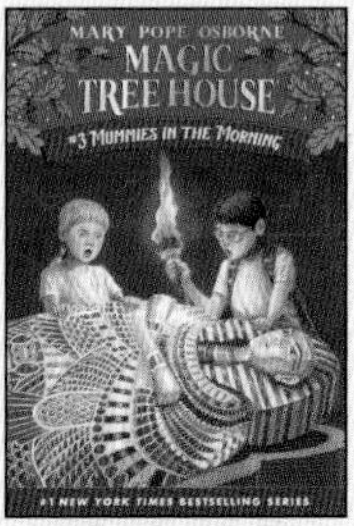

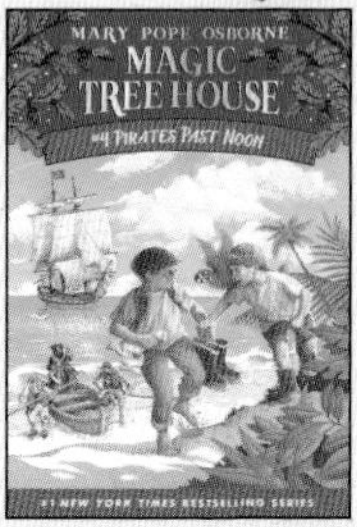

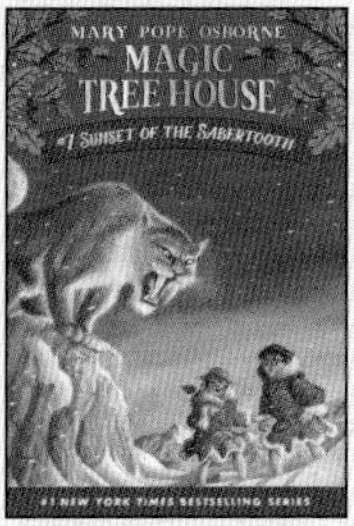

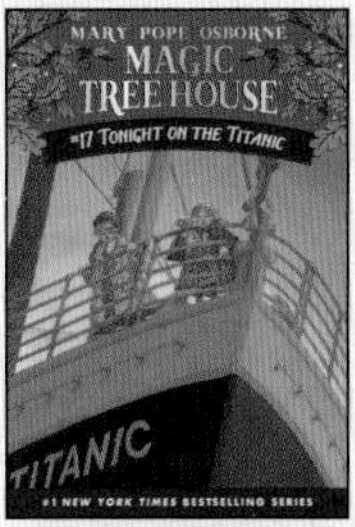
MARY POPE OSBORNE
MAGIC TREE HOUSE
#17 Tonight on the Titanic
TITANIC
#1 NEW YORK TIMES BESTSELLING SERIES
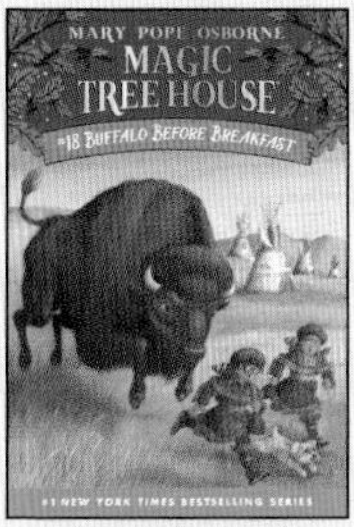
MARY POPE OSBORNE
MAGIC TREE HOUSE
#18 Buffalo Before Breakfast
#1 NEW YORK TIMES BESTSELLING SERIES
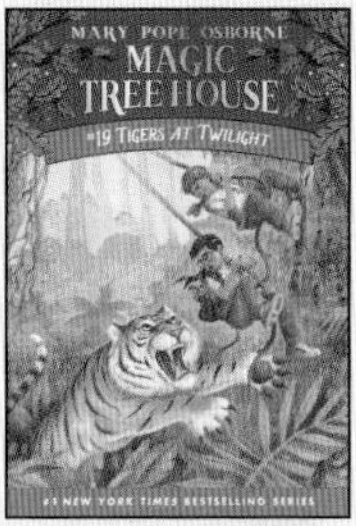
MARY POPE OSBORNE
MAGIC TREE HOUSE
#19 Tigers at Twilight
#1 NEW YORK TIMES BESTSELLING SERIES
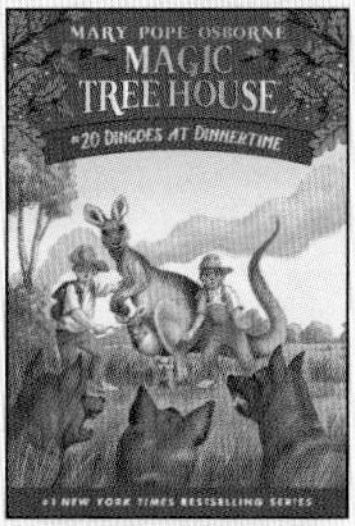
MARY POPE OSBORNE
MAGIC TREE HOUSE
#20 Dingoes at Dinnertime
#1 NEW YORK TIMES BESTSELLING SERIES
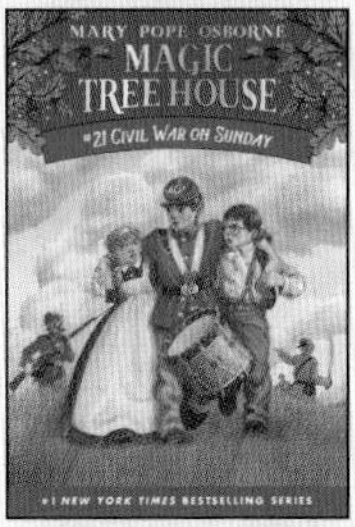
MARY POPE OSBORNE
MAGIC TREE HOUSE
#21 Civil War on Sunday
#1 NEW YORK TIMES BESTSELLING SERIES
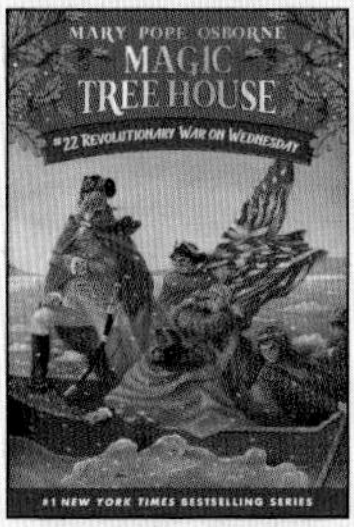
MARY POPE OSBORNE
MAGIC TREE HOUSE
#22 Revolutionary War on Wednesday
#1 NEW YORK TIMES BESTSELLING SERIES
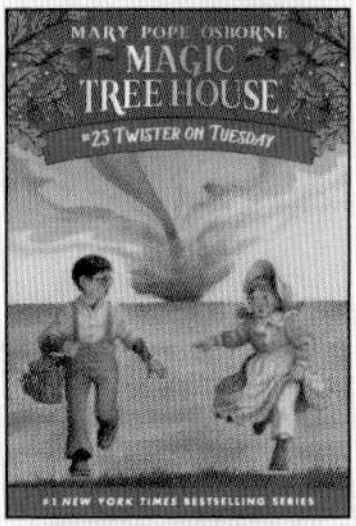
MARY POPE OSBORNE
MAGIC TREE HOUSE
#23 Twister on Tuesday
#1 NEW YORK TIMES BESTSELLING SERIES
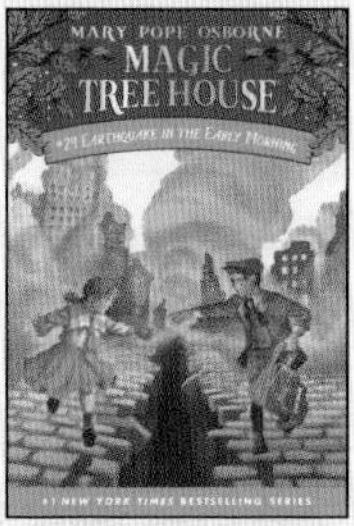
MARY POPE OSBORNE
MAGIC TREE HOUSE
#1 NEW YORK TIMES BESTSELLING SERIES
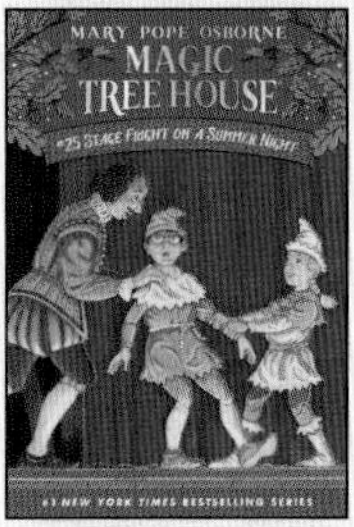
MARY POPE OSBORNE
MAGIC TREE HOUSE
#25 Stage Fright on a Summer Night
#1 NEW YORK TIMES BESTSELLING SERIES
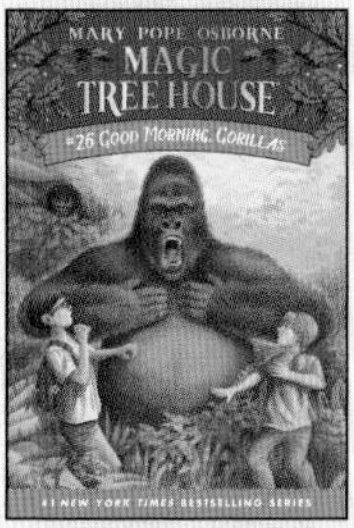
MARY POPE OSBORNE
MAGIC TREE HOUSE
#26 Good Morning, Gorillas
#1 NEW YORK TIMES BESTSELLING SERIES
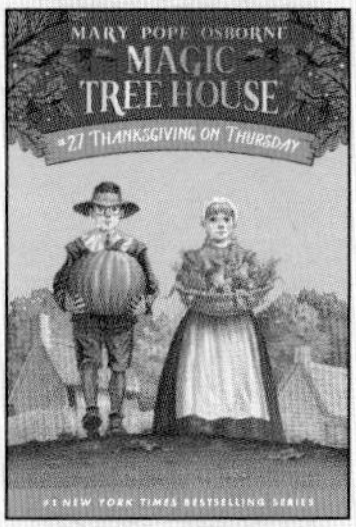
MARY POPE OSBORNE
MAGIC TREE HOUSE
#27 Thanksgiving on Thursday
#1 NEW YORK TIMES BESTSELLING SERIES
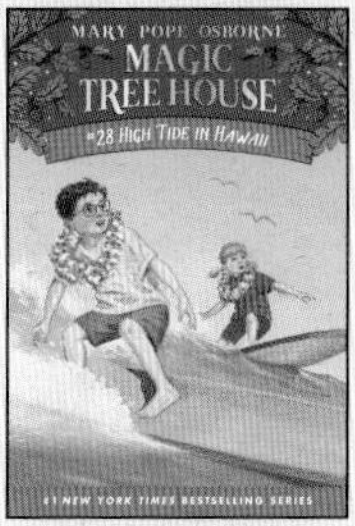
MARY POPE OSBORNE
MAGIC TREE HOUSE
#28 High Tide in Hawaii
#1 NEW YORK TIMES BESTSELLING SERIES
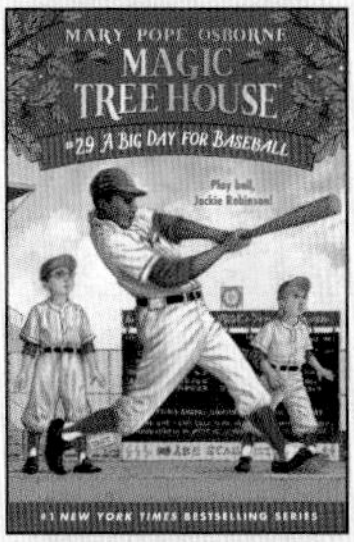
MARY POPE OSBORNE
MAGIC TREE HOUSE
#29 A Big Day for Baseball
Play ball, Jackie Robinson!
#1 NEW YORK TIMES BESTSELLING SERIES
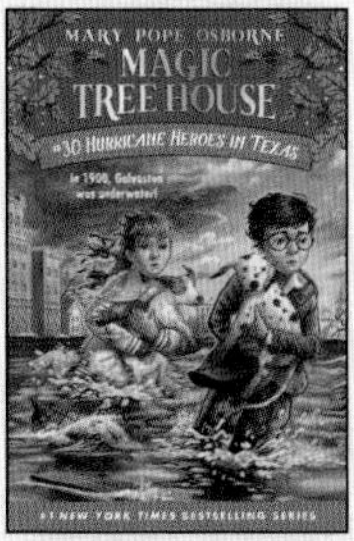
MARY POPE OSBORNE
MAGIC TREE HOUSE
#30 Hurricane Heroes in Texas
#1 NEW YORK TIMES BESTSELLING SERIES
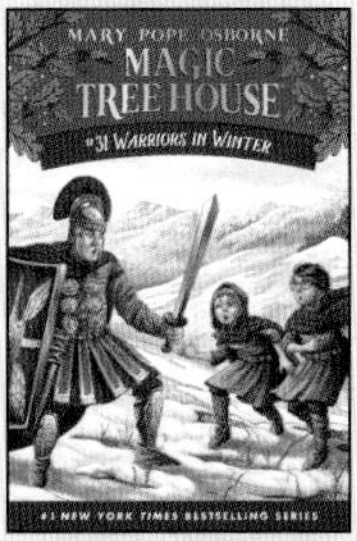
MARY POPE OSBORNE
MAGIC TREE HOUSE
#31 Warriors in Winter
#1 NEW YORK TIMES BESTSELLING SERIES
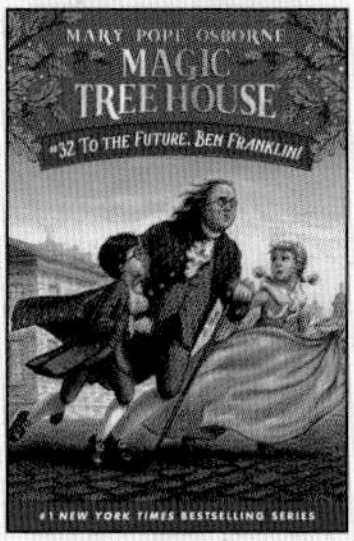
MARY POPE OSBORNE
MAGIC TREE HOUSE
#32 To the Future, Ben Franklin!
#1 NEW YORK TIMES BESTSELLING SERIES
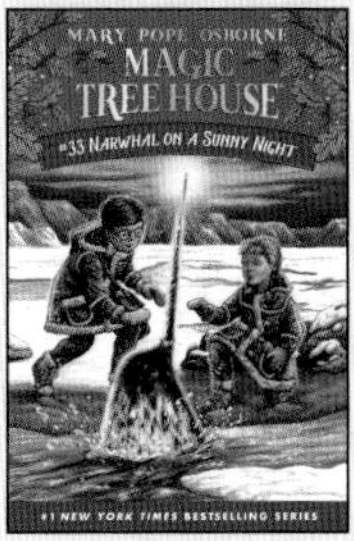
MARY POPE OSBORNE
MAGIC TREE HOUSE
#33 Narwhal on a Sunny Night
#1 NEW YORK TIMES BESTSELLING SERIES
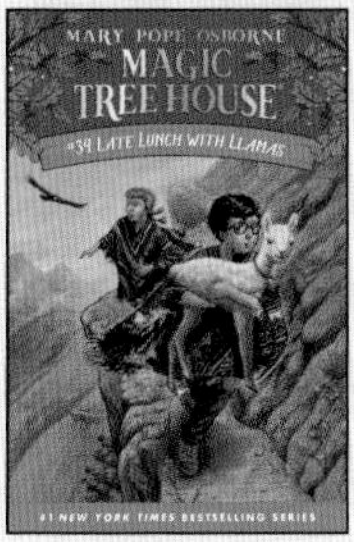
MARY POPE OSBORNE
MAGIC TREE HOUSE
#34 Late Lunch with Llamas
#1 NEW YORK TIMES BESTSELLING SERIES
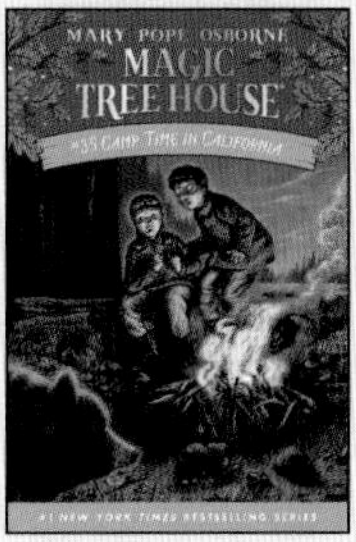
MARY POPE OSBORNE
MAGIC TREE HOUSE
#35 Camp Time in California

Read all the novels in the #1 bestselling chapter book series of all time!

TRACK THE FACTS WITH JACK & ANNIE!

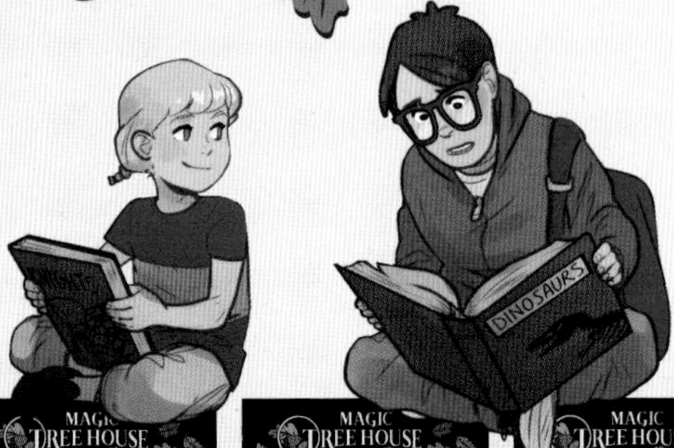
DINOSAURS

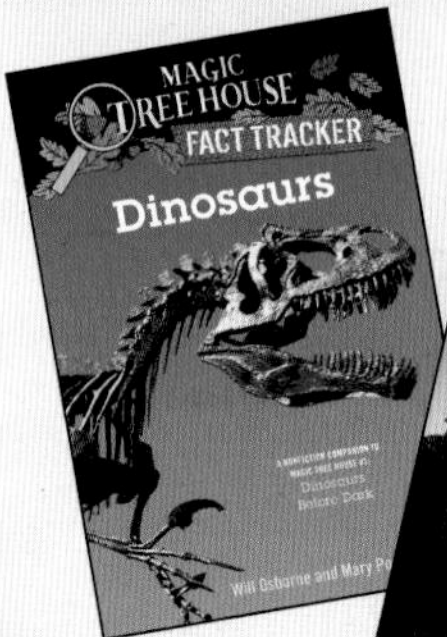
MAGIC TREE HOUSE
FACT TRACKER
Dinosaurs

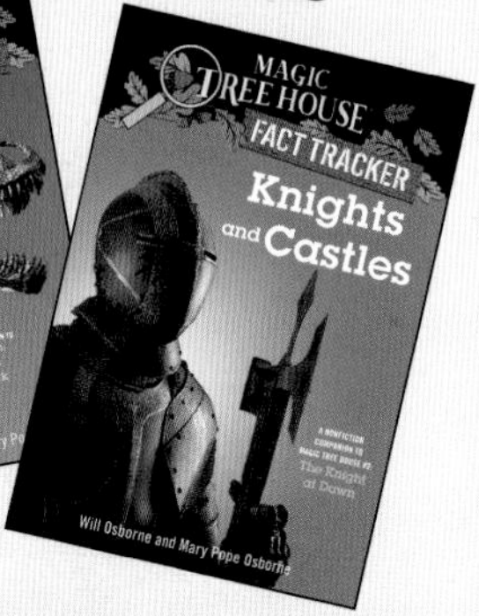
MAGIC TREE HOUSE
FACT TRACKER
Knights and Castles
Will Osborne and Mary Pope Osborne

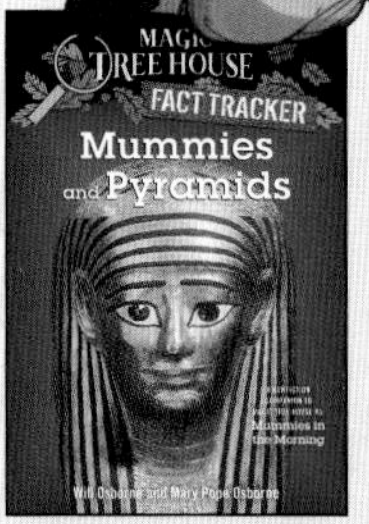
MAGIC TREE HOUSE
FACT TRACKER
Mummies and Pyramids
Will Osborne and Mary Pope Osborne

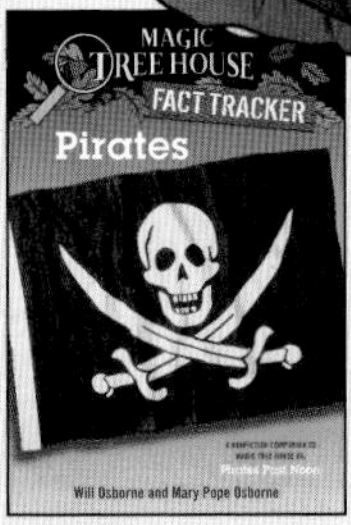
MAGIC TREE HOUSE
FACT TRACKER
Pirates
Will Osborne and Mary Pope Osborne

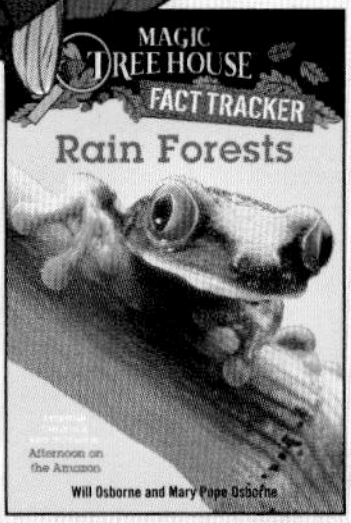
MAGIC TREE HOUSE
FACT TRACKER
Rain Forests
Will Osborne and Mary Pope Osborne

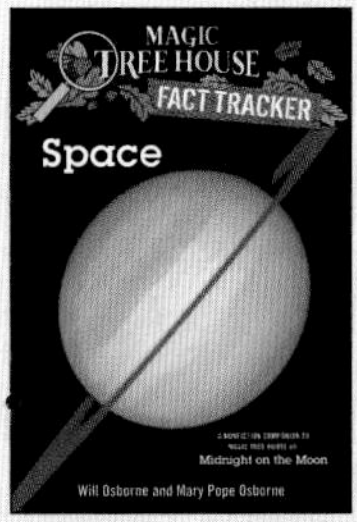
MAGIC TREE HOUSE
FACT TRACKER
Space
Will Osborne and Mary Pope Osborne

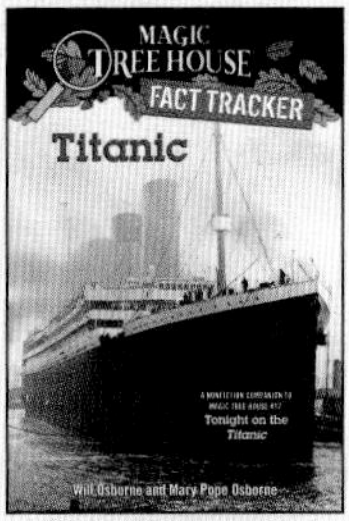
MAGIC TREE HOUSE
FACT TRACKER
Titanic
Will Osborne and Mary Pope Osborne

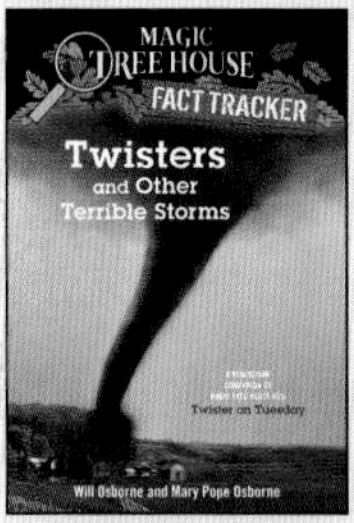
MAGIC TREE HOUSE
FACT TRACKER
Twisters and Other Terrible Storms
Will Osborne and Mary Pope Osborne

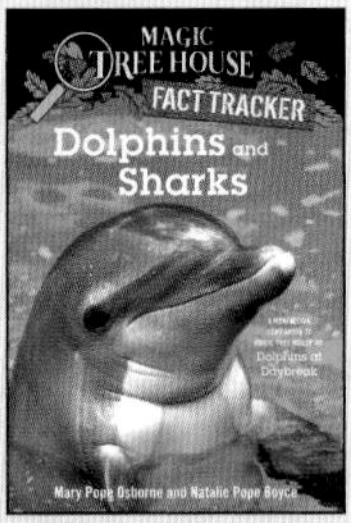
MAGIC TREE HOUSE
FACT TRACKER
Dolphins and Sharks
Mary Pope Osborne and Natalie Pope Boyce

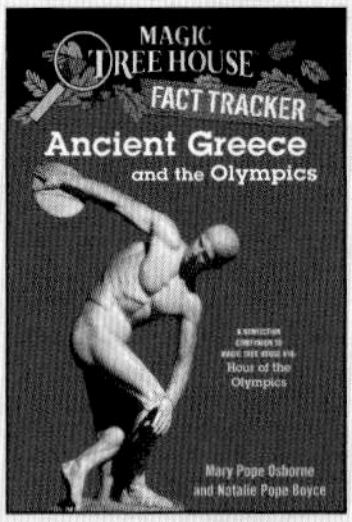
MAGIC TREE HOUSE
FACT TRACKER
Ancient Greece and the Olympics
Mary Pope Osborne and Natalie Pope Boyce

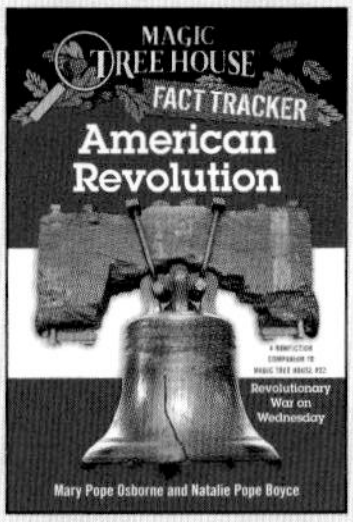
MAGIC TREE HOUSE
FACT TRACKER
American Revolution
Mary Pope Osborne and Natalie Pope Boyce

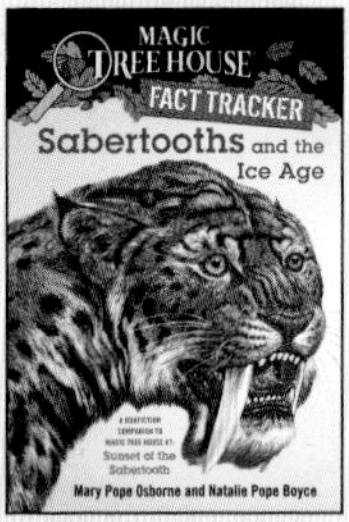
MAGIC TREE HOUSE
FACT TRACKER
Sabertooths and the Ice Age
Mary Pope Osborne and Natalie Pope Boyce

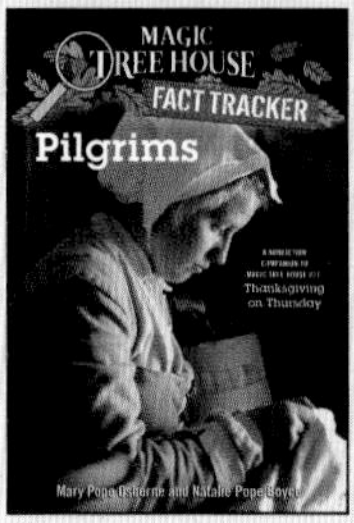
MAGIC TREE HOUSE
FACT TRACKER
Pilgrims
Mary Pope Osborne and Natalie Pope Boyce

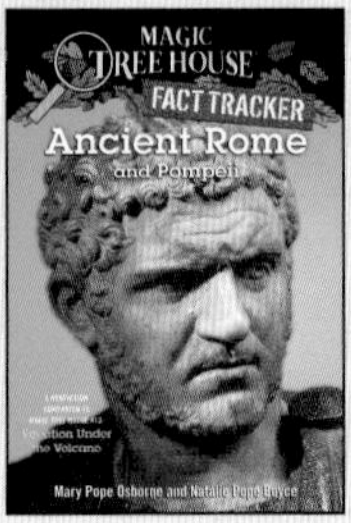
MAGIC TREE HOUSE
FACT TRACKER
Ancient Rome and Pompeii
Mary Pope Osborne and Natalie Pope Boyce

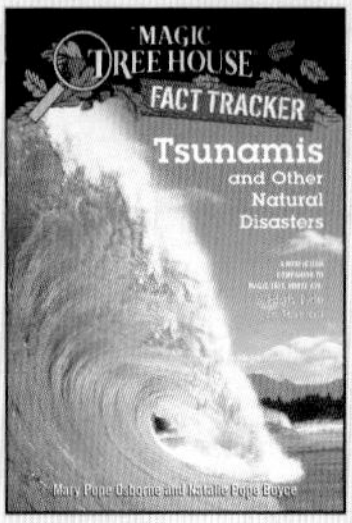
MAGIC TREE HOUSE
FACT TRACKER
Tsunamis and Other Natural Disasters
Mary Pope Osborne and Natalie Pope Boyce

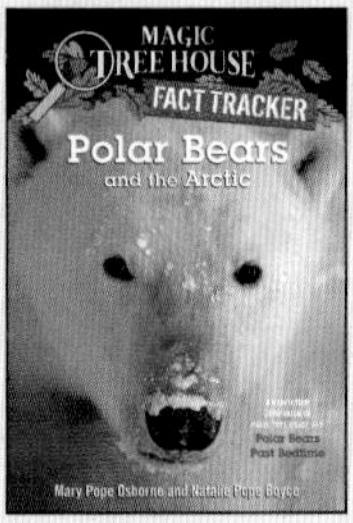
MAGIC TREE HOUSE
FACT TRACKER
Polar Bears and the Arctic
Mary Pope Osborne and Natalie Pope Boyce

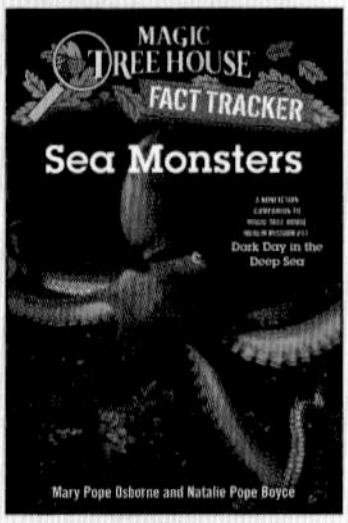
MAGIC TREE HOUSE
FACT TRACKER
Sea Monsters
Mary Pope Osborne and Natalie Pope Boyce

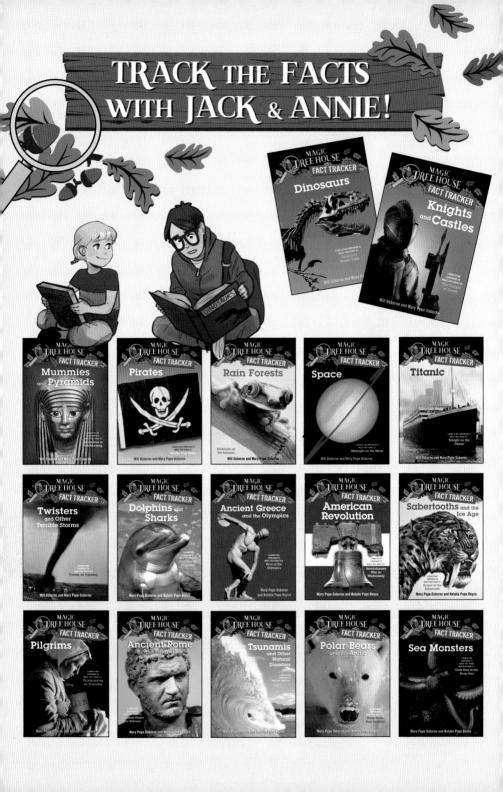

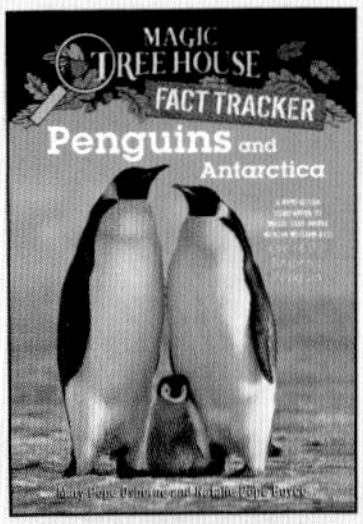
MAGIC TREE HOUSE
FACT TRACKER
Penguins and Antarctica
Mary Pope Osborne and Natalie Pope Boyce

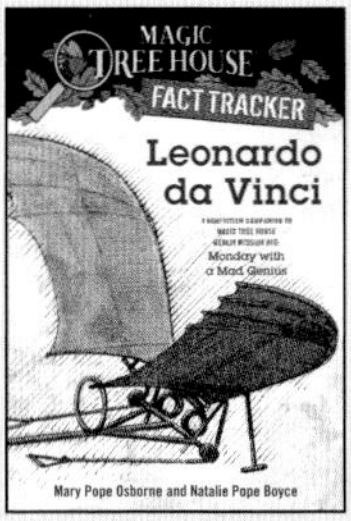
MAGIC TREE HOUSE
FACT TRACKER
Leonardo da Vinci
Mary Pope Osborne and Natalie Pope Boyce

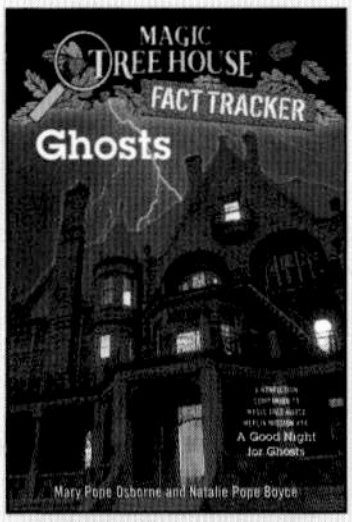
MAGIC TREE HOUSE
FACT TRACKER
Ghosts
Mary Pope Osborne and Natalie Pope Boyce

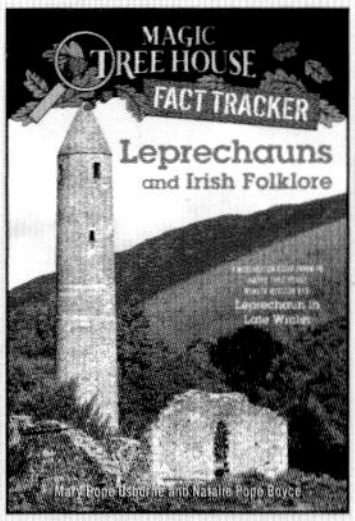
MAGIC TREE HOUSE
FACT TRACKER
Leprechauns and Irish Folklore
Mary Pope Osborne and Natalie Pope Boyce

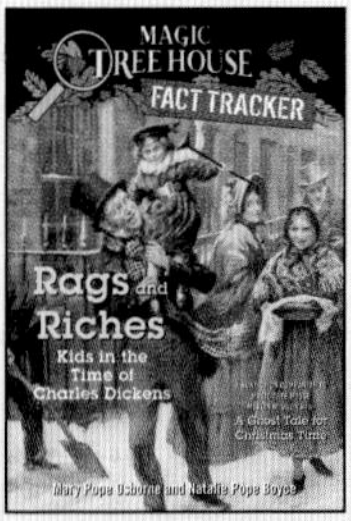
MAGIC TREE HOUSE
FACT TRACKER
Rags and Riches
Kids in the Time of Charles Dickens
Mary Pope Osborne and Natalie Pope Boyce

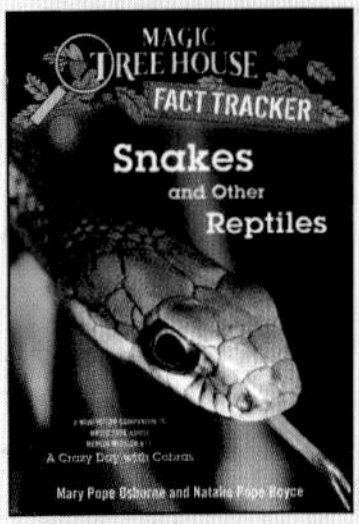
MAGIC TREE HOUSE
FACT TRACKER
Snakes and Other Reptiles
Mary Pope Osborne and Natalie Pope Boyce

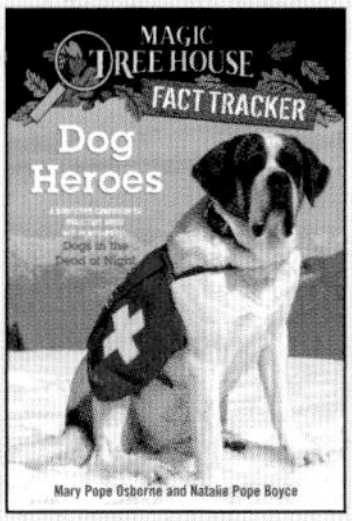
MAGIC TREE HOUSE
FACT TRACKER
Dog Heroes
Mary Pope Osborne and Natalie Pope Boyce

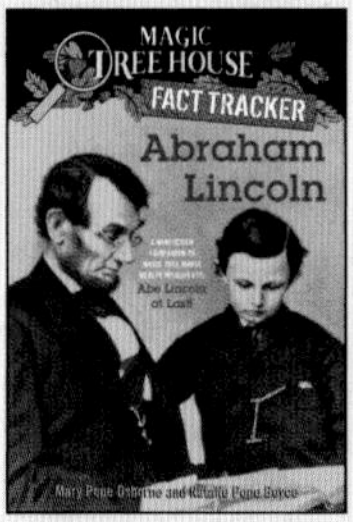
MAGIC TREE HOUSE
FACT TRACKER
Abraham Lincoln
Mary Pope Osborne and Natalie Pope Boyce

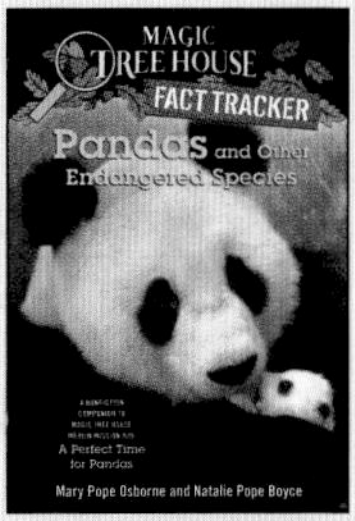
MAGIC TREE HOUSE
FACT TRACKER
Pandas and Other Endangered Species
Mary Pope Osborne and Natalie Pope Boyce

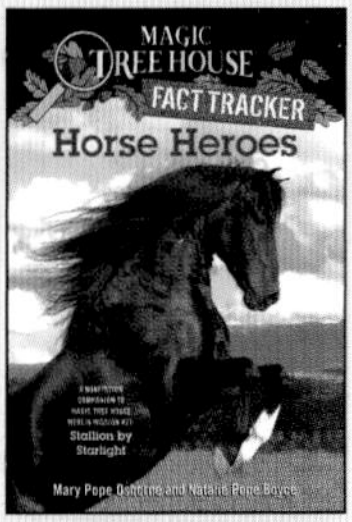
MAGIC TREE HOUSE
FACT TRACKER
Horse Heroes
Mary Pope Osborne and Natalie Pope Boyce

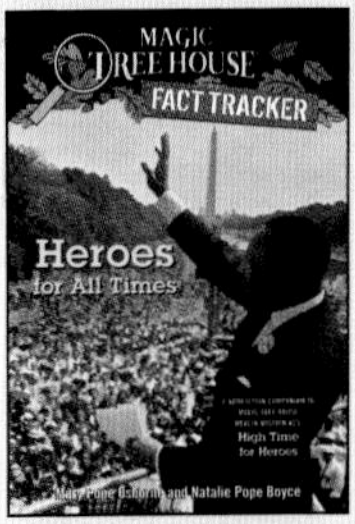
MAGIC TREE HOUSE
FACT TRACKER
Heroes for All Times
Mary Pope Osborne and Natalie Pope Boyce

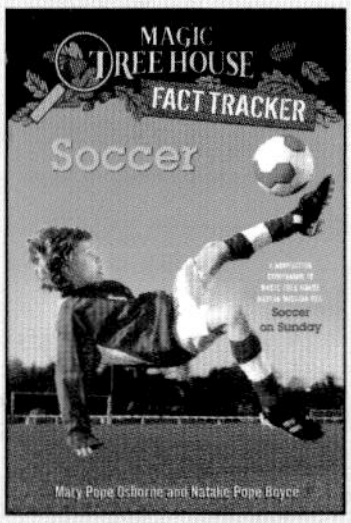
MAGIC TREE HOUSE
FACT TRACKER
Soccer
Mary Pope Osborne and Natalie Pope Boyce

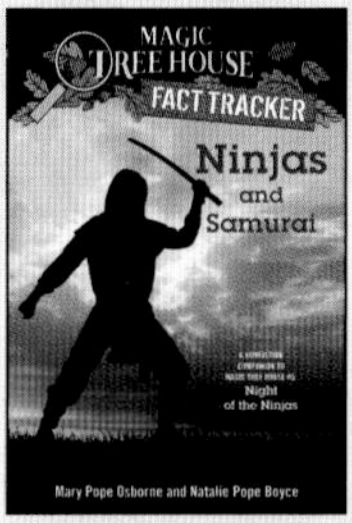
MAGIC TREE HOUSE
FACT TRACKER
Ninjas and Samurai
Mary Pope Osborne and Natalie Pope Boyce

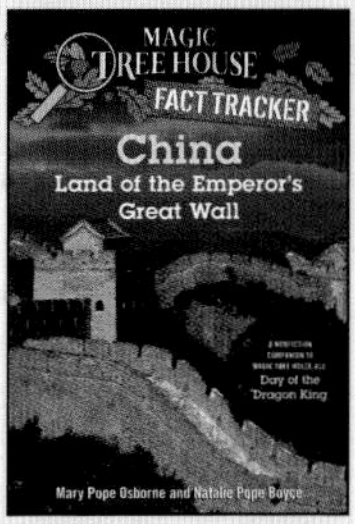
MAGIC TREE HOUSE
FACT TRACKER
China
Land of the Emperor's Great Wall
Mary Pope Osborne and Natalie Pope Boyce

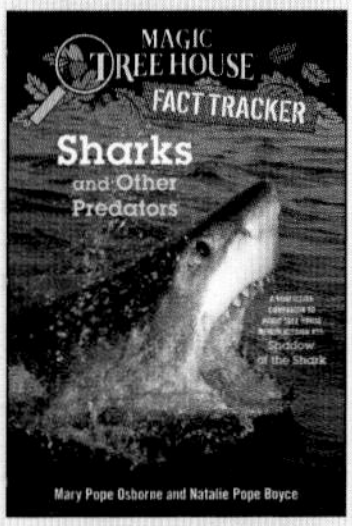
MAGIC TREE HOUSE
FACT TRACKER
Sharks and Other Predators
Mary Pope Osborne and Natalie Pope Boyce

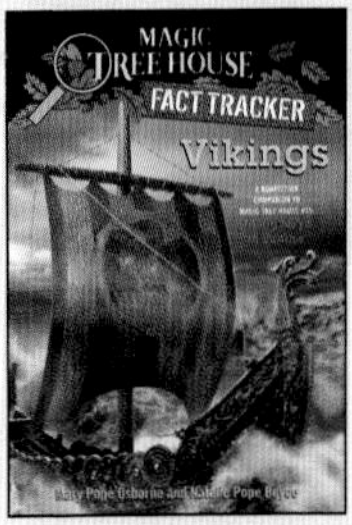
MAGIC TREE HOUSE
FACT TRACKER
Vikings
Mary Pope Osborne and Natalie Pope Boyce

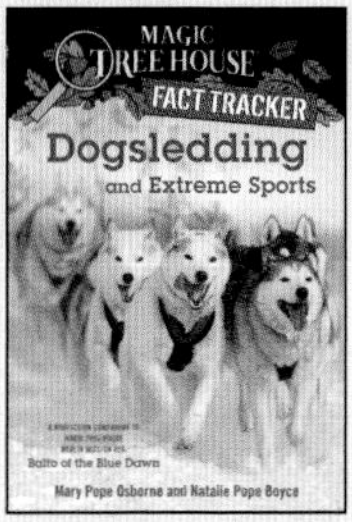
MAGIC TREE HOUSE
FACT TRACKER
Dogsledding and Extreme Sports
Mary Pope Osborne and Natalie Pope Boyce

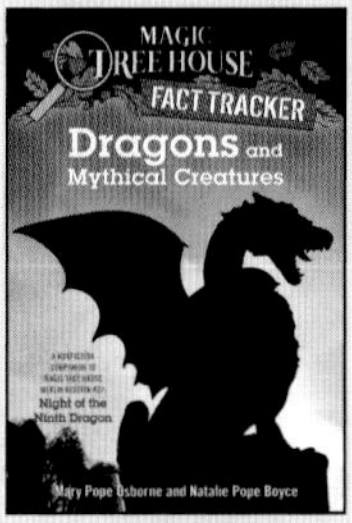
MAGIC TREE HOUSE
FACT TRACKER
Dragons and Mythical Creatures
Mary Pope Osborne and Natalie Pope Boyce

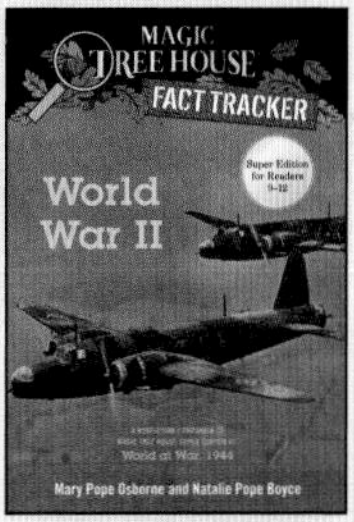
MAGIC TREE HOUSE
FACT TRACKER
World War II
Super Edition for Readers 9-12
Mary Pope Osborne and Natalie Pope Boyce

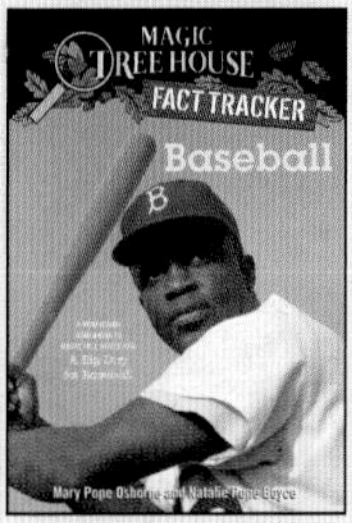
MAGIC TREE HOUSE
FACT TRACKER
Baseball
Mary Pope Osborne and Natalie Pope Boyce

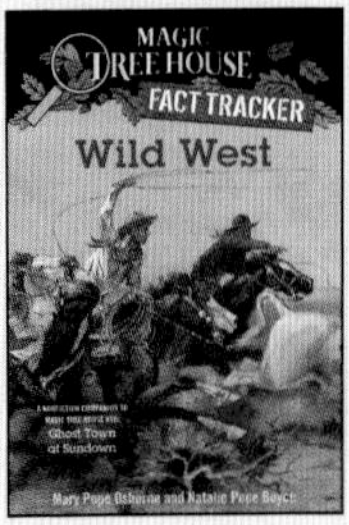
MAGIC TREE HOUSE
FACT TRACKER
Wild West
Mary Pope Osborne and Natalie Pope Boyce

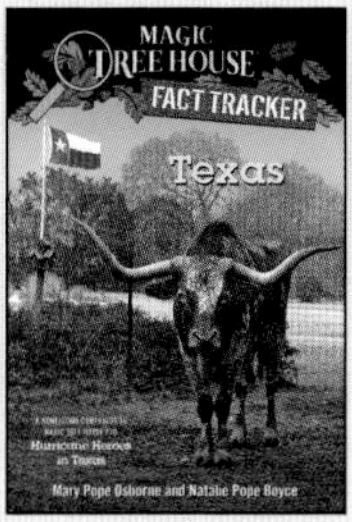
MAGIC TREE HOUSE
FACT TRACKER
Texas
Mary Pope Osborne and Natalie Pope Boyce

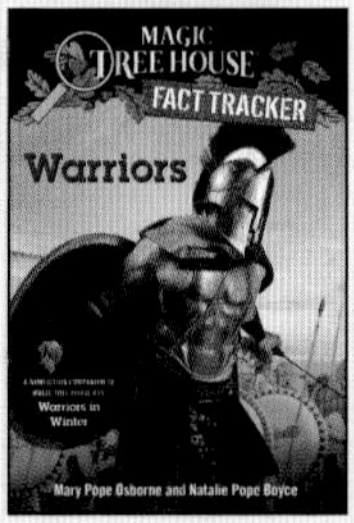
MAGIC TREE HOUSE
FACT TRACKER
Warriors
Mary Pope Osborne and Natalie Pope Boyce

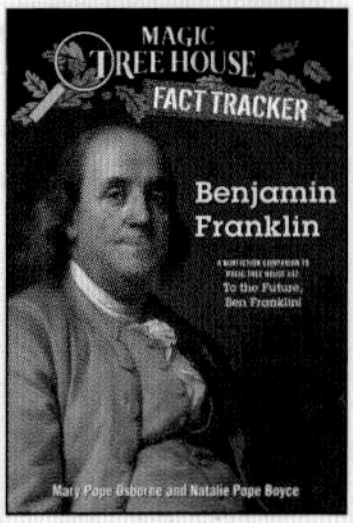
MAGIC TREE HOUSE
FACT TRACKER
Benjamin Franklin
Mary Pope Osborne and Natalie Pope Boyce

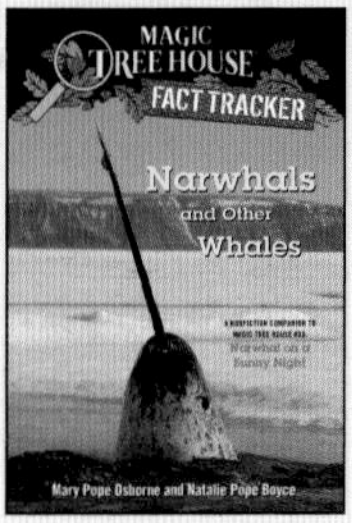
MAGIC TREE HOUSE
FACT TRACKER
Narwhals and Other Whales
Mary Pope Osborne and Natalie Pope Boyce

MARY POPE OSBORNE is the author of many novels, picture books, story collections, and nonfiction books. Her #1 *New York Times* bestselling Magic Tree House® series has been translated into numerous languages around the world. Highly recommended by parents and educators everywhere, the series introduces young readers to different cultures and times, as well as to the world's legacy of ancient myth and storytelling.

JENNY LAIRD is an award-winning playwright. She collaborates with Will Osborne and Randy Courts on creating musical theater adaptations of the Magic Tree House® series for both national and international audiences. Their work also includes shows for young performers, available through Music Theatre International's Broadway Junior® Collection. Currently the team is working on a Magic Tree House® animated television series.

KELLY & NICHOLE MATTHEWS are twin sisters and a comic-art team. They get to do their dream job every day, drawing comics for a living. They've worked with Boom Studios!, Archaia, the Jim Henson Company, Hiveworks, and now Random House!